On Wheels of Love

Heartlines

Books by Pam Lyons

A Boy Called Simon
He Was Bad
It Could Never Be
Latchkey Girl
Danny's Girl
Odd Girl Out
Ms Perfect

Books by Anita Eires

Tug Of Love
Summer Awakening
Spanish Exchange
Star Dreamer
Californian Summer
If Only . . .
Teacher's Pet
Working Girl

Books by Mary Hooper

Love Emma XXX
Follow That Dream
My Cousin Angie
Happy Ever After
Opposites Attract
A Love Like Yours
Blondes Have More Fun and Other Stories

Books by Barbara Jacobs

Two Times Two

Books by Jane Pitt

Loretta Rose
Autumn Always Comes
Stony Limits
Rainbows For Sale
Pia
The Boy Who Was Magic

Books by Ann de Gale

Island Encounter
Hands Off

Books by Anthea Cohen

Dangerous Love
Substance and Shadow

Books by David S. Williams

Give Me Back My Pride
Forgive and Forget
My Life to Live

Books by Jill Young

Change Of Heart
Three Summers On

Books by Ann Ruffell

Friends For Keeps
Secret Passion
Baby Face

Books by Lorna Read

Images
The Name is Zero
A Taste of Fame

Books by Jane Butterworth

Spotlight On Sam
Wild in the Country

Books by John Harvey

Wild Love
Last Summer, First Love

Books by Anita Davies

Stepsisters

Heartlines

Lorna Read

On Wheels of Love

A Pan Original

First published 1987 by Pan Books Ltd,
Cavaye Place, London SW10 9PG

9 8 7 6 5 4 3 2 1

Printed in Great Britain by
Richard Clay Ltd,
Bungay, Suffolk

Chapter 1

The only thing I really loved more than my bicycle was Tom West. Tom, with his thick black hair which always looked so healthy and shiny, his nose with that bit of a bump in it from where he broke it at rugby, his lips, which were neither too thin nor too thick but just in between, just right. His deep, almost navy-blue eyes sparkled under a fringe of eyelashes so thick and sweeping that, if he'd been a girl, you'd have said they were false.

I'd have given anything for eyelashes like that. I'd have given anything to go out with Tom. So would half the girls in our school.

As I polished my bike and tested the tyre pressures, I couldn't stop thinking about him. Tom was a keen cyclist, too, but he was two years older and much better than me. He went on proper cycle tours, whereas I just went on days out with Dad – Mum didn't cycle – or my friends, Julie, Kim, Martin and Dave. My best mate of all was Van. Her name was Vanessa but nobody ever called her that, just like nobody ever called me Teresa. I was always Terry.

Unknown to anyone, even Van, I'd cut Tom's picture off a school photo and carried it in my wallet, tucked behind my bus pass. Well, we all have to have someone to dream about, don't we?

'I don't know why you don't go out with Dave,' Van had said dozens of times. 'I'm sure he's crazy about you.'

'He's got a funny way of showing it, then,' I'd replied. 'Anyway, he's never even asked me.' I'd grown up with Dave. He really, truly was the boy next door. Had been, anyway. Two years ago his parents had split up and they'd moved away to the other side of town. He now lived in a flat with his mother and younger brother, and his older sister had got married. I hadn't really missed him because I still saw him at school and still talked bikes with him. But he had never asked me out and I've never felt anything special for him. He was great, a fabulous friend, but that was all. I'd never fancied Martin, either. Some girls I knew thought it impossible to be platonic friends with boys. They only ever spent time with them if they were going out with them. I'd done a bit of research and found out that they were mainly girls who didn't have brothers with a houseful of mates. Funny, isn't it? I've never seen any articles about that.

I had a brother, Mark, but he was eight years older than me and worked for an engineering firm in Coventry, which was miles away. I really missed him. He only came to visit us about once every two months, which wasn't nearly enough. He had his own flat and I really envied him, and was dying for two years' time when I'd be eighteen and free to do what I wanted. I sometimes fantasised about applying to the same college as Tom. But I suppose there would be plenty of other girls in my class with the same idea! We wouldn't all get in!

I was out in the front garden with the bike. I looked up when I heard the gate go, and there was a delivery boy with a sackful of our local free newspaper, the Gazette.

'I'll take it,' I said. He was only about twelve, and he jumped in fright, as he hadn't seen me crouching down behind the privet hedge. I must try this dodge again, I thought. I'll get our rotten milkman next time, the old misery. He'd actually had the cheek to tell my mum off because she didn't have the right change last time she'd paid his bill, and I'd had to open my piggy bank to help her out!

It was a breezy day in late March, quite warm if you were out of the wind. I propped my bike against the front wall of the house, sat down on the windowsill and opened the paper . . . and that's when I saw the picture and felt a wave of lump-in-the-throat tears, the sort you can't cry even though you want to.

It was a little boy's face. His eyes were huge, like the children in those rather yukky greetings cards that some people think are cute but which make me want to throw up. But these eyes were real, so it was different. His little face was all pinched and pitiful and there were big smudges like thumbprints under his eyes. He was beautiful – and so, so sad, because he was dying; it said so in the paper. It would take an awful lot of money to save him, to send him for an operation which he could only get in America, and his mother, who was a widow, hadn't got it.

'Our only hope is that some company, or some generous person, will help to save my son's life,' appealed his brave mother, Linda Morgan. 'Since his father died, Tony is everything to me.' Without the six-hour operation, doctors say that three-year-old Tony will be dead within six months . . .

An address followed, to which donations could be sent.

I stared and stared at that poor little boy until the newsprint blurred before my eyes. I did a mental calculation of all the money I'd got in the world, which amounted to about £30 since I'd bought my wonderful second-hand Dawes touring bike. I could send that, but what good would £30 do? It was a mere drop in the ocean. If everyone in our town sent £30, that would be different. Perhaps I could go round collecting door to door . . .

'*Terry!*' Mum called from inside the house. 'Dinner's ready!'

I wheeled my bike into the hallway and shut the door. Dad was already sitting at the table.

'Wash your hands, you're all oily,' he said.

'No, don't bother, love, your soup will get cold,' said Mum. A quick glare passed between them as neither of them liked to be contradicted. Normally, I'd have laughed out loud, but today, I couldn't. Not after reading the paper.

'Why were you doing your bike out the front? What's wrong with the back yard?' Dad wanted to know.

'She can't see the boys walking past if she's in the back yard,' Mum pointed out shrewdly, but giving me a teasing look at the same time.

'Oh, *Mum*!' I said exasperatedly. 'I do think of other things sometimes, you know.'

'Give me an example?' she challenged.

'Like what it must be like to be struck down by a fatal disease when you're only three,' I replied.

'Not at mealtimes, please,' said Dad. 'Death and asparagus soup don't mix.'

'It's not funny, Dad. Not at all funny. I'm serious. You read the paper and you'll see what I mean,' I told them. Maybe I sounded a bit pompous – I don't know.

'I thought about death a lot when I was sixteen,' Mum said thoughtfully.

'Yes, you wanted to be a nun. That would have been a *living* death!' Dad said, and they started having a heated discussion about religion, which was great because I could get on with eating and thinking without having to talk. I had a lot to think about. The plight of little Tony Morgan had stirred something deep inside me. I'd never been what you would call a 'do-gooder', like some of my friends who were members of Greenpeace and CND and went to meetings and did things for charity. Maybe I was too selfish. Though I'd bought all my Christmas cards from Oxfam last year.

'Going out this afternoon? Terry, wake up, I'm talking to you,' Mum's voice suddenly intruded into my thoughts.

'Uh-huh. I'm going to Van's,' I told her.

'Hadn't you better do some homework before you go?'

Oh, that ominous word, *homework*. Home*torture*, homepenance, home-interferer-with-everything-else-you-wanted-to-do. Okay, so my GCSE's were looming. Hideously close, in fact. I heaved a great, heartfelt sigh. They were right – I really should do some work.

'Okay,' I assured them, 'I'll work till three and then go to Van's. Then I'll come back about eight and do some more.' After all, it was Sunday and I had a Geography test tomorrow. I always had been a last-minute swot, not like these people who could learn it all months before and still remember it on the day of an exam. I had to cram it into my brain hours beforehand, and then I could just about remember it before it fell out again the day after.

Van was washing her hair in the bathroom when I arrived. Not that she had much hair to wash; she'd had it cropped short at the sides, and left a bit longer and spikier on top. Her sister let me in and then Van emerged, rubbing her bristles vigorously with a red towel.

'Done your Geog?' she asked.

I grimaced and gave her a thumbs-down. 'How about you?'

She grinned smugly. 'Got Ginny to test me, didn't I?' Ginny, her sister who'd let me in, was studying A-level Geography. It wasn't fair. No wonder Van was streets ahead.

'Been out on the bike today?' she asked.

'No, I was doing some work on it. How about you?'

'Dave called round and we went for a ride up Buckhurst Hill.' She grinned.

'Oh, *really*!' I waggled my eyebrows as an invitation to tell more.

'Oh, it's nothing like that. Dave and me – well, it's like Dave and you. Just friends. He's very nice, though. He's heaps better now than he was last year. His clothes are a bit trendier – '

'And he washes his hair a lot more often,' I put in, remembering how he used to leave his dark red hair so long between washes that it looked lank and revoltingly greasy.

'He's not so spotty now, either,' Van observed. I really hadn't noticed.

'*You* are, though,' I pointed out cruelly, referring to the giant-size pimple on her chin.

'Beast! Isn't it ghastly? I keep squeezing it and it just comes back again,' she said dolefully.

'It's probably your mum's cooking. Oops . . . sorry, Mrs Philips!' I hadn't heard Van's Italian mum come out of the kitchen, but she couldn't have heard because she was smiling and asking if I was staying for tea.

'Yes, she is,' Van answered for me.

'Yes, it's okay, I've told Mum,' I confirmed.

Van and I went up to her bedroom. 'I'm depressed and it's nothing to do with the test tomorrow,' I told her, and then recounted the story of Tony Morgan.

When I'd finished, Van's pretty, pointed face looked really mournful. 'I can't bear hearing about things like that,' she said. Suddenly her face brightened. 'Hey, why don't we do something in school to raise money? A jumble-sale or something?'

''Cos if we did, it might have to go into the school funds,' I reminded her. 'They'd need it for textbooks, or something. We wouldn't be allowed to raise money for something else . . .'

The subject changed, partly because it was too depressing to go on thinking about, and partly because Van wanted to show me her new jumper which she'd got in a Top Shop sale. It was big, baggy and striped in mustard and black. 'It's great with my black leggings,' she said. 'I wore it today and Dave said how nice I looked.'

'Pity it wasn't Tom West saying it,' I observed, and we both sighed. I almost showed Van my picture, but changed my mind, because if she knew I had one, she'd get one, too, and I hated being copied. There was a kind of privileged feeling about carrying round a secret photo and I wanted to hug it to myself. I also didn't want Van to know that I kissed Tom's picture every night before I went to sleep. That's why it had the odd lipstick mark on it, from when I hadn't taken off my make-up properly.

It was more than just a crush that I felt for Tom – much, much more. I couldn't have explained my feelings to anyone. When I first became aware of him, which was last year some time, I had this jolt of recognition, as if all my life I'd been carrying a portrait of the man I was fated to love in my heart, and at last the person who fitted the picture had emerged. It was like the Prince carrying round the glass slipper until he found the only person who could fit it, Cinderella. Tom fitted my ideal image in every way. It wasn't just the way he looked, he was nice too, not like those boys who hang around in a gang and shout and tease you.

But there was one huge, mammoth, mighty, ginormous problem about Tom: he simply had no idea whatsoever that I existed. Or Van, for that matter. Neither of us knew who his girlfriend was. He kept his love-life right out of school. We had visions of him dating someone really glamorous, a singer in a group, perhaps, or a model, or perhaps a champion sportswoman, because he was so good at sports himself.

I was neither brilliant at sports, nor dazzlingly good-looking. There was no reason whatsoever why any boy should look at me twice – or even once. It would take an absolute miracle for Tom to take an interest in me, and it was my firm belief that miracles stopped happening the day they finished writing the Bible.

Van and I played records and talked till half-seven, then I had to go home and do some more swotting. I didn't pack it in till about midnight. Then I lay wide-awake in bed with the light out, rain forests and glaciated valleys and the names of different kinds of rocks tumbling through my brain.

Then, in the middle of the scrambled egg state of my brain cells, I suddenly saw Tom Morgan again; that little, pinched face, those haunted eyes which seemed to be pleading, 'Help me . . . please help me live.'

By the morning, I knew what I had to do . . .

Chapter 2

I was dying to tell someone, but I didn't bump into any of my friends on the way to school and I was late anyway, because I had to take a last look at my notes, and the register was already being marked as I sidled in.

After Assembly, the unfortunate Geography lot headed gloomily for Room 12.

'You look as though you've been up all night swotting,' Van said.

I shook my head. 'No, I didn't sleep much but it wasn't that.' I didn't want to tell her my great idea just before the test. In fact, I didn't really want to talk at all.

Adam Welch – Welch the Squelch as he was known

– confessed that he was going to cheat, as he'd written some stuff down in fine-tipped pen on his wrist, so all he had to do was roll his cuff back a bit.

'Do you think we ought to tell on him?' Van hissed in my ear, and I shook my head again. Squelch was so hopeless that he'd never pass, even if he had notes written all the way from his hand to his armpit. He never seemed to be able to correlate it all properly.

Miss Sundera handed out our question sheets and told us we had an hour in which to complete them. A chorus of groans went up from all of us who'd swotted up on the wrong things and Miss Sundera frowned.

'You should know all these subjects perfectly well by now,' she snapped.

John Moore did an imitation of her 'perfectly well' and got told off. It was our Geography teacher's catch-phrase. She glanced at her watch. 'You can all start . . . now.'

My biro scrawled furiously across the page, but I did make an effort to control my writing so she could at least read it. Our English teacher called my scribble, 'barbed-wire entanglements' and remarked that he ought to sent it to a graphologist. I didn't need any handwriting expert to tell me that I was just plain untidy, with thoughts that ran well ahead of my hand.

After I'd answered three questions at lightning speed I paused for a rest and a think. It was nearly my undoing. I was sitting by the window and as I happened to glance out, who should be striding purposefully across the yard towards the drive but . . . Tom

West! He had dazzling white shorts on, a yellow school sports shirt and a squash racquet under one arm. A regulation grey sweatshirt was draped carelessly over his shoulders.

My heart gave a kind of double beat and I could hardly catch my breath. I longed to be able to dive out of the window, sprout wings and fly so as to catch him up, just to have ten minutes private conversation with him on his way to the school squash courts.

Miss Sundera clearing her throat brought me back abruptly to reality. I finished the rest of the questions as best I could, acutely aware of all the sighs and rustlings around me, as people agonised over their work.

Then at last it was break, followed by a study period. In the cloakroom, I was hailed by Julie and Kim, who wanted to tell me about this great new club they'd been to over the weekend.

'Kim's sister took us,' Julie told me breathlessly while she tugged a comb through her blonde curls.

'She didn't want to, but Mum made her because she was having some friends round and wanted us out of the house,' Kim explained, with a grimace. Her mother played competition Scrabble and organised fiendish Scrabble nights where middle-aged people almost came to blows over whether to allow *re* and *qua* or not.

'Was anyone from school there?' I enquired, only listening with half an ear, really, because I'd just spotted Van and was desperate to talk to her.

'*Mario* was there – he would be!' Kim giggled. Mario was this really flirty Italian boy who fancied himself something rotten and always wore gorgeous clothes. He had a motorbike, too, and had loads of girlfriends. 'He was with Tom West, surprise, surprise. Oh, and Stefan was around somewhere but we only saw him vaguely, when we went to get some Cokes from the bar.'

I felt the colour leave my face, then flood back in a tell-tale crimson wave. Was Tom – *with* anybody? I didn't want to know, and yet I did. Desperately.

'Er . . . did anybody get off with anybody?' I hedged.

'Kim did.' Julie snorted with laughter and Kim belted her.

'No I did not!' Kim yelled.

'That guy in the leather jacket – what was his name? Diana or something?' Julie screeched. 'You must have been desperate!'

'His name was Dai, and he was Welsh, and I know we danced a few times, but that was all. He didn't even kiss me,' Kim said crossly.

'Hard luck!' Julie teased.

'Look, I've got to have a word with Van, I must go,' I said. I knew I'd never get any sense out of them with regard to Tom. Not without making it plain that I fancied him – and that would be more than my life at school was worth. Kim and Julie, good friends though they were, were awful chatterboxes.

Van was waiting for me. I linked arms with her and we went out and paced round the yard. The weather was just like Sunday, crisp and sunny, and my heart lifted at the sight of all the bursting buds on the trees, and the yellow clumps of crocuses that had come out in the flowerbed outside the Head's room.

I was glad that the younger kids had their own playground round the other side, because at least, in the area reserved for seniors, you could hear yourselves speak.

'You know I mentioned raising some money to send to the fund for that little boy that needs the operation?' I asked Van. 'Well, I think I've hit on a way it could be done. You know all those charity walks people do? Well, it'll be the Easter hols soon; so why couldn't we do a charity cycle ride?'

Van's jaw dropped. 'You mean, just the two of us?' she asked incredulously.

'No, idiot. I mean, get a whole gang of us together. Dave, Martin . . . to name but a few.'

'Here comes one of the few now.'

'So here you are!' It was Martin, gold-rimmed specs glinting in the sunshine. He was a real bike ace. He'd built his own racing bike from spare parts and bits of dead bikes, and was now constructing a tourer to end all tourers. He said he was going to call it a 'Paws' as it was mainly a mixture of Peugeot and Daws, with the odd bit of Raleigh thrown in.

I outlined my idea to him, but he hardly had a chance to comment before the bell rang and we had to go back inside.

'It's sports all afternoon, so I probably won't see you. Tell you what, I'll tell Dave and we could all meet round at my house after school to discuss it later, if you like,' he offered.

So by quarter to five, there were eight of us crammed into Martin's dad's shed, admiring his half-built bike.

'I don't know if it'll be finished in time for the hols, though,' he said doubtfully, 'though I could use the racer. It depends where you're thinking of going . . .'

'I hadn't thought – not yet,' I confessed. 'First, though, does everyone approve of the basic idea?'

There was a chorus of assent; I wasn't the only one who'd seen Tony Morgan's picture in the paper, and read the harrowing article.

'Second question; how many of us would be able to come?'

'Would your parents let you?' Van enquired. 'I'm not sure mine would. They would if it was just a day trip, but not for a weekend or anything . . .'

The thought hadn't occurred to me and I bit my lip. Van was right. They probably *wouldn't* let me go. Not unless there was someone older with us, who was capable of taking charge.

'It's got to be longer than a day, otherwise why should people sponsor us?' I said dolefully.

'I was sponsored for every length of the baths I swam when I raised money for Sports Aid,' Julie said.

'But that had loads of publicity anyway. We want to do something that will fire people's imaginations and make them feel that we're making a worthwhile effort,' said Dave, who had been silent up until now. 'A day of cycling up and down Buckhurst Hill's hardly going to do that. Now, if we were cycling all the way to Tibet – '

'You couldn't fit that in over the Easter holidays,' sniggered Dave's friend Ross.

Dave shot him a withering look. 'Let's be serious,' he said. 'I was about to add, or even over some lonely moors somewhere.'

'Dartmoor,' said George Kyriakou. 'I've never been there, but it's supposed to be pretty wild.'

'I've been there, but only in summer, and in a coach,' confessed Kim. 'It was very beautiful.'

'I remember reading about teachers taking a school party to Dartmoor. They got caught in a blizzard and some children died,' Martin said, with unnecessary relish.

'That sounds like our sort of place!' Dave said, smacking his hands together enthusiastically. 'Anyway, surely, if we all do our homework – '

'Don't mention that word!' I interjected.

'As I was saying, if we all read up on survival techniques and prepare ourselves properly with the right clothes and equipment, then it should be all right. I'm sure my parents would let me go. Martin and I went cycling together last summer for a week, and we were only fifteen then. They let us go camping – '

'Yes, but you're *boys*!' Julie pointed out. 'You know what parents are like with girls. They wouldn't like us going on holiday with boys, for a start, let alone camping out. Anyway, my bike's not good enough, so that's me out, I'm afraid.'

'And me,' chimed in Kim. 'My dad says I've got to study really hard all over Easter because he wants me to get good exam passes in June. It's not very long off, you know.'

'We know. Don't remind us!' the rest of us chorused.

My idea was beginning to look impossible, with first one person backing out, then another. George's parents ran a restaurant and George was needed to help out when he wasn't doing school work, so that left me, Van, Dave, Martin and Ross. But first of all Van and I had to persuade our parents to agree, which would be a near-impossible task. Unless my dad could take time off work and come with us . . . Whose crazy idea was Dartmoor, anyway? Why couldn't it just be a 'cycle up and down Buckhurst Hill till you drop' marathon? If we could each find fifty people to sponsor us at 10p per ascent, that would make – if we managed ten ascents each – £250 between five of us. Maths wasn't my best subject. It was bit like one of those mind-boggling problems starting, *If it takes ten trips up a hill to earn one cyclist £50, how many cyclists and how many trips,* etc etc.

I'd check it on my calculator later. One thing was for sure, though: £250 wasn't nearly enough money. I'd hoped to raise £1000 somehow. But what was the use of straining my brain? The whole thing looked impossible, anyway. My parents would never agree.

When I got home, first of all Mum was mad because I

was late for tea – I knew she'd worry or get cross if I didn't phone her, but somehow, it went right out of my head – and secondly, we had a peculiar phone call.

It was Mum who answered it. I heard her going, 'Yes . . . erm . . . I beg your pardon? Yes, I have a daughter called Terry Mitchell. No, not a son, a daughter. She's called Teresa . . . No, I've no idea what you're talking about. I think you must have the wrong family. Goodbye.'

She put the phone down, came back, and gave me a very peculiar look. 'That was the Gazette,' she said. 'They wanted to speak to you about some charity cycle marathon you're organising in Dartmoor. I told them they must have got it wrong, that it wasn't us.'

There was a tense, horrible silence and I knew Mum was challenging me to spill the beans, if there were any to spill. I swallowed hard.

'Er, Mum . . .' I began.

She folded her arms and got that glint in her eye which she always gets when a storm is brewing.

'You see, it was like this . . .' And I told her. It wasn't a bit easy. 'I don't know how on earth the paper found out though,' I concluded. 'We only started discussing it this evening. I mean, we haven't made any plans yet, because we didn't think there was much of a chance of you – our parents – letting us go.'

'Who exactly is us?' Mum demanded to know.

'Me, Van, some of the other girls from school . . . oh, and Dave, Martin and Ross Sayers, that friend of

Dave's,' I said quickly. Well, it wasn't an out and out lie; maybe quite a few other girls *would* want to go.

'I see. And who exactly will be in charge of this . . . expedition?'

My mind whirled round in circles, grasping at straws. 'Well, it was my original idea, but I thought someone like, well, Dad, for instance, might want to come,' I mumbled. It might be a good idea, if he could get time off work. But would it have the same impact as a group of sixteen and seventeen year-olds living rough and crossing difficult terrain in order to draw attention to the fund for little Tony? It did seem to spoil it a bit if there was a parent along . . .

When Dad came in, we all sat down and talked it over and, as I'd expected, Dad put his foot down and Mum backed him up. 'I'm not averse to giving money, if it'll help, but I can't have you doing anything risky, Terry, especially with your GCSEs coming up.'

It was funny to think that we were the first year to be doing GCSEs. I suppose we were pioneers really. I felt sure they must be more difficult than O levels because it was all so new and no one really knew what to expect the first time round.

I was sadly thinking that I'd better abandon the whole scheme when the phone rang and it was Van's father, wanting to speak to mine.

I strained my ears, but Mum ruined my eavesdropping by continuing to talk to me, despite all my efforts to shut her up. 'It's rude to listen to other people's conversations, dear,' she reminded me.

'Even if it's about me?' I protested, but it had no effect.

When Dad came back into the living-room, I pounced on him right away.

'What did he say? Was it about the charity ride? Are they letting Van go?'

'They wanted to see if we were letting you go, before making their minds up,' he told me.

My heart sank. That meant my rotten father had ruined it for both of us. Van would never forgive me!

I started to slink away in the general direction of my homework. Then Dad called after me. 'We thought we should ring around the other parents to get their views too.'

Oh no! I thought wildly. They'd find out that Kim and Julie weren't going, then they'd want to know who the other girls were, and I wouldn't be able to tell them. 'Only Dave, Martin and Ross are absolutely definite so far,' I confessed. 'You'd better leave it a few days till I know a bit more.'

'You are awfully young to be going away on your own,' Mum said doubtfully. 'Isn't she, Graham?'

'I'm nearly sixteen!' I pointed out. My birthday was in May.

'We don't want any funny business with boys, either,' Mum added.

That made me furious. 'You *know* I'm not like that!' I shrieked. 'It really is about time you put a bit more trust in me!'

'Dave King's a good lad. He's always been reliable,' Dad thought aloud. 'And Martin Cross seems a sensible boy. He's certainly very knowledgeable about bikes. You wouldn't have any trouble if he was with your team.'

I held my breath, wondering if Dad was about to soften.

But then he went on: 'I still don't hold with this camping out idea, though. Not at Easter – it's much too early. And not on Dartmoor. It's a very dangerous place – very boggy, and a lot of it is used by the army as firing ranges. Now, why don't you go somewhere a bit safer and closer to home?'

'But *Dad*!' I wailed. 'It's supposed to be a challenge, a test of our endurance skills! A quick pedal round the local lanes won't inspire people to give money to our cause. We need to do something a bit more exciting, and a *teeny* bit dangerous, otherwise how can we get any publicity? We'll plan it all properly, I promise. After all, it's not as if we're going to hang-glide off the top of Everest, or even do a parachute jump! We simply want to cycle down to Devon, spend two or three nights on Dartmoor, whatever the weather, and then come back. We should make it there and back in under a week.'

'You must give your mum and me time to talk about it,' Dad said firmly. 'Now, go off and do your homework . . .'

When I talked to Van before our first class next day, she told me there was very little chance of her parents letting her go. It wasn't only the usual arguments about her age, and going on a trip with boys, but the added aggravation that her parents wanted her to have extra Maths tuition in the Easter holidays, because the Maths teacher had told them that she stood little chance of getting a good grade in her Maths GCSE if she didn't.

This was a devastating blow to me, as it meant that so far there were no other girls going – just me and three boys, Dave, Martin and Ross.

By the end of the day, I'd learned two more things. Firstly, that it had been Martin who had let the local paper know what we were planning – or, to be more precise, Martin's stepfather, who was one of the printers.

Secondly, there was one more boy going, so it would be me and *four* boys – and that extra person was . . . Tom West!

Chapter 3

Predictably, Van went mad when she heard the news. 'You lucky beast!' she yelled.

'Perhaps. I still don't know if I can go yet,' I pointed out.

We had an after-school meeting round at Dave's –

Van came even though she was out of the trip, just to be under the same ceiling as Tom – and we were joined later by Ross.

I didn't know him very well as he wasn't at our school, so I didn't know if I liked him or not. I was quite prepared to hate his guts after what he did that evening, though. He brought along two girls – very attractive ones, at that – and told the assembled crowd that they were keen cyclists and wanted to join us.

I seethed when I saw Tom giving them the once-over, especially the plumper one with the curly red hair. The other girl was tall, blonde and pretty skinny – though I suppose some people would have said that she had a model's figure. My dream of being the only girl in Tom's field of vision for a whole week was shattered. Why couldn't rotten Ross have found some ugly girls? Anything but these two!

They told us all that they belonged to a local cycling club near where they lived, which was a small village about six miles from our town. The blonde was called Sue and the redhead was Lorraine. Dave told me later that he thought Sue was Ross's ex-girlfriend – though they seemed very friendly for 'exes'.

Martin suggested that we all went for a practice run at the weekend. They were carrying on as if I was definitely part of the team. But then, it had all been my idea, even if it had now got a bit out of hand. This Dartmoor business, for instance. No one would hear of us going anywhere else. Martin had already bought an Ordnance Survey map and a book about cycling in south-west England. I decided that the best thing for me to do would be to go along with everything, until I knew for sure whether or not I could go.

By Saturday, Mum and Dad still hadn't said any more on the subject, so I cycled off to meet the others as planned, to see if we could all last a thirty-mile route.

It's all pretty flat round our way but our route home took in Buckhurst Hill, which is a long killer of a slope up one side and a steep charge down the other. Only we were doing it in reverse!

I didn't get much of a chance to talk to Lorraine and Sue that day, as they tended to stick together and whenever there was an opportunity, to ride two abreast. So mainly Dave rode next to me and chatted, while Martin, Tom and Ross did their own thing. I was pretty cross with Dave for monopolising me, as I didn't want Tom to think he was my boyfriend. Though surely someone would tell him? After all, if you're about to pitch in your lot with a gang of people for a week, spending every day and every night together, the first thing you do is find out who is who, and especially who is going out with who!

But I didn't like my competition at all. Lorraine was everything I wasn't. She had that glorious long, curly, auburn hair, for a start, and she had a bust whereas my chest was woefully flat. Mum kept saying I still had plenty of growing to do, but I felt sure that didn't include sprouting 36 C's overnight! I was neither particularly short or especially tall and my hair was what people tactfully call brunette probably meaning boring dark brown. I had it cut often so that it didn't get in the way when I was riding and everyone said it suited my turned up nose! The only bits of me I really liked were my eyes. They were pale turquoise like my Dad's, and seemed to change colour to match the clothes I wore. I made a point of always choosing blue or green sweaters to set them off.

When Buckhurst Hill reared up in front of us at about four o'clock, there was an audible groan from Sue.

'Oh, come on, don't be wet,' Lorraine chivvied her. Then she muttered something which I couldn't catch but which might have been to the effect that none of the boys would fancy them if they didn't make a good show of getting up the hill.

Even my legs were feeling the strain. The weather had been lousy for ages and I hadn't really done much cycling, just a long run with Dad in the previous month. Martin and Tom seemed to be sailing up with no trouble, but I could see Dave puffing a bit, and Lorraine and Sue had their heads down, their mouths grimly set and were standing on the pedals. Lorraine's face was so red that I wondered if she ought to give up and walk, but she earned my admiration by struggling to the top.

After that, we could all take our feet off the pedals and swoop down the other side, gloriously freewheeling. 'This'll test our brakes!' Dave yelled over his shoulder to me as, with a whoop of joy, he took off like a bird. There was hardly any traffic about, so we burned down the hill, scorching our tyres and coming to a gravel-spinning halt before the long bend at the bottom.

'That was great!' panted Tom. 'Everyone okay?'

'Fine,' we chorused.

'There'll be an awful lot of steep hills in Devon,' Martin pointed out. 'We need to practise till we can take Buckhurst in our stride.'

'We ought to make it a stipulation of the marathon that no hill is to be walked unless the going's really rough,' I said, hoping that hearing such a tough proposition might put Sue and Lorraine off.

But I should have known better. 'I'm game,' piped up Sue, and Lorraine nodded brightly, and they both stared directly at Tom, as if seeking his approval. And they got it, too, because he grinned at both of them and said, 'That's the spirit!'

I'll probably be happier if I don't go now, I thought gloomily as I cycled home. For a start, Dave would probably monopolise me and would get all hurt if I told him to shove off because I fancied Tom. Worse, he might tell him. Then, there was my double problem, Lorraine in particular. Why couldn't she fall madly in love with Dave, or Martin? Fat chance of that, though, with someone as stunning as Tom around.

With these kinds of jumbled up thoughts spinning round my head, it wasn't perhaps surprising that I got a shock when I got home and Dad promptly collared me in the hall and said he and Mum had talked it over now and had decided that I could go, after all. Apparently the reporter from the Gazette had been on to them again, trying to get some information for a piece for the next issue.

'You ought to be proud of your daughter,' he'd told Dad. 'Not many teenagers today are so thoughtful and caring. They're mostly out for themselves. I'd like to come round with a photographer and talk to all of them, and take their photograph. I'm sure they'll get a lot of local support . . .'

After that, Dad had felt he couldn't really say that he'd vetoed my taking part – robbing the heroine of her brief hour of fame and glory!

'I still wish there were rather more girls going, and rather fewer boys,' Mum said anxiously. I'd told her about Lorraine and Sue. 'I hope you'll invite everyone round here, so that we can meet them.'

Which is exactly what I did. Next afternoon, all seven of us were lined up outside the house, next to our gleaming bicycles which we'd all spent Sunday morning polishing.

The photographer, a rather gorgeous blonde bloke of about twenty, took several pictures, and two individual ones of me – thank heavens I didn't have any spots! – and the reporter, a fat man of about Dad's age, asked me how I'd thought up the idea for the Dartmoor Challenge, as it had started to be called. He then chatted to all of us and it all went quite well, I thought.

I dashed to the newsagent's on my way to school and bought three copies, so I could pass them round at school. To my embarrassment, when I got there, someone had forestalled me by pinning the cut-out article up on the main noticeboard! There was a crowd of people around it. Some of them dashed up excitedly as I walked in, asking questions and offering to sponsor me. That night, I borrowed Mum's old typewriter and painfully bashed out a prototype sponsorship form, the kind I'd seen lots of times floating round school when people did various things, and Mum promised to take it to work and photocopy some for me.

There was just two weeks to go till the start of the Easter holidays. I was really sorry Van wasn't coming with us, as I was so busy with plans and preparations that I hardly saw her out of school time.

Martin had issued us all with lists of things we had to get, such as first aid equipment, tools, a spare inner tube and a set of panniers for the back of the bike.

When I checked the price of the panniers, I found the ones I really wanted were about ten pounds, which meant a third of my remaining life savings would have to go. But then Mum and Dad decided to give me a birthday present in advance – so I got my panniers, and most of the other things on my list! I needed spending money, too, of course, but I partially solved that problem by doing a few nights' babysitting for a friend of Mum's.

Fortunately, I already had all the cycling clothing I needed, but I still made list after list trying to decide what to pack. I kept thinking – or rather, hoping – that

I might need just one slightly more glamorous outfit than my special windproof jacket and cycling trousers and a couple of thick jumpers. Maybe one evening we might – just might – end up in some lovely country pub or restaurant where they had music and a roaring log fire, and Tom and I could sit in the inglenook, our faces lit by the flames' dancing glow, and swap life histories . . .

Ah well! I dismissed those impractical ideas. After all, I had things like a sleeping bag and a tent to fit in somehow.

'Now, you are to share the tent with the other girls,' Mum said firmly.

Unfortunately, our family possessed one which was just about big enough but I didn't relish the thought of sharing with two girls who were best friends one little bit. I'd feel an alien, an interloper. Maybe they'd gossip about me and shut up when I crawled in. There would be secret looks, codes and giggles and I'd just have to ignore it and put up with it. I just hoped I would manage to convince them that we should all take turns carrying the blasted tent. It wouldn't be fair if I was lumbered with it for the whole trip.

Dave and Martin, being good mates, were going to share, and Ross and Tom would also share. It seemed ironic that the three people who could be relied upon to take the most stuff with them were the ones with the most cramped quarters. But still, I was going and that, after all, was the most important thing.

We were going to avoid Easter weekend like the plague. We were planning to set out on the Monday after Easter Monday when, hopefully, there wouldn't be so much holiday traffic on the roads. It seemed unlikely that many people would want to go to Devon so early in the year, not unless there was some freak sunshine.

To our amazement, there was! The week before Easter was like a picture postcard April, with blue skies, puffy white clouds like reflections of the lambs in the fields, and lots of blossom everywhere. It was warm enough to roll your sleeves up, though not to discard your sweater. I was really looking forward to our trip now, even though Dave and Martin kept reminding us not to think of it as a holiday.

Mum and Dad had specially asked Dave to look after me – to be *in loco parentis,* as they put it. I'd had to look that up in the dictionary to find out that it meant 'in the place of a parent'. Just as well I didn't have a crush on Dave!

The day after school broke up, I was humming away to myself as I helped Mum dust the living-room, when Dave rang up. I knew straight away, from the tone of his voice, that something had happened.

'I'm afraid Ross can't make it,' he said. 'He's bust his ankle playing football. It's a real blow because we'll lose all his sponsors – '

'Unless we can persuade them to transfer to us,' I said quickly, fighting off the urge to dash for my calculator that very moment, to work out exactly how much we would lose. Then, realising I hadn't sounded very sympathetic towards Ross, I said, 'I do feel sorry for him. Is he in a lot of pain? I bet he's really upset about not coming to Devon.'

'He is,' Dave replied. 'I'm going round to see him this afternoon. Would you like to come?'

'Yes, of course,' I responded automatically. It was only after we'd made our arrangements about where and when to meet that I found myself guilty yet again of having done something with an ulterior motive in view, even if I'd hardly realised it. I was hoping Tom would be there . . .

But he wasn't. Ross was sitting in a chair with his leg propped up on a small coffee table, his ankle and foot in heavy plaster. He said he'd phoned as many of his personal sponsors, such as relatives, as he could, and they had all promised to transfer their sponsorship to us. That way, he didn't stand to lose too much money. It was obvious that our hope of raising £1,000 was much too high. We would be lucky to make £500, but we were keeping our fingers crossed. I had plucked up courage to ring our local radio station and a very nice lady said that she would give us a mention on the air, together with my address so that people could send money and pledges. She also said that if we phoned with news of our expedition, she would broadcast it.

We would be leaving in ten days' time. Martin had mapped out our route for us, which involved two days spent getting there, three nights on Dartmoor and two days cycling back – and Ross wished us luck.

Our parents held a meeting to check our plans and

preparations. Everyone met in Martin's house and then most of them drifted off for a drink at the Red Lion, apart from Sue and Lorraine's folks, who drove off taking their daughters with them. I cheered inwardly, and hoped I'd get a chance to talk to Tom, who was looking particularly heart-stopping in well-fitting jeans and a jacket in soft black leather.

Martin poured a bottle of cider and we all had a glass each, but Tom was discussing some problem Dave had with his Physics A level – Tom, being two years ahead, knew just that bit more – and I couldn't get a word in and ended up discussing the merits of various types of bike wheels and tyres with Martin. An interesting enough subject, but utterly frustrating when Tom was inches away and that part of my body which was nearest him was tingling with electricity.

So when Mum and Dad came back and offered me a lift home, I went with them gladly.

After that, the days seemed to whizz by. The Gazette published Martin's map of our route, and another request for sponsorship, and we heard from a lot more people, including Mrs Morgan, who sent a brief, sweet little note thanking us for everything we were doing and saying that Tony seemed to be holding his own at the moment. I crossed my fingers and prayed that nothing would happen to him in the next two weeks, before we could do our share to help him. The weather turned wet, windy and cold again.

Each night I watched the weather forecast on TV and punched up the predictions on Teletext, hoping for another glimpse of spring in the air. But bad weather seemed to have set in, which got me wondering how on earth we were going to dry our clothes. Seven days in soggy socks and trousers was a depressing thought . . .

I was too excited to get much sleep, the night before our departure. I had everything packed and ready – Sue and Lorraine had agreed to take their turn carrying the tent – and I lay in bed listening to the wind booming and howling in the chimney flue and imagining scenes from *Wuthering Heights* transferred to Dartmoor, with me as Cathy and Tom as Heathcliffe. Just the two of us against the elements, and at the moment when the storm was at its worst, flashing and crashing all around us, Tom would suddenly take me in his arms and tell me he loved me for all time.

'You'll be lucky!' I snorted to myself. More likely, I would have to watch him and Lorraine cycling off handlebar to handlebar into the sunset!

Then I must have fallen asleep, because the next thing I knew, I was waking up in an exceptionally light bedroom. Light, because there was a certain golden quality filtering through the curtains, a sight I hadn't seen for ages and ages.

The sun!

Chapter 4

I had never ridden such a heavily loaded bike before and it felt very strange, almost like riding a motor scooter, except that my legs were the engine!

Riding down mile after mile of dreary main road was very tiring and we had no chance to speak to each other, partly because of the noise of the traffic, and partly because we had to ride single file.

I blessed the change in the weather. If enormous lorries and buses had been splattering us with muddy water, it would have been miserable. Instead, I was able to admire the blossom in the front gardens of the houses we passed, and the stretches of green fields between towns were refreshing both to my eyes and to my spirit.

We all stopped for drinks and sandwiches at mid-day, then ploughed on, heading for the youth hostel where we had arranged to spend the night. I hadn't been a member of the YHA and had had to join specially, but luckily my membership had come through in time.

It was just as well that our route was flat for most of the first day. I had never ridden more than fifty miles in

a day in my whole life, and that day we did sixty-six. Sue and Lorraine were trailing badly throughout the last twenty miles. Lorraine's face was scarlet with effort, and Sue's was grey with fatigue, and I've no idea what colour mine was because all I could think about was keeping the pedals spinning round, and I think the only thing that kept me from admitting defeat and wailing for frequent rests was the sight of Tom riding in front of me, his broad back and powerful legs like a guiding beacon.

We found the hostel eventually and registered, then Dave insisted that we all stagger out and get some food, though all I wanted was to take a hot shower to ease my aching legs, and then collapse into bed.

'We'll only regret it in the night, or tomorrow morning, if we don't eat now. We need to eat to keep our strength up,' he said sensibly.

But my eyelids were drooping and my head was nodding as I crammed down my chips, and I noticed Lorraine could hardly eat a thing. She just took three bites out of a saveloy, ate half a dozen chips, then sat in her chair with her eyes closed while the boys divided her meal out between them.

Sue was sitting next to me and, right out of the blue, she asked me a question that woke me up with a start.

'Are you going out with Dave, Terry?'

I shook my head, grinning. 'No. We've been friends all our lives, but we've never gone out together. Why?'

'Oh, nothing. Just wondered, that was all,' she said quietly, and continued to eat in silence, while I tossed

her question around in my head and wondered if this meant that Dave had an admirer! He was a great guy; he deserved to have girls chasing him, though surprisingly he hardly ever did. It was a pity I didn't feel that way about him, because he would have been so easy to go out with, and our parents would have approved, and all that.

I think they approve of Tom, though, I mused hopefully. As he was the oldest and most experienced of us, my father had sort of assumed that he would be leading our expedition, and had commented on how mature, sensible and practical he seemed. Maybe, if Sue did fancy Dave, it left only one rival for Tom's affections. Now there was only Lorraine in the way.

I glanced at her pale, tired face and closed eyes, and gave myself a little shake and tried to think of something lively to say to make Tom notice me – he was talking to Martin about tomorrow's route. But by the time I had remembered the joke that Van had told me last week, people were on their feet and chairs were being scraped back and the opportunity had gone.

I think I fell asleep even before my head had hit the cast-iron pillow on my bunk. I awoke to a chorus of groans . . . The rain was back!

'Oh, no!' I exclaimed, staring out at the dirty grey sky. No doubt yesterday had been a fluke and now we were fated to suffer the worst April weather in history. Why hadn't someone invented umbrellas or tarpaulins

that would stay up, attached to your bike, while you cycled?

By lunchtime, we were all thoroughly damp and disgruntled.

'Look at this!' Sue snapped, undoing her shoe and rolling down the heel of her sock to display a large blister.

'I told you we must all wear comfortable shoes,' Martin droned.

'Well, they were all right yesterday. How was I to know they'd rub today?' she retorted. 'I'm not clairvoyant!'

'Pity,' Martin said, in the same laconic tone. 'We would have asked you to be our weather forecaster – '

'And to find us a good camp site,' Dave chipped in.

I saw Sue glance quickly at him to see if he was getting at her, too, but Dave's face bore its usual amiable grin.

'I think I've got rheumatism, with all this water about,' Lorraine moaned. 'My right wrist's really bad. I can hardly keep it on the handlebar when I need to signal left.'

'Blister . . . rhuematism,' said Tom, ticking off the complaints. Then he turned to me. 'You might as well have your go, Terry. What have *you* got? A headache? Boils on your bottom?'

Fury flushed my face scarlet. 'You sexist pig!' I hurled at him. 'I suppose you think all girls are hypochondriacs? I bet you'd soon moan if you got saddle-sore or something. I know what babies men are. Every time my dad has a cold he thinks he's dying. My brother is just the same!'

'Oh, let's stop arguing and try and find something to eat in this lousy place,' Dave said. He put a hand on my arm and I shook it off. Although I was mad at Tom, I didn't want him to see Dave touching me. There was still a chance that he had the wrong idea about us.

Trust us to pick the only town which had early-closing that day. We had to mount our bikes again and cycle seven miles to the next one, but there we were lucky and found a great little café and had fresh Cornish pasties, followed by apple pie and custard. Good job we were going to start camping soon. Our money would run out if we had to eat in cafés all the time.

By nightfall, we had reached Exeter and checked into our hostel there.

'Won't we have to stock up with rations tomorrow morning?' I reminded Martin. 'There won't be any shops in the middle of Dartmoor . . .'

'You're right. We'd better all get together and make out a shopping list,' he said.

Dave had brought a camping stove, and the boys had a selection of lightweight alloy pans and plates between them. I'd packed a combination tin-opener and bottle-opener, as that was just the kind of thing that was easy to forget. But as it turned out, all great minds had thought alike. We ended up with no fewer than five tin-openers!

Next morning, we found a supermarket, bought half a dozen loaves, sliced ham, sausage, beans, fruit, powdered milk, juice, big bars of chocolate, packet soups, loads of mushrooms as they were so light to carry, margarine and a few other necessities and brainwaves. Soon we were heading for the tourist town of Chuddleigh, with its famous caves.

Dave wanted to stop and have a look round. I would have liked to have done, too, only Tom rightly reminded us that we weren't on a pleasure trip but had a schedule to stick to, and it was vital that we found a good campsite before dark.

By now, the road was a lot hillier and we passed through wooded gorges where fast streams, full of rain, poured down the hillside and passed beneath hump-backed bridges. We stopped to consult the map.

'Once we're past Widecombe, we'll be in the real wilds, up in the moors,' Martin said. 'Look!'

We all crowded round. 'Is that the same Widecombe that the song's about?' Lorraine demanded, and we all blasted out what we could remember of Widecombe Fair, getting stuck on who came after Peter Davey and before Old Uncle Tom Cobleigh.

'Oh, look! There's Buckfast Abbey!' Sue squeaked excitedly. 'I saw pictures of it in the book I read about Devon before we came. Couldn't we just go and have a look? It wouldn't take long . . . We can't come all this way and not see anything.'

I sighed. Was it going to be like this from now on? One contingent wanting to sightsee, forgetting what our trip was really about, and the rest of us having to remind them?

'Look, we'll just have to come again, in the summer holidays, maybe, when the weather will be better and we can take our time. We could take the bikes on the train as far as Exeter,' I suggested.

'That's not a bad idea, but all the same, we're so close and it would have been nice to – ' Sue started up again, but Tom silenced her.

'We can't stand around talking all afternoon, we've got to get on, up to the moors . . .'

'People have cycled over Dartmoor before,' Sue said acidly, determined not to let the subject drop. 'We're not doing anything that unusual. What does it matter if we spend just a couple of hours here and there doing something we want to do? It's not as if anyone will know . . .'

'My dad cycled all the way from Liverpool to Scotland once,' Lorraine chipped in.

'And my grandad went all the way down the M1 on his penny-farthing,' Tom said, straight-faced.

'But they hadn't built the M1 then,' Lorraine responded, falling right into his trap.

'Exactly. I was just trying to make you hear how daft you sounded. It's no good trying to make comparisons. Britain's a small country. I should think that just about every cycleable inch has been cycled over. It doesn't matter where we're going, what matters is the spirit in which we're doing it.'

Tom paused and I stared at him admiringly. I'd never heard him make a speech before.

'We musn't lose sight of why we're here, that's what I'm trying to say. If we start getting in the holiday spirit instead it won't work and we'll have let our sponsors down.'

'Ve are not here to enjoy ourselves,' said Martin, in a mock German accent. That eased the tension and we all chuckled.

We took swigs from our water canisters, I broke off a couple of squares of chocolate, and we got back on our bikes. Once more, I found myself behind Tom. It was my favourite place, if I couldn't be alongside him. When he turned the pedals, his track suit trousers pulled tight over his muscular calves and thighs and displayed how perfectly-shaped and strong they were. He had a neat, firm bottom, then his back broadened out to a set of powerful rugby-player's shoulders. I would feel so safe in his arms, snuggled against his hard chest, protected from the wind and rain, I thought, grimacing as a blast of wind carried a flurry of rain into my face. It hadn't let up all day.

We hit a hill that was particularly steep. 'Oh God!' I heard Sue wail. 'I'll never get up that!'

'There's worse to come,' Dave promised lugubriously.

The final stretch to Widecombe was the most exciting. Already, we could see the undulating moors with their craggy tors.

The landmark of the famous village turned out to be its spectacular church with its pinnacled tower. It seemed incredible that such a small place should have such an imposing church.

'They call it the Cathedral of the Moors,' Tom informed us, consulting his guidebook. 'It was built in the fourteenth century and there's a legend that it was once visited by the devil.'

Sue let out one of her piercing squeaks. 'Ooh! I hope it's not spooky round here. I'm terrified of ghosts.'

Dave had sneaked up behind her. He placed his thumbs against his lips, cupped his hands together, blew and a *whooooo* sound like an owl hooting made her jump out of her skin.

'I'm sure there must be a few dead highwaymen haunting the moors,' Martin suggested cheerfully.

'To say nothing of millions of dead sheep,' Tom added. I shuddered at that. I had a phobia about bones, they made me feel really peculiar. My uncle had taken Mark and me to the Natural History Museum in London once, and I'd taken one look at the skeletal dinosaurs and run out screaming!

We did sneak a very quick look at the church, but it was getting late. Beyond the village stretched the rough moorland we had come to find. My heart gave a leap of excitement. The rain had died down and was more like a soft mist which felt almost pleasant on my skin, and gentle, purplish shadows lay on the bracken-speckled moorland.

We took a track which led off the road and I felt the road surface deteriorate and the tyres bump over stones and hollows, and had to steer carefully.

'We shouldn't really be doing this, you know,' Dave said. 'Dartmoor is a National Park and people are only supposed to camp on the proper sites. I know *we're* a responsible bunch, but lots of people aren't. They're the sort who would light fires without taking any precautions to prevent them spreading, and leave litter all over the place.'

'That guy from the Gazette brought that subject up when I told him we were thinking of camping, but he thought that, as we were kind of in the public eye, no one would bother us. I hope not, anyway,' I said.

We'd all dismounted now and were pushing our bikes up the rocky track, searching for an ideal camp-site, which was difficult as a lot of the ground was very boggy.

'We need somewhere that's sheltered but not wet,' Tom said.

'Huh. Fat chance of that!' snorted Lorraine.

'Can't say I relish the idea of sleeping out in this. Couldn't we go back to the village and find a nice Bed and Breakfast?' Sue said, in a plaintive tone. Oh dear, I thought; Dave will soon go off her if she goes on complaining like this. Then I had the more cheering thought that so would Tom – if he fancied her at all, that was.

Personally, I was looking forward to a wild night on the moors, with the tent flapping in the gale and the wind singing in the rocks.

'How about over there?' Martin suddenly called. 'Those rocks will give us some shelter from the wind and the ground's well-drained and shouldn't be too boggy –'

'There's a stream over there, too,' Dave noticed.

There was a mad scramble to inspect the site – and suddenly, I was left behind with Tom, the two of us standing propping up our bikes as a gentle shawl of mist settled on our hair and faces.

My stomach turned over in a nice way, the kind of excited way you feel when a lift zooms upwards, and my pulse was racing. I could feel my arm trembling where it rested on my bicycle saddle.

'It's beautiful, isn't it?' he said, sweeping out his arm and indicating the gently rising upland with a blue hilltop in the distance. Somewhere, a curlew was singing its spiralling song and I could feel the peace and solitude settling around me.

I took a deep breath, wishing I could think of a poetic quotation. 'Yes,' I agreed, thinking how dumb I sounded.

Then Tom said something which surprised me so much that I nearly let go of my handlebars. 'You know, you look really good on a bike, Terry.'

I didn't think he'd ever really looked at me and the revelation set my heart hammering, my spirits soaring with hope. Could this be the beginning of a romance? It was the ideal setting, he'd come out with the ideal first words. All I needed was the perfect reply. But, as usual, I had to spoil it by turning it into a joke.

'You mean arms like handlebars and legs like spokes and a wedge-shaped behind?' I chuckled. Well, I was embarrassed. I always cracked stupid jokes when I was unsure of myself.

He laughed. Then we were hailed by the others to come and start unpacking. The magic moment was over, perhaps never to be repeated. What could I do? How could I make him see how much I felt for him? How could I make him see that I was something special – that, even if I didn't have long, curly, red hair and a spectacular figure I did have humour, tenderness, a superb imagination (absolutely true, just think of all the things I'd imagined about *him*!), warmth, understanding . . . in short all the qualities that would make me the ideal girlfriend. If only I knew what he was looking for.

In the meantime, I felt an acute pang as he moved away from me, guiding his bike round the rocks and ruts, leaving me to plod in his wake wishing . . . wishing we could sit up till late talking, finding out about each other. Wishing, in fact, that there was nobody else on the whole of Dartmoor except Tom and me . . .

Chapter 5

Sue approached me with a peculiar expression on her face, friendly yet apprehensive.

'I don't want you to be insulted or anything, Terry. I honestly brought this thinking it might give us all more room to spread out.'

'What is it?' I inquired, staring at the roll of green nylon with metal poles sticking out of the middle. I'd seen the polythene-wrapped roll strapped to her saddlebag and assumed it was just a sleeping bag.

'You can see what it is. It's a – a tent. I know you've got one already, but this is a little single-person one and I thought . . . Oh dear, I don't want you to take this the wrong way.' She gazed at me pleadingly. I smiled encouragingly.

'You don't know Lorraine and me very well and I thought you might feel awkward sharing a tent with us, so I brought this along thinking you might like to use it and we could have yours. I don't want to deprive you of the big tent, but . . .'

She was floundering, so I stepped in to save her. 'I think it's a fantastic idea, Sue. To tell you the truth, I was a bit nervous about sharing with you two, knowing you were best friends and would have lots you wanted to talk about that you mightn't want me to hear.'

'Oh, it's not that!' she insisted and I had to admit she did seem sincere.

'Look, I know that if Van and I were sharing a tent, someone else might feel weird because we talk in a special code sometimes, and we've got all kinds of little in-jokes and things.' Sue looked relieved. 'Thanks very much. Tell you what, I'll put my tent up for you, because I've done it before, and you can put this one up,' I suggested.

Twenty minutes later, my big blue tent was billowing in the breeze and Sue was prone beneath something which looked like a collapsed balloon. The boys came over in fits of laughter.

'You look as if you've never put a tent up before in your life!' gasped Martin, bent double with mirth.

'She hasn't,' Lorraine confessed. I saw looks pass between the boys and held my breath.

All the amusement vanished from Martin's face and the look in his eyes was accusing as he said, 'You did understand that one of the pre . . . pre . . .'

'Prerequisites?' supplied Tom.

'Yes, prerequisites of this expedition was that everyone should have camped out before.' He waited for Sue's reply.

'I'm sorry, Sue,' wailed Lorraine. 'I didn't mean to drop you in it.' She gazed wide-eyed at Tom, as if appealing for his support, and I scowled, hoping he wasn't being melted by those big blue eyes. 'We *have* camped before, honestly we have. But it was on a campsite in Spain where tents were already supplied and all we had to do was crawl into them and swot the mosquitoes!'

'Well, it's too late to worry about it now,' said Dave brusquely, and strode forward to help Sue. He had the tent up in seconds and she thanked him profusely and let her hand linger on his arm for a bit longer than was necessary, which just confirmed my suspicions that she fancied him. If only Ross had been here, he might have kept these two in order, I thought crossly. After all, they were *his* friends . . .

Dave and Martin were sharing a tent, Sue and Lorraine had my double one, and only Tom and I had our own. The thought gave me an excited shiver as I shook out my sleeping bag and tried to make my tiny shelter as comfortable as possible. By no stretch of the imagination could my – or rather, Sue's – tent have held two. But Tom's . . .? No, I couldn't think things like that. I musn't. Any hint of a scandal and it would be bound to get back, maybe even to my parents, once we got home. The person I trusted the least was Dave. As he knew me best, and was out to protect my interests, he'd be the most angry if anything went on.

I hadn't had all that much experience with boys. Quite the opposite, in fact. I'd never even been kissed properly, except for one rather slobbery kiss at a school disco from a boy I didn't even fancy.

I stretched myself out on top of my sleeping bag, my

tummy pleasantly full of the burgers and beans Dave had served up – Lorraine and Sue had volunteered to do the next meal, as a way of apologising for the tent incident, and I had offered to help them. It had been Martin and Tom who'd rinsed the pots and plates in the clear, fast-running stream tonight.

Why was I such a failure with the opposite sex, I wondered? Van had had a boyfriend for a whole nine months when she was fifteen, and was always being invited out. The most I had managed was the odd date and never with anyone really nice.

'Perhaps you're not romantic enough,' Van had suggested. 'Maybe you don't flatter the boy enough. Perhaps all you want to talk about is cycling . . .'

Maybe she had a point there. If a boy wasn't interested in cycling, then I had nothing in common with him, because it was the thing I enjoyed most in the world.

Somewhere to my right, I could hear murmurs and giggles coming from Sue and Lorraine's tent, but the boys were camped a bit farther away and I couldn't hear anything from their direction.

I was growing sleepy in spite of my soul-searchings. So I took off my shoes and sweatshirt and crawled into bed with my stretch trousers still on, but I soon got too hot so I had to unzip my sleeping bag and wriggle out and take them off, nearly knocking the main tent support down in my sleepy, disgruntled clumsiness. It had gone all wonky and I didn't want it collapsing on me in the night so, cursing to myself, I dragged my trousers back on, put my shoes and sweatshirt on, and crawled out of the flap.

In the half hour I'd been inside, the clouds had rolled back and the rain had ceased. I glanced over towards the boys' tents. Dave and Martin's was in darkness but I could see flickering torchlight coming from Tom's tent. Perhaps he was lying in his sleeping bag reading, unable to get to sleep for thinking of me! Scarcely had the wicked, delicious thought crossed my mind than his torch was abruptly switched off. So much for that theory!

I stretched my aching arms upwards and stared at the black, blank sky. There was no moon to light it, but the longer I stared, the more tiny stars I saw emerging from their opaque backcloth.

Something rustled in a bush somewhere and I jumped, my breath catching in my throat. I shone my torch bravely towards the sound, but there was nothing there, not even a mouse. I didn't mind mice, they were quite sweet. It was rats I was terrified of. I imagined a monster one cruising the moors – The Rodent of the Baskervilles! I sniggered out loud at the image, and was mortified at how loud my voice sounded, and hoped I hadn't woken anyone up.

I centred my tent pole again, pulled the whole thing taut, crawled back inside and did up the flap, removed my clothes carefully this time, and snuggled down into my sleeping bag.

And that's all I remember before I was woken by the scream . . .

I thought I'd dreamt it at first, that long, piercing shriek of terror, followed by a shuddering moan of horror. Perhaps I'd been having a nightmare and it was my own dream scream that had woken me up. Yet I couldn't recall any nightmare, or any dream at all.

Then, as I lay there, a bit cross at having woken up, it came again and immediately I thought of ghosts, the spirits of the highwaymen that Martin had mentioned, perhaps, and I felt my flesh creep. All at once I remembered Dartmoor Prison, and that thought was even more terrifying than spooks! Maybe, right this second, an escaped convict was threatening Sue and Lorraine with a knife – because it was their tent that the screams had come from, no doubt about that.

Quick as a flash, I was out of my sleeping bag and pulling on my trousers and sweatshirt. Then, very cautiously, I poked my nose out of my tent and peered towards Sue and Lorraine's. As I hadn't put my torch on, my eyes were accustomed to the dark and the stars cast a faint silvery glow, outlining something large, dark and bulky moving about in front of their tent.

Now it was my turn to gasp! Maybe the Hound of the Baskervilles story was true and any minute now the monster would turn towards me, with glowing red eyes and dripping fangs!

'Hey! What's going on over there? Are you all right?'

I could make out the shapes of two of the boys, Dave and Martin probably, coming towards us, with the third one, Tom, just visible in the background. At the sound of their shouting, there was the clattering noise of hooves hitting pebbles, and the creature reared up its head, snorted, and went skittering off. It was the first wild Dartmoor pony I had ever seen – but in what circumstances! Loud sobs were coming from the next-door tent and I realised guiltily that I hadn't exactly done much to help. They could have been bitten, or trampled upon for all I knew. I crawled out of my own tent still shaking and went over to theirs, arriving there just ahead of the boys.

'Are you okay?' I enquired. 'It was only a pony, you know . . .'

'A what?' came Sue's voice. 'Did you hear that, Lorraine? Lorraine . . .? Oh, come on . . .'

Dave was beside me, shining his torch into their tent, illuminating Lorraine lying face-down in her sleeping bag, sobbing hysterically.

'Calm her down, Sue, can't you?' he asked irritably. I couldn't help noticing that Sue was wearing a pair of pink pyjamas that left very little to the imagination. Trust her!

'Well, you seem in a better state than your friend,' Tom joined in from the background, making me tingle to the sound of his voice in the night. 'Tell us what happened.'

'I don't know!' Sue said wildly. 'I just woke up to hear Lorraine screeching her head off and something scrabbling around inside the tent. I was terrified. I actually put out my hand and felt something hairy and huge. It was ghastly!'

Lorraine took a deep, shuddering breath and raised a scarlet, tear-streaked face. 'I was having a nightmare and I . . . I thought something was going to k-kill me,' she stammered, her voice all wobbly. 'It woke me up with its whiskers and hot breath on my face . . . It was trying to – to *eat* me!'

'Not you, it was that sandwich it was after,' observed Martin drily, and we all peered in and spotted the last bit of bread lying in the sandwich wrapping.

'We bought some sarnies in that shop this morning and forgot to eat them,' Sue explained. 'Then, when we got into bed, we decided to have a midnight feast.'

'Piglets!' snorted Dave. 'What was wrong with my beefburgers, eh?'

'Lorraine doesn't like beefburgers,' revealed Sue, and Lorraine promptly snapped, 'Shut up!' at her.

Martin glanced at the luminous dial of his watch. 'Look, it's five o'clock. The sun'll be up soon. We'd better get some more sleep while we can, okay?'

There was a chorus of assenting grunts. As the boys ambled off, I could hear a bit of sniggering going on. Oh, yeah – very funny! I thought crossly. I bet they'd have yelled if some horrible, hairy face stuck itself into their tent and breathed all over them in the dark. I hoped it wasn't Tom doing the sniggering . . .

Two hours or so later, four out of the six of us were up and having breakfast. Of Sue and Lorraine, there was no sign at all.

'Better have a look to see if they're still in their tent,'

Martin suggested. 'Perhaps they were so scared, they thumbed a lift home at dawn – '

'Or perhaps a herd of horses ate them for breakfast,' Dave chuckled.

'Horses aren't carnivorous,' I reminded him.

'You could have fooled me. The only time I ever tried riding, the blasted animal put its head round while I was trying to get up on its back and took a chunk out of my backside,' he told us.

I laughed so much, my fried egg slithered off my plate and landed on the grass, right by a neat pile of rabbit droppings. Dave noticed and roared.

I put down my plate, feeling thoroughly cheesed off. I had a feeling that it wasn't going to be a good day for me. 'Anyway, I thought Lorraine and Sue were supposed to be cooking breakfast?' I said.

'So did we,' replied Tom, vigorously clinking his teaspoon in his tin mug.

It was freezing. The sky was a leaden grey colour and a nasty, nippy wind was getting up, rustling the grasses and rattling the sparse bushes. 'I'll go and get them up,' I said shortly, knowing my stomach would miss that egg later, but I certainly wasn't going to pick it up and eat it; the ponies were welcome to it!

'Oh, leave us alone,' Lorraine groaned, when I told them what time it was. 'Don't we deserve a lie-in after last night?'

'I'm aching all over. I don't think I could cycle to save my life,' Sue added.

'So am I, but we've got to keep going, we can't give

up. We promised,' I reminded them.

'Maybe you did,' Lorraine said ominously.

'What's that supposed to mean?' I asked spikily, but just then a body shouldered me aside. Tom.

'Morning girls,' he said cheerfully. 'Two huge mugs of tea, one with sugar, one without, correct?'

'Oh, fantastic!' I heard Lorraine sigh.

'I don't think that's a good idea,' I hissed at him, as soon as he'd handed the mugs inside. 'You can't start spoiling those two. They're not exactly pulling their weight as it is . . .'

'Give them a chance, Terry. Just because you're Superwoman . . .'

He marched off to pack up his camping stuff, leaving me staring after him. What did he mean? Was he being sarcastic? Somehow, his dig implied that he thought of me as practical, capable and all muscly, rather than feminine. I had always been a bit of a tomboy, but there was no point in lamenting now. I wasn't about to start looking for dewponds to bathe myself in at this time of year, and I hadn't brought any make-up with me . . . though Sue and Lorraine probably had. I expect they've brought perfume, too, I thought morosely.

Was that sort of stuff really important to boys? Was that why I didn't get many dates? I thought sadly that, if I could only put on a bit of eyeshadow and lipstick, maybe Tom would start seeing me as a girl, rather than just as a super-efficient cyclist.

Tom's cups of tea did the trick because soon the two emerged, looking remarkably untousled. I spotted a small ant running up the back of Sue's jumper, and decided I wouldn't tell her, but Dave spotted it and brushed it off, and seeing him touch her in such an easy, familiar fashion made me feel shut out somehow, as if I'd lost my best friend to somebody else.

'Right, folks,' announced Martin, 'we leave in half an hour.' He had his map in his hand and described our route, which would take us past some prehistoric stones. He glanced up at the sky. 'Doesn't look very promising,' he said, voicing the gloomy thought of all of us. 'I think we'd better go as far as we can before the heavens open.'

If I'd begun feeling depressed, pretty soon my spirits were at rock bottom, and it was all because of Lorraine and Sue. Martin had begun by setting the pace, but soon he'd dropped back and was shouting instructions at me while he joined Tom and Dave in chatting up my tawny-haired rival and her blonde friend. Although it was very cold, they were both wearing shorts and I thought how utterly stupid they were. Here was I, dressed practically, feeling warm and comfortable, whereas Lorraine's knees were purple with cold and Sue's legs looked red and blotchy.

As I rounded a corner, the wind knifed around a crag and brought tears stinging to my eyes. I had to stop my bike and wipe them, or else I'd have fallen off. But nobody else noticed.

'Come *on*, you lot!' I shrieked. 'We won't get anywhere unless you get a move on!' From my vantage point higher up the steep track we were on, it appeared that Dave and Martin were vying for Sue's attention, and Tom was off his bike, pushing it, deep in conversation with Lorraine, who was also walking. They all seemed so very engrossed in one another while once again I was completely on the outside. I felt the grip of depression swiftly taking a hold again.

I got back on my bike, hunched my shoulders over the handlebars, drove my bike up the last few yards to the top of the hill and paused. Despite the cloudy sky, the view was marvellous, the brown peat bogs with their hummocks of sedge gradually rising and giving way to tors which, in the lowering light, loomed silver and purple. A line of bushes and stunted trees gave away the path of a stream and, far to the right, I could see the sheen of water, a lake of some sort.

I widened my nostrils, feeling like a pony myself, and inhaled the sweet, chilly air. It hit me like a dash of spring water, clearing my head and lungs. I got back on my bike, pushed off, took my feet off the pedals and freewheeled down the hill . . . then disaster! My speedy descent came to an abrupt end as my front wheel hit a rock. The bike behaved like a bucking bronco and I found myself hurtling through the air.

The ground I landed on was soft, and very, very wet. So wet that, as I stumbled to my feet feeling a bit dazed from my fall, I realised I was soaked through to the skin.

At that moment, Sue reached the top of the hill ahead of the others and saw what had happened.

'Terry!' she called. 'Have you hurt yourself?'

'No, I'm all right,' I called back, but she came belting down, skidded to a halt beside me and almost fell off herself.

'You look a bit wet,' she observed, and I saw her lips twitch. Unsympathetic cow! To think of how cross I'd been when the boys had laughed at her and Lorraine last night!

'I'm all right,' I repeated gruffly, and went over to examine my bike, aware that boggy water was squelching over the sides of my shoes and my socks were wet.

The others had all caught up now and were taking advantage of the halt in the proceedings to nibble chocolate and swig drinks. Tom didn't even look my way, he was so intent on catching something Lorraine was saying. I felt really miserable. Suddenly the rumble of a car engine made us all look up and we saw a Landrover coming towards us. It pulled up by us and a man in a ranger's uniform got out.

'Where are you heading?' he asked us, and Martin got his map out and showed him. 'You do know some parts of the moor are quite dangerous?' he said, and proceeded to show us where exactly all the army firing ranges were. He handed Martin a leaflet with all the out-of-bounds areas marked on it.

'Which campsite are you heading for tonight?' was his next question.

'I, er . . . We're not exactly sure,' Tom said.

The man gave us a keen look. 'You know you're only allowed to camp on the official sites?' he reminded us.

'Yes, we know,' Tom assured him.

'Good. Well, I'll be on my way then. On your bikes!' he laughed, and got back in the Landrover, slamming the door with a loud clunk that echoed round the empty moors like a pistol shot.

I was glad I'd brought three pairs of socks. I changed into my red towelling ones and knotted the wet ones round one of the straps of my saddlebag, where they could stream out in the wind and dry as I rode. Then, fiercely, I turned on my companions.

'Look, I hate to say this but everybody had better buck their ideas up,' I said. My cheeks burned when I saw the mixture of startled, affronted and amused looks I was getting, but I ploughed on: 'This isn't a cycle club outing, it's the Dartmoor Challenge. We've got to put our backs into it.'

'You sound just like an old-fashioned Girl Guide,' sneered Sue.

'No, more like a Sergeant-Major! Come down off your high horse, Terry,' Dave said, exchanging an amused glance with Martin.

'Her high bike, you mean,' Tom put in. Oh, why were they *all* turning against me? Wouldn't just one person stick up for me and see the sense in what I was saying?

I bit my lip. I felt a bit sick. What was going on? I caught Martin looking at Sue's mottled legs and my temper just went wild.

'Look at you!' I said disgustedly. 'The two of you are complete idiots – amateurs! No real cyclist wears shorts in weather like this. It's only Easter, for God's sake. Do you want to catch pneumonia?'

'There's nothing wrong with my central heating system. I haven't got ice in my veins like you've obviously got, Miss High and Mighty!' snapped Lorraine haughtily.

I tried to keep calm. 'I was only thinking of your own good, and ours. If you catch a cold, it will be rotten for you, and it might hold the rest of us up.'

'You're just a slave-driver!'

I stared at Sue, my eyes almost popping out of my head. The boys were listening to us, slightly embarrassed, but amused nevertheless.

'I have to be,' I reminded her, as calmly as I could. 'This trip was my idea, even if Martin took over organising the actual route. Now it appears he's abandoned his post so someone's got to take over and chivvy the rest of you up, otherwise it'll be time to pitch camp again and we won't have gone half a mile.'

'I thought our only goal was spending three or four nights on the moor?' Lorraine had one pencilled eyebrow raised and was looking down her snub nose at me.

'It was crossing the moor both ways, then cycling back home, if you remember. We've got to call the paper when we get to the other side, and they'll tell that woman at the radio station. We've got to give our parents a ring, too, otherwise they'll be worried about us. So it's no use dithering about in the middle of Dartmoor because there's no phone boxes here.'

Dave came up and patted me on the head, which

made me cringe with fury. He was treating me just like a stupid little schoolgirl. 'Had our say, have we? Shall we get our wet bottom back on our bicycle seat and carry on . . .?'

'Oh, you're horrible!' I tore myself away from him, leapt onto my bike and pedalled off down the rough, bumpy track at a furious rate, not caring if I fell off again, just desperate to get away from all of them, with their sniggers and their mocking eyes.

I didn't bother looking back to see how far behind the others were, until I heard a succession of curses. Then I stopped, and was glad I had because I was so tense that my arms and legs were trembling slightly.

Dave was bending over his bike, examining the rear tyre. 'I've got a puncture,' he groaned.

'Tea-break!' shouted Tom, waving a thermos flask. So he'd filled it at breakfast time. That was bright of him. Why hadn't I thought of it? My left hip was aching and I rubbed it. It hurt. I must have bruised it when I fell off my bike. Still, I couldn't examine it now.

I noticed Lorraine was rubbing the side of her stomach. She saw me looking and called over that she'd got a stitch. I couldn't really feel any sympathy. Those two were useless. If only Ross had been here, I thought for the umpteenth time. Even better, if only Van had been here instead of Lorrainc and Suc. Van and Kim and Julie. That would have been fun.

Then a sudden thought struck me. You know those moments when the whole of the known universe gives a sort of jolt, and all at once you're seeing your life differently, as if someone's given you a big shake? It was like that. I suddenly saw myself from the outside, as the rest of them saw me. *I was no fun*! That was it! Because I had no special friend with me, now that Dave had started spending all his time chatting up Sue, I couldn't smile, I couldn't laugh, because I had no one to laugh with. I was being a big drag and the awful thing was that Tom could see it, too.

I took an enormous breath and pushed my bike over to join the others. 'Hello stranger,' Tom said, and gave me a quizzical look of surprise which turned my insides to jelly.

'Hello,' I said. And smiled.

Chapter 6

I'd seen Tom smile before, but never the way he smiled back at me just then. It was more than a smile. He was putting feelings into it, feelings which I could see in his eyes, which came out as a kind of sparkle and lit a little fire in me. Was this what love was like? As if everything around had suddenly become brighter, louder and more colourful? It had been a real effort for me to swallow my pride and come over. I knew it and Tom knew it, but now I was so glad I had. The others were all talking loudly amongst themselves but I couldn't make out any words they were saying, they just faded into a background babble as I concentrated on what, if anything, Tom was going to say to me.

I was amazed at how little I knew about him. Martin and Dave talked about themselves a lot. I'd known when Dave had had crushes on girls. I'd acted the sympathetic sister and told him all kinds of lies to soothe him when he got upset because he'd asked someone out and been turned down. I bet Tom had never been turned down in his life. A girl would have to be mad not to go out with him.

'Do you like the countryside down here?' he asked me. It was the kind of question a boy who was shy of girls and couldn't think of anything else to say would have asked – or a boy who was just making polite conversation . . .

I nodded. 'I prefer bigger mountains though.'

'Not to cycle up.' He grinned and I felt as if I had no bones in my legs.

I saw Lorraine glancing at us and tossed my head, hoping she'd see my insolent gesture and Tom wouldn't. 'Do you prefer the mountains or the sea?' I asked him.

'Oh, the seaside, I think. I love swimming and last year my dad and I took a yacht out in the Isle of Wight. I tried some water ski-ing but couldn't quite get the hang of the balancing, though.'

'I would have thought that you'd have been good at

that,' I said. 'How about surfing? I can just picture you in California, riding the crest of a wave.'

'I think I'd be terrified. Have you seen surfing programmes on TV? Those waves are as high as a house! They can knock you down and pulverise you.'

'So can an opposing rugby team!' I joked.

'Don't remind me!' He tapped the bump on his nose.

'Terry! Do you want some tea? I think there's half a cupful left. We've all had some,' Dave yelled, coming over to return Tom's flask. I'd been so busy talking to Tom that I'd hardly noticed how everyone was helping themselves to Tom and Martin's flasks.

'Sorry,' Tom apologised. 'If that selfish swine hadn't grabbed it . . .'

'Thirsty swine,' Dave corrected him. 'Okay, Terry?' he enquired, giving me a sharp look as if daring me to start lecturing them all again. Why couldn't he just go away and allow me to get on with chatting to Tom? But Dave sat on a rock near us and started talking rugby to Tom while I silently cursed him. After a while, bored and fed-up, I wandered off, up a little hill. Tom didn't look up; I was sure he hadn't even noticed that I'd gone.

As I walked away from them and the distance between us lengthened, I wished I could keep on walking, walking away from a disaster area. I just couldn't do a thing right, and everybody knew it. I thought back to my conversation with Tom and, try as I might, I couldn't regard it as anything other than social chitchat, meaningless and impersonal.

Tears stung my eyes as I gazed out over the panorama of hills and hidden valleys. I watched a pack of grazing ponies for a while, then Martin yelled for me and, reluctantly, I had to go back and join the group. As usual, Martin had his guidebook in his hand and everyone was standing round him.

'Does anyone know what a *kistvaen* is?' he asked us all.

'What's the prize for guessing?' said Sue.

'It's the way fishes greet each other. "Kissed fin." Get it?' Dave joked.

Everyone groaned.

'We give up,' I said. Martin explained that it was a sort of ancient burial chamber made of flat stones.

'There's one over here somewhere, according to my guidebook,' he said.

A chill shiver rippled down my back. I really did hate anything to do with death, but I also hated being a wet blanket. I had now become determined to cheer up and join in more with everybody else, so I forced myself to tiptoe across the boggy ground, testing each footstep to make sure I wouldn't sink into the marsh and disappear for ever.

When we found it, it wasn't much to look at, just a rough, jumbled rectangle of stones, but unmistakably a tomb. I thought of the poor soul that had been laid to rest in such a lonely spot, and shivered again. The wind moaned in the rocks and I felt a flicker of fear, thinking of ghosts again. The place even *smelt* of death, a rotten, sweetish, decaying smell. Yet the corpse, if it was still under there, must have been dead thousands of years, so how could it smell?

I took a few steps back and nearly tripped over something which moved as I stumbled against it. I jumped and turned round, and found myself staring at a very dead sheep.

'Ugh!' I exclaimed, feeling suddenly sick. I averted my eyes, trying not to look at it, just as I had to look away from the TV screen every time they showed a close up of ants or maggots eating something dead. Yet, as always, some kind of fatal, perverse fascination drew me to look again. Its eyes had been pecked out, and some animal had been working on it, so that the ribs gleamed through the red gash in the ragged grey wool.

A wave of nausea welled up from the pit of my stomach and, letting out a gasping sob, I staggered away, feeling faint and ill. Next moment, I was joined by Lorraine, only she was actually sick. Her horrible noises alerted the others, who all came dashing up, issuing a series of 'Ughs!' and 'How horribles' as they, too, passed the corpse.

'I . . . I'm sorry,' Lorraine muttered.

'Here,' Tom said, handing her a plastic beaker of water. She sipped it gratefully. 'Are you all right, Terry?' he asked me.

'I haven't been sick, if that's what you mean,' I answered tartly. I had to be sure he knew that.

'How are you?' I asked Lorraine, who was looking terribly pale.

'I'm okay, I think,' she replied uncertainly.

'At least I'm not the only squeamish person round here,' I said.

Sue came over and put an arm round Lorraine and started leading her back to where the bikes were. Tom was still hovering around in my immediate vicinity.

'You'rc not going to be sick, are you, Terry?' he enquired, looking at me quizzically. 'You're looking a bit green. That sheep was grisly enough to make anyone feel ill. I don't feel too good myself.'

'I'm fine,' I told him firmly. 'I'd be happy to leave here, though. Do you think the others are ready?' Dave and Martin were still discussing the history of the tomb.

'I'll ride next to you in case you feel a bit wobbly,' Tom offered. That made me feel better straight away! What a weird day it was, I thought. So many ups and downs, good things and bad things, all mixed up. But this was definitely one of the good ones.

My stomach soon settled down as we all straggled off along our chosen track, having to get off and push every so often, when the ground got too steep or rocky. It was pretty exhausting, but I hardly noticed because I was talking to Tom. And this time we weren't talking about trivialities, but about important things, about us, about our likes and dislikes.

Every so often, I'd hear scraps of the conversations

that were going on behind me, where Martin was chatting to Lorraine and helping her push her bike. Dave and Sue were bringing up the rear. I didn't know what stage they'd reached in their relationship and I was dying of curiosity. They were doing a lot of laughing about something, anyway. Sue had one of those raucous laughs that you could hear for miles. No wonder we hadn't seen any wildlife apart from the odd sheep and pony. Every animal for miles had run for cover when it heard that screech owl coming!

'I'm hoping to get into university,' Tom was saying.

'Which one?' I enquired.

'Depends what grades I get at A level. I'm not quite sure at the moment. I'll decide when the results come through. You've got your GCSEs in a few weeks' time, haven't you?'

'Don't remind me,' I said with a grimace. 'I'm dreading it.'

'Don't worry too much. If you fail something, you can always take it again in November. I had to do that with English Literature. I never had time to do any reading as I was always out playing rugby, or practising. I started working at it in the lower sixth and passed it last November – just!'

'English Lit's one thing I hope to do well at. I've always got my nose in a book,' I told him. Then, not wanting to sound boring, I added: 'Pity you can't take an A-level in cycling.'

We tossed that idea around for a couple of minutes, making a lot of silly jokes about papers in Oil Efficiency and Gear Theory. Then he asked me about my family and I asked about his. Whereas I'd got Mark, he had two older sisters, both married.

'So we're both the baby of the family,' he said teasingly.

'You don't look much like a baby,' I said, and immediately felt myself blushing in case he'd read any other meaning into it, because it sounded a bit flirtatious and I found it hard to make that kind of teasing, semi-sexy conversation with boys.

'I have been known to cry,' he said unexpectedly. 'Big boys aren't supposed to, are they?'

I thought about that seriously, then said, 'I don't see why not. Crying means admitting you've got feelings, that you're sad, or upset. It's different from being a cry-baby, howling every time you've cut your finger.' The thought of tears in Tom's eyes filled me with an indescribable tenderness. My feelings for him took a jump off the diving board into the deep end.

'What kind of things have made you cry?' I asked, and had to clear my throat because I'd suddenly developed a frog in it. 'I cry over sad films and books – even records, sometimes.'

'The last time was when our dog died,' he confessed. 'We'd had Rags since I was about two. He had to be put to sleep when I was sixteen. The funny thing was, we'd given him an official birthday, the sixteenth of December, because that was when we'd got him, just before Christmas, and – do you have a dog, Terry?'

'No. No animals.'

'Well, it might sound stupid then, but we all used to give him cards and presents, just as if he was a human member of the family, and last December I was about to get him something, out of habit, when I remembered he wasn't there any more and I just broke down. It was crazy. Do you think I'm mad?'

'No. I think you're . . .' I wanted to say 'fantastic', or 'lovely', or 'just my sort of person', but I didn't dare say any of those in case I gave away my feelings towards him, so, after a slight pause, which he must have noticed, I just said, 'completely normal. Boys have just as much right to cry as girls.'

We came to a really steep bit of road and had to stop talking, needing our breath to heave our bikes over some rocks.

'Look at that view!' Sue yelled, and we all stopped, glad of a breather. It really was amazing. It was exciting to see so much sky. At home, you only saw the patches between next door's chimney pots. But there was so much here, my eyes couldn't take it all in. Great boiling grey clouds with vivid patches of blue between, the shapes changing all the time as the wind sped them across the sky. As they went, they cast shadows on the undulating ground below, patches of dark and light which chased each other, dappling hillsides, darkening bogs, flicking across us so that one minute we were bathed in sunshine, and the next we were shivering in shade.

Martin got his camera out – he hadn't used it much yet – and took a photograph of the landscape, then asked us all to stand close together so that he could take one of us with the moor in the background.

I had to get next to Tom, so I squeezed myself in between him and Dave. Then Lorraine came round and stood on the other side of him, which upset me. Martin asked us all to get even closer together . . . and I seethed as Tom draped his left arm around Lorraine. He couldn't put his other round me as he was propping his bike up with it. I had to be content with Dave's shoulder rubbing against mine. He had his spare arm round Sue, of course.

'Shall we do another one, just in case this one doesn't come out? How about one with you in?' I suggested to Martin, intending to oust Lorraine somehow, and get Tom's arm round me!

'Good idea. You take it then, Terry,' Martin said. Just my luck!

There was a longish stretch of fairly even track ahead, so we all mounted our bikes and set bumpily off. I was glad when Lorraine dropped back to talk to Sue, leaving Tom and me together again.

'Terry . . .?'

Some sixth sense made me aware of a slightly different tone in his voice, and I gripped my handlebars hard. When his question came, it was even more important than anything I could have imagined.

'Is there anything going on between you and Dave?'

I burst out laughing, but my brain was whirling. Why was he asking? My heart began to thud. Could it be he *was* interested in me?

'No,' I chuckled. 'Does it look like it?'

'I've seen you around together a lot . . .'

'We used to live next door to each other. Our families are very friendly. That's all.'

'Oho! The boy next door, eh? We all know about those romances . . .'

'Well, there isn't one in this case. There never has been. Anyway, he's got his eye on Sue. I'm surprised you haven't noticed. They are making it rather obvious . . .'

'Mm. I did wonder. Well, that clears one thing up,' he said enigmatically.

'What's that?'

'There's no obstacles in my path.'

I pretended to think that he was referring to the physical path we were cycling over, and I squinted down it pink with embarrassment.

'No, you're right,' I observed.

'Good. That means I can ask you out one night when we get back.'

Everything swam in front of my eyes and my front wheel did a swerve and my bike took me off the track and down a little incline, where I skidded to a halt just before hitting an enormous rock.

'Hey . . .' Tom came swooping down to find me. 'Is the prospect that grim?' he panted, coming to a bouncing stop.

'No,' I croaked. 'Not grim at all. I . . . it would be lovely.'

'You know I like you a lot . . .'

'No, how could I?' I murmured, thinking: this isn't happening, it can't be. I've come off my bike, hit my head, and now I'm unconscious and dreaming.

'Well, I do,' Tom said. 'I hope you like me a bit. Do you . . .?'

'Mmm.' What else could I say? At a moment like this, every word was a potential bomb. It was better to say nothing, just nod, and let my face and eyes do the talking.

It was quiet and sheltered where we were, out of the wind, with no sign of the others, though doubtless they'd find us before long. Tom leaned his bike against the big rock, then did the same thing with mine. He put his hands on my shoulders and looked into my eyes, and my whole body started trembling so much that I felt sure he could feel it, too.

His hands slid down my back and he pulled me towards him. I closed my eyes. It was as if we were in a time capsule and we'd left the unknown universe behind. We were suspended in space. I felt Tom's lips in my hair, felt his warm breath on my forehead. I felt myself collapsing against him, his arms taking my weight.

His lips travelled down my nose, gave the tip a little peck. He paused, moved his head back a little way. 'Terry,' he said, very quietly, as if to himself. It was almost a question.

Then he kissed me . . .

'Hey there! Terry . . . Tom . . . where are you?'

'Oh, hell!' Tom cursed, springing away from me the instant he heard Martin's voice.

'Down here!' he called back.

I was aware of my fiery cheeks, and of the four sets of eyes on us as the others pushed their bikes down to the little sheltered hollow where we were.

'Er . . . Terry's bike hit a bump and spun off the road, and this is where we ended up,' Tom explained.

'A likely story,' Sue responded, but her teasing tone held a hint of genuine disbelief, and there was a hurt look in Lorraine's eyes.

Did I look like a girl who had just been kissed? I wondered. What did people who had just been kissed look like, anyway? In books, they had rumpled hair, flushed faces, and a sparkle in their eyes. I was sure I had all of those.

'Time we stopped for lunch, anyway,' Martin announced. 'I'm starving.'

'I could eat a horse,' Dave said.

'There were some over there. I'll go and get you one,' Tom offered, and we all laughed. That lightened the atmosphere and I found I could breathe again, though I still felt all trembly and tingly inside.

'I'm not very hungry,' said Lorraine, refusing the piece of currant loaf that Sue offered her. 'I've still got this blasted stitch in my side.'

'I'll have it then, if it's going spare,' I said. I was ravenous myself. Then I remembered dropping that egg at breakfast time. No wonder I was hungry.

We all found rocks to sit on and I got out the

tomatoes I had in my saddlebag and added them to Sue's packet of ham slices, and helped her make some sandwiches which we passed round. Tom had a bag of apples, and they got passed round, too. I noticed Lorraine helping herself to one of those. She would, if it was Tom offering it to her, I thought jealously. Not hungry, indeed! All she wanted was a bit of Tom's attention. I really would have to watch her from now on.

Chapter 7

Funnily enough, that afternoon I actually got talking to Lorraine, and it was nothing to do with boys, either.

Martin had produced some cans of lager, and I'd had some. So maybe I was feeling just a little bit more relaxed and outgoing than normal. I'd noticed that, although Lorraine had accepted that apple from Tom, she'd only nibbled it a little bit and not really eaten anything, and Sue had finished it off herself.

I found myself bringing up the rear with her as we all pushed our bikes back up the hill to the track. Lorraine appeared to be having some trouble with hers.

'Are you okay?' I asked her. She had been very quiet all day – much quieter than usual.

'I've got these awful cramps in my stomach. I think it's my period coming on. I do get a lot of pain with it sometimes,' she confided.

I smiled sympathetically. I'd had the occasional bad pain with mine, too.

'Have you got anything for it?' I asked.

'I haven't got any painkillers, no. I didn't think it was due till next week. Luckily, Sue's brought some things with her.'

'I've got some, if you run out,' I said. I'd just been at the end of my period the day we'd set out.

'Thanks, Terry.' She smiled gratefully and I gave her a hand with her bike. 'It's not a thing you can talk about when the boys are around, is it?'

'No, not really.'

We caught up with Sue and those two immediately started talking, which left me out, so for a while I was happy to ride along in a contented haze on my own, watching Tom talking to Dave, nursing my – our – secret to myself. Whatever else might happen now, I had the assurance that Tom wanted to see more of me once we got back home.

Suddenly, I realised that it wasn't just because I felt a bit drunk, and in a happy daze, that things seemed hazy. We were riding into a thick, damp mist which had fallen without warning. All landmarks were blotted out and we couldn't see the sky, the hilltops, or anything further away than about six feet all around us.

‘Blimey!’ I heard Dave exclaim.

‘Er . . . I’m scared, folks!’ piped Sue; she put on a funny voice, but you could tell she was a bit alarmed.

‘Everyone move closer, so we can all see one another,’ ordered Tom sensibly.

We clustered together and Martin switched on his torch in order to map-read. It was only about four o’clock but it might as well have been midnight, it was so foggy and dark.

I glanced hopefully at Tom and moved nearer to him, wondering if he was brave enough to put his arm round me in public, but he didn’t. So, swallowing my disappointment, I racked my brains to recall everything I had read about what to do in blizzards and fogs.

‘We must all stick together and not wander off the road. That’s vital,’ I said, remembering what I’d read in the book about cycle touring which I had at home. ‘You’ve seen what the ground’s like, with those sudden ruts and gulleys and treacherous bogs. Remember that bit in *Lorna Doone* where that guy steps in one and sinks, and nobody can save him?’

‘Oh, don’t!’ Lorraine wailed. She actually looked close to tears, though I wondered if it was all an act, put on specially for the benefit of the boys. Tom was standing on one side of her and Sue on the other. For once, I felt safe. Tom had made his choice – it was me he wanted, not her. I took a deep breath.

‘There’s no ground fit to camp on just here, so what I suggest is that we all carry on on foot, very slowly, keeping the person in front of us in sight, and maybe the mist will clear up, once we reach higher ground.'

'It won't,' forecast Martin. 'It actually came down on us, so it must have started up there.'

Lorraine gave a sniff and I gritted my teeth. Why was she such a wimp? Okay, so she had period pains, but all she had to do was ask one of us for a pain-killer. She knew I had some. Maybe I should offer her one, I thought – then my thoughts stopped dead as my mind went into a kind of seizure. Tom was walking with his arm around Lorraine's shoulders.

I felt as if all the breath had been knocked out of me. How could he? What kind of a game was he playing, the conceited, smug, big-headed rat? Did he think he could go round privately flirting with all of us? Did he hope to end the week with Sue, Lorraine and me all helplessly in love with him?

I felt sick and noticed I was shivering, with shock as much as cold. And the mist was growing even thicker.

'Oh Dave, I'm so scared,' I heard Sue say in a weak voice.

'Well, I'm not!' I responded scornfully, striding out, pushing my bike by the saddle, left hand on the handle-bars. I was furious – seething in fact. I cast a dark look in Tom's direction and he must have felt it because he suddenly looked back at me and I quickly turned my head away. He still had an arm round Lorraine, though she certainly didn't need helping along. I loathe girls who put on a little-girl act when there's a strong boy around. They're the type who give other girls a bad name. From now on I just wasn't going to speak to her if I could help it.

I was so angry that I was striding along at a terrific pace, passing the others without realising it.

'Oi, Terry! Come back – don't get yourself lost!' I heard Dave call from somewhere in the swirling yellow blanket. I looked back and people and bicycles were vague grey shapes wading through gloom.

I remembered I'd actively hoped Sue and Dave would get together. Well, that seemed to be taken care of. He was being the perfect gent now and pushing both their bikes, while she walked by his side, clutching his arm.

Once more, I plunged forward . . . and suddenly my feet and tyres were bumping over rough ground. I'd left the track somehow. Scrubby clumps of heather snagged my trousers, pulling at the material. It was horribly, ominously silent. I strained my ears, listening for the voices of my companions. Nothing. Panic began to rise inside me. They couldn't be far away. I'd only been ahead by a few yards. But the mist was so thick now, and it had got dark, too, and my cycle lights were useless. I got my torch out and snapped it on, directing it at the ground. I shone the beam in every direction but there was no sign of the track I had recently left.

My teeth began to chatter. I could *die* here, I realised! Hypothermia could quickly set in and when the weather cleared tomorrow they'd find my body, just two yards from the track, huddled in the heather.

Don't be so wet! I rebuked myself. I had a small tent, a sleeping bag and my spare clothes. All I needed to do was put the tent up and keep myself warm and I'd be all right.

But I felt so desperately alone, even Tom and Lorraine, hand in hand, would be welcome now; anything rather than face a minimum of thirteen hours till dawn – and more if the fog didn't lift – absolutely alone.

Panic got the better of me, surging up from the pit of my stomach into my throat, into my vocal chords.

'Help!' I shrieked. 'Where are you? *HELP!*'

I began to ring my bicycle bell and carried on shouting. Then suddenly – miracle of miracles! – I heard a voice.

'Hey!' it called, faintly, then louder: 'Terry!'

'I'm over here!' I yelled, ringing my bell frantically.

It was answered by another tinkling bell, then suddenly Martin materialised by my side.

'Thank God I've found you!' he said.

'Phew! My thoughts exactly,' I replied, an inane grin splitting my features. I almost felt like hugging him, I was so pleased to see him. 'Are you going to lead me back to the others?'

'No. I thought perhaps you were going to lead me back,' he replied, and my high spirits plummeted.

'You don't mean you've got lost, too?'

'Looks like it,' he answered cheerfully, laying his bike down in the heather. 'I was following you, then all at once I looked back and the others had vanished. I couldn't even hear them.'

'So much for my warning everyone to stick together,' I said dolefully.

'Well, they were sticking together. Quite successfully too. I felt quite left out.' Martin took off his gold-rimmed specs and wiped them with his glove. 'Damn! It's all the moisture in the mist. I can't get them clear,' he grumbled.

'What shall we do?' I had put my bike down, too. I had my hands jammed in my pockets and I began hopping up and down, trying to warm myself up.

'I think the worst thing we could do is to go any further. We might just stumble into a bog. Even worse, we might end up on an army firing range and there could be unexploded bombs around,' Martin announced unhelpfully.

'That's right. Cheer me up,' I said. 'I suppose you're saying we should pitch camp right here and stay here till it's cleared up.'

'You're quite right,' said Martin, in his careful, precise way. 'I think that *is* the best thing to do. In fact, it's the only thing to do. Have you got any food?'

I shook my head ruefully, cursing my stupidity. One of the most important rules of survival is to split the food up equally, so that if there's an emergency and a group gets split up, everyone has some. 'I might have a bit of chocolate,' I said doubtfully.

'I've got a can of luncheon meat and two oranges, and I might have a packet of gingernuts,' Martin said enthusiastically. Then, in the thin beam from my torch, I saw his face cloud over. 'There's one very important thing I haven't got though. A tent . . .'

It felt very strange having somebody else – someone larger than me – trying to squash into my tiny single-person tent. No matter how we moved, we overlapped.

'This is ridiculous!' snorted Martin when, for the umpteenth time, a sharp bit of me met an unyielding bit of him, and vice versa. The fact that we'd turned our torches off to save the batteries only made things worse.

My teeth felt all furry and nasty. I longed to get my toothbrush out and give them a clean, but Martin had said that we must conserve the water we had. I thought that was a bit daft. If we were that thirsty, we could go out and lick it off the bushes, or spread out some plastic and catch the water droplets from the air. I had to make do with a fast brushing using the minimum of toothpaste, and a surreptitious gulp of water and a spit.

'I'm starving,' I moaned, aware that I must sound just like Lorraine.

'Have an orange,' offered Martin. 'I think I can just about reach them if I stretch my arm . . . Oh!' As he tried to extend his arm beneath the side of the tent and reach the saddlebag of his bike, which was lying prone on the ground right outside, he got his sleeve caught and tipped our shelter sideways.

'Oh, hell, Martin, you've got me all wet now!' I

exclaimed furiously, frantically brushing raindrops off my sweatshirt and my sleeping bag.

'It was you who wanted the wretched orange!' he hurled back, and suddenly we were having the most awful argument.

'I think I'll go and sleep outside and catch pneumonia!' Martin stormed. 'Even that would be better than sharing this hamster cage with you!'

'You might as well put it back up seeing that it was you that knocked it over,' I said acidly.

He barged past me, treading on my finger, and I screamed, but he didn't even apologise. I could feel tears pricking at my eyes. Here I was, marooned in an impenetrable moorland mist, having the row to end all rows with boring old Martin, and somewhere Sue and Dave, and Lorraine and Tom, were snuggled oh-so-cosily in *my* double tent, murmuring sweet nothings to each other, keeping each other warm in the best kind of way.

Lorraine in Tom's arms. Tom's fingers tangling in her red curls, Tom's lips brushing her head like they did mine, but moving downwards and settling on her lips . . . I will not cry! I told myself, grimly gritting my teeth while above me the nylon flailed as Martin attempted to pull it straight. I wasn't a baby. I was the one who'd started this whole thing, therefore I had to be the bravest of the lot. I drew back my shoulders and stuck out my chin. I wouldn't cry – not over Tom, or over being stranded. I was perfectly all right, I had nothing wrong with me, apart from being ravenously hungry, and I could remedy that right this minute.

I savagely ripped the peel off the orange Martin had hurled in to me and began sucking it noisily.

Martin finished rebuilding our shelter and crawled back inside.

'Pooh! It stinks of oranges in here,' he grumbled.

'What do you expect, stupid?' I spat a pip towards the flap, missed, and it hit Martin's hand instead.

'Ugh! Look out!' he said in disgust, rubbing his hand on his other sleeve.

'Oh, for goodness sake let's stop this,' I said wearily. 'It's going to be a long night. Why don't we try and get some rest?'

'How?' he grunted crossly. He arranged himself on his side, with his back to me. His feet pushed mine into an uncomfortable position, but I didn't dare complain. Instead, I did my best to arrange myself into the space that was left. And, to my surprise, I eventually drifted off to sleep.

But not for long.

'Tom . . .?' I mumbled dreamily. I thought I was still asleep, reliving that magical moment before Tom had proved to be such a rotten swine. Warm lips were brushing my cheek, seeking my mouth hungrily, and an arm was clasping me, pulling me firmly towards an unmistakably masculine body.

I kept my eyes closed, surrendering to the embrace, allowing my mouth to be greedily pressed until my lips parted under the pressure.

'Oh Terry . . .' He was panting noisily, crushing me

with his weight. I felt stifled, trapped in my sleeping bag, but a hand was worming its way down inside the padded interior, groping for my breast.

'Martin! Get *off*!' Suddenly, I was wide awake, shrieking in horror, pushing him away – an impossible manoeuvre in that confined space. The tent was holding well now, the nylon taut and resisting, almost pushing him back to me like elastic.

'No, Terry. Please let me . . . You've got to. I've never been so close to a girl before in the dark. We've got all night. I've always fancied you. We must keep warm . . . Let me kiss you . . . Oh Terry . . . '

Martin's mouth crushed down on mine again. I could feel his teeth brusing my lips. His tongue came out, all spitty. I knew my breath smelt foul but he didn't seem to mind. He was past noticing little things like that. His hand was pushing further down inside my sleeping bag. He was hurting me.

I screamed, and lashed out with both hands, hammering at his shoulders. I couldn't fight back with my legs trapped in my sleeping bag, so I drew my knees up, trying to push him off. He was still hanging on to me, but the nylon sleeping bag was slippery and he was gradually sliding off. Any minute now . . .

Crunch! Suddenly something crackled beneath my shoulder and I cried out as I felt something sharp stick into me. With a superhuman effort I shoved Martin off and struggled to sit up. He collided with the tent frame, cursing as he banged his elbow. Then there was a blast of cold, damp air as he pushed his way out of the tent.

I rolled onto my side and gingerly patted the groundsheet, my fingers encountering needle-sharp fragments. I couldn't find the torch so, using my shoe which I'd placed behind my head with its partner, I carefully brushed whatever it was up to the edge of the tent and off the end of the groundsheet, out of harm's way. But my shoulder was stinging and suddenly I burst into tears I couldn't control.

Outside there was silence. Maybe Martin had stomped off in the mist and left me to fend for myself. He'd probably pinched my torch, too. I couldn't hear anything but the rasping sound of my own shuddering breaths, and the gulping sound of my sobs. I was weeping for everything that had happened today, all the nasty things like the dead sheep, the depressing tomb, Tom's uncaring behaviour, the fog, losing the others, and Martin's completely out of character attack. He had acted like a total stranger.

Yet, I suddenly realised, he *was* a stranger. I'd only ever seen the 'Dave's mate' side of him. I'd never talked in depth to Martin proper. I'd never seen any sign of this darker side of him. Would he have raped me if I hadn't stopped him?

Gradually, my sobs dried up and my shoulders stopped heaving and I found a tissue screwed up in my pocket and blew my nose, and wiped my wet face on my sleeping bag.

It was difficult to go back to sleep because I soon began to worry about Martin. I had the tent, but he had nothing, not even his sleeping bag which was still in here. He was the one who was going to die of cold, not me. I forced myself to wake up. I had to do something. I couldn't let anything happen to him, in spite of what he'd tried to do. Perhaps I'd taken it too seriously, I thought worriedly. Maybe all he'd wanted was a kiss and a cuddle, nothing more.

I held my breath and listened. Was I mistaken, or was that a human sound outside?

I stuck my head out. The mist had cleared a bit and I could see Martin huddled across his bike, his head on his arms. His shoulders were moving and he was making harsh grunting noises. He was crying – Martin was crying!

Quietly, I tiptoed over and laid a tentative hand on his shoulder. 'Martin . . .? Are you all right?'

He lifted his face, and I caught the gleam of tears. 'I'm sorry, Terry,' he choked out. 'God, I'm sorry . . . I didn't mean to . . . Oh, you know. I . . . I don't know what happened.' He was shivering violently and I could actually hear his teeth chattering.

'Look, you've got to come back inside,' I said. 'We'll both freeze out here.'

'Can you ever trust me?'

'Of course.' We were both in the same boat, lost, tear-stained and completely miserable. He didn't look a bit like a rapist, just like a frightened, cold boy.

I held out a hand to him. 'Come on.' I almost had to drag him into the tent.

When he'd crawled into his sleeping bag and his shivers had begun to subside a little, I tried to crack a joke.

'I thought for a minute you'd gone cycling back to Exeter to find that nice warm hostel!'

'I would have gone off somewhere but I had a bit of a problem,' he said.

'What?'

'I think you broke my glasses . . .'

Chapter 8

I woke up with cramp in one leg and an extremely apologetic Martin trying to crawl out of the tent without waking me.

'Oops, sorry,' he said as he accidentally kicked me.

I was right over against one wall of the tent, so it was little effort to stick my fingers beneath the bottom edge, prise up the taut nylon and peep out. When I saw green grass and shiny white stones, I let out a little cheer.

'Hooray, the mist's gone!'

'Let's get this lot packed up, then, and try and find the others,' Martin said. Then he looked me straight in the eye, which was difficult for him, as he was so short-sighted. 'I, er . . . About last night. I'm really sorry. I didn't intend to act like that, it was just that . . . you were so near, and I was so cold, and I thought maybe – '

'Maybe you'd chance your luck,' I finished, not without a hint of sarcasm.

'I suppose so.' He grinned sheepishly. 'I'm really sorry. I've never been so close to a girl before. I don't suppose you would understand . . .'

'No, I don't.' I shrugged huffily. But I did, really.

'As long as we can forget it and still be friends,' he continued.

'Why not?' I said resignedly. 'I'm not going to tell anyone.'

'Neither am I.'

'What about your specs?' I asked, changing the subject. 'How will you manage? I suppose I'll have to pay for a new pair when we get back.'

'I wouldn't expect you to do that. It was all my fault!' he insisted, looking quite shocked at the idea. 'Anyway, I've got a spare pair in my saddlebag. I'll go and find them.'

By now, I was standing outside the tent. A powerful wind was whipping back my hair.

'I'd give anything for a shower,' I said.

'Mm. Me too.' Martin gave a sudden sneeze. 'That'll teach me to sleep in damp socks,' he said glumly.

'Change them now, before we set out,' I suggested.

'Good idea.'

While he was rummaging, I walked up the rising

ground, until I was standing on a ridge from which I could see quite a panorama of sweeping hills and spreading moorland.

'There's a road over there!' I yelled, pointing.

To get to it, we had to splash through a stream, with Martin being extra careful not to get his fresh pair of socks wet, and walk carefully round a patch of quagmire. As we pushed our bikes with difficulty over the roughest ground we'd encountered yet, Martin said knowledgeably, 'We got mazed last night.'

'What?' I queried.

'Mazed. It means lost in the mist. It's a dialect word. I found it in the guidebook this morning.'

'You and your guidebook! Why don't you check your compass instead? Then perhaps you'd have some idea of which way we're going. No. Let me do it. I haven't used my compass yet,' I added, producing it from my saddlebag.

I took the lid off it and found we were heading due north. 'Isn't that where the firing ranges are?' I asked Martin.

'I don't think we're that far north. See those houses way over there?'

I squinted into the distance, reflecting that Martin's spare specs gave him much better vision than my own unaided eyes, and wondering if I needed specs myself.

'I think that could be Postbridge, and that's the road which runs to Yelverton. On the other hand, I could be entirely wrong,' he admitted cheerfully.

'Great,' I said bleakly.

'Look, it's civilization, so we'll make for it, anyway, and if there's a shop or something open, we could ask if there's been any sign of the rest of our party.'

'What if there hasn't been?'

Martin sighed thoughtfully and ran his hand through his fair curls. 'Dunno . . .'

'If only we'd fixed up some plan for what to do if we got separated,' I said, suddenly feeling very tired and depressed, even though it was only a quarter to nine. After that disturbed night, though, and all the strain of yesterday, thinking Tom was keen on me and then realizing he was only playing with me, it wasn't surprising if I felt a bit miserable.

It took half an hour to reach the distant road and the village. It turned out to be Two Bridges, right in the centre of the moor with the River Dart running through it – and, wonder of wonders, we found a little shop open and bought a pie each, and a couple of cans of Coke. Food had never tasted more delicious!

As we sat on a wall munching away, raised voices made us look up. Some cyclists were coming down the road. 'It's Dave!' I yelled. 'Look, Martin!'

The others came into view, too, and when Dave saw us waving he braked violently.

'Well, look who it isn't!' he exclaimed excitedly, and we were immediately subjected to a barrage of questions. Tom gave me an odd sort of look, his eyes switching to Martin, then back to me, and I felt myself flushing. So he was trying to put two and two together, was he? Well, he was totally wrong. And anyway, after his abandonment of me in favour of Lorraine yesterday, he didn't have a leg to stand on.

'. . . and we suddenly found ourselves on a road, and this car came along and the man stopped and said we were only a mile from Postbridge, where there was a Youth Hostel,' Dave was telling Martin.

'Lucky devils!' I put in.

Sue gave a toss of her blonde hair. 'Yes, weren't we?' she crowed. 'We all had a lovely hot shower and it was great to sleep in a bed, even if it was only a hard old bunk.'

Lorraine wasn't smiling, though. Maybe her bunk had bed bugs! I thought hopefully.

It was a brilliant morning. After yesterday's rain, everything seemed incredibly fresh and green, and the river was full and fast as it tumbled over its stones.

Martin had noticed a phone box and suggested that we made a few calls, one to one of our parents, so they could spread the word to the others that we were okay, one to the guy on the Gazette, and one to the lady at the radio station who had promised to put out a little newsflash about us. All at once, I recovered my spirits and began to feel quite excited. We only had to see out one more night on the moor and then we'd be heading for home to collect all the cash we'd been promised, and send it to the fund for little Tony. I hoped he was still all right. It suddenly occurred to me that none of us had seen a newspaper for days . . .

I made the call to the Gazette and told the reporter, Mr Taylor, all about our ordeal in the mist, exaggerating a bit to make it sound even more scary than it was. I didn't say anything about my personal ordeal with Martin, of course! He told me that Tony was holding his own, which cheered me up.

Tom spoke to the radio station lady, Dave called his mum, and then we were on our way again, at an ambling pace, sticking to the main road, treating ourselves to an easy time for a change.

The lady who served us in the shop had asked us if we were going to Wistman's Wood, a patch of real prehistoric oak wood with ancient, gnarled trees and tumbled stones, and Martin insisted on seeing a standing stone called Beardown Man. We decided to take a short break before resuming the route.

There was no way we could take our bikes into the wood as it was far too steep and rocky, so we padlocked them and were about to leave them when Lorraine piped up, 'Do you think it's safe, leaving all our gear like this? Someone could rifle our bags while we're gone.'

'She's right, you know,' Tom said thoughtfully and I felt a stab of jealous anger. Perhaps they were plotting to stay behind so they could have some time alone. Well, I'd see about that!

'Tell you what, I'll stay behind,' I offered. 'I'm pretty done in after last night and I'm not that mad about seeing a few oak trees and a standing stone. Not after the tomb episode yesterday!'

Lorraine gave me a dubious look and spoke in a firm, urgent kind of way: 'Honestly, Terry, I'd like to stay with the bikes, I really would. I . . . I've hurt my ankle a bit and I don't think scrambling over fallen stones will be a good idea. You lot go on, I'll be okay. I'll get my diary up to date, and make the most of the sun.'

As soon as I heard Tom say, 'Okay then, we'll see you later,' a sense of relief washed through me and I walked off gladly. The sun really did seem to have a bit of power in it for the first time since last autumn, and I soon had to take off my jacket and roll the sleeves of my sweater up a bit.

The trees in the wood were incredible, twisted by the wind into shapes which, if you've got an imagination like mine, became witches, dinosaurs, stags with enormous, many-pointed antlers, triffids, hunchbacked old crones – and they were all velvety green with moss. If Lorraine really did have a sore ankle, she'd done the right thing in refusing to come with us, though, as the ground was really treacherous, with slippery moss and loose stones, and places where you had to squeeze yourself between rocks and branches as there were no proper tracks. Once, we all jumped when a series of sharp cracking sounds echoed through the rocks ahead of us. It turned out to be a big bird, a pheasant or something. Dave swore he saw a rabbit.

All I saw was Tom. His wide shoulders and powerful back swinging between the branches, pushing through confined spaces between trees, ducking and weaving athletically, while I followed in his wake, reliving yesterday and wishing I could forget it. All I wanted now was to get home. If I didn't have Tom around all the time, it wouldn't be so bad. Well, not quite . . .

'Do you need a hand, Terry?' Without even noticing, I had paused at the foot of a rocky ledge I had to climb up – and there was Tom at the top, his eyes twinkling down at me, his arm extended. I didn't need any help, but I pretended I did, just to get hold of that warm, reliable hand and imagine, for a moment, that we were a couple and could hold hands all the time.

But of course, as soon as I'd got up the rock, he let go.

We never saw the standing stone because we decided it wasn't fair to leave Lorraine for so long, so after half an hour we all turned and came back, nearly getting lost a couple of times. Fortunately, Dave had had the sense to mark our trail by doing what the gypsies do and arranging twigs in a pattern at every place where we could go wrong.

When we got back, Lorraine had dozed off and was curled up with her back to a tree.

'She didn't get a lot of sleep last night,' Sue explained. 'She was really restless, grunting and tossing and turning. I think she must have been having nightmares.' But Lorraine denied it, just saying the bed was uncomfortable.

It was still only twelve o'clock and we had the rest of the day ahead of us. We carried on down the road towards Yelverton, and were just passing through

Princetown, where the famous Dartmoor Prison is, when Sue let out a shriek and her bike started wobbling.

'Oh no, I've got a puncture!' she yelled.

We all got off for a rest. Sue made one or two feeble attempts to lever her front tyre off, then Dave went to her rescue, recalling the one he'd had.

'Honestly!' I said in a loud voice, not caring who heard. 'Come on a cycle tour and you can't even change your own tyre?' But I wasn't so much cross at Sue as at Dave. If it had been me who'd had the puncture, everyone would have thought, 'Oh, Terry knows how to do it. Terry can manage for herself,' and nobody would have lifted a finger. Not that I'd have wanted them to. Sue couldn't have much pride, I thought crossly.

Sue held the bike up while Dave applied the patch to the inner tube, pumped it up to ensure it wasn't still leaking, then pressed the tyre back on. Princetown gave me the shudders and I was glad to leave it behind, but its dark shadow must have pursued me because, only a mile and a half down the road, a huge lorry thundered past us and I felt my bike sway, caught in the slipstream. But when the lorry had passed, my bike was still jumping and juddering.

'Hey!' I called to the others. 'I've got to stop!'

Tom was the first to reach me. 'What's the trouble?'

I shook my head. 'I don't know. It happened when I put my brake on. I thought that meant the wheel rim was bent, but it can't be. The problem's only just started . . .'

'Let's have a look,' he said, so I dismounted and handed over the bike. Tom crouched down in the road, holding the bike and squinting down its length. 'Doesn't *look* bent,' he said. 'Mind you, you did have that fall yesterday.'

'Yes, I suppose so,' I said gloomily. 'But why didn't it show up sooner, if I'd bent something?'

'It could have been just a slight fault, something just a bit out of line, and riding the bike has made it worse.'

Seeing him crouching, his tousled dark head so close to my hip, made me long to touch his hair. His brow was furrowed slightly as he looked up at me, and I felt my heart give a lurch. I can't help it, I thought; Tom West, I do really love you in spite of everything.

It was Martin, the cycle boffin, who solved the mystery of my bike wheel. 'Your front brake's loose,' he said. 'See that bolt? Just tighten it a little, then try the bike again.'

I did as he said and, lo and behold, my machine worked perfectly. I gave it a pat, like you would a pony.

By the time we reached Yelverton, we would have truly crossed Dartmoor. We had done it the hard way, by going cross-country in an almost complete circle. Of course, we had planned to reach Yelverton without resorting to a proper road, then take the road back, reaching Exeter, just over forty miles away, all in a day.

We'd hoped to stay there overnight, then head for home. But now our route had gone a bit awry.

'Can we have a rest please?' The panting little voice belonged to Lorraine. She looked pale. She had hardly spoken all day. There was her disturbed night, of course, and her ankle, and probably her period as well . . . but it struck me that there might be another reason for Lorraine's misery. Maybe she was as madly in love with Tom as I was. Maybe she was feeling just as jealous of me as I was of her. If this was the case I could understand only too well why she was feeling subdued. I felt pretty subdued myself when I thought of Tom. All kinds of reasons and dramas played through my mind as we stood around resting while Martin studied his maps and guidebook.

I gave up trying to unravel the mystery and turned back to the discussion about our route.

'We're not far from Yelverton,' Martin was saying. 'We'll go there, then sprint off towards Okehampton where we can pick up some supplies, then wander down to Giddleigh. It's only about twenty-five miles.' I saw Lorraine give a grimace. 'Right – everybody ready . . .?'

Martin went off in the lead, with me following, then came Sue and Lorraine, with Tom bringing up the rear. We'd only gone about five miles when Lorraine yelled that she wanted another rest.

'Oh, come on!' I snapped at her. 'We've all got things wrong with us, if we think about it. Sue's got her blisters, I've got a headache, and I know Martin's feeling pretty shattered.' I wondered afterwards if that remark had been wise, considering the circumstances of the previous night! 'Don't be so wet, Lorraine,' I added. 'We've only got one more day, then you can go home to your nice warm bed and never have to get on a bike again!'

Sue was scowling at me. 'Who do you think you are? The school head-girl? Well, we can't all be perfect! You're so hard, aren't you? How do you expect mere mortals to live up to your high standards? God, I wouldn't like you for a P.E. teacher.'

'And I wouldn't like you two as my pupils!' I screeched back. 'I'd have enjoyed this trip if it hadn't been for you. Yes, I'm well aware that you can't stand me – I've felt it all along. But I thought I might be able to put up with it as we had a greater purpose in mind – helping save that little boy, if you haven't forgotten? I'm really glad I didn't have to share that Youth Hostel dormitory with you last night, and I'm delighted that we'll be on our way home tomorrow. I might just take the train so as not to have to spend the last few ghastly hours in your company.' I was seething.

Sue looked disdainful. 'Then you'd be letting down your own ideals, wouldn't you? It was you who decided we should cycle all the way here and back, so you'll just have to force yourself to spend those last ghastly hours with us – just like we'll have to spend them with you!'

I noticed Lorraine was looking quite tearful. She really was wet.

'All right! I'm sorry,' I said, realizing that I had gone completely over the top. 'I think we've all been under a lot of stress. Let's just get on, shall we?'

The boys had refused to take part in our argument. They were standing around, looking embarrassed and a bit stunned.

I had my back to everybody as I cycled off, so I had no idea what glances were passing between them. I didn't want to know. Maybe I *was* a slave-driver and a perfectionist, but I just wanted to get this mission completed and get us all back home again. When that sponsorship money came in, I knew I'd feel that I'd really earned it, as this trip really had been an endurance test. Just then I felt I hadn't enjoyed it a bit . . . except for those few intimate minutes when Tom took me in his arms. And now it seemed that that perfect moment, which had been the best experience of my life, had meant nothing to him.

Chapter 9

It was great to be leaving the main road again and turning our bikes down a minor road, with the Dartmoor tors rising up on either side of us. I'd had to slow down and wait for the others – especially Lorraine – to catch up and now we just had seven or eight miles to go until we could start looking for our final campsite.

At about four o'clock, the sunshine had abruptly left us. We'd noticed the odd grey cloud since about three, blowing up and obscuring the sun and blotting out the warmth, and finally a cloud had appeared that was so big that the weak April sun didn't stand a chance. So it was on with the warm jackets again – and now it had started to rain!

Not only that, but a wind had got up too, blowing from the north-west in powerful bursts which, when it suddenly whistled down a ridge, caused my bike and its load to sway alarmingly.

Since the outburst between Sue and me, I hadn't said a word to anyone and they all seemed to be ignoring me. Still, I felt a bit above them in a way, the only one still carrying the spirit of the Dartmoor Challenge inside me, even if I had descended to a bit of petty bickering. Now, I was cycling towards my goal – getting back and collecting in the money for Tony – and I didn't care if I never spoke to any of them again. I'd be heartily glad to get back with friends like Van and Kim and Julie – friends I could trust, whom I knew wouldn't suddenly act out of character, or let me down.

Then I thought of Dave. I'd always looked on him as a good friend, yet since he'd fallen for Sue he'd practically ignored me. He should have been my ally on this journey, the one person I could confide in. But I hadn't had a chance to get close to him and talk because Sue was always hovering somewhere. Would Dave and I ever get back that nice, easy companionship we'd had for so many years, I wondered sadly. I should have been prepared for the fact that, sooner or later, he'd get involved with a girl and not want to see so much of his friends.

The rain grew steadily worse. I thought I heard a voice behind me but didn't dare turn round as I was leaning into the wind, feeling somewhat like a sail on a boat adapting to the air currents, and trying not to skid on the slippery road surface.

'Oi, Terry!' A bike came alongside mine – Tom's – and my insides started the usual fluttering I experienced when he was near, but I tried to ignore them.

He leant towards me, his bike making an alarming swoop. 'Dave thinks we should find a campsite very soon, then go back for a drink at that nice pub we just passed. He wants to try some real Devon cider. I've heard two pints are enough to get you under the table!'

'Look, I don't go in pubs,' I pointed out, hoping I didn't sound too priggish. 'I'm not even sixteen yet, let alone eighteen. I'd hate to get into trouble. My parents would hit the roof!'

'You can have a Coke and *I'll* slide under the table!' he shouted cheerfully.

Even dripping wet, even though I knew what a tease he was, he still looked absolutely gorgeous, with tiny beads of rain hanging on his long eyelashes, making me want to catch each one on the tip of my tongue. His hair was plastered to his cheekbones and forehead in dark strips and the cold wind and exercise had whipped glowing colour into his face.

A car overtook us and Tom had to drop back, but seconds later he was at my side again. 'About yesterday, Terry . . .' he began tantalisingly, but, at that crucial moment of revelation, confession or whatever, Martin suddenly whizzed up to us and began going on about how we had to make sure we weren't in the path of any running water when we pitched our tents, and how a track started a bit further on. The track appeared as he was speaking, and we all shot past it and had to go back. We could only ride a few hundred yards up it, then we had to dismount and push, our feet sloshing and sliding on the mud-covered stones and puddles.

What had Tom been going to say? Martin was alongside me now, yakking on, making it clearer than ever that he was making up for his behaviour on the previous night, and Tom was talking to Sue, with Dave and Lorraine bringing up the rear. As I glanced over my shoulder, I saw Lorraine stumble and Dave put his hand under her elbow to save her and her bike from landing in the mud. Seeing Dave do that, I felt nothing. If it had been Tom, of course, I would be feeling madly jealous. Funny, isn't it, how just one boy can stir your feelings to such a ridiculous pitch?

We found the perfect place to camp just as it was growing dark. It was a sheltered spot on high ground, by some big rocks which acted as a windbreak. The surface of the ground was very wet, though, and it was horrid having to put the groundsheet down on top of a thin layer of slime; but then, the groundsheet was covered in mud from the previous night, anyway.

Sue and Lorraine had got the hang of putting the big tent up now, I was pleased to see. Not that Lorraine did much to help. She was leaving all the work to Sue.

'It might be more sensible to see if we can get a meal in that pub, rather than trying to brew up in this weather,' Dave suggested.

'But we've got to pay for a meal tomorrow night. It'll be awfully expensive to eat out twice running,' I objected. 'Anyway, we've got things that will go off if we don't finish them, like the remains of the bacon and sausages we bought yesterday.'

Sue agreed with me and thought we should eat up what we'd got. By tomorrow night, we'd be back in civilization and, like me, she hated wasting food. She'd even offered to do the cooking! Dave instantly offered to help her, of course and I was happy to retreat into my tiny tent, out of the rain, though it was foul having to take my dripping wet jacket in with me; there seemed to be nowhere to put it where I didn't brush against its damp surface all the time.

It was beginning to rain harder and it was difficult keeping the camping stove going. We couldn't eat outside, we had to snatch things and dash back in before they got wet. It wasn't until the first few mouthfuls of scalding tea were making me glow, that I realised quite how chilled I was, and decided I'd better change into my dry trousers. I was just peeling off my wet ones with difficulty when there was a male voice at my tent-flap.

'Do you mind!' I yelled. 'I'm not decent!'

'Oh.' From the preciseness of the tone, I knew it had to be Martin. 'I was just going to ask you if you were coming to the pub with us.'

'Not now,' I wailed. 'I've just taken my wet trousers off. I couldn't bear getting back into them.'

'Well, we're going – us, the lads, I mean. Dave's just asking Sue and Lorraine if they're coming.'

'Well, you can count me out. I'll stay here with the tents and stuff,' I said. 'That pub was miles away. You'll get drenched!'

'It's worth it for a taste of that zoider, oooh-arrr!' he replied, trying to sound like a country yokel.

He went away and I heard the guys talking. Then I heard Sue's penetrating voice saying, 'No way. I'm not going out in that!'

There was another babble of conversation, then I heard her say, 'Anyway, Lorraine's not feeling very well. I think I'd better stay with her.'

There was a chorus of goodbyes, followed by the squelching of feet and bike tyres, then silence. I heaved a great sigh. Sometimes it was wonderful to be on your own for a bit, especially when you had as much to think about as I did. I wished I'd brought a book with me to read, but I didn't have one, so instead I braved the rain for a few seconds, dived under the plastic sheeting I'd covered the bike with to protect the saddle and panniers from the rain, and got my notebook out of the saddlebag. This was the ideal time to write an account of our travels. Maybe the school magazine would publish it – or, even better because it meant instant fame, the Gazette! I'd always fancied myself as a travel writer, having to fly off to the Seychelles or Mozambique at a moment's notice and be invited to write it up for one of the Sunday supplements when I got back.

Maybe one day I'd own a good camera and be able to take the photographs to go with my article . . . I dreamed for a moment longer, then started scribbling. It occurred to me that we wouldn't have any good pictures to accompany the account of this trip because Martin had hardly bothered to get his little Olympus out and take any. The weather had been too bad, for one thing; but, for another, the atmosphere between us all hadn't been right. There had been too many tensions. We hadn't once experienced a feeling of unity and togetherness, and I couldn't help feeling that Sue and Lorraine had been the ones who had rocked the boat. As far as I was concerned anyway.

I glanced at my watch: twenty past eight. The boys hadn't gone until after seven, they wouldn't be back till at least half nine or ten. I shrugged. It was their business if they wanted to cycle with hangovers tomorrow. I had some Alka Seltzer in my bag. No doubt there would be a run on it in the morning, if Devon cider was as strong as all that.

In fact, I needed my Alka Seltzer and my medical kit much sooner than I'd expected . . .

It *would* have to be when I was right in the middle of trying to sort out my feelings towards Tom, that Sue suddenly called my name and started to undo my tent flap.

'What is it?' I asked, looking up crossly and shutting the book with a snap so that she wouldn't see anything I'd written about her.

'It's Lorraine. She's not very well at all. It's her stomach. I wondered if you had anything?'

'Has she got the trots, or what?'

'The trots?'

'The runs – you know.'

'She's just got a pain and feels sick. It's probably something she ate.'

I passed Sue the Alka Seltzer, but a minute later she was back.

'I really would like you to take a look at her, Terry, a sort of second opinion. I don't like the look of her. I think she might be really ill. I couldn't even get her to take any of these.' She handed the Alka Seltzer back.

'Maybe a painkiller would be better.' I took a packet of Paracetamol out of my first aid kit, groaned at the thought of getting wet again, threw my waterproof over my shoulders and followed Sue to the other tent.

Lorraine was lying curled up in a ball in her sleeping bag. Her face was dead white. 'I . . . I feel terrible,' she whispered.

'I've got something here that should help,' I said cheerfully. 'Sue . . . have you got any water?'

Sue poured me a cupful from her plastic bottle and I

knelt down beside Lorraine, with the glass and tablets.

'I . . . I don't think I can swallow them,' she muttered through gritted teeth. 'I feel too sick and it hurts to move. I just want to lie here.'

'Well, I'll leave them here then and you can have them as soon as you've stopped feeling sick,' I suggested.

Lorraine was obviously feeling too bad even to manage a smile. Even I had to admit she looked a very sick girl indeed.

Sue and I exchanged glances. 'Nothing more I can do, if she won't take Doctor Terry's magic pills,' I said jokily. 'Let me know how the patient gets on. See you.' And I splashed out into the rain again and dived back into my own tent.

By ten, the wind was howling, the rain was lashing down – and there was still no sign of the boys. I was just getting ready to crawl into my sleeping bag and have an early night when Sue disturbed me again.

'Lorraine seems worse. I'm really worried about her.'

'Oh dear. What on earth are we going to do? Damn this weather!' I said, pulling my shoes and jacket back on.

Sue hadn't exaggerated. Lorraine was rolling around, moaning, and her face was no longer pale but looked flushed and feverish. I knelt down and felt her forehead, which was burning hot. She obviously had a high temperature.

'We've got to get some of these down her,' I insisted, indicating the painkillers which were still sitting there untouched. 'It looks like she's caught some kind of chill on her stomach. Maybe, when the boys get back, we ought to send one of them out for a doctor . . .'

'Oh, I don't like doing that. How would he get here, anyway? I'm sure she'll be better tomorrow. She's been a bit off-colour for the last couple of days. She's probably been gradually going down with something.'

'Well, I hope she doesn't give it to us. Thing is, if she's this bad tomorrow, how are we going to get her home?'

Lorraine opened her eyes and blinked at us hazily, then closed them again, screwed her face up, clutched at her stomach and groaned.

'She was sick before. I had to clean up,' Sue said dolefully.

'She was sick yesterday, too, remember?' I said. 'It could have been coincidence or it might be something she's eaten. Did either of you drink any stream water?' I had visions of typhus and cholera!

She shook her head.

'I remember being horribly sick once after I'd eaten some chocolate that had gone off. It had gone all white and funny,' I said.

'We did buy some chocolate at one of those little village shops . . .'

'But you're all right,' I pointed out.

'Yeah. I feel fine. Oh dear . . .' Sue ran her hand worriedly through her fair hair.

'I think we'll just have to wait a bit longer till the boys get back, and see what they think,' I said. 'There's nothing we can do at the moment except wait.'

But the boys didn't get back . . .

Chapter 10

The wind had really got up now, and I thought once or twice that my tent was going to blow away, and had to hang onto the sides. The rain was absolutely crashing down, we were in the middle of a violent storm, and I couldn't help worrying about both Lorraine *and* the boys. What if she really *was* seriously ill? We were miles from a doctor or a hospital. Anyway, no ambulance could get to where we were. We'd have to try and find some way of transporting her back to the nearest road, about a mile away.

And Tom, Dave and Martin? What if they'd had an accident? One of them could have been blown off his bike, sent hurtling over a bridge down to the rocky riverbed beneath. Or else there could have been a landslide, great rocks tumbling down onto the road, and them.

There was no chance of sleep for me now. Instead, I lay on my stomach facing the front of the tent, with the bottom corner of the flap pinned back so that I'd see the flicker of the boys' torches as they came across the moor. But it was now nearly midnight. Where *were* they? Something *must* have happened!

Then I heard Sue calling to me. 'Terry . . . Terry!' There was a wobble in her voice and she sounded tearful – or afraid.

I dreaded having to go out into the wild, wet, blustery night again, but I shoved my feet into my damp trainers, my arms into my waterproof jacket, and ducked out of the tent, flinching as the full force of the gale and the rain hit me between the eyes.

Sue popped back inside her tent as soon as she saw me, and I joined her. 'I . . . I don't know what to think . . .' she stammered. Lorraine was looking terrible, pale and sweating, dark round the eyes. Every so often a kind of spasm of pain would go through her and she'd knot herself up and cry out. She didn't open her eyes once.

I felt her forehead. It was clammy and very hot. I turned back to Sue. 'I think she has to have a doctor,' I said gravely, biting my lip, the magnitude of the problem boggling my mind.

Sue's 'But how . . . ?' simply echoed my own thoughts. How, in this ghastly, dangerous weather, at this hour of night, and miles from civilisation, were we going to find a doctor and bring him to Lorraine?

I remembered the phone box we'd made our calls from earlier that day. No, that was miles away. I'd never get there in this. I'd be blown off my bike in the pitch darkness and they'd find *me* dead in the morning, as well as Lorraine.

I crouched down on the groundsheet, my chin on my hands. 'Just let me think . . .' I said, while Sue bathed Lorraine's face with a rainwater-soaked sponge. If only the boys would come back. They'd know what to do. But right now I was the only one who could help.

I took a deep, sighing breath and somehow felt a bit stronger afterwards. 'You stay here with Lorraine and I'll ride back to the road and hammer on the door of the first house I see and ask to use their phone,' I said decisively.

'What if they won't let you in? It is after midnight, after all. They might think you're an escaped convict,' Sue quavered.

'I'll just have to take a chance on that, won't I? Getting Lorraine some help is the most important thing, and I'll just have to shout through the letterbox and convince them.'

'Maybe I ought to go . . .'

'No, it's best if you stay with Lorraine. She'd prefer seeing a familiar face when she opens her eyes. I know I would.'

Sue raised her index finger to her mouth and began chewing nervously on it. 'I – I don't know what I'd have done if you hadn't been here, Terry. I'd really like to – to apologise for picking a quarrel with you.'

'That's okay. I owe you some apologies, too. Any-way, no time to talk now. See you later – hopefully with a doctor in tow,' I said as I backed out of the tent and nearly came to grief on the skiddy mud.

It wasn't at all easy trying to hurry over rough ground with a force ten gale blowing, rain lashing in my face, and absolute pitch darkness all around me. The glow from my bike lamp was hopeless because it couldn't possibly show up every bump and rut on the track.

My face was streaming with water. It was running in icy rivers down my neck and up my sleeves, chilling me to the bone as I ploughed on, doing a mixture of cycling and getting off and pushing.

It seemed like hours before the track, well used by hikers in the summer, widened and flattened out – and then I came to a fork in it and my heart sank. Why hadn't I thought to take a compass bearing before I started? I swore, dismounted, found my compass and, with the help of the wind direction, and my memory of where the nearest village was from having glanced at Martin's map earlier, chose the right-hand path.

The noise of the wind had risen to a piercing howl and as it came rushing between rocks and through gulleys I was buffeted this way and that. I felt as though I was trapped inside a concertina with discordant tunes wailing in my ears and powerful punches knocking the breath out of me. My face and hands were so cold – even though I had my gloves on and my hood pulled well down over my forehead, and my collar turned up as far as it would go – that I couldn't feel them any more. My feet were so numb that they kept slipping off the pedals.

I prayed that nothing would go wrong with my bike. If the chain were to slip now, that would be it. My hard physical struggle against the elements gave me plenty of time for thought. And I began to think more clearly than I had since this holiday began. Lorraine and Sue hadn't been a problem at all. I was the one out to cause trouble. They were just two ordinary girls out for a few days of fun – maybe they hadn't got my cycling capabilities or grit but they had done their best and I had been set against them from the start. I would have disliked them whatever they did. And all the time Lorraine was feeling so ill, I had given her no sympathy and considered her a nuisance. I felt thoroughly ashamed of myself.

I bent low over the handlebars, forcing a passage through the gale for myself and my bike, cleaving a hole in the solid wall of rain, powering my machine – my lifesaver, maybe – on and on. I allowed my body to absorb the bumps and I leaned with the angles, just riding, riding, while my breath heaved hoarsely in my lungs and my mouth became set in a grimace of effort. Tears of desperation mingled with the rain that was sluicing down my cheeks. I had to get help – had to get help. My mind chanted these words in a kind of regular rhythm that urged my feet along.

The lamp picked up a solid sheet of water in front of me, a stream that had overflowed and burst its banks. I slammed on the brakes just in time and drew to a skidding halt at the brink of the flood.

Dry, racking sobs burst out of me. This was the end!

However was I going to get past this particular obstacle? My torch beam couldn't even reach the other side.

Spotting some higher ground on my left, I hauled the bike up it, my feet slipping and sliding, my shoes filling with mud and slime. I was past caring about physical discomfort as so many parts of me were either cold, wet, numb or aching. If I dared to think about my body I'd give up.

I gained the top of the ridge – and then I spotted it, down in a hollow. *A light*! It was about a quarter of a mile away and no doubt acres of boggy land lay between me and it, but a fresh surge of hope and energy filled my muscles and, leaving my bike where it was on the ridge, I began to run.

By some miracle, I didn't twist my ankle, or even fall over. Past a collection of tumbledown outbuildings, in the shelter of which huddled a small herd of shaggy ponies, was a low, white-painted house. I heard a dog begin to bark furiously.

A light was on in a front room. I banged on the window, then dashed round to the door, couldn't find a bell, and rapped as loudly as I could with the knocker, over and over again.

There was no reply, but the dog barked even louder. My heart sank. Whoever lived there must be out, and have left the dog there and the light on to deter burglars.

I tried again, but there was still no sign of life, apart from the frenzied barking. My burst of energy drained away from me, leaving me exhausted and utterly depressed. And frightened. What was happening to Lorraine? Had the boys got back? If Sue told them I'd gone to get help, what would they do? Would they go off on a separate errand of their own, or would they stay put, relying on me?

All I knew was that I'd never felt so alone and so completely at a loss. Yet people were relying on me – perhaps I was Lorraine's only hope. I had to think of something . . .

There was no way I'd even dream of trying to break into the house. Not with that savage-sounding dog there. But, if there was a house, there had to be a proper lane leading to it. There was. Then I had to make the decision as to whether I should go back for my bike, or leave it where I hoped I'd be able to find it later and go on on foot. There was little point in cycling under these conditions. In a way, the bike only impeded my progress. I decided to press on without it.

I must have gone about three-quarters of a mile before the bumpy track, rutted and churned by car tyres, reached a proper road. By then, my torch had started to cause me some concern because the battery kept fading, then recovering. I kept switching it off to conserve its energy, and only putting it back on when I was scared of walking into, or falling over, something.

It was a fantastic relief to hit tarmac! Now I could do with my bike, I thought regretfully as I strode out, feeling sure of reaching civilization soon.

My ears picked up a sound above the wailing of the

wind. An engine . . .

A van was coming towards me, blinding me with its headlights. I leapt up and down, shouting and waving, and it braked to a halt a few feet in front of me. Nobody got out, as the rain was still lashing down, so I dashed over to the driver's window, not thinking for a second of what danger *I* might be in by stopping strange men in cars on lonely roads late at night.

This man had a woman with him. They had waterproof coats and wellies on, but the woman had make-up on and I could smell her perfume, so they had obviously been out somewhere. Maybe they were the people who lived in the house I had just come from.

I spoke as simply and precisely as I could. 'I'm with a party of young people camping on the moors. One of us has been taken ill. I think it's serious. We need medical help quickly. Is there anything you can do . . .?'

The man glanced at his watch and started to mutter doubtfully, but the woman interrupted him. 'Jump in. We'll drive home and ring the police from there. There's a rescue service. They'll know how to make contact.'

I apologised for my bedraggled, soaking state, explaining about walking miles over the open moor, leaving my bike, not being able to get an answer at the house. It turned out they were the people who lived there, and they'd been visiting friends for dinner at Widecombe.

The savage dog turned out to be a benign labrador

who jumped up and licked my face. I patted and stroked her while the man dialled. It seemed ages before he got a reply, and in the meantime I started shivering from head to foot, my teeth chattering so loudly that the woman went off to make me a hot drink.

Then the man asked if I would speak to the police and give them the location of the campsite and I felt a dart of terror and guilt, knowing we were camping illegally. Would we be prosecuted? A fine could take up all the money we'd hoped to raise and render all our efforts useless. I sniffed back some hopeless tears as I took the telephone receiver.

The officer at the other end was calm and business-like. He didn't utter one word of rebuke, just wanted me to be as precise as possible about where we were. I told him about passing the pub, going on through the village, passing a small grocer's shop, a bridge, a sign-post, a boarded up garage, then taking a lane which led to the left. I marvelled at how I could remember these details which I didn't think I had taken in at the time.

However, it was a lot more difficult trying to describe exactly how far we had pushed our bikes before pitching camp. I mentioned the large rock formation that had sheltered us from the wind, and the stream that ran behind it.

'Oh, that's probably Goat Brook,' the policeman said. 'If you looked around, what landmarks could you see?'

I racked my brains. There had been two rocky hilltops, like twins, close together. I told him about those. He said he thought he knew the spot. He asked me what Lorraine's symptoms were, and I described them as best as I could.

'We'll try to take a helicopter out, though it'll be difficult in this gale,' he said. 'And we'll take a vehicle as close as we can.'

'What shall I do? Do you need me to show you the way?' I asked, my voice was beginning to crack with weariness, tension and tears.

'No, dear,' the policeman said in his soft Devon accent. 'If Mr and Mrs Castle will be good enough to keep you there, we'll contact you later. You've done all you can for now.'

As soon as I put the receiver down, I burst into tears. Immediately, Mrs Castle was at my side, making me take off my dripping jacket and unlacing my sodden shoes.

'You're coming upstairs with me and you're going to have a nice, hot shower,' she ordered firmly. I was too weak to protest. She pushed me into the bathroom, provided me with a big, soft bath towel and her own dressing-gown and told me to help myself to anything I needed, like shampoo and shower gel.

About half a mile of mud washed off me and there were big clods of it all over the bath as they didn't have a proper shower cubicle, just a hose suspended above the bath like we had at home. I washed my hair and could hardly raise my hands above my head, they were so tired and trembling. I longed for a nice, soft bed to sink into, and thought longingly of my bed at home.

I dried myself, shook some of her lovely, honeysuckle-scented talc over me and fastened the dressing-gown round me, yawning as I did so. Then I padded out to where she was waiting on the landing.

Mrs Castle knocked on the door and asked if I was all right.

'I've made up the guest bed for you, Teresa,' she told me. She must have heard me telling the policeman what my name was.

'It's extremely kind of you,' I said, yawning again.

She showed me into a small room with pretty yellow and blue wallpaper and turned down the sheet. Then we both stopped still, hearing the helicopter droning overhead.

'Do they have to use it often?' I asked her, feeling guilty at having caused so much trouble. What if Lorraine only had indigestion? But then I remembered that burning hot forehead, and her grey face, and knew I'd done the right thing.

'When there's an escaped convict, or someone's got lost or had an accident. But it doesn't happen very often, thank goodness,' she assured me. 'There was somebody who had a heart attack, and a child who fell off a rock and fractured his skull. And of course people have wandered into the bogs occasionally. This area has a lot of dangers. It needs to be treated with respect.'

'I know,' I sighed, clambering into the welcoming bed. 'Have there been any escaped convicts since you've lived here, Mrs Castle?'

I don't remember her reply because her voice slowly faded into the distance as I instantly fell asleep, wet hair and all.

Chapter 11

I awoke suddenly, hearing a great bustle going on in the house, voices and footsteps coming from downstairs, the front door opening and closing and the telephone ringing. It took me a few minutes to piece together the events of the night before.

Suddenly I remembered Lorraine and sat bolt upright in the old-fashioned single bed with its iron bedstead. I swung my legs out of the bedclothes and winced as they reached the floor. My calf muscles were aching dreadfully. My shoulders and arms hurt too. I had a moment of panic trying to recall where I'd left my bike, but I thought I could remember.

I padded over to the window, pulled the curtain, and the storm of the previous night might have never happened. Out there, it was a glorious early spring day, the sky a pretty light blue with puffy white clouds, though raindrops still hung on the budding branches of the tree outside my window.

I had to find out whether they had rescued Lorraine

and got her to hospital, and if she was okay. Putting on the dressing-gown which Mrs Castle had lent me the previous night, I cautiously opened the bedroom door, still a little bit afraid of the dog, in case it had forgotten who I was, and made my way barefoot across the landing.

It sounded as if a party was going on downstairs, there was so much loud chatter. Most of it sounded male, I noticed. I decided to beat a retreat and get dressed before proceeding any further, but just then Mrs Castle came to the foot of the stairs and called up to me.

'Teresa? Oh, there you are, dear. I've got some friends of yours down here. If you hurry, you can have breakfast with them.'

Friends? My heart gave a thump. Perhaps Tom was there! Then my spirits sank again as I figured he was more likely to be at Lorraine's bedside – that's if she was in hospital. She could even have been taken home by now.

Driven by curiosity, I threw on my mud-stained clothes and went downstairs. Through an open door, I could see a cluster of people round the kitchen table. Dave and Martin were there, with their backs to me. They had mugs in their hands and were talking to Mrs Castle and another man whom I didn't know.

'Come along,' bustled Mrs Castle. 'There's some bacon and egg in the pan. Feel okay, do you? No chills?'

'I'm fine,' I assured her.

As I entered the kitchen, heads turned and the next thing I knew, I was being greeted by a round of applause.

'Hey, Terry, you're an overnight star! You're a heroine!' Dave yelled, throwing his arm round my shoulders.

'I've known this girl all my life,' he told the man I didn't know. 'This chap's from the local radio station. He wants to talk to you.'

'And I'm from the Courier. I'd like to do a piece on your trip, and what you did last night,' said a girl of about twenty, stepping forward with a notebook in her hand.

My eyes moved apprehensively from one to the other. My brain was spinning. Was this what being a celebrity was all about? Pass me my dark glasses, I thought.

'Let the poor girl have a cup of tea, at least,' insisted Mrs Castle, thrusting a steaming mug towards me.

'Look, do you mind if I sit down? This is all a bit much, first thing in the morning,' I said, feeling very bewildered. 'Anyway,' I added, 'what I really want to know is, how's Lorraine?'

'Oh, she's had her appendix out and she's doing fine. Sue's with her at the hospital, and Lorraine's parents have come down. They'll be giving Sue a lift back,' Martin explained.

Appendicitis! No wonder she was looking so awfully ill. 'What exactly happened? Did the helicopter find her? Where were you? And where's Tom?'

My questions came tumbling out, while Mrs Castle placed a plate of bacon and eggs in front of me. Where was my comb? I needed one if they were going to start taking photographs, I thought confusedly. And what about my clothes? I looked a sight, with half the Dartmoor bogs all over me. I must apologise to Mrs Castle about mud flaking off my clothes onto the carpet, I reminded myself as I shoved a forkful of food into my mouth. I was suddenly ravenous, and eating allowed me to listen while Dave and Martin vied to answer my queries.

'No, the weather was too bad for the helicopter,' Dave began.

'I lost my front light on the way to the pub. Martin had a puncture. By the time we arrived the weather had become impossible. The landlord said it was much too dangerous to ride back and made us sleep in the pub. We were so worried about you girls.'

'Apparently they took Sue and Lorraine to the hospital in a Landrover. We got back this morning to find nothing but the tents and a note from Sue. Where's your bike by the way?'

'Up the hill,' I told Martin, with my mouth full.

'If I could just take a few pictures,' said the Courier woman. The man meanwhile was fiddling with his heavy tape recorder.

There was a loud knock on the front door and Mr Castle strode off to answer it. I saw a huge mass of flowers first, then Tom's familiar hair and eyes appearing above them.

'Well done, Terry,' he said quietly, holding out the bouquet to me.

I dropped my knife and fork with a clatter. 'Shouldn't . . . shouldn't these go to poor Lorraine?' I faltered, aware of a flashbulb going off.

'I'm sure her parents and Sue will have got her some. You deserve these.'

'I . . . Oh, thank you!' Tears were welling up in my eyes and there was a big lump in my throat as I laid the large bouquet of spring flowers on the empty chair beside me.

Needless to say, I couldn't eat any more breakfast as I was far too excited. Mrs Castle quietly removed my plate as I allowed myself to be interviewed by the radio man with the tape recorder, while the newspaper lady took notes, then answered a few extra questions which she put to me. But all the time I was talking, I was aware of Tom looking at me. No, not just looking, gazing . . . staring. He hardly took his eyes off me.

Shouldn't he have been at the hospital with Lorraine? I asked myself. Surely, if he was really fond of her . . . I mean, if *he'd* suddenly been taken ill, I would have fought for a place in the ambulance!

Once the two reporters had gone, things quietened down a bit and I was able to eat a piece of toast and marmalade.

'I'm glad you managed to get in the bit about this being an official trip to raise money for the Tony Morgan fund,' Martin said.

'Would I abandon the Dartmoor Challenge?' I cried,

striking a melodramatic pose with one hand on my chest. Then I choked over a toast crumb and ruined the effect.

'What are we going to do now, though?' I enquired of all and sundry.

'Go home, I suppose, just like you told those reporters, and collect our sponsorship money,' Dave said, looking a bit deflated. I felt that way, too. A lot had happened this last week, not all of it good, but it was a pity to have been through the hardships we had been through and have to end up like this.

'The thing is, if Sue and Lorraine don't complete the course on their bikes, they can't collect their money,' Martin pointed out. 'Oh, I know it's impossible for Lorraine to – she couldn't help getting appendicitis – but it's sort of made the whole thing fizzle out, hasn't it?'

'Yes, true,' I agreed sadly. 'It's a real shame.'

Mr Castle had been standing by, listening to us. While I was speaking that last sentence, he had turned round to the dresser, and was scribbling something. Then he came over to me with something in his hand, and held it out. It was a cheque.

'My wife and I really admire what you've tried to do,' he said, 'and we'd like to contribute something to the fund. Please accept it from us.'

'But you've been kind enough already,' I began, then: 'Twenty pounds? Oh, that's much too much. We can't – '

'Oh yes, you can!' Mr Castle wouldn't hear of any

objection, and Mrs Castle joined in.

'It's me who should be paying you for bed and breakfast!' I said. 'I'll never be able to thank you enough for helping me last night – and I'm sure Lorraine's really grateful, too. When you think she might have died . . .' I gave a shudder. 'Well, suppose I'd better go and look for my bike. It'll be a patch of rust by now!'

'We've brought all the stuff from the campsite,' Tom told me. 'It was a bit difficult loading it all on to our bikes because there was Sue and Lorraine's stuff too, but her parents say that if we can get it up to the hospital this afternoon, they'll take it back in the car.'

'I think we should visit her,' I suggested. As I spoke, I glanced at Tom's face, but he didn't show any particular emotion, though everyone agreed it was a good idea.

'How am I going to cycle with these flowers?' I wondered. Then I had a brainwave, and hoped Tom wouldn't mind. 'Please let me give you these as a tiny thankyou for last night,' I said, handing the bouquet to Mrs Castle. She looked delighted, and a bit touched, and promptly began arranging them in a yellow vase that complemented the bright colours perfectly.

'That was a nice thing to do,' Tom whispered in my ear as we gathered ourselves together to leave. 'I'll buy you some more when we get home.'

I'll believe it when I see it, I thought, but smiled happily at him anyway.

Fortunately, the hospital to which Lorraine had been admitted was on our route home. We got there during visiting hours, having first found a hostel to stay in that night, and as they would only allow us in two at a time, Dave and Martin went first and stayed about ten minutes, leaving me to go to her bedside with Tom.

I hadn't been sure whether or not to buy her any fruit, as I didn't know if she would be allowed to eat it yet, so I had bought her a couple of magazines instead.

She was lying back against the white pillow, her hair spread around her like a Pre-Raphaelite painting. She looked very beautiful. I glanced guardedly at Tom. He could hardly help falling in love with her now, surely? That was if he hadn't fallen already . . .

'How do you feel?' I asked her.

'Mum and Dad say I owe my life to what you did last night,' she said, her voice faint and husky. She had only come round from the anaesthetic that morning.

I blushed. 'Anyone would have done the same. Sue would have gone . . .'

'I don't remember a thing, apart from having this appalling pain,' she whispered. 'I . . . I don't know how to thank you.'

'Just get better. That'll be thanks enough,' I assured her. I still felt very guilty about the rude, uncaring way I had behaved. Then I got up to go, thinking that Tom would probably appreciate a few moments alone with her, but, to my amazement, he said, 'See you when you get home, then. We'll all have a get-together as soon as you're up to it.'

Well, that didn't sound particularly intimate, I thought. If he'd just said, 'See you when you're back home,' that might have implied that he intended seeing her on his own. Or maybe he was trying to throw me off the scent – playing a double game as I had suspected . . .

We all telephoned our families from the phone in the hospital reception area. Mine were most concerned about Lorraine, but I didn't tell them the full story, of course, and I hoped Lorraine's parents wouldn't drop me in it. If they heard that I'd been tramping over dangerously boggy moors after midnight, in a howling storm, and banging on strange people's doors, they would have been utterly horrified!

After a fish and chip meal, we returned to our hostel feeling rather subdued. It was a big anticlimax, somehow. There should have been six of us celebrating the last night of our successful fund-raising trip. Instead, there were four fairly depressed people, doing precisely nothing. It was too early to go to bed, none of us had much money, and there was nothing we felt like doing, anyway. We certainly didn't have the right clothes to go to a disco, even if there was one in the vicinity.

'I don't know,' Martin sighed at last. 'Maybe I'll go for a walk. Anyone else fancy one?'

'Not me,' I said. I wanted to write all the latest developments down in my diary before I forgot the details.

'I'll come,' Tom said.

That left Dave and myself.

'I've got a pack of cards,' he told me. 'Fancy a game of something?'

'Okay,' I said, not terribly enthusiastically, I have to admit. With Tom not around, I'd kind of lost interest in the rest of the evening. Then I told myself off soundly for being such a wimp. Tom West is not interested in me as anything other than a good friend. There. I repeated the sentence again to myself, then once more for luck.

'. . . and so I thought, maybe you'd like to come with me. As my date, I mean. I know we've been friends all this time, but – '

'What?' I suddenly tuned in to what Dave was saying. Date? Had he gone mad? 'Sorry, I was thinking about Lorraine,' I lied, so that he wouldn't think I was rude for not having listened to him.

Dave was sitting opposite me at a rickety table in the almost deserted common room of the hostel, twisting his fingers round, twiddling with the cuff of his sweater and looking awkward and nervous.

'A mate of mine is having a party next Saturday. I was inviting you,' he said stiffly.

'That's very nice of you. But I didn't quite catch . . . you were saying something about a date?' I was completely baffled. Dave and I just didn't have that sort of relationship. We never *could* have.

'Well, we've always been friends, but we've never . . . gone out.' He bit his lip and raked his fingers through his auburn hair, then looked me in the eye. 'Terry, could you possibly fancy me as a boyfriend?'

The horrible thing was, I wanted to burst out laughing. But I daren't, because it would have hurt him terribly.

'I thought you were very keen on Sue,' I pointed out.

He went red. 'Oh . . . well . . . If you must know, Martin beat me to it. He's asked her out as soon as we get back.'

'Oh! Of all the – how could he! What a swine! After the night we got stuck in the fog together, too!'

'Terry . . .?' Dave was staring at me through narrowed eyes. 'What really happened on that night? I did wonder.'

'Forget about it. It was nothing,' I fibbed. 'Just a slight mistake when we were both half asleep. He probably thought I was Sue!'

We both laughed.

Then Dave grew serious again. 'Have you . . . I mean, is there anybody else?'

I took a deep breath. This was one way of putting Dave off. It also happened to be true: there was somebody else, although he didn't appear to recognise it. 'I'm afraid there is,' I said, in a small voice. 'I'm really sorry . . . '

Dave put his hand out and touched mine for a moment. 'Oh well. Just my luck. Maybe it wouldn't have worked out, anyway. We probably know each other too well . . .'

'Yes, we probably do,' I said. 'Look, do you mind if we forget that card game? I think I'd just like to get to bed.'

Chapter 12

Coming from our direction, there was only one logical way to enter our small town, which was directly along the high road. We got there shortly before half-past three and our spirits rose as we passed the familiar shops and office blocks.

'What's this? Something must have happened,' Dave exclaimed, pointing to a small knot of people and a large van with what looked like a television camera in front of it.

'Maybe Charles and Diana have been here and we've missed them,' I said.

'Hey! Are you Teresa Routledge?' somebody called out.

I frowned. 'Yes,' I hurled back. What had I done? My heart gave a sudden lurch. Perhaps the house had burned down since last night, with Mum and Dad in it, and I was just about to find out.

Then the group of people sped towards us and suddenly there was the sound of cameras clicking. I recognised our friend from the Gazette. Then I saw that the TV camera was trained on us!

There was no way we could carry on cycling. We got

off our bikes, with the traffic having to detour round us, and somehow we all ended up safely on the pavement.

'Me first!' shouted the Gazette man. 'We were the ones who gave them publicity.'

'Yes, that's true,' I agreed.

But as I spoke to him, I could see Martin, Tom and Dave being bombarded with questions. Then I was pulled in front of the television camera.

'Can't I even comb my hair?' I asked, my mind whirring in confusion. I spotted Mum and Dad then, and gave them a wave. But there was a microphone in front of me and a girl was asking me about the trip.

I was too tired, and it had all happened too suddenly, for me to be nervous.

'Do you think it has been a success?' the girl asked, when I'd finished recounting some of our adventures, such as that first night when the pony had stuck its head into Sue and Lorraine's tent.

'The Dartmoor Challenge will have succeeded as long as we have made a significant contribution to the Tony Morgan Appeal Fund,' I replied, trying to sound as businesslike as possible.

'I think you and our viewers will be pleased to hear that a date has been fixed for Tony and his mother to fly over to America and consult the top specialist on his condition,' the television reporter said.

My face fell. 'Do you mean they didn't need us, after all?' I blurted out, immediately kicking myself for sounding like a disappointed kid.

Her face broke into a grin. 'On the contrary. If the local West Country papers hadn't spread the news, and raised a lot of extra interest so that money started pouring in from all over Britain today, it might have taken a lot longer. And it's all thanks to you and your mercy dash.'

I felt myself blush scarlet and hoped they had some way of toning down my cheeks on the film, before it was televised.

I was relieved when the press of people subsided and the questions stopped, and I could go over and give Mum and Dad a hug and kiss.

'I'm sorry you had to find out about all those dangerous things I did,' I apologised.

'We're proud of you, Terry,' Mum said, and gave me another big hug.

'In fact, we thought we'd throw a bit of a party for you tonight,' Dad said gruffly. My eyes widened in surprise as I remembered the trouble I'd had trying to get him to agree to my having a birthday party.

'We've contacted some of your friends, like Vanessa and Julie, and they are coming, and I thought you might like to ask those boys,' he said, nodding towards Martin and the others, who were still standing talking.

I spotted Tom about to get on his bicycle. 'Tom . . . hey, Tom! *Stop!*' I shrieked. Giving Dad my bike to hold, I went tearing after him.

He stopped and was gaping at me, his eyebrows raised. 'What is it?'

'We . . . Dad . . . That is, we're having a party

tonight. It won't go on late because we're all tired, but you must come. Dad says ask your parents along if you like . . .' Mum and Dad seemed rather to have taken to Mr and Mrs West when they had met to discuss our trip – though this invitation was pure invention on my part, in the hope of persuading him.

It worked. By seven-thirty, everyone had arrived, including Tom. It was very embarrassing, having to pretend to be a heroine. I didn't feel like one in the slightest. Yet I had done some risky things, and I had been very scared. I just hadn't thought about it at the time.

My moment of fame was nothing in comparison to how I felt when Tom put his arm round me and asked me to dance with him. 'I've wanted to do this ever since that day when we were alone by the rocks,' he murmured. 'Before we got so rudely interrupted.'

'By whom! Lorraine?' I said miserably. I just couldn't help myself. I had to make him see what was upsetting me, without having to put it into words, and I couldn't be more obvious than this. He would have to be really dense not to twig instantly what I was on about.

It appeared that he was. He simply stared at me and furrowed his brow. 'What do you mean?' he enquired.

Oh heavens, this was dreadful! There was no way out of it – I'd have to go on and explain. 'I . . . I thought you must fancy her,' I admitted, my head drooping. 'You had your arm round her. You stayed close to her. I felt so left out, after what had happened between us. I was really hurt. I didn't know what you were playing at . . .'

There was a sound above my head. Tom – laughing. Scandalised, I jerked my head up to look at him, my eyes blazing.

'Oh, women!' he said. 'You're all so sensitive.'

'No, we're not!' *Yes, we are* . . .

'You didn't see what was right under your nose. Surely I wasn't the only one who noticed that Lorraine was feeling a lot worse than she was letting on. I thought she was being very brave. She didn't want to hold us up. I gave her a bit of help and encouragement, that was all. It was purely platonic. But even I didn't realize that she was seriously ill. We all make mistakes . . . '

'Yes, don't we?' I threw him a rueful grimace. And the next second, I was in his arms . . .

Lorna Read

A Taste of Fame £1.50

Would Janice ever get the chance to play the romantic lead?

When Stevo began to sing at the audition, Janice was entranced by his beautiful voice and his pop star looks. But when Shaz was cast as the heroine in the show, leaving Janice with the comic role, her only consolation was her growing friendship with Stevo. The night he kissed her, she was left in no doubt – this was love.

The next day, Stevo ignored her, and Shaz clung to him possessively. All the dislike she'd ever felt for Shaz returned one hundredfold. From now on, this was war . . .

Images 95p

Belinda's friends are mad with jealousy when she lands a holiday job working for a company that manages pop groups. But the fact that she isn't a raving pop fan got her the job in the first place, and she remains calm and level-headed – until the day singer Flip Sauvage walks up to the Reception desk . . .

Association

Registered as a charity (No. 266754)

The Association was formed by Philip and Mary Carter in 1973, to promote the interests of users of the South West Coast Path

SOUTH WEST COAST PATH ASSOCIATION
Bowker House, Lee Mill Bridge, Ivybridge, Devon PL21 9EE
Tel: 01752 896237 Email: info@swcp.org.uk
Visit our website at www.swcp.org.uk

CHAIRMAN - ANDREW LACK
421 Bury Street West, London, N9 9JR
Tel: 0208 360 8423 Email: swcpa.chair@gmail.com

TREASURER - JOHN MILLS
Bowker House see above. Email: johnmills49@btinternet.com

SECRETARY - STEVE CHURCH
4 Wheal Speed Road, Carbis Bay, St Ives TR26 2QG
Tel: 01736 791777 Email: steve.church1@googlemail.com

ADMINISTRATOR - KATE HOLLAND
Bowker House see above

Published by: The South West Coast Path Association

Designed and printed by Swiftprint, Dawlish, Devon www.swiftprintsw.co.uk
ISBN 978-0-907055-20-4

Jacket photography:
Inner Hope to Salcombe - photographer Phil Andrews
Victoria Clock, Weymouth - photographer Dave Westcott
Beach Huts at Seaton - photographer Steve Pattemore
Padstow Boats - photographer Jennifer Rowlandson

Welcome to the Annual Guide

Welcome to the South West Coast Path Association's Annual Guide to the wonderful experience of England's longest National Trail. This superb walk encircles the coastline of the entire South West Peninsula of England. In its 630 miles it encompasses high cliffs, breezy dunes, wooded estuaries, saltmarshes, picturesque fishing ports, sedate seaside towns, holiday resorts and all the interest of the major seaside city and naval port of Plymouth.

No matter what your interest, be it in the landscape, wildlife, history or just a wish to get away from it all, the South West Coast Path has the answer.

The South West Coast Path Association is the charitable body set up to represent the interests of all those who walk on the Coast Path. It doesn't matter whether you're an afternoon stroller or a long-distance walker who intends to walk all 630 miles, or has done so, the Association is there for you.

The Association campaigns for the best possible standards for the Coast Path and its immediate corridor and financially assists where appropriate to ensure the best possible experience for those using the route. And, of course, it also provides help and information to walkers, including this Guide and the other publications mentioned in these pages.

So, if you've not already done so, why not join 5,000+ Coast Path enthusiasts and become a member. Then -

-your subscription will help the Association promote, protect and enhance the Coast Path, including providing funds for specific improvement projects;

- You will receive your copy of the Annual Guide free and keep up to date with what's happening on the Path via our two free Newsletters each year plus regular e-newsletters.

- you will be part of the "family" of those who love the Coast Path by knowing that your input is important to the Path's well-being.

Funding provided by members' subscriptions have enabled the Association to play a vital part in getting bridges replaced, re-constructing the Path when it has been lost to cliff falls, improving its alignment and a host of other improvements. That's all thanks to the Association's members....well done everyone!

In 2013 the Association marked its 40th anniversary by organising the Great South West Walk. This event took place during April and May and took the form of a series of guided walks along the whole length of the Trail, acting as two relays from the two ends, Minehead and Poole Harbour, the two meeting for a "birthday party" at Land's End on 7th May 2013. The event attracted sponsorship and match funding to deliver a programme of improvements around the 630 miles of the Coast Path and was successful in encouraging partner organisations such as the local authorities, National Trust, holiday companies and accommodation providers to work with the Association in celebrating the anniversary, raising the profile of the Association and the Coast Path and raising funds.

The event was incredibly successful, with over £650,000 being raised in all, supporting over 100 improvements to the Coast Path. Nearly 1,100 walkers took part in the event, helped by 14 bus companies, 62 walk leaders and 73 backmarkers. Indeed, it was so successful that the Association is now looking to see if a similar, if smaller, fundraising event can be organised for September 2014, possibly this time involving a series of circular walks based on the Coast Path. Keep an eye open during the year for information on this event.

Sign at Berry Barton , East Devon

Contents

Photography courtesy of:
Phil Andrews, Fiona Barltrop, Ralf Buscher
Kate Holland, Ted Foreman, Barry Lockwood
Lucy Masterton, Mark Owen, Steve Pattemore
Jennifer Rowlandson, Liz Wallis and Dave Westcott

Introduction to The South West Coast Path

The South West Coast Path National Trail is a 630-mile adventure around the coastline of the south-west peninsula. From Minehead in Somerset all the way to Poole Harbour in Dorset, it is simply the best way to enjoy the scenery, wildlife and heritage of this wonderful coastline.

The sheer variety of the South West Coast Path means that there are plenty of gentle stretches as well as dramatic headlands and steep coastal valleys where the going can be strenuous and demanding. Relaxation, challenge, tranquillity or inspiration - the choice is yours!

National Trails are walking routes (and some also for riding) through the country's finest scenery and heritage. They are created and mainly funded by Natural England and managed by Highway Authorities and the National Trust. They receive a high standard of care and are the flagships of the rights of way network. No one in England and Wales lives more than 50 miles from a National Trail.

As a result of the 1999/2000 survey of the full length of the Coast Path using a global positioning system, we now have access to very precise distances - the Coast Path is 630 miles (1014km) long. The survey carried out by the South West Coast Path Team included the Isle of Portland.

During a survey in 2011-12 of the entire Coast Path, an Association member used a sophisticated altimeter to calculate that the walker who has completed the whole Coast Path will have climbed 115000 feet (35024m), which is just a little short of walking the height of Mount Everest from sea level four times!

The path passes through some of the finest coastal scenery anywhere, and has enormous variety and contrast between bustling resorts and quiet coves. The path is the longest National Trail in the country; we think it is the finest, and hope you will too. We know of no other that has as much contrast and variety as ours and urge you to try it.

So here it is - England's longest and most beautiful walking trail - read about it, then go for it!

Padstow

Dedicated to helping everyone enjoy the path

The Association was formed in 1973 by a group of enthusiasts to encourage the development and improvement of the South West Coast Path. This is still one of the main aims of the Association, and it works closely with Natural England, local authorities, the National Trust and other more general user groups such as the Ramblers' Association and the Long Distance Walkers' Association.

Over those years the Association has continuously campaigned for maintenance, signing and alignment improvements.

Of primary importance is to have the Coast Path removed from roads. There have been many improvements as long-standing members will know, and the Association has strongly influenced the implementation of these.

The Association has been instrumental in the placing of markers at each end of the trail, and also a half-way marker.

Today one of the Association's functions is to assist and advise all those who wish to walk along this wonderful coastline - whether in short, relaxing strolls around a headland, or by more demanding long distance walks lasting several days, or by heroic attempts at covering the whole length of 630 miles (1014km) in one go!

The Association currently has a programme of funding improvements to the Coast Path and encourages all who walk and enjoy the trail to join as members and support this very important work. To see how Association funding grants have helped improve the South West Coast Path in recent years see page 182.

Funding provided by our members' subscriptions have enabled the Association to play a vital part in a range of necessary Coast Path projects, including getting bridges replaced, improving the path alignment, replacing the path where it has been lost to cliff falls and other general enhancements. That's all thanks to our members...
well done everyone!

So if you haven't already done so, why not join 5,000+ other Coast Path enthusiasts and become a member of the Association? Then...

- Your subscription will help the Association promote, protect and enhance the Coast Path, including providing funding for specific projects;
- You will receive your copy of the Annual Guide free and keep up to date with what's happening on the path via our two free Newsletters and regular E-newsletters each year.
- You will be part of the "family" of those who love the Coast Path and know that your input is important to the path's well-being.

And remember, the Association represents ALL Coast Path walkers, not just the hardy long-distance walkers. Whether you plan to walk all 630 miles, or have already done so, or are happy to stroll along the coast on a Sunday afternoon or a couple of days a year when on holiday, if you love the Coast Path the Association is for you.

Our thanks also to all who took part in the Great South west Walk in 2013 and helped us to raise over £650,000 for Coast Path improvements. Look out for news of a further event in 2014 and help us raise more funds for the Path.

Aims and Objectives

1. To secure the protection, improvement and preservation of an acceptable South West Coast Path and public access thereto in order to improve the conditions of life of the users of the South West Coast Path.
2. To educate users of the South West Coast Path to a greater knowledge of, respect and care for the coast and the countryside.

In furtherance of these objectives the Association aims to work for and assist in:

1. Providing information about the South West Coast Path and its corridor to the public;
2. The organisation directed at the improvement and maintenance of the South West Coast Path.
3. Providing a forum in which different interests connected with the South West Coast Path (including its corridor) and its use can discuss problems of mutual concern.

Membership

Members receive an Annual Guide as part of their membership plus two Newsletters and regular E-newsletters each year, with up-to-date information on the state of the path and special offers.

Subscriptions

Single	**£14.50**
Joint	**£16.00**
Life Membership	**£220.00**
Joint Life Membership	**£250.00**
Non-UK Membership	**£22.00**

Payment may be made at www.swcp.org.uk or by telephoning 01752 896237 or by using a cheque or postal order made payable to the South West Coast Path Association.

We can accept the credit/debit cards shown below.

A Word to Beginners

Long distance path walking

These words are not for those hardy veterans who have all the gear, have done several paths already, and know all about it. However, we do get a number of letters each year from those who have not ventured before on long distance paths and need some advice. This we are pleased to try and provide and we do hope those who read this will find it helpful. However, it is easy to miss out things that folk wish to know, so if you who are new read this, and are still baffled, please contact us and we will try to provide the answers. As well as perhaps helping you, it will enable us to improve this section for another year and so be of help to more people.

Newcomers to the Coast Path

To get the feel of the Coast Path you are advised to take some day walks along it - there are some very good ones on the coast. Better still, look for the sections marked 'Easy' - start at one end and stop and turn back before you have half had enough. We say before half because it is always better to do a bit less and really enjoy it.

You can soon progress to setting out to walk a whole section either by using two cars or using public transport. One point here - if possible use the public transport to go out and walk back to your car or base; this means that you do not get yourself in a position of having to race the clock if you should take a bit more time than you thought.

If you are walking on your own, do please take additional care, for as you will appreciate, if you fall or twist an ankle there can be problems. If you are on your own therefore, you should leave a note with someone to make sure that you arrive at your destination. Not everyone is happy walking on their own and can feel lonely. There is also an added problem that you may try to do too much, so please bear this in mind.

There is no need to buy expensive equipment for the easy sections at the start; a pair of stout shoes and a rainproof jacket is all you need. As you progress, a small rucksack for 'eats' will be needed next.

Obviously if you can join a walking club and go out with them you will collect lots of friendly advice on all sorts of gear you may care to purchase as you become more serious about walking. Maps, guides, etc., are all listed in their appropriate sections.

For those who have walked, but not on long distance trails

Having stated the two big points, we will elaborate. You will not be able to accomplish in daily distance the same amount you normally cover in a day walk; you will have to settle for less. The first reason is that you will be carrying more equipment; you must for instance, have a complete change of clothing and footwear, possibly nightwear and toilet kit. For this you need a bigger rucksack so you will be carrying quite a bit more weight than you normally do. Secondly, there is what we call the 'wear' factor. For the first few days until you are really fit, it is just simply more tiring having to walk each day. The last point could be called the 'interest' factor. Usually, if you are walking a long distance path, you are further from your home base, in fresh fields and pastures new; there is more to see so you will need more time to look around.

If you usually accomplish 15 miles (24km) a day, aim, say, for 12 miles (19km). This is particularly important if you are booking ahead. You can find yourself tied to a treadmill which you cannot get off. Booking ahead has the advantage that you know there is a bed ahead. On the other hand, it does mean even if you are tired, have developed blisters, and the weather is diabolical, you have to go on. Be guided too by our `Trail Description' section and

Naughty sheep close to Portwrinkle

Zennor

the terrain you are tackling. 6 miles (10km), say, of a `Severe' section can equal in effort 10-12 miles (16-19km) of an 'Easy' one.

Planning Your Walk

We have stated you must carry more gear and this is true. Having said that, think long and hard about every item you imagine you may need. You will be surprised - you may find you will not want it at all. Watch particularly those extras such as cameras and binoculars - they are often a source of considerable weight. One little additional point, many rucksacks, even modern ones, are not as waterproof as you think. A plastic liner, which can be obtained quite cheaply from rambling shops, etc., as an additional inner layer, may save you that most unpleasant discovery after a long day spent in the rain that your only change of clothing is no longer dry. We would also recommend that in addition to this liner, your dry clothing should then be enclosed in further plastic bags to ensure dryness. Trainer shoes are useful for wearing at the end of the day and can be worn on some parts of the path.

A sensible idea before undertaking a long walking holiday is to take, say, a weekend of two or three days first, walking continuously as a practice.

Another point to watch especially on our Coast Path is the availability of refreshments. At main holiday times, you will get them nearly everywhere, except for the few places we especially mention in our 'Coast Path Walk' section. Out of season, you will find them in surprisingly few places on long stretches of coast. The usual remarks about carrying stand-by supplies, therefore, certainly apply; better to carry an extra couple of bars of chocolate than to go hungry.

Walking alone

The Association has long had a scheme that enables single female members who are a little nervous about walking alone to team up with other single female members.

Contact the Administrator for information.

It has also been suggested that we start a similar Men's Walking Companion scheme. If you'd like to find out more, contact the Administrator.

Guides

Path Descriptions

Path Descriptions written by our Association are detailed accounts on all aspects of short sections of the Coast Path and include hand-drawn maps and illustrations. They cover in detail what cannot be included in our Annual Guide book.

- **Minehead to Porlock Weir** (9.5 miles/15.3km)
- **Porlock Weir to Lynmouth** (12.3 miles/19.8km)
- **Lynmouth to Ilfracombe** (18 miles/30km)
- **Ilfracombe to Croyde Bay** (13.6 miles/21.9km)
- **Croyde Bay to Barnstaple** (14.4 miles/23.1km)
- **Barnstaple to Westward Ho!** (19.1 miles/30.7km)
- **Westward Ho! to Clovelly** (11.2 miles/18km)
- **Clovelly to Hartland Quay** (10.3 miles/16.6km)
- **Hartland Quay to Bude** (15.4 miles/24.8km)
- **Bude to Crackington Haven** (10.2 miles/16.4km)
- **Crackington Haven to Tintagel** (12 miles/20km)
- **Tintagel to Port Isaac** (8 miles/13km)
- **Port Isaac to Padstow** (11.7 miles/18.9km)
- **Padstow to Porthcothan** (13.6 miles/21.8km)
- **Porthcothan to Newquay** (11.1 miles/17.9km)
- **Newquay to Perranporth** (10.8 miles/17.5km)
- **Perranporth to Portreath** (12.2 miles/19.7km)
- **Portreath to Hayle** (12.4 miles/19.9km)
- **Hayle to Pendeen Watch** (19.5 miles/31.3km)
- **Pendeen Watch to Porthcurno** (15.6 miles/25.2km)
- **Porthcurno to Penzance** (11.5 miles/18.5km)
- **Penzance to Porthleven** (14 miles/22.5km)
- **Porthleven to The Lizard** (13.9 miles/22.3km)
- **The Lizard to Coverack** (10.6 miles/17.1km)
- **Coverack to Helford** (13.1 miles/21.1km)
- **Helford to Falmouth** (10 miles/16.1km)
- **Falmouth to Portloe** (13.7 miles/22km)
- **Portloe to Mevagissey** (12.3 miles/19.8km)
- **Mevagissey to Charlestown** (7.2 miles/11.6km)
- **Charlestown to Fowey** (10.3 miles/16.6km)
- **Fowey to Polperro** (7.1 miles/11.5km)
- **Polperro to Looe** (5.0 miles/8.0km)
- **Looe to Portwrinkle** (7.6 miles/12.2km)
- **Portwrinkle to Plymouth** (13.3 miles/21.4km)
- **Plymouth (River Tamar) to Wembury (River Yealm)** (14.8 miles/23.8km)
- **Wembury (Warren Point) to Bigbury-on-Sea** (13.5 miles/21.8km)
- **Bigbury to Salcombe** (13 miles/21km)
- **Salcombe to Torcross** (12.9 miles/20.8km)
- **Torcross to Dartmouth** (10 miles/16km)
- **Dartmouth to Brixham** (10.8 miles/17.3km)
- **Brixham to Torquay** (8.4 miles/13.5km)
- **Torquay to Shaldon** (10.8 miles/17.3km)
- **Shaldon to Exmouth** (7.9 miles/12.7km)
- **Exmouth to Sidmouth** (13.1 miles/21km)
- **Sidmouth to Lyme Regis** (17 miles/27km)
- **Lyme Regis to West Bay** (9.7 miles/15.6km)
- **West Bay to Abbotsbury** (9.4 miles/15.2km)
- **Abbotsbury to Ferry Bridge** (10.9 miles/17.5km)
- **Isle of Portland** (13.2 miles/21.3km)
- **Ferry Bridge to Lulworth Cove** (13.2 miles/21.3km)
- **Lulworth to Kimmeridge, Lulworth Range** (7 miles/11km)
- **Kimmeridge to South Haven Point, Poole Harbour** (20.9 miles/33.6km)
- **Alternative Inland Route, West Bexington to Osmington Mills** (18 miles/28km)

These Path Descriptions are all available to buy on our web site at www.swcp.org.uk or by phone on 01752 896237.

The Reverse Guide

The Association has written a description of the Trail for those walking in the Poole to Minehead direction. It deals only with the path so this Annual Guide will be necessary for all the other information. Our Reverse Guide supplement was comprehensively revised in 2008.

Price £4.00 plus UK postage

Maps

We are sometimes asked if you require a map sheet as well as a guide book and our advice is certainly yes. One does not get as badly lost on the Coast Path as you can on inland paths, but a map is an asset nonetheless. Furthermore many walkers derive much interest from looking at their route in relation to the rest of the countryside on ordinary walks, and the same applies just as much, if not more so, on our Coast Path. The National Trail Guides offer a partial solution with their maps, but even these are not as useful as a map sheet.

Harvey Maps

Walk for a week with just one map - those who have walked in the Scottish Highlands or the Lake District will know of Harvey Maps.

Produced at a scale of 1:40 000 the walkers' maps for the South West Coast Path are ideal for this National Trail which, because it is following a geographic feature, i.e. the coast, route finding does not usually present any real difficulties.

Six maps cover the entire route of the Coast Path compared with fourteen OS Landranger maps or seventeen OS Explorer/Outdoor Leisure maps. The maps have a similar amount of detail as Landranger maps for the walker yet without the administrative symbols that sometimes obscure the detail. The maps are of a more manageable size (folding to approx 240 x 120mm or 9.52" x 4.68") and are waterproof. Weight wise (without the wallet) they are a mere 84g compared with Landrangers at 74g and Explorers at 110g (without their card covers). Another useful feature is the provision on areas of the map not needed for walking (in this case the sea) of much important information about the Trail and services along the way.

Map 1	Minehead to Bude
Map 2	Bude to Portreath
Map 3	Portreath to Lizard
Map 4	Lizard to Plymouth
Map 5	Plymouth to Sidmouth
Map 6	Sidmouth to Poole

They are priced at £10.95 each and are becoming more widely available at branches of Waterstone's and Cotswold Outdoors (or direct from Harvey Maps). For further details visit www.harveymaps.co.uk or telephone 01786 841202, fax 01786 841098, sales@ harveymaps.co.uk

They offer the complete set for £55.75.

1:50 000 Ordnance Survey Maps

The Metric 1:50 000 Landranger Series needed to cover the coast from Minehead in Somerset to Poole Harbour in Dorset are as follows, working round the coast from Minehead.

181	Minehead & Brendon Hills
180	Barnstaple & Ilfracombe
190	Bude & Clovelly
200	Newquay & Bodmin
204	Truro & Falmouth
203	Land's End & Isles of Scilly
204	Truro & Falmouth
200	Newquay & Bodmin
201	Plymouth & Launceston
202	Torbay & South Dartmoor
192	Exeter & Sidmouth
193	Taunton & Lyme Regis
194	Dorchester & Weymouth
195	Bournemouth & Purbeck

Levant Mine

Geographers A-Z Maps

The Geographers A-Z Map Company has now mapped the entire 630 miles of the South West Coast Path and covered the entire route in five new and convenient Adventure Atlases.

The maps use 1:25,000 mapping, updated by A-Z cartographers, and each one includes a comprehensive index, outdoor information and QR barcodes to provide an instant connection to the latest local information including weather and tide times.

The five maps cover North Devon and Somerset (Minehead to Bude), North Cornwall (Bude to Land's End), South Cornwall (Land's End to Plymouth), South Devon (Plymouth to Lyme Regis) and Dorset (Lyme Regis to Poole). The maps cost £7.95 each – check them out and order them on our web site at www.swcp.org.uk

1:25 000 Ordnance Survey Maps

In path order, from Minehead the Coast Path is on 2½" maps.

- **Outdoor Leisure 9** Exmoor
- **Explorer 139** Bideford, llfracombe and Barnstaple
- **Explorer 126** Clovelly and Hartland
- **Explorer 111** Bude, Boscastle and Tintagel
- **Explorer 109** Bodmin Moor (depicts Coast Path from Boscastle to Portgaverne)
- **Explorer 106** Newquay and Padstow
- **Explorer 104** Redruth, St Agnes, Camborne and Perranporth
- **Explorer 102** Land's End, Penzance & St Ives
- **Explorer 103** The Lizard
- **Explorer 105** Falmouth and Mevagissey
- **Explorer 107** St Austell and Liskeard
- **Explorer 108** Plymouth & Tavistock
- **Explorer OL20** South Devon
- **Explorer 110** Torquay and Dawlish
- **Explorer 115** Exmouth and Sidmouth
- **Explorer 116** Lyme Regis and Bridport
- **Outdoor Leisure 15** Purbeck and South Dorset

All A-Z, Harvey and OS maps can be obtained from most bookshops. They, including Harvey Maps, may also be obtained from KenRoy Thompson Limited, 25 Cobourg Street, Plymouth PL1 1SR
Tel: 01752 227693
Email: maps@kenroythompson.co.uk
Website: kenroythompson.co.uk

POST FREE TO UK MEMBERS OF THE SOUTH WEST COAST PATH ASSOCIATION (Credit cards accepted).

The above is a comprehensive list of maps for the South West Coast Path. In Section 3 you will also find the relevant maps listed for each section of the Coast Path.

Books

These publications are available from bookshops.

This list is not exhaustive; there are a number of other books available but we have tried hard to list all those which are really useful and even those not really useful that you might think would be.

South West Coast Path - Minehead to South Haven Point (ISBN 1-85284-379-9)
An excellent pocket sized book by Paddy Dillon (March 2003). We can recommend it as most useful. It has stunning photographs and OS maps. Available from Cicerone Press, 2 Police Square, Milnthorpe, Cumbria LA7 7PY at £12.95 and bookshops. Note that Association members receive 20% discount. See our members' newsletters in 2013 for details or contact the office. Third print 2007 ISBN 978-1-85284-379-3.

National Trail Guides -
published by Aurum Press in association with Natural England. They are available from bookshops, or in case of difficulty, from Aurum Press, 74-77 White Lion Street, London, N1 9PF. These are good guide books with good maps. An excellent venture by those involved.

Minehead to Padstow
by Roland Tarr (May 2013)

Padstow to Falmouth
by John Macadam (April 2013)

Falmouth to Exmouth
by Brian Le Messurier (May 2013)

Exmouth to Poole
by Roland Tarr (May 2013)

Most Tourist Information Centres (see our Accommodation section) have good supplies of leaflets and books relating to their local areas. We suggest you telephone or write to them and ask what is available.

Please also see the Association's shop on pages 186-189 and remember that Tourist Information Centres (see page 179) are a source of local leaflets and books.

Railways

Help in planning your journey to the south west can be obtained at www.transportdirect.info

Throughout the year there is a regular service of direct First Great Western High Speed services linking London Paddington with Taunton, Exeter St. David's, Newton Abbot, Plymouth and Cornwall. There are also regular Arriva Cross Country Trains services linking Birmingham, the North West, North East and Scotland with Taunton, Exeter St. David's, Plymouth, Cornwall and Bournemouth.

There is also a First Great Western overnight sleeper service between Paddington and Penzance.

All these services offer a range of on-train facilities including catering and on most First Great Western High Speed services during the school holidays, coach E is dedicated for the use of families. During the high season (May to September), demand for seats is high so it is recommended that seats are reserved in advance to ensure a comfortable journey. There is a half hourly South West Trains service linking London Waterloo, Woking, Basingstoke and Southampton with Bournemouth, Poole, Wareham (for Swanage), Dorchester (for Bridport and Lyme Regis) and Weymouth for those intending to walk the Dorset end of the Coast Path.

East Devon is also served by South West Trains with an hourly service from London Waterloo to Exeter St David's calling at Woking, Basingstoke and Salisbury to Axminster (for Lyme Regis & Seaton), Honiton (for Sidmouth), and Exeter Central (for Exmouth branch).

First Great Western West offers long distance and most local trains in the South West. The long distance trains link Cardiff and Bristol with Exeter, Penzance, Plymouth, Portsmouth, Salisbury, Southampton and Weymouth. The local services on the branch lines of Devon and Cornwall offer connections into and out of First Great Western and Arriva Cross Country services, and South West Trains at Exeter for the Exmouth branch.

For those walking the Coast Path in the far west, why not consider using the First Great Western night sleeper service from Paddington to Penzance? This is a unique way to arrive on the Coast Path ready to walk fully refreshed.

First Great Western West local routes run Sunday services on the routes listed below

- **Westbury - Yeovil - Weymouth**
- **Liskeard - Looe**
- **Exeter - Barnstaple**
- **Par - Newquay**
- **Exeter - Exmouth**
- **Truro - Falmouth**
- **Newton Abbot -Torquay - Paignton**
- **St Erth - St Ives**
- **Plymouth - Gunnislake**

The web address for First Great Western High Speed and West services is **www.firstgreatwestern.co.uk**

To obtain train information, book tickets and reserve seats call the National Rail Enquiries Service on 08457 484950 (24 hours a day) or via the website **www.nationalrail.co.uk** or go to **www.thetrainline.com**

The web address for Arriva is **www.crosscountrytrains.co.uk**

The web address for South West Trains is **www.southwesttrains.co.uk**

Bus Services

A National Transport Enquiry Service has been established. For all timetable enquiries in South West England, call Traveline on 0871 200 2233 or www.travelinesw.com

The main bus operative contact details are: First Devon and Cornwall Tel: 0845 600 1420 **www.firstgroup.com.**

Tourist Information Centres can be very helpful with bus enquiries. For details of all coastal TICs see our Accommodation section at the back of this book.

Access to the start of the Path

Access to the start of the path can be made locally and from outside the region, with First's bus service 28 linking Minehead to the mainline railway station at Taunton. Service 28 Taunton - Minehead currently operates on an half-hourly frequency up to the early evenings from Monday to Saturdays.

On Sundays service 28 operates less frequently. For service 28 timetable enquiries telephone First - Taunton. Tel: 01823 272033. National Express operates some direct services to Minehead and others to Taunton where passengers can change to First Service 28 for Minehead. For more information about national coach services to the South West, telephone National Express Tel: 08717 818181

Airports

There are airports in or near towns close to the Coast Path. In path order, they are:

Newquay Airport
Flights to and from the Isles of Scilly, Gatwick and Manchester. Many more flights for Summer only.
St Mawgan, Newquay TR8 4RQ
Tel: 01637 860600 www.
newquaycornwallairport.com

Land's End
For flights to the Isles of Scilly:
Information from Isles of Scilly Travel,
Steamship House, Quay Street,
Penzance TR18 4BZ
Tel: 0845 710 5555
www.islesofscilly-travel.co.uk

Exeter
Exeter International Airport,
Exeter, EX5 2BD
Tel: 0800 655 6526
www.exeter-airport.co.uk

Bournemouth
Bournemouth Airport Ltd.,
Christchurch, Bournemouth BH23 6SE
Tel: 01202 364000
www.bournemouthairport.com

Sea Transport & Coastal Cruises

Brittany Ferries provide a ferry link as follows to the South West Coast Path: Plymouth/Roscoff; Poole/Cherbourg (Not Dec - Feb); Plymouth/Santander.
Tel: 0871 244 0744
www.brittany-ferries.co.uk, or contact by mail to Brittany Ferries, Millbay, Plymouth, Devon, PL1 3EW

The famous pleasure steamers Waverley and Balmoral provide both cruises and transport, to and from the Exmoor Coast.

From May until September these sea-going ships provide transport to South Wales, Bristol, North Somerset, Lundy Island and the Exmoor Coast.

Sailings are to and from Ilfracombe & Minehead. The timetable is subject to the Bristol Channel tides which have the second highest rise and fall in the world. Free copies of the full programme are available from:
Waverley Excursions Ltd.,
The Waverley Terminal,
36 Lancefield Quay, Glasgow G3 8HA
www.waverleyexcursions.co.uk
Tel: 0845 1304647, or from Tourist Information Centres in West Somerset and North Devon.

Porlock Weir

Planning your walking holiday in the south west can be helped at www.travelinesw.com or telephone 0871 200 2233.

Private Branch Line Railways

Bishops Lydeard to Minehead

The West Somerset Railway runs steam trains through 20 scenic miles (32 km) to Minehead. Bishops Lydeard is 4 miles (6 km) outside Taunton and easily accessible by bus. The service operates between February & December. For details contact the company at 'The Railway Station', Minehead TA24 5BG
Tel: 01643 704996 Book online at
www.west-somerset-railway.co.uk

Paignton to Kingswear (Dartmouth)

For the rambler who is also a railway enthusiast, the Paignton and Dartmouth Steam Railway is a `must'. This most attractive line runs from Paignton to Goodrington, Churston and Kingswear and operates preserved Great Western steam locomotives and rolling-stock. The line passes through some delightful coastal and river scenery, and a trip on the railway could easily be combined with a walk to make a very pleasant day out. Steam trains operate on selected dates in Feb & March, April - Oct; Daily April to October; Santa specials in December. For details contact Queens Park Station, Torbay Road, Paignton TQ4 6AF
Tel: 01803 555872
www.dartmouthrailriver.co.uk

The Bodmin & Wenford Railway

runs between Bodmin Parkway to Bodmin General is a service that could prove useful for those requiring bus transport to the coast.
Tel: 0845 125 9678
www.bodminrailway.co.uk

The Swanage Railway

which links a large park and ride facility at Norden, north west of Corfe Castle to Swanage, could also prove useful for those requiring car parking (not long stay) with access by rail to the Coast Path. If you require information contact the enquiry line on
Tel: 01929 425800
www.swanagerailway.co.uk

Bus Information

Listed below, in path order, are details of services and information available from County Councils and local bus operators; it is intended for guidance use only. All information provided is correct at the time of going to print; responsibility for any inaccuracies or changes cannot be accepted by County Councils or bus operators. For up to date bus service information, telephone the relevant numbers given in the following paragraphs.

Somerset

For service 28 from Taunton to Minehead and services 30/30A from Taunton to Lyme Regis and Weymouth via Axminster (change buses) contact First, The Bus Station, Tower Street, Taunton, TA1 4AF
Tel: 0871 200 2233
www.firstgroup.com

For service 18 from Taunton to Minehead contact sales@webberbus.com
0800 096 3039 or 01278 452086
www.webberbus.com

For service 39/300 from Minehead to Porlock/ Lynmouth contact Quantock Motor Services, The Coal Yard, Broadgauge Business Park, Station Road, Bishops Lydeard, TA4 3BU
Tel: 01823 430202.
www.quantockmotorservices.co.uk

Somerset County Council produces booklets detailing the timetables of all public bus services in Somerset which can be downloaded at www.somerset.gov.uk/timetables, or requested from Transporting Somerset, County Hall, Taunton, TA1 4DY
Tel: 0845 345 9155
Email: generalenquiries@somerset.gov.uk
www.somerset.gov.uk

North Devon

The North Devon coast has a range of bus services which may be of use to coastal walkers. The greatest choice of coastal destinations is provided from Barnstaple. The principal services are: 309/310 Barnstaple to Lynton; Services 21 and 301 Barnstaple to Ilfracombe and Combe Martin; 308 Barnstaple to Georgeham; 303 Barnstaple, to Woolacombe; 21 & 372 Barnstaple to Bideford and Westward Ho!; 21A Barnstaple to Bideford and Appledore and 319 Barnstaple to Bideford, Clovelly and Hartland. Also 21 Barnstaple to Bideford and Westward Ho! and

21A Ilfracombe, Barnstaple to Bideford and Appledore. Note that the number prefix refers to the bus route number. During the Summer, Exmoor Coastlink 300 operates daily from Ilfracombe to Lynton, Lynmouth (changing at Lynmouth) for Porlock and Minehead, with glorious coastal views along much of the route.

Those who are walking between North Devon and North Cornwall may find First Devon and Cornwall X9 service or Western Greyhound 599 from Exeter to Bude a useful link.

The above services are operated by First Devon and Cornwall, Filers Travel, Quantock Motor Services, Stagecoach South West, TW Coaches and Western Greyhound. For timetable enquiries telephone Traveline - 0871 2002233, 07:00-21:00 daily, www.traveline.org.uk

Devon County Council produces an annual timetable guide from May each year, entitled 'North Devon Public Transport Guide'. They are available from Tourist Information Centres, Libraries, bus operators or by telephoning the DevonBus enquiry line Barnstaple: 01271 382800 or Exeter 01392 382800, Monday - Friday 09:00-17:00. Email: devonbus@devon.gov.uk www.journeydevon.info
Also see www.journeydevon.info where there is a new interactive bus map.

Cornwall

Cornwall Council, in conjunction with local bus operators, produces a public transport guide, published in May each year, covering the whole of Cornwall. It is available by post, price £2.50, from The Passenger Transport Unit, Carrick House, Pydar Street, Truro, Cornwall, TR1 1EB. Telephone 0300 1234 222. The timetable can also be obtained, free of charge, locally from bus stations, tourist information centres and libraries as can a county public transport map showing all bus and rail routes with a summary of frequencies. Full details on all the services contained in the guide can also be obtained from www.cornwallpublictransport.info

Public transport information can also be obtained from Traveline 0871 200 22 33, www.traveline.org.uk. The main bus operator contact details are: First Devon and Cornwall, Tel: 0845 600 1420 www.firstgroup.com Western Greyhound, Tel: 01637 871871, www.westerngreyhound.com

The principal routes serving coastal areas are:
First Services: 1 Penzance - Land's End, 2 Penzance - Helston - Falmouth/Truro, 10 Penzance - St Just, 16 Penzance - Nancledra - St Ives, 17 St Ives - Penzance, 27 Truro - St Austell - Par , 34 Helston - Redruth, 35 Helston - Helford Passage - Falmouth, 36 Helston - Coverack, 37 Helston - The Lizard, 81 Cremyll to Plymouth, 85 Truro - St Agnes, 88 Truro - Falmouth, 300 Penzance - Land's End - St Just - St Ives (summer only), 500 Truro - Falmouth - Helford Passage

Western Greyhound services:
See their web site for many more routes too www.westerngreyhound.com
501 Penzance - Land's End,
504 Penzance - Mousehole - Porthcurno - Land's End - St Just, 508 Penzance - Zennor - St Ives, 510 Wadebridge - Camelford - Exeter
515 Penzance - Hayle - Gwithian - St Ives,
524/526 Fowey - Par - St Austell - Mevagissey - Gorran Haven, 525/526 Fowey - Par - Charlestown - Mevagissey - Gorran Haven,
547 Newquay - Perranporth - St Agnes - St Ives, 550/551 Truro - Veryan - St Mawes,
555 Bodmin Parkway - Bodmin - Wadebridge - Padstow, 556 Newquay - Padstow,
572 Polperro - Looe - Plymouth,
573/574 Polperro - Looe - Liskeard - Callington, 584 Wadebridge - Port Isaac - Camelford, 591/592/594/597/598 Newquay - Perranporth - St Agnes - Truro - Newquay
595 Wadebridge - Camelford - Boscastle - Tintagel - Bude, 599 Bude - Exeter

Travel Cornwall:
403 Newquay - Perranporth - St Agnes - Truro

Stagecoach:
X9 Bude - Exeter
Information correct as of December 2012

South Devon

The coastline between Plymouth and Exeter is accessible by bus from many inland towns. The principal services are:

81 Plymouth to Torpoint; 34 Plymouth City Centre and Admirals Hard for Cremyll Ferry (buses meet ferry and through ticket available); 2 Plymouth City Centre to Mount Batten; 54 Plymouth to Bovisand (Summer holidays only); 49 Plymouth to Heybrook Bay; 48 Plymouth to Wembury; 94 Plymouth to Noss Mayo; 93 Plymouth to Kingsbridge & Dartmouth; X80 Plymouth to Paignton & Torquay; X38 Plymouth to Exeter; X64 Exeter to Totnes (Kingsbridge and Salcombe on Sundays), 164 Totnes to Kingsbridge; X81 Torquay and Totnes to Dartmouth;
162 Kingsbridge to Hope Cove; 606 Kingsbridge to Salcombe; 120 Kingswear to Paignton;

22, 24 Kingswear to Brixham; 12 Brixham & Paignton to Torquay and Newton Abbot; 11 Torquay to Teignmouth; 2 Newton Abbot to Teignmouth, Dawlish and Exeter. 25 Goodrington to Paignton and Stoke Gabriel; 17 Brixham to Furzeham, Wall Park and The Quay; X46 Paignton to Torquay and Exeter; 88 Paignton to Totnes, Buckfastleigh, Ashburton and Newton Abbot; X80 Torquay to Paignton, Totnes, Ivybridge and Plymouth.

The above services are operated by First, Tally Ho, Plymouth Citybus, Stagecoach South West and Dart Pleasure Craft.
For timetable enquiries telephone Traveline on 0871 200 2233.

Devon County Council produces annual timetable guides, from May each year for the South Hams and Teignbridge areas. They are available from Devon bus on Traveline 0871 200 2233, or from Salcombe TIC 01548 843927.

Plymouth Citybus map and services are available from from Plymouth Citybus on 01752 662271 or www.citycoach.co.uk
Also see www.devon.gov.uk where there is a new interactive bus map.

East Devon

The East Devon coastline is accessible by bus from Exeter, Ottery St. Mary, Honiton and Axminster. The principal services are:

X53 Exeter to Beer, Seaton, Lyme Regis, Bridport, West Bay and Weymouth;
X53 Exeter to Wareham, Poole, 20 Taunton to Seaton; 57 Exeter to Exmouth, 157 to Budleigh Salterton and Sidmouth; 52A Exeter to Sidmouth & Seaton; 52B Exeter to Sidmouth & Honiton; 382 Ottery St. Mary to Sidmouth; 885 Axminster to Seaton; 30 Taunton to Axminster change at Axminster for service 31, 31 Axminster to Lyme Regis (and continues to Bridport, Dorchester and Weymouth); 899 Sidmouth to Branscombe, Beer and Seaton. On Summer Sundays service 56B operates between Sidmouth, Honiton, Ottery St Mary & Exeter.

The above services are operated by Stagecoach South West, Axe Valley Mini-Travel and First Hampshire and Dorset. For timetable enquiries telephone Traveline public transport info.(Tel: 0871 200 2233) daily 08:00-20:00.

Devon County Council produces an annual timetable guide from May each year, entitled 'East Devon Public Transport Guide'- they are available from Tourist Information Centres, libraries, bus operators or by telephoning the DevonBus enquiry line on Exeter (Tel: 01392 382800) Monday-Friday 09:00-17:00.

Bus Map - Other useful information provided by Devon County Council includes the public transport map. This depicts all bus routes and railway lines throughout the county and gives a summary of service frequency. It is available from Tourist Information Centres, libraries and bus stations or by telephoning the DevonBus enquiry line on Barnstaple (Tel: 01271 382800) or Exeter (Tel: 01392 382800) Monday-Friday 09:00-17:00 or www.devon.gov.uk.

Dorset

The Dorset Coast is accessible by bus from various inland points with train connections for the distant traveller. The principal routes are listed below.

Service 31 provides hourly journeys from Mondays to Saturdays between Weymouth-Dorchester-Bridport-Lyme Regis and Axminster, calling at Axminster and Dorchester South rail stations for onward travel. The service operates until late in the evening. There is a two hourly service along the same route on Sundays. Passengers benefit from low floor buses that provide easy access and greater comfort. Contact First Hampshire and Dorset. Tel: 0870 010 60 22.

Services 103 and 104 provide journeys between Dorchester-Wool-Bovington/ Wareham. Operated by Damory Coaches and Dorset Community Transport respectively the services run Monday to Saturday with four services a day serving Lulworth Cove.

Service X53 is fully accessible and operates several journeys each day between Poole-Wareham-Weymouth-Lyme Regis and Exeter. During the winter, the Sunday service is reduced and operates until December between Weymouth and Lyme Regis. Details from First Hampshire and Dorset, see above.

Service X43 operates between Weymouth, Wareham and Swanage during the summer months.

Service 40 runs daily between Poole, Swanage and Wareham. Service 44 operates between Swanage, Harmans Cross and Worth Matravers from Monday to Saturday. Details from Wilts & Dorset Bus Company, Tel: 01202 673555.

Service 50 operates daily between Bournemouth and Swanage via the Sandbanks Ferry. Service 52 runs from the Sandbanks ferry into Poole town centre daily, (not winter Sundays) details from Wilts & Dorset Bus Company,
Tel: 01983 827005.

Frequent services run to Portland from Weymouth and Dorchester. They are mainly operated by First Hampshire and Dorset and South West Coaches, details above.

Dorset County Council produces comprehensive timetable information including a countywide Bus and Rail Map.

All information is available from Tourist Information Centres or Dorset Passenger Transport, County Hall, Dorchester, DT1 1XJ. Tel: 01305 225165 or Email: publictransport@dorsetcc.gov.uk

Timetables can be downloaded at www.dorsetforyou.com/bustimes

Important Information: There may be changes to services and/or operators. For up to date information, visit www.dorsetforyou.com/bustimes or contact Dorset Passenger Transport - details as above.

Ferries & River Crossings

The nature of the Coast Path means that many ferries must be used to cross estuaries along the length of the path. It is recommended the ferry operator be contacted direct for the service to be used. Please do this especially when a fairly late timing is expected and it is necessary to confirm the time of the last run. Also do this when using outside the main tourist season or if use by a party of walkers is planned.

Full ferry details are shown here. Less detailed ferry information is also included in the relevant Walk Section text.

The walker tends to view feet as the only certain method of progress - and why not? Unfortunately, the absolute purist would need to be an olympic-class swimmer not to have to use ferries on the South West Coast Path. However, a certain amount of scepticism is helpful, absolute reliance on ferries is not advised. There are other ferries available on the path which walkers may wish to use for diversions or shortcuts. We have attempted to list those directly necessary.

The ferry crossings encountered, in path order, are: River Torridge (Instow/Appledore) (optional); River Camel (Rock/Padstow); River Gannel (Newquay/Crantock); Helford River (Helford/Helford Passage); Fal Estuary (Falmouth/St Mawes and St Mawes/Place); River Fowey (Fowey/Polruan); River Tamar (Cremyll/Plymouth); River Yealm (Wembury/Noss Mayo); River Avon (Bigbury-on-Sea/Bantham); River Dart (Dartmouth/Kingswear); River Teign (Shaldon/Teignmouth); River Exe (Starcross/Exmouth, Turf/Topsham); Weymouth Harbour.

Instow/Appledore (River Torridge)

This ferry service, an optional means of crossing the Torridge without passing through Bideford, has recently been revived after many years. It runs generally for 2 hours either side of high tide.
Website: www.appledoreinstowferry.com
Email: contact@appledoreinstowferry.com
The ferry will operate from early April 2014 until October.

Rock/Padstow (River Camel)

Black Tor Ferry, Padstow Harbour Commissioners, Harbour Office, West Quay, Padstow, Cornwall PL28 8AQ
Tel: 01841 532239 Mobile: 07773 081574
Fax: 01841 5333346
Website: www.padstow-harbour.co.uk
Email: padstowharbour@btconnect.com
Ferry operates all year at 20 min intervals
08:00 to 18:50 (Summer)
08:00 to 19:50 (mid July-end August)
08:00 to 16:50 (winter) Some Sundays in winter, no ferry

Water taxi

A water taxi service operates between Rock and Padstow between 19:00 and midnight from Easter to 31st October, weather and tides permitting. Contact: GB Smith&Son
Tel: 01208 862815 (office hours)
Fax: 01208 863090
Website: www.rock-watertaxi.co.uk
Email: info@rock-watertaxi.co.uk
Or contact the boat direct on 07778 105297.

Newquay/Crantock (River Gannel)

Fern Pit Café & Ferry, G A Northey and G King (Proprietors), Fern Pit, Riverside Crescent, Newquay, Cornwall TR7 1PJ
Tel: 01637 873181 Website: www.fernpit.co.uk
Email: mail@fernpit.co.uk
Ferry operates as follows: 18th May to mid September continuous, 7 days a week, 10:00-18:00. Weather dependant.

Gillan Creek

Anthony Jenkin Tel: 01326 231357
Ferry operates most days Easter, and April 1st to 31st October
Website: www.stanthony.co.uk
Email: anthony@stanthony.co.uk

Helford River
River Boats, Helford Passage, Falmouth, Cornwall Tel: 01326 250770
Website: www.helford-river-boats.co.uk
Email: ian@helford-river-boats.co.uk Ferry operates Good Friday/1st April to 31st October 09:30 to 17:00 daily on demand. July & August on Tues & Weds until 21.00
It is possible to use local taxi services if the ferry is not operating - Autocabs, tel: 01326 573773 or Cove Cars, tel: 07980 814058.

Falmouth/St Mawes (River Fal)
Cornwall Ferries, 2 Ferry Cottages, Feock, Truro, Cornwall TR3 6QT
Tel: 01326 270917 - Kiosk (summer)
Tel: 01872 861910
Website: www.falriver.co.uk
Ferry operates all year.
June-October inclusive 3 ferries per hour, fewer at other times. Ferries operate from Falmouth Prince of Wales Pier all year and Custom House Quay summer only.

St Mawes/Place (Percuil River)
Cornwall Ferries (see above)
Mobile: 07791 283884
Ferry operates Easter to early Jan 2015 09:30 to 17:00, every half hour.
There is also Falmouth Water Taxi service which operates between Falmouth and St Mawes or Place, weather permitting, between March and October, 9am - 6pm (until 10.30pm May-Sept). If needed, it is best to telephone a day in advance.
Tel: 07522 446659.
www.falmouthwatertaxi.co.uk

Fowey/Polruan (River Fowey)
Polruan Ferry Co Ltd, Toms Yard, East Street Polruan-by-Fowey, Cornwall PL23 1PB
Tel: 01726 870232
Ferry operates all year at 5-10 min intervals.
07:00 to 23:00 1st May-30th September (Saturdays 07:30 start, Sundays 09:00 start)
07:00 to 19:00 1st October-30th April (Saturdays 07:30 start, Sundays 10:00 to 17:00). Website: ctomsandson.co.uk
enquiries@ctomsandson.co.uk

Cremyll/Plymouth
Cremyll Ferry, Cremyll Quay, Cremyll, Torpoint, Cornwall PL10 1HX
Tel: Tel 0774 6199 508
The ferry operates depending on weather, tides and other circumstances permitting.
All year round at 30 minute intervals.
Summer Service from 1st April to 30th September.
From Mt Edgcumbe:
Weekdays 06:45 to 20:30, Saturdays 08:00 to 21:30, Sundays 09:00 to 21:00.
From Plymouth: Weekdays 07:15 to 20:45. Saturdays 08:15 to 21:45, Sundays 09:15 to 21:15.
Winter Service from 1st October to 31st March.
From Mt Edgcumbe:
Weekdays 06:45 to 18:30. Saturdays 08:00 to 18:30, Sundays 09:00 to 18:00.
From Plymouth:
Weekdays 07:15 to 18:45, Saturdays 08:15 to 18:45, Sundays 09:15 to 18:15.
Closed Christmas, Boxing & New Year's Days
We urge you to contact the ferry operator direct if you are relying on this service, particularly if you are anticipating a fairly late finish and need to confirm the time of its last run. Further information about the Cremyll ferry can be found at www.cremyll-ferry.co.uk

Sutton Harbour/Mount Batten
Mount Batten Ferry 0751 537 0000
www.mountbattenferry.com
info@soundcruising.com
All year round, every ½ hour. Summer weekdays 07:15 to 23:00 and weekends 08:45 to 22:30. Winter weekdays 07:45 - 18:15 and weekends 08:45 - 23:00.
We urge you to contact the ferry operator direct if you are relying on this service, particularly if you are anticipating a fairly late finish and need to confirm the time of its last run.

Wembury (Warren Point)/Noss Mayo (River Yealm)
Bill Gregor, Mobile: 07817 132757
Ferry operates the Monday before Good Friday until last Sunday in Sept, 10:00 to 16:00. In bad weather, school, term-time & weekdays, 10:00 - 12:00 & 15:00 - 16:00 BUT use the signal board to call ferry if required.
Eco-Taxi based in Kingsbridge will carry walkers between Plymouth and Dartmouth and from all estuaries in South Devon.
Tel: 01548 856347 or 07811 385275.
Alternatively, Ivy Cabs may also carry walkers round the South Hams estuaries.
Tel: 01752 696969

Bigbury/Bantham (River Avon)
Marsh Dawes, The Boathouse,
Bantham, Kingsbridge, Devon.
Tel: 01548 561196 Mobile: 07837 361306
Ferry operates 29th April - 28th September, daily except Sundays, 10:00 to 11:00 and 15:00 to 16:00. Eco-Taxi based in Kingsbridge will carry walkers between Plymouth and Dartmouth
and from all estuaries in South Devon.
Tel: 01548 856347 or 07811 385275
Alternatively, Ivy Cabs may also carry walkers round the South Hams estuaries.
Tel: 01752 696969

Salcombe to East Portlemouth Ferry
The Salcombe Ferry
Tel: 01548 842061/560558
Simon Shortman
All year round.
Nov - March: ½ hourly between 08:00 to 1800 hrs. April - Oct half term: Continuous service 08:00 to 18:00 hrs. (July & August) 08:30 hrs start weekends and bank holidays. Please note that the ferry point is Jubilee Pier in summer & Whitestrand Pontoon in winter. We urge you to contact the ferry operator direct if you are relying on this service, particularly if you are anticipating a fairly late finish and need to confirm the time of its last run.

Dartmouth/Kingswear (River Dart)
Sat Nav Codes - Kingswear TQ6 0AA.
Dartmouth TQ6 9AP
Tel: 01803 752342
www.southhams.gov.uk/
DartmouthLowerFerry Email pat.webb@
southhams.gov.uk
Ferry operates all year on a continuous service 07:00 to 22:45, Sundays 08:00 to 22:45

Dartmouth Passenger Ferry (River Dart)
Dartmouth Steam Railway & River Boat Co.
5 Lower Street, Dartmouth TQ6 9AJ
Tel: 01803 555872
www.dartmouthrailriver.co.uk
Ferry operates all year on a continuous service 07:30 to 23:10, Sundays 09:00 to 23:10.
Check web for specific times.

Shaldon/Teignmouth
The ferry operates:

April - Mid July	08:00 to 18:00
Mid July - End August	09:00 to 20.30
September - October	08:00 to 18:00
November - January	08:00 to 16:30
February - March	08:00 to 17:00

Special event finish time is posted on the day on the ferry notice board.
Closed Mon & Tues in Dec & Jan. Call Mr Allen on ferry mobile: 07896 711822
Tel: 01626 215617
www.teignmouthshaldonferry.co.uk
leisure@teignbridge.gov.uk
If operating, the ferry runs from the beach opposite the Ferry Boat Inn.

Starcross/Exmouth (River Exe)
Mr Mark Rackley, Starcross Pier and Pleasure Company, 26 Marine Parade, Dawlish, Devon EX7 9DL
Tel: 01626 774770 or 07974 022536
Ferry operates mid-April - end October, hourly, 7 days a week. From Starcross,
on the hour from 10:10 until 16:10, until 17:10 (mid-May to mid September). From Exmouth, on the half hour from 10:40
until 16:40 (Easter and October), until 17:40 (mid-May and June-mid September).

Turf/Topsham (River Exe)
Steve Garrett Tel: 07778 370582
www.topshamtoturfferry.co.uk
Email: seadreamferry@btinternet.com
Ferry operates 7 days a week, Easter holiday, mid-May - mid-September and weekends April-September; from Turf 11:45 to 15:00 and from Topsham 11:30 to 14:15.

Topsham Ferry (River Exe) (between Topsham Quay riverside and Topsham Lock canalside)
Exeter City Council
Canals and Rivers Department
Tel: 01392 274306 (office); 07801 203338 (ferryman).
Ferry operates Easter-September daily except Tuesdays, 9:30 to 17:00; October-March Saturdays, Sundays and Bank Holidays 11:00 to 17:00 or sunset. Wave or phone for service. Between April and September the ferry may be available outside these hours, weather and tides permitting; phone for details.

Weymouth Harbour
Weymouth and Portland Borough Council,
Harbour Master's Office,
13 Custom House Quay, Weymouth DT4 8BG
Tel: 01305 838423
Ferry operates (rowing boat):

Easter-June	11:00 to 15:00
July	09:30 to 17:00
August	09:30 to 19:00
September-October	11.00 to 15.00

All weather permitting.
www.harbour.weymouth.gov.uk
www.harbour.weymouth.gov.uk

South Haven Point to Sandbanks, Poole
See end of Walk 70, page 130.

South Haven Point/Sandbanks
Shell Bay/Sandbanks
(Mouth of Poole Harbour) Bournemouth - Swanage Motor Road & Ferry Company, Shell Bay, Studland BH19 3BA
Tel: 01929 450203 Fax: 01929 450498
www.sandbanksferry.co.uk
All year round. Daily every 20 mins.
Sandbanks 07:00 to 23:00 hrs
Shell Bay 07:10 to 23:10 hrs
Christmas Day every half hour.

If you are relying on a ferry service we urge you to contact the ferry operator direct, particularly if you anticpate a fairly late finish and need to confirm the time of its last run.

Tide Times

The tide tables included in this edition refer to the times of low water at Devonport.

These tables will act as a guide for those wishing to paddle across the Gannel (Newquay) or the Erme. Please be sure to read the warnings given under each section. We have been criticised for being too cautious over the times we suggest for paddling across the rivers, and know that some walkers cross at other times.

We believe our attitude is correct as there certainly are dangers, but you may wish to try at low tide on other occasions to see if conditions will permit a safe crossing. Variations in barometric pressure can affect tide levels. Remember there are different levels daily of low water; if in doubt seek local knowledge.

- Newquay (The Gannel) deduct 30 minutes
- River Erme as at Devonport

The tidal information for the port of Devonport is reproduced by permission of the Controller of Her Majesty's Stationery Office and the UK Hydrographic Office (www.ukho.gov.uk)

MARCH 2014 LOW WATER *From 30th March add 1 hour for BST*			
1	Sat	1159	****
2	Sun	0020	1245
3	Mon	0104	1327
4	Tues	0144	1406
5	Weds	0221	1441
6	Thurs	0255	1515
7	Fri	0329	1549
8	Sat	0406	1628
9	Sun	0454	1722
10	Mon	0559	1833
11	Tues	0720	1959
12	Weds	0901	2123
13	Thurs	0958	2215
14	Fri	1041	2256
15	Sat	1119	2333
16	Sun	1154	****
17	Mon	0007	1227
18	Tues	0040	1258
19	Weds	0111	1328
20	Thurs	0141	1358
21	Fri	0212	1429
22	Sat	0246	1506
23	Sun	0328	1552
24	Mon	0424	1656
25	Tues	0546	1831
26	Weds	0729	2011
27	Thurs	0853	2125
28	Fri	0957	2223
29	Sat	1050	2313
30	Sun	1138	2359
31	Mon	****	1222

APRIL 2014 LOW WATER *Add 1 hour for BST*			
1	Tues	0041	1303
2	Weds	0120	1340
3	Thurs	0156	1414
4	Fri	0229	1446
5	Sat	0302	1518
6	Sun	0337	1555
7	Mon	0421	1645
8	Tues	0522	1752
9	Weds	0635	1907
10	Thurs	0752	2022
11	Fri	0903	2125
12	Sat	0955	2214
13	Sun	1038	2256
14	Mon	1118	2336
15	Tues	1156	****
16	Weds	0013	1233
17	Thurs	0050	1308
18	Fri	0125	1343
19	Sat	0201	1419
20	Sun	0240	1459
21	Mon	0325	1548
22	Tues	0423	1653
23	Weds	0539	1818
24	Thurs	0710	1949
25	Fri	0830	2101
26	Sat	0933	2159
27	Sun	1026	2249
28	Mon	1114	2335
29	Tues	1157	****
30	Weds	0017	1238

MAY 2014 LOW WATER *Add 1 hour for BST*			
1	Thurs	0057	1315
2	Fri	0132	1349
3	Sat	0205	1420
4	Sun	0237	1452
5	Mon	0311	1526
6	Tues	0351	1610
7	Weds	0444	1710
8	Thurs	0550	1820
9	Fri	0658	1928
10	Sat	0803	2031
11	Sun	0901	2127
12	Mon	0953	2217
13	Tues	1041	2303
14	Weds	1126	2347
15	Thurs	****	1209
16	Fri	0030	1251
17	Sat	0113	1332
18	Sun	0155	1415
19	Mon	0239	1459
20	Tues	0327	1549
21	Weds	0422	1648
22	Thurs	0528	1758
23	Fri	0643	1917
24	Sat	0758	2030
25	Sun	0903	2131
26	Mon	0959	2224
27	Tues	1048	2311
28	Weds	1133	2355
29	Thurs	****	1214
30	Fri	0034	1252
31	Sat	0111	1326

JUNE 2014 LOW WATER *Add 1 hour for BST*			
1	Sun	0145	1358
2	Mon	0217	1429
3	Tues	0248	1500
4	Weds	0322	1536
5	Thurs	0402	1622
6	Fri	0457	1725
7	Sat	0604	1835
8	Sun	0710	1941
9	Mon	0813	2043
10	Tues	0912	2140
11	Weds	1007	2234
12	Thurs	1059	2325
13	Fri	1149	****
14	Sat	0015	1238
15	Sun	0103	1324
16	Mon	0150	1411
17	Tues	0237	1457
18	Weds	0324	1544
19	Thurs	0413	1634
20	Fri	0506	1731
21	Sat	0608	1838
22	Sun	0718	1952
23	Mon	0829	2101
24	Tues	0931	2200
25	Weds	1024	2250
26	Thurs	1111	2335
27	Fri	1154	****
28	Sat	0016	1233
29	Sun	0053	1307
30	Mon	0127	1338

JULY 2014 LOW WATER *Add 1 hour for BST*			
1	Tues	0157	1407
2	Weds	0225	1435
3	Thurs	0253	1504
4	Fri	0324	1538
5	Sat	0403	1624
6	Sun	0457	1730
7	Mon	0612	1851
8	Tues	0728	2004
9	Weds	0837	2110
10	Thurs	0940	2211
11	Fri	1038	2308
12	Sat	1133	****
13	Sun	0001	1226
14	Mon	0052	1315
15	Tues	0140	1401
16	Weds	0226	1445
17	Thurs	0310	1528
18	Fri	0353	1611
19	Sat	0438	1659
20	Sun	0529	1756
21	Mon	0631	1908
22	Tues	0749	2030
23	Weds	0904	2138
24	Thurs	1003	2232
25	Fri	1052	2317
26	Sat	1135	2358
27	Sun	****	1213
28	Mon	0035	1248
29	Tues	0107	1318
30	Weds	0135	1344
31	Thurs	0200	1410

AUGUST 2014 LOW WATER *Add 1 hour for BST*			
1	Fri	0225	1436
2	Sat	0252	1506
3	Sun	0326	1545
4	Mon	0409	1637
5	Tues	0512	1758
6	Weds	0644	1932
7	Thurs	0809	2048
8	Fri	0921	2154
9	Sat	1023	2254
10	Sun	1120	2348
11	Mon	****	1211
12	Tues	0037	1300
13	Weds	0124	1344
14	Thurs	0208	1426
15	Fri	0248	1505
16	Sat	0327	1544
17	Sun	0406	1626
18	Mon	0451	1716
19	Tues	0547	1823
20	Weds	0701	1956
21	Thurs	0836	2118
22	Fri	0942	2212
23	Sat	1031	2256
24	Sun	1112	2335
25	Mon	1150	****
26	Tues	0010	1223
27	Weds	0041	1253
28	Thurs	0108	1319
29	Fri	0134	1345
30	Sat	0159	1411
31	Sun	0226	1441

SEPTEMBER 2014

LOW WATER

Add 1 hour for BST

1	Mon	0258	1517
2	Tues	0338	1606
3	Weds	0435	1721
4	Thurs	0609	1909
5	Fri	0750	2032
6	Sat	0907	2140
7	Sun	1009	2239
8	Mon	1104	2330
9	Tues	1154	****
10	Weds	0018	1240
11	Thurs	0103	1323
12	Fri	0144	1402
13	Sat	0222	1439
14	Sun	0258	1516
15	Mon	0334	1554
16	Tues	0414	1641
17	Weds	0506	1744
18	Thurs	0617	1908
19	Fri	0752	2047
20	Sat	0911	2143
21	Sun	1001	2226
22	Mon	1042	2304
23	Tues	1119	2338
24	Weds	1153	****
25	Thurs	0010	1224
26	Fri	0040	1254
27	Sat	0108	1322
28	Sun	0136	1351
29	Mon	0205	1423
30	Tues	0238	1500

OCTOBER 2014

LOW WATER

Add 1 hour until 25th for BST

1	Weds	0320	1550
2	Thurs	0417	1705
3	Fri	0548	1851
4	Sat	0734	2017
5	Sun	0851	2124
6	Mon	0952	2220
7	Tues	1045	2310
8	Weds	1133	2356
9	Thurs	****	1217
10	Fri	0038	1259
11	Sat	0119	1338
12	Sun	0156	1414
13	Mon	0230	1449
14	Tues	0304	1525
15	Weds	0341	1609
16	Thurs	0430	1707
17	Fri	0536	1820
18	Sat	0654	1945
19	Sun	0816	2055
20	Mon	0916	2143
21	Tues	1001	2223
22	Weds	1042	2301
23	Thurs	1119	2337
24	Fri	1155	****
25	Sat	0011	1230
26	Sun	0045	1303
27	Mon	0118	1337
28	Tues	0152	1414
29	Weds	0229	1455
30	Thurs	0313	1547
31	Fri	0412	1659

NOVEMBER 2014

LOW WATER

1	Sat	0534	1831
2	Sun	0711	1954
3	Mon	0828	2101
4	Tues	0930	2157
5	Weds	1022	2247
6	Thurs	1110	2332
7	Fri	1155	****
8	Sat	0015	1237
9	Sun	0055	1315
10	Mon	0131	1351
11	Tues	0205	1426
12	Weds	0238	1501
13	Thurs	0313	1540
14	Fri	0354	1629
15	Sat	0451	1732
16	Sun	0601	1842
17	Mon	0712	1949
18	Tues	0817	2048
19	Weds	0913	2138
20	Thurs	1001	2223
21	Fri	1045	2305
22	Sat	1128	2346
23	Sun	****	1209
24	Mon	0026	1250
25	Tues	0106	1330
26	Weds	0146	1412
27	Thurs	0228	1457
28	Fri	0314	1548
29	Sat	0409	1649
30	Sun	0516	1803

DECEMBER 2014

LOW WATER

1	Mon	0637	1922
2	Tues	0757	2032
3	Weds	0903	2132
4	Thurs	1000	2224
5	Fri	1050	2311
6	Sat	1135	2354
7	Sun	****	1218
8	Mon	0034	1257
9	Tues	0111	1333
10	Weds	0145	1407
11	Thurs	0217	1439
12	Fri	0248	1512
13	Sat	0321	1549
14	Sun	0401	1636
15	Mon	0457	1738
16	Tues	0609	1848
17	Weds	0720	1953
18	Thurs	0824	2053
19	Fri	0922	2147
20	Sat	1015	2238
21	Sun	1105	2326
22	Mon	1153	****
23	Tues	0013	1240
24	Weds	0058	1325
25	Thurs	0143	1410
26	Fri	0227	1455
27	Sat	0312	1542
28	Sun	0359	1632
29	Mon	0452	1729
30	Tues	0556	1839
31	Weds	0715	1957

On long trips it is a good idea to:

Send guides, maps etc. ahead to larger post offices Poste Restante.

The only snag is if you arrive on a Saturday evening.

Start out with a few map-sized envelopes and the smallest available roll of sellotape so that you can despatch finished guides, maps, books etc. home.

Kit Transfer

Coast Path walking can be arduous in places but some of the hard work can be eliminated. One of the harder tasks can be having to carry a heavy pack from one B&B to the next. There are, however, potential ways around this. For transfer of kit anywhere on the Coast Path, the Association has an agreement with Luggage Transfers Ltd.

Luggage Transfers South West

Luggage Transfers Ltd, started in 2008 by two SWCPA members, moves up to 10,000 bags a month for walkers on the Coast Path, and is the only comprehensive service covering the entire Path.

The large volume of deliveries means that they can combine and "daisy chain" transfers which has kept the cost of the service low at an average of £8 for each bag movement. The effect of volume delivery also saves an estimated 200 tons of carbon emissions each season.

In addition, Luggage Transfers encourages walkers to donate 25p per transfer to the Association in order to raise funds for the Path. It also encourages its accommodation providers to become Business Members of the Association, which brings us a membership fee to be used for Path improvements. In return, Business Members get an enhanced entry in the accommodation list of the Annual Guide and on the website. Try and use them if you can to repay their support for us.

To book your luggage transfers with them, go to their website at www.luggagetransfers.co.uk. Alternatively, click on the accommodation list at the Association's own website. For telephone enquiries, call 01326 567247. The office is open 9.00am to 7.00pm 7 days a week from March until October inclusive, and office hours November until February.

Walking Holiday Companies

For those who require a Coast Path walk without carrying rucksacks and have their accommodation fixed in advance there are several businesses that will arrange everything. All you have to do is let them know your requirements and pay them. Also there are some excellent organisations that run walking holidays with guides. The South West Coast Path Association realised that there are too many to be listed in this guide so we have now listed them on our web site at www.swcp.org.uk

The Countryside Code

- Be safe - plan ahead and follow any signs
- Leave gates and property as you find them
- Protect plants and animals, and take your litter home
- Keep dogs under close control
- Consider other people

Because our Coast Path is so special and so popular, it is important to treat it with care and to use it in an environmentally sensitive way by employing the following principles:

- Use guidebooks and information
- Keep to the path to minimise erosion
- Report problems to the South West Coast Path Association
- Always consider the interests of landowners and other users
- Take special care where the Coast Path is routed onto roads

Supporting Local Businesses

- Use public transport to reach the path wherever possible
- Support local shops and services

Website News

Any news concerning the state of the Coast Path received after this book is printed will be published in newsletters and on our web site www.swcp.org.uk

Coast Path Safety Advice

Your safety is your responsibility - please look after yourself and other members of your group. Keep to the path and stay away from cliff edges - please follow advisory signs and waymarks. Supervise children and dogs - please look out for your children and pets at all times. Be prepared and well equipped - wear suitable clothing and footwear and be ready for possible changes in the weather.

Stay within your capabilities - some sections of the Coast Path can be strenuous and/or remote. In an emergency dial 999 and ask for the coastguard.

Weather

The South West Coast Path is more exposed to wind than any other long distance trail, so please pay attention to gale forecasts as well as rain. Along some sections, strong winds can be dangerous, especially when rounding exposed headlands and crossing bridges; a high backpack can act like a sail.

Always use sun protection especially on bright cloudy or breezy days when the risk of sunburn seems lower.

Detailed local forecasts are available from the UK Meteorological Office on 0870 900 0100 (24 hours) or www.metoffice.gov.uk/weather/uk

Military Ranges

Two lengths of the Coast Path may be affected by the use or otherwise of military ranges. The use of one, at Tregantle in south east Cornwall, only means that a more inland and less pleasant route must be used for a length of some 1.25 miles/2km in Section 46, Portwrinkle-Cremyll (Plymouth Ferry). However, if there is military use of the other, east of Lulworth Cove in Dorset, this means the whole of Section 67 between Lulworth Cove and Kimmeridge Bay will be impossible. Generally the Lulworth ranges are closed to walkers Monday to Friday during school term time and also up to six times a year at weekends. Try to arrange your walk so as not to miss this superb but tough section.

Information details for the ranges are included in the relevant Section descriptions.

Telephones

Mobile phones sometimes will not work in remote places and it's reassuring to see a public telephone box just when you need it. However, many of these remote telephones have recently been converted to only take debit cards. You can use the following cards in these boxes - Switch; Maestro; Delta; Solo; Visa Debit but not Electron. There are still some telephone boxes which will accept BT Phonecards and all boxes will accept BT Chargecards (these are only available to BT landline customers). Mobile phones are always useful to have whilst on the Coast Path. However, do not rely on them as coverage is not always good in the South West. You may also have difficulty in obtaining top-up in some areas.

Banks

There are small Post Offices in most villages. Overseas visitors, we suggest, will find their cashpoint cards very useful. ATM machines are widely available along the Coast Path and can be sourced at www.link.co.uk/atmlocator/Pages/ATMLocator.aspx

Dogs

1. Beaches

Most district councils and unitary authorities have implemented dog bans on beaches generally from 1st May to 31st October. Our Association and most of the general public regard this as a sensible measure.

There are several sections of the South West Coast Path that cross beaches and are officially marked as such. These beaches are Croyde Bay in Devon, Harlyn Bay, Constantine, Treyarnon, Perranporth and Penberth slipway in Cornwall, and Studland in Dorset. The routing of the Coast Path (with its designation as a National Trail) across these beaches means that they are public rights of way. A public right of way DOES carry precedence over seasonal regulations banning dogs, and ultimately any walker in the process of walking along, but not stopping on, these sections of the path may be accompanied by a dog under TOTAL control.

However we strongly recommend the following:

a) If an alternative route is provided and signposted, that you use it.
b) That residents near to dog ban beaches use other walks and do not use the beach path during the ban period.
c) Total control means that the dog should be on a short (not extendable) lead.
d) That your progress should be as unobtrusive as possible to other beach users. To aid this, close attention should be paid to the actual route marked on the map.
e) Lastly, but most importantly, should the worst happen, any dog mess MUST be removed from the beach.

2. Along the Coast Path

Many walk the Coast Path with their dogs and all have an enjoyable time and we receive many reports of dogs completing the whole path.

However we do urge caution because the Coast Path is very high along many sections, and it takes only an excited dog to go chasing after a rabbit, to cause much grief if it goes over the edge. If your dog is well-trained and you can trust it, then please enjoy your Coast Path walk with your four-legged friend. If it is not and you cannot, then do take care.

Many sections along the South West Coast Path will have farm livestock grazing.

Again, walkers should maintain proper control of their dogs.

Important - Please Note

Information included or available through the South West Coast Path Association (SWCPA) is given in good faith and is believed to be accurate and correct at the time of going to print - however it cannot be guaranteed not to include inaccuracies or typographical errors.

Advice received via the SWCPA should not be relied upon for personal decisions and you should take into account the weather and your own capabilities before following the walks set out in this Guide. It is for the individual concerned to weigh up the risks of each of the walks described in this book.

The SWCPA makes no representations about the suitability of walks to any one person and will accept no liability for any loss or damage suffered as a result of relying on this book; it should be used for guidance only.

In no event shall the SWCPA be liable for any personal injury or any loss suffered as a result of using this publication.

Week 1 (Seven days)

Day	Distance		From - to
1	10mi	15km	**Minehead - Porlock Weir** *Take National Rail main line to Taunton; bus Taunton - Minehead; or National Express coach to Minehead*
2	12mi	20km	**Porlock Weir - Lynton**
3	13mi	21km	**Lynton - Combe Martin**
4	13mi	20km	**Combe Martin - Woolacombe**
5	16mi	27km	**Woolacombe - Braunton**
6	12mi	20km	**Braunton - Instow**
7	11mi	18km	**Instow - Westward Ho!**
Total	**87mi**	**141km**	*Take bus Westward Ho! - Barnstaple; train Barnstaple - Exeter; National Rail main line from Exeter; or National Express coach from Westward Ho!*

Week 2 (Seven days)

Day	Distance		From - to
1	11mi	18km	**Westward Ho! - Clovelly** *National Rail main line to Exeter; train Exeter - Barnstaple; bus Barnstaple - Westward Ho!; or National Express coach to Westward Ho!*
2	10mi	16km	**Clovelly - Hartland Quay**
3	15mi	25km	**Hartland Quay - Bude**
4	10mi	16km	**Bude - Crackington Haven**
5	11mi	18km	**Crackington Haven - Tintagel**
6	9mi	15km	**Tintagel - Port Isaac**
7	12mi	19km	**Port Isaac - Padstow**
Total	**78mi**	**127km**	*Bus to Bodmin Parkway; National Rail main line from Bodmin Parkway.*

Week 3 (Six days)

Day	Distance		From - to
1	14mi	22km	Padstow - Porthcothan *National Rail main line to Bodmin Parkway; bus Bodmin Parkway - Padstow.*
2	11mi	18km	Porthcothan - Newquay
3	11mi	18km	Newquay - Perranporth
4	12mi	20km	Perranporth - Portreath
5	12mi	20km	Portreath - Hayle
6	6mi	9km	Hayle - St Ives
Total	**66mi**	**107km**	*Train St Ives-St Erth; National Rail main line from St Erth; or National Express coach from St Ives.*

Week 4 (Six days)

Day	Distance		From - to
1	14mi	22km	**St Ives - Pendeen Watch** *National Rail main line to St Erth; train St Erth - St Ives; or National Express coach to St Ives.*
2	9mi	15km	**Pendeen Watch - Sennen Cove**
3	12mi	19km	**Sennen Cove - Lamorna Cove**
4	9mi	15km	**Lamorna Cove - Marazion**
5	11mi	17km	**Marazion - Porthleven**
6	13mi	22km	**Porthleven - Lizard**
Total	**68mi**	**110km**	*Bus Lizard Town - Helston; bus Helston - Redruth; National Rail main line from Redruth*

It is possible to use one accommodation base in summer between St Ives and Marazion as summer bus service 300 travels in a circuit both ways around the Land's End peninsula. See page 15 Local Transport.

Week 5 (Six days)

Day	Distance		From - to
1	11mi	17km	**Lizard - Coverack** *National Rail main line to Redruth; bus Redruth-Helston; bus Helston - Lizard Town.*
2	13mi	21km	**Coverack - Helford**
3	10mi	16km	**Helford - Falmouth**
4	14mi	22km	**Falmouth - Portloe**
5	12mi	20km	**Portloe - Mevagissey**
6	12mi	19km	**Mevagissey - Par**
Total	**72mi**	**115km**	*National Rail main line from Par.*

Week 6 (Seven days)

Day	Distance		From - to
1	13mi	21km	**Par - Polperro** *National Rail main line to Par.*
2	12mi	20km	**Polperro - Portwrinkle**
3	13mi	21km	**Portwrinkle - Plymouth**
4	15mi	24km	**Plymouth - Wembury (ferry crossing)**
5	14mi	22km	**Wembury (ferry crossing) - Bigbury on Sea**
6	14mi	22km	**Bigbury on Sea - Salcombe**
7	13mi	21km	**Salcombe - Torcross**
Total	**94mi**	**151km**	*Bus Torcross - Plymouth; National Rail main line or National Express coach from Plymouth.*

Week 7 (Six days)

Day	Distance		From - to
1	10mi	16km	**Torcross - Dartmouth** *National rail main line or National Express coach to Plymouth; bus Plymouth - Torcross.*
2	11mi	17km	**Dartmouth - Brixham**
3	11mi	17km	**Brixham - Babbacombe**
4	16mi	27km	**Babbacombe - Exmouth**
5	13mi	21km	**Exmouth - Sidmouth**
6	11mi	17km	**Sidmouth - Seaton (Devon)**
Total	**72mi**	**115km**	*Bus Seaton - Exeter; National Rail main line or National Express Coach from Exeter.*

Week 8 (Seven days)

Day	Distance		From - to
1	14	23	**Seaton (Devon) - Seatown (Dorset)** *National Rail main line or National Express coach to Exeter; bus Exeter - Seaton.*
2	12	19	**Seatown (Dorset) - Abbotsbury**
3	11	17	**Abbotsbury - Ferry Bridge (Wyke Regis)**
4	13	21	**Isle of Portland**
5	14	23	**Ferry Bridge (Wyke Regis) - Lulworth Cove**
6	14	23	**Lulworth Cove - Worth Matravers**
7	14	22	**Worth Matravers - South Haven Point (Poole Harbour)**
Total	**92mi**	**148km**	*Ferry South Haven Point-Sandbanks; bus Sandbanks-Poole or Bournemouth; National Rail main line or National Express coach from Poole or Bournemouth.*

Other breakdowns are obviously possible, although the above is probably the best one for individual full weeks. A good alternative to use with direct nationwide public transport access at both ends of each stage would be:-

- Stage 1: Minehead to Barnstaple (68 miles/110km)
- Stage 2: Barnstaple to Bude (56 miles/90km)
- Stage 3: Bude to St Ives (108 miles/174km)
- Stage 4: St Ives to Falmouth (103 miles/165km)
- Stage 5:Falmouth to Plymouth (81 miles/131km)
- Stage 6: Plymouth to Exmouth (98 miles/158km)
- Stage 7: Exmouth to Weymouth (60 miles/97km)
- Stage 8: Weymouth to Poole (via Portland) (56 miles/90km)

Those interested in devising their own lengths might wish to know the locations of train access points on the Coast Path. On the national network, these are at Barnstaple (branch line from Exeter), Newquay (branch line from Par), St Ives (branch line from St Erth), Penzance, Falmouth (branch line from Truro), Par, Looe (branch line from Liskeard), Plymouth, Paignton, Torquay, Teignmouth, Dawlish, Exmouth (branch line from Exeter), Weymouth and Poole (for access to South Haven Point). Other locations are served during the summer by private railways, usually with steam-powered trains - Minehead (West Somerset Railway), Kingswear and Paignton (Dartmouth Steam Railway) and Swanage (Swanage Railway).

Reporting Problems on the Path

Be our Eyes and Ears on the Ground

With 630 miles of path to cover, it is impossible for the path wardens and rangers or the Association's local representatives to keep up with everything on the path at all times. So, if you encounter any problems, be they broken or missing signposts or waymarks, broken stiles or gates, real difficulties with the path surface, or anything else you think we should know about, contact us at our office address or phone number on page 3, or e-mail us. We will get in touch with the relevant path ranger with your concerns.

Undercliffs

Background

The South West Coast Path is one of the "family" of National Trails. It is generally well signposted and waymarked, using the National Trail symbol of the acorn. In some parts of the Coast Path waymarking relates to the local environment, for example the use of granite waymarks in parts of West Cornwall and Purbeck stone signs in Dorset. Be sure when walking the route to follow any such directions on the ground rather than relying on literature - things change over time, even including the route of the South West Coast Path, literature can become out-of-date.

Those who set out to walk all or any of this beautiful trail should remember that much of it is a cliff-top path - in places a very high cliff top. Those who manage the Coast Path want to keep it safe, but walkers should be reminded that it is unwise to leave the path at any point on the seaward side. Sometimes the edges of cliff tops away from the path can be unstable and unsafe.

Now and again the descriptions suggest an alternative path away from the officially designated route. These alternatives will themselves follow rights of way or, occasionally, "permitted routes" maintained by the landowner for use by the public. They are suggested for a more scenic and enjoyable experience than the formal route.

Once again, the Association stresses that ANYONE USING THE PATH SHOULD NOT WANDER OFF IT, ESPECIALLY ON THE SEAWARD SIDE. TO DO SO WOULD BE PUTTING YOURSELF AND POSSIBLY OTHERS IN DANGER OF SEVERE PERSONAL INJURY, OR EVEN DEATH.

Always follow the National Trail Waymark.

That said, the South West Coast Path is a wonderful environment enjoyed by millions. Choose a length, long or short, and undertake one of the greatest walking experiences the country has to offer.

The Environment of the South West Coast Path

The South West Coast Path is one of the country's National Trails; it is, indeed, the longest of them at 630 miles/1,105km. In common with all National Trails, the Coast Path passes through an outstanding environment. In the Coast Path's case, this outstanding environment is recognised by the large number of formal designations throughout its length. These include both international and national designations.

International Designations

i. **North Devon Biosphere Reserve**
   Biosphere Reserves are places with world-class environments designated by UNESCO to promote and demonstrate a balanced relationship between nature and people. They are places where conservation and sustainable development go hand in hand. North Devon is a UNESCO Biosphere Reserve because of its blend of special landscapes and wildlife areas, rich cultural heritage and communities that care about it and want to sustain it into the future. The core area of the Biosphere Reserve is at Braunton Burrows (Section 7 of the Trail Descriptions following), but including the outer areas the Reserve covers the Coast Path between Lynmouth and Marsland Mouth (Sections 3-13).

ii. **Cornwall and West Devon Mining Landscape World Heritage Site**
   World Heritage Sites are designated by UNESCO for their "Outstanding Universal Value". This World Heritage Site is defined by the mining landscape which was formed by the cultural tradition of non-ferrous hard-rock mining. It contributed to developing the Industrial Revolution in Britain and pioneered its transfer overseas. The designation covers ten distinct areas, of which five relate to the Coast Path. These are the St Agnes Mining District (Section 24), the Port of Hayle (Sections 25 and 26), the St Just Mining District (Sections 27 and 28), the Tregonning and Gwinear Mining District with Trewavas (Section 32) and the Luxulyan Valley and Charlestown (Section 41).

iii. **Jurassic Coast World Heritage Site**
   This was England's first World Heritage Site designated for its natural properties. Is it designated as it clearly depicts a geological "walk through time" of 185 million years of Earth's history in 95 miles/152km. Geological history of the Triassic, Jurassic and Cretaceous periods are successively exposed and are accessible over the length of the Site, which stretches between Exmouth and Swanage (Sections 58-70).

National Designations

Most of the South West Coast Path is covered by the national landscape designations of National Park or Area of Outstanding Natural Beauty (AONB). In landscape terms these designations are regarded as equal, representing the country's finest landscapes.

i. **Exmoor National Park**
Minehead - Combe Martin (Sections 1-3).

ii. **North Devon AONB**
Combe Martin - Marsland Mouth, excluding Ilfracombe, the Taw-Torridge Estuary and Westward Ho! (Sections 4-8, 11-13).

iii. **Cornwall AONB**
The entire coast of Cornwall, excluding Bude and its environs, Polzeath and Rock, Carnewas - Newquay, Gwithian - St Ives, Newlyn - Marazion, Charlestown - Par and Looe - Rame Head (Sections 13-25, 27-44, 46).

iv. **South Devon AONB**
Plymouth - Brixham (Sections 48-54).

v. **East Devon AONB**
Exmouth - Lyme Regis, excluding Sidmouth and Beer - Seaton (Sections 58-61).

vi. **Dorset AONB**
The entire coast of Dorset, excluding Weymouth - Portland (Sections 62-64, 66-70). The South Dorset Ridgeway (Section 71) also falls within this designation.

The Landscape of the South West Coast Path

The wealth of landscape and environmental designations outlined above gives some idea of the quality of the landscape through which the South West Coast Path passes. However, this hides the fact there is a wide range of landscape types to be experienced. For those not over-familiar with the South West, we have divided the Coast Path into seven areas, shown on the map on page 2, and noted on each of the Section descriptions. This will help to pinpoint geographically the various path Sections, but can also be used to describe the path's landscapes.

The various areas are identified by using a colour coding system as shown on the map on page 2 and set out in the Contents page 5. The colour code is used on the corner tabs of the Walk Sections, the title information and the page numbers.

i. Exmoor

Minehead - Combe Martin (Sections 1-3)

The Exmoor length is characterised by two main landscape types. The first is the meeting of the rolling expanse of high moorland and the sea. The coastline itself is one of high cliffs, some of them among the highest sea cliffs in England, but this height is sometimes disguised by the cliffs' convex shape, usually referred to as "hog's back". Views are often extensive inland, over the undulating moorland, while seaward in good visibility the coast of Wales may be seen across the Bristol Channel. In contrast, substantial lengths of the Exmoor coast comprise deep and steep valleys cutting across the high land. These valleys, locally known as "combes", are typically wooded, often with ancient oak woodland. Often this woodland spreads along the adjacent cliff faces, also convex in shape. Views from the Coast Path here are inevitably less extensive, and sometimes quite limited by the woodland, but the nature of the ancient woodland makes for an environment of considerable ecological interest. The combes and the height of the cliffs in this length result in some notable gradients in places.

ii. North Devon

Combe Martin - Marsland Mouth

(Sections 4-13)

Most of the North Devon coast faces north over the Bristol Channel. Much of this length comprises cliffs of moderate height with, in the east, some prominent headlands like Morte Point and Baggy Point which offer fine coastal vistas. In the centre of this length is the large joint estuary of the Taw and Torridge Rivers, flanked by areas of sand dunes and marshland. Adjacent to the estuary and just east of it are extensive sandy beaches, popular with surfers and families. Seascapes typically have the coast of Wales beyond the Bristol Channel as the backdrop in the east of this length. In the centre and west the offshore island of Lundy, at the "mouth" of the Bristol Channel, is the focal point. At the west end of this length is Hartland Point, one of the Coast Path's major headlands (referred to as the Point of Hercules in a Roman geography). It marks an abrupt change in direction from the east-west typical of most of North Devon (and Exmoor) to the north-south length beyond. This north-south length is very dramatic, with high cliffs fronted by jagged fingers of rock stretching into the Atlantic. Deep and steep valleys cut into this coastline, but there are no bays or harbours - an historic attempt to make a harbour at Hartland Quay was foiled by the elements. This is a section of great atmosphere.

iii. North Cornwall

Marsland Mouth - Portreath (Sections 13-24)

This section of coast trends either north-south or north east-south west. As such, it faces the prevailing Atlantic westerlies, making for a sometimes exposed landscape. This is exacerbated by the fact that much of the length comprises high cliffs, often quite sheer, with prominent headlands giving excellent coastal vistas. In places the feet of these cliffs are fronted by extensive sandy beaches, as north of Bude or at Watergate and Perran Beaches, north and south of Newquay. The cliff line is also punctuated by numerous sandy coves. There are also two main breaches in the cliff where river estuaries reach the sea, the Camel at Padstow and the Gannel at Newquay. These estuaries are also flanked by extensive sandy beaches. The uncompromising nature of the cliffs means there are few ports or harbours. Padstow, sheltered within the Camel estuary, is an ancient port and Newquay has a medieval origin, sheltered behind the promontory of Towan Head. Newquay has now, of course, expanded into a major holiday centre. Smaller 19th century harbours at the north-east end at Bude, originally largely based on its canal, and at the south-west end at Portreath, originally based on exporting mineral ores, have also expanded into tourism centres. These are very much exceptional settlements on this coast.

iv. West Cornwall

Portreath - Falmouth (Sections 25-37)

Most of this part of the coast is occupied by the two great peninsulas of Penwith, the westernmost part of England, and the Lizard, the southernmost. Both are composed of hard, resistant rocks making for a rugged cliff coastline, but their characters differ. Penwith is largely granite and inland of its impressive cliffs, frequently marked by rock pinnacles and solid jointed slabs, is a rough semi-moorland landscape. The Lizard has a much smoother profile, with its inland landscape an unusual flat-topped plateau. The exposed locations of these two peninsulas result in harsh, weather-beaten coastlines with a lack of large-scale tree cover, though both are magnificently dramatic. Only on the eastern, lee side of the Lizard does the coastline become a little more lush. Flanking these two peninsulas are lower, more sheltered lengths - St Ives Bay on the north-east side of Penwith, Mount's Bay between Penwith and the Lizard and the Helford - Fal estuaries east of the Lizard. It is in these sheltered areas the only ports and harbours of any size are found, principally Penzance and Falmouth.

v. South Cornwall

Falmouth - the Tamar (Sections 38-46)

The South Cornwall stretch of coast is relatively sheltered being either south-east or south-facing and being largely in the lee of the large peninsula of the Lizard. Cliffs of moderate height are found along most of the length, and there are numerous intimate little bays and some quite prominent headlands. In the eastern half of the length the coast is cut by wooded river valleys, at Fowey, Looe and Seaton. In the centre is the major feature of St Austell Bay, the only part that lacks the otherwise ubiquitous cliffs. This bay also has the only major length of coastal development in South Cornwall, based on the town of St Austell and its extensions. Elsewhere, small ancient fishing ports such as Mevagissey, Fowey and Looe are scattered along the coast, all of them very picturesque. Major estuaries, of the Fal and Tamar, mark the two ends, each of them of great historic maritime importance.

vi. South Devon

Plymouth - Lyme Regis (Sections 47-61)

This section of coast may be conveniently subdivided into three landscape types. In the west, between the Rivers Tamar and Dart, is an area of largely slate cliffs, sometimes quite rugged, these being cut by the drowned mouths of wooded river valleys. This area is usually referred to as the South Hams and extends south to the major headland of Prawle Point, west of this headland being relatively exposed and the east of it much more sheltered. To the east, between the Dart and the Exe, is an area of low, mostly red sandstone cliffs. This length, the "Riviera", is largely occupied by towns based on tourism such

South of Morte Point

as Paignton, Torquay, Teignmouth and Dawlish, and being east-facing is mainly sheltered. Much of this length presents an almost continuously developed coastline. Further east still, between the Exe and the Dorset border at Lyme Regis, the cliffs rise again. This section, East Devon, has a slightly different character to the rest of the south coast of Devon. The red sandstone cliffs continue across the Exe for a while. Then, halfway along the East Devon coast, chalk and greensand make for a change in the landscape, to a mixture of white cliffs and extensive undercliffs and landslips. South Devon has many holiday resorts, some of the earliest in the country such as Exmouth and Teignmouth, some famed for their elegance such as Torquay, and some based on historic towns and villages such as Dartmouth and Beer. The biggest urban area of all on the South West Coast Path is Plymouth. Its historic importance is, of course, largely based on the Royal Navy.

vii. Dorset

Lyme Regis - South Haven Point (Poole Harbour) (Sections 62-70)

South Dorset Ridgeway (Section 71)

Geology is both the curse and the boon of the Dorset part of the South West Coast Path. As a curse, the geology means the Dorset cliffs are vulnerable to slippage, especially at the western end. This has meant that several diversions, necessary but hardly ideal, have had to be put in place for the Coast Path. There is currently no clear idea of when permanent solutions will be found for these problems. The Marine and Coastal Access Act 2010 may resolve the matter of replacement or alternative routes in the longer term but, apart from the Weymouth area, there is currently no programme for implementation. However, as a boon, Dorset's exposed and accessible layers of geological history have made it a textbook example for a wide range of coastal features. These features are also landscape highlights - the great shingle bar of Chesil Beach backed by the semi-freshwater lagoon of the Fleet; the fortress-like monolith of the Isle of Portland, jutting into the English Channel; the textbook arch of Durdle Door; the erosion of soft rock once the harder limestone has been broken through forming hollowed-out bays, as at Lulworth Cove; the offshore Purbeck stone stacks at Handfast Point. Inland, the rolling green hills evoke the spirit and landscape of Thomas Hardy, a worthy addition to the range of South West Coast Path landscapes.

Bugle Hole

Key to Walk Descriptions

Based on the Suggested Itinerary on page 27, the South West Coast Path has been divided into 70 Sections. Each Section represents a day's or half-day's walk of the Itinerary. However, it must be emphasised that these Sections should not be confined to use by those walking long stretches of the Coast Path. Each Section is designed to be used on its own as a one-off if so wished, as well as by those planning long walks of several days. The Sections are arranged in anti-clockwise order, from Minehead to Poole, with an additional Section 71 for the alternative inland South Dorset Ridgeway.

Each Section entry follows in the following format:

Distance - length of the Section in miles and kilometres;

Cumulative distance - total length of the Coast Path from Minehead to the end of the Section in miles and kilometres;

Ascent - height climbed during the Section in feet and metres;

Cumulative ascent - total height climbed on the Coast Path from Minehead to the end of the Section in feet and metres;

Grading - each Section is graded as Easy, Moderate, Strenuous or Severe. Inevitably, such grading is subjective to an extent, and not all of any Section will be identical throughout, but the grading will give an idea of the effort required;

Timing - this is an estimated fair average for completing the Section. Times will vary depending on weather, number in party, gear carried, number of refreshment or photograph stops. The estimate should be an aide in planning.

OS Maps - the reference numbers of the OS Maps needed to walk the Section are given. Both Landranger (1:50,000) and Explorer (1:25,000) maps are given;

Area - for those not geographically acquainted with the South West, the Coast Path has been sub-divided into seven areas for ease of identification of each Section's location; see map on page 2 and area descriptions on pages 31-33.

Path Description booklet - the Association has published a series of Path Description booklets which give detailed walking directions as well as pointing out items of interest along the route; see page 10. The relevant Path Description booklet title for the Section is given.

There is then an overview of each Section. This covers the landscape, its general character and some of its highlights.

Next, there is a short description of how the Section can be undertaken as a day or part-day walk with public transport or a local circular walk. For more details about local public transport see pages 15-21.

Finally, the main body of the Section description contains simplified instructions for walking in a Minehead - Poole direction, generally only highlighting those locations where it is possible to go astray.

Remember, as a National Trail, the South West Coast Path is usually well signed and waymarked throughout its length, using the National Trail acorn symbol. Bear in mind that things change over the years, including the actual route of the Coast Path, so using out-of-date literature can be misleading. If in doubt, follow the signs and waymarks on the ground.

The various areas are identified by using a colour coding system as shown on the map on page 2 and set out in the Contents page 5. The colour code is used on the corner tabs of the Walk Sections, the title information and the page numbers.

1. Minehead to Porlock Weir

Week 1 - Day 1

OS Maps: **Landranger 181; Explorer OL9**

	This Walk	Cumulative	This Walk	Cumulative	Grading	Timing
Ascent	1,824ft	1,824ft	556m	556m	Official: Moderate Alternative: Strenuous	4.5 hours
Distance	9.5mi	9.5mi	15.3km	15.3km		

For detailed directions see our Minehead to Porlock Weir Path description booklet.

This is a classic example of where moorland meets the sea. Inland, the high expanse of Exmoor rolls away, broken by deep wooded valleys; where it meets the Bristol Channel there are high, convex cliffs, cut by deep and narrow "coombes". This is a lonely, remote length, away from main roads and settlements, with often the only evidence of modern life being development far away on the opposite shore of the Bristol Channel on the South Wales coast. At the western end is the contrasting landscape of Porlock Vale, a flat-floored area of farmland and marshland behind its shingle ridge, quite different in character from the rest of this Section.

Directions

Minehead and Porlock Weir are connected by a year-round bus service. However, there are no "staging posts" along this length although there are possible circular walks based on Minehead or Porlock via Selworthy Beacon, on the inland "official route".

The South West Coast Path starts from the celebratory marker on the sea front, approximately 100 yards/91m beyond the Quay Inn. The current route, which may not be shown on older maps, proceeds along the sea front, past the quay. Just before Greenaleigh Farm it turns left on ascending zigzags to North Hill.

At the summit of North Hill follow the acorn sign towards Selworthy and Bossington. At the next Coast Path sign there is a fork, the route to the right being marked "Rugged Cliff Top Path", and either option can be taken. Do not be put off by the description of the seaward path as "rugged" - it is a splendid alternative and not difficult, and gives much better sea views than the inland "official" path. It is well waymarked, and dogs are permitted but must be under very close control. There is likely to be cattle grazing.

On the "rugged" path, at the stile, take the left fork towards a bench, then continue downhill to take the lower path by a "Rugged Path" signpost. From Grexy Combe (GR 937 481) take the well-defined diagonal path up the hill to a wall, which is then followed first towards the sea then parallel to it to Western Brockholes. Here it turns inland to re-join the inland "official" path behind Hurlstone Point. (This seaward path will add about an hour to the estimated time.)

The inland route, meanwhile, follows good tracks parallel to the sea. Joining the "rugged" path on Bossington Hill, the now-combined route descends Hurlstone

SWCP marker, Minehead

Combe. There is an optional diversion out to Hurlstone Point which gives a superb view. From Hurlstone, take care not to follow the obvious path to the left which contours round Bossington Hill.

The path descends and goes inland to Bossington village and then just past the car park out towards the sea again. The route now crosses the marsh to Porlock Weir, easy to follow the whole way. At high spring tides it can become impassable, and signs to Porlock village should be followed. (For tidal information consult Minehead TIC.) If the diversion via Porlock village is taken, leave the village on the Toll Road then bear right on a footpath that goes behind West Porlock to Porlock Weir.

Week 1 - Day 2

OS Maps: Landranger 181 (eastern half); Landranger 180 (western half); Explorer OL9

	This Walk	Cumulative	This Walk	Cumulative	Grading	Timing
Ascent	3,156ft	4,980ft	962m	1,518m	Moderate, strenuous in parts	5.5 hours
Distance	12.3mi	21.8mi	19.8km	35.1km		

For detailed directions see our Porlock Weir to Lynmouth Path Description booklet.

Worthy Combe Toll House

This is a Section of two halves. In the east, approximately between Porlock Weir and the Devon/Somerset border, Exmoor meets the sea at a run of high, convex but well-wooded cliffs. The Coast Path here is a woodland walk with frequent glimpses of the sea, quiet and remote in character. To the west the cliffs become more open and steeper and the area around The Foreland and Countisbury is a spectacular viewpoint with panoramas over the double-decker towns of Lynton and Lynmouth.

Directions

A summer bus service links Porlock Weir to Lynton. It is possible to divide the walk at County Gate, mid-way along, which is on the bus route.

The official route is signposted left of the Anchor Hotel at Porlock Weir but it is possible to go in front of the hotel, past the shops then left signposted to Culbone. Reaching Culbone turn right to visit the charming tiny church, which is recommended. From the church retrace steps and turn right uphill on the Coast Path. After about 300 yards/275m bear right into Culbone, Embelle and Yenworthy Woods. This route may not be shown on some older maps. Unfortunately, recent land slippages towards the end of Yenworthy Wood have forced an inland diversion via Yenworthy Combe. Continue to Sister's Fountain, where the access path to the bus route at County Gate on the A39 leaves the Coast Path. Go uphill through a pair of wild boar head gateposts, then take care not to miss the narrow signposted path 300 yards/275m past the cottage as the drive bears left.

An alternative waymarked route may be taken between Culbone and Yenworthy Wood. Although slightly more inland, it offers better views than the mainly woodland more coastal route.

At Coddow Combe, the route is signposted left off the lighthouse track "Countisbury 1.5 miles". From Countisbury the now spectacular path continues down the seaward side of the A39 road. Lower down it joins the road for a short way before descending on zigzags to the foreshore. Walk into Lynmouth, crossing the footbridge, then turn right to the sea front. Lynton is vertically above Lynmouth and is reached by turning left up the steps before the cliff railway (which can be taken as an interesting alternative). A new route is also available past the Esplanade car park at the end of the sea front, where a pleasant path, signposted to Lynton, goes left up the steep wooded hillside to emerge on the Coast Path west of Lynton. Both Lynmouth and Lynton have all facilities.

It is interesting to know that from Lynmouth it is possible to walk Devon's Coast to Coast route using the Two Moors Way and its southern extension to the south coast at Wembury. Guide books are available from Lynton TIC.

Week 1 - Day 3

OS Maps: **Landranger 180; Explorer OL9**

	This Walk	Cumulative	This Walk	Cumulative	Grading	Timing
Ascent	3,766ft	8,746ft	1,148m	2,666m	Strenuous	7 hours
Distance	13.3mi	35.1mi	21.4km	56.5km		

For detailed directions, see our Lynmouth to Ilfracombe Path Description booklet.

This generally quiet and remote Section passes through a series of spectacular coastal landscapes: the Valley of Rocks with its rocky crags and pinnacles; the steep wooded cliffs at Woody Bay; the breathtaking scenery of the deep and steep crevice carved through the cliffs at Heddon's Mouth; the wide open spaces of Holdstone Down; and the heights of the Great Hangman, the highest point on the entire Coast Path and one of the highest coastal locations in the country.

Directions

Lynton and Combe Martin are connected by a summer bus service (year-round at weekends). Heddon's Mouth (6.5 miles/10.5km from Lynton) makes a good break in this length (though not on the bus route). It has refreshment facilities at Hunter's Inn and as there is a parallel higher path between here and Woody Bay there is scope for a scenic circular walk.

The Coast Path out of Lynton is on North Walk, and this path leads to Castle Rock in the Valley of Rocks. The next section follows a minor but sometimes busy road, but a diversion to the right from the turning circle at the end of the Valley avoids its first length. Continue past the Toll House and up the hill. A permissive path on the right to Crock Point then avoids another length, and also gives stunning views.

The Coast Path leaves the road just before the Woody Bay Hotel opposite the Red House. Arriving at another road turn left uphill. Follow the next Coast Path sign ahead. When this superb stretch reaches the dramatic Heddon's Mouth valley follow it down to the valley floor. On reaching the stone bridge over the Heddon River turn right, over the river, and at the next path turn hard left. Continue for 100 yards/91m to the signpost on the right to Combe Martin. (Inland on either side of the river the path leads to the pub and shop at Hunter's Inn.)

Climb steeply away from the valley floor, keeping right at the top where the path levels off. Continue round the headland (take care in windy conditions) then the path heads inland to reach a stone wall; this is followed parallel to the sea. The wall ends and the signed path continues across the heathland of Holdstone Down. At Sherrycombe the route follows the grass track along the top of the combe to the inland end and then down. Ascending Great Hangman from Sherrycombe bear away from the wall on the left and ignore the many paths going to the right, meeting the wall higher up. From Great Hangman the path is obvious to Little Hangman and beyond to Combe Martin.

Goats near Lynton

Week 1 - Day 4 (half day)

OS Maps: Landranger 180; Explorer 139 or OL9

	This Walk	Cumulative	This Walk	Cumulative	Grading	Timing
Ascent	1,280ft	10,026ft	390m	3,056m	Moderate, strenuous in parts	2.5 hours
Distance	5.3mi	40.4mi	8.6km	65.1km		

For detailed directions see our Lynmouth to Ilfracombe Path description booklet.

This is a Section of rocky inlets, one of which, Watermouth, is spacious enough for boats to be moored. These bays are divided by rugged headlands. The cliffs here are grey and slatey, making for a forbidding looking coastline, notwithstanding the little bays. At the western end the site of a prehistoric hill fort gives a panoramic view over Ilfracombe. This Section is never far from the A399 coast road and various tourist facilities, so despite the impressive cliffs it is not a lonely length.

Ilfracombe Harbour

Directions

Combe Martin and Ilfracombe are linked by a regular bus service, allowing a bus-walk to be easily undertaken on this Section.

The Coast Path leaves the Lime Kiln car park in Combe Martin, passing the TIC, then forks right to join the A399 road. Turn right (Seaside Hill Road) above the beach. Turn right onto a narrow tarmac lane which climbs steeply to re-join the A399 road. Walk on the slightly raised path along the roadside through two gates. Go along a path beside a field to a flight of steps, then turn left up the slip road back to the main road and on to the brow, passing the bus shelter. Turn right to follow the road down to the old main road, with a bus shelter, now used as an Information Point, over to the right. Here turn left beside the entrance to the Sandy Cove Hotel to follow a track towards Watermouth Cove.

Looking back to Little & Great Hangman

At Watermouth it is possible to cross the foreshore for some 110 yards/100m to a flight of steps at most states of the tide; take care, as the rocks can be slippery. However, if the tide is high, it is necessary to walk alongside the main road. (Check the Watermouth tide timings by contacting Ilfracombe or Combe Martin TICs.)

There has been a recent great improvement here to avoid walking along the carriageway of this busy road. Because of the Association's concerns here, we offered £50,000 from our reserves towards the cost of the new off-road route. This offer enabled the South West Coast Path Team to secure the remainder of the funding required to build the new path from the Rural Development Fund for England and Devon County Council, who also oversaw the work.

The next pleasant section of path passes the western side of Watermouth Cove and on around Widmouth Head and then Rillage Point. There is then a roadside section into Hele. Turn right here then climb some steps on the far left of the beach. The path zigzags up past Beacon Point to the top of Hillsborough. Follow the waymarks down the hill to Ilfracombe Harbour.

Watermouth improvements opened in December 2013 after over a decade of pressure

Week 1 - Day 4 (half day)

OS Maps: Landranger 180; Explorer 139

	This Walk	Cumulative	This Walk	Cumulative	Grading	Timing
Ascent	2,037ft	12,063ft	621m	3,677m	Easy to moderate; strenuous west of Lee Bay	3.5 hours
Distance	7.3mi	47.7mi	11.7km	76.8km		

For detailed directions see our Ilfracombe to Croyde Bay Path Description booklet.

Most of this Section is characterised by grass-topped cliffs fronting numerous small coves and a foreshore of rock ledges. Half-way along is the focal point of Bull Point lighthouse. At Morte Point the character of the coastline changes abruptly as the enormous beach of Woolacombe Sands in its vast bay comes into view, often dotted with surfers. The dark jagged rocks of Morte Point give this headland a superb brooding atmosphere.

Directions

Ilfracombe and Woolacombe are linked by a regular bus service, allowing a bus-walk to be easily undertaken on this Section.

From Ilfracombe Harbour pass the Sandpiper Inn into Capstone Road. After some 170 yards/150m turn right to pass around Capstone Point. At the far end take a flight of steps that goes up behind the back of the Landmark Theatre. Follow this path to the top of the gardens and through a gate by a shelter. Bear right along Granville Road then right again onto an unmetalled road which leads to the Torrs Walk on the right; the Torrs Walk is well waymarked.

At the top of the Torrs Walk bear right and follow the path down the field to the stile in the corner. Continue ahead around the hill to another stile then cross the field to meet the old coach road ahead. Bear right on this track, which later becomes a minor road into Lee Bay. Refreshments are available year-round at the Grampus Inn in Lee village, a short way inland.

The next length from Lee Bay is quite strenuous. Proceed up the road from Lee, turning right at the top of the hill through a brick-pillared gate. Two steep valleys are crossed before Bull Point and its lighthouse are reached. The path continues on and out around Morte Point, a spectacular jagged slate ridge like a dinosaur's back emerging from the sea. The path leaves Morte Point and continues beneath the cliffs past small sandy bays to arrive at Woolacombe.

Rockham Bay, Mortehoe

Week 1 - Day 5 (half day)

OS Maps: Landranger 180; Explorer 139

	This Walk	Cumulative	This Walk	Cumulative	Grading	Timing
Ascent	725ft	12,788ft	221m	3,898m	Moderate	3 hours
Distance	6.3mi	54.0mi	10.2km	87.0km		

For detailed directions see our Ilfracombe to Croyde Bay Path Description booklet.

The main feature of this Section is the vast sandy beach of Woolacombe Sands, backed by a substantial line of dunes. Busy with families and surfers close to the town, it becomes surprisingly empty away from the facilities. Beyond the beach is the superb headland of Baggy Point, a contrast to the beach with its steep cliffs and broad, grassy top. Rounding the headland another, smaller sandy bay comes into view, Croyde Bay, with the wider vista of Bideford Bay beyond.

Directions

Croyde Bay is an excellent centre for a circular walk using the Coast Path, around Baggy Point to Putsborough, giving views over Woolacombe Sands while experiencing the superb character of the headland.

At Woolacombe the Coast Path leaves the Watersmeet Hotel parallel to the Esplanade road, then turns up Challacombe Road. It leaves this road on the right at approximately the National Trust sign - there may be no waymark here. The path continues through the enormous dunes of Woolacombe Warren - the waymarking means that going astray is unlikely. An alternative is to follow Marine Drive and the track beyond, which gives better views. If the tide is low many walk the length of Woolacombe Sands but this should not be attempted on a high or rising tide.

The official path leaves the Warren by a set of steep steps, joining the extension to Marine Drive and the alternative route.
It continues along the track then a road, leaving it to the right after the caravan site. As an alternative, take the earlier path on the right to the car park at Putsborough, where there are seasonal refreshments and toilets (the beach route joins here). Go left of the caravan site to a stile and up the cliff slope to re-join the official path.

The excellent high level path continues to the end of Baggy Point, giving superb views. At the end of the headland, bear right to join the lower path towards Croyde. Follow the road, partly on a parallel path. Do not leave the road at the first slipway. The official path leaves the road a little further on to cross the beach, but many will continue on to visit Croyde and its facilities.

Woolacombe from the North

Week 1 - Day 5 (half day)

OS Maps: **Landranger 180; Explorer 139**

	This Walk	Cumulative	This Walk	Cumulative	Grading	Timing
Ascent	506ft	13,294ft	154m	4,052m	Easy	3.25 hours
Distance	8.8mi	62.8mi	14.0km	101.0km		

For detailed description see our Croyde Bay to Barnstaple Path Description booklet.

The length immediately adjacent to Croyde Bay follows a low cliff and gives stunning views over the truly enormous length of Saunton Sands with the dune complex of Braunton Burrows behind. Beyond is the sweep of Bideford Bay, with the possibility of seeing as far as Hartland Point lighthouse, many miles away. Offshore on the horizon is the isle of Lundy. The remainder of this Section is low and level, through a huge range of dunes (the official route) or along the seemingly endless Saunton Sands. Then comes the twin estuary of the Rivers Taw and Torridge, with mudbanks and reclaimed marshes making for a birdwatcher's delight. This is a length displaying a relatively rare aspect of the South West coast.

Directions

Croyde Bay and Braunton are linked by a regular year-round bus service, making this a good bus-walk possibility.

The Coast Path leaves Croyde Bay via the beach (no dogs May-September) and on to the low cliffs at Down End. Turn left at the old coastguard lookout to the B3231 road. Cross the road with care here, turn left then climb some stone steps. The path now contours round Saunton Down, parallel to and above the road. This ends opposite the large white building of the Saunton Sands Hotel.

From here there are optional routes. The first option is to cross the road and pass around the hotel to the Saunton Sands car park, where there are toilets and seasonal refreshments. Leave the car park by the entrance road and after 55 yards/50m bear right along a sandy lane to the B3231. Continue carefully along the road for some 400 yards/365m, past the Golf Club driveway, turning right at a red brick partially rendered house.

If there is no need for the toilets or refreshments, a better option is to turn left uphill opposite the hotel, away from the road. Follow the path as it bears round to the right until it arrives at the B3231 opposite the red brick house described above. Cross the road to continue on the same route as above.

This route now enters the Braunton Burrows nature reserve, designated a UNESCO Biosphere Reserve for its nature conservation importance. The route through the Burrows is well waymarked; it then follows a clear track to arrive at the car park at Broad Sands, at the mouth of the estuary of the Taw and Torridge rivers. From here head for the white cottage on the estuary side, a well-known local landmark known as the White House.

Many walkers prefer to miss the Burrows and walk from Saunton Sands car park the length of the beach, for some 3.5 miles/5.5km. Near the end of the beach, just after a wooden groyne, look out for a slatted wooden catwalk entering the dunes to the left. Follow this to arrive at the Broad Sands car park. This beach route keeps the sea in sight, not the case with the Burrows route.

From the White House follow the estuary side on top of the Great Sea Bank. This is followed, between estuary and reclaimed marshes, to the old quay at Velator on the edge of Braunton. To visit Braunton and its facilities, turn left at Velator along the footpath and cycleway, following the former railway track.

Boardwalk from Airy Point

Week 1 - Day 6 (half day)

OS Maps: Landranger 180; Explorer 139

	This Walk	Cumulative	This Walk	Cumulative	Grading	Timing
Ascent	16ft	13,310ft	5m	4,057m	Easy	2 hours
Distance	5.6mi	68.4mi	9.1km	110.1km		

For detailed directions, see our Croyde Bay to Barnstaple Path Description booklet.

This is a flat, low-level Section, following the line of the former railway track once used by the Atlantic Coast Express. As well as the Coast Path, it is also used by Devon's Coast to Coast Cycle Route. At the Braunton end, the main item of interest is the Royal Marines air base at Chivenor, next to the path, but further on the path runs alongside the estuary of the River Taw, with its interplay of water and sand and mud banks. This makes for a pleasant environment; in character, however, this length is semi-urban.

Directions

There is a regular and year-round bus service between Braunton and Barnstaple, which can also be accessed at Chivenor and at the Braunton Inn, approximately mid-way along the route, giving various short walks options.

From Braunton's main car park the signed route to Barnstaple leads to the Coast Path at Velator and from here the path follows the former railway past Chivenor Royal Marines base and then alongside the Taw Estuary all the way to Barnstaple.

A new bridge over the river offers an alternative crossing point, but using this misses Barnstaple and its facilities though it does give a superb view down the river.

Approaching Barnstaple on the former railway the path crosses a bridge over the tributary River Yeo and then passes the old railway station to a riverside embankment. Leave this at steps climbing to Barnstaple's Long Bridge. Barnstaple, North Devon's major centre, is a pleasant and interesting historic town well worth exploring, as well as offering a range of facilities, including a branch line railway to the main line at Exeter.

Braunton Inn

Week 1 - Day 6 (half day)

OS Maps: Landranger 180; Explorer 139

	This Walk	Cumulative	This Walk	Cumulative	Grading	Timing
Ascent	36ft	13,346ft	11m	4,068m	Easy	2.5 hours
Distance	7.4mi	75.8mi	11.9km	122.0km		

For detailed directions see our Barnstaple to Westward Ho! Path Description booklet.

This is a flat, low-level Section, much of it following a former railway line on the south side of the Taw Estuary. It passes through a landscape of marshland and pastures, with the tidal expanses and sand banks of the river never far away. This is an area of great value for birdlife. Approaching Instow the estuary opens out as the Taw's sister river, the Torridge, joins and there are wide areas of sand bars and dunes. This Section, despite its proximity to "civilisation" and the use of the former railway as part of the Devon Coast to Coast Cycle Route, is nevertheless one of much interest and character.

Directions

There is a regular and frequent all-year bus service between Barnstaple and Instow, which can also be accessed at Fremington, approximately mid-way along the route. A variety of short walk options is therefore available.

Cross Barnstaple's Long Bridge then keep to the right of the large roundabout, pass the factory buildings, then cross a mini-roundabout to a path which curves around to a subway under the approach road for the high-level bridge. A link path to the railway station goes off to the left here. In addition, this link path gives access to the Station Master's Cafe, which usefully also carries a range of local walking information. The main path, signed Coast Path and Tarka Trail, then links to the former railway line. The short cut across the high-level bridge joins here.

The former railway continues past the delightfully restored Fremington Quay, with its all-year cafe and Information Point. At Yelland look out for the path leaving the railway to the right which takes the Coast Path behind the site of an old power station. It then crosses an area of dunes to arrive at the estuary-side road through Instow, which has all facilities.

Appledore from Instow

Week 1 - Day 7

OS Maps: **Landranger 180; Explorer 139**

	This Walk	Cumulative	This Walk	Cumulative	Grading	Timing
Ascent	528ft	13,871ft	160m	4, 228 m	Easy	4.5 hours
Distance	11.7mi	87.5mi	18.8km	140.8km		

For detailed directions see our Barnstaple to Westward Ho! Path Description booklet.

Much of this Section follows the estuary of the River Torridge, first on its east bank then turning back on its west. The estuary is largely enclosed by green hills, but houses and roads are ever-present and a high-level road bridge over the estuary is a major feature. The Coast Path crosses the river at the charming old port of Bideford. Passing beyond the estuary and through the characterful old fishing town of Appledore, the path crosses the open spaces of Northam Burrows and its surrounding marshlands and then alongside an enormous pebble ridge as it arrives again at the open sea. As an alternative option, missing out Bideford, a ferry service is now operating from April to October between Instow and Appledore; tel: 07757 620999 for details (and see page 18).

Directions

A regular bus service links Instow and Westward Ho! and another connects Instow to Appledore, both via Bideford. These services allow for a range of Coast Path-based walk options.

From Instow go through the old railway station and follow the former railway, passing underneath the high-level bridge, to the restored Bideford station. Leave the station to cross Bideford Long Bridge, then turn right along the bustling quay. Bideford has all facilities. Keep alongside the river past the car park then next to the rugby club to a lane which passes under the high-level bridge. Follow the waymarked tracks to a riverside lane then, after the old tank traps, fork right to a small woodland area.

Descend to a boardwalk then, if the tide is low, continue on the old sea wall. At high tide a well waymarked route circles the marshy area. Follow the waymarked route round Appledore shipyard and at the road turn right into Appledore via Myrtle Street. Continue along the quay and on into the charming old part of the town, along Irsha Street and past the lifeboat station to a path along the edge of low cliffs and across a field to a slipway, where the route joins a road. Follow the road for approximately 0.3 mile/0.5km to a crossroads and here turn right.

Follow the track ahead alongside the marshes then on the seaward side of the dunes to the pebble ridge. Continue ahead on the landward side of the ridge to Westward Ho! (At most states of the tide it is possible to walk along the beach next to the ridge.)

Week 2 - Day 1

OS Maps: Landranger 180 (eastern half) ; Explorer 139 (eastern half); Landranger 190 (western half); Explorer 126 (western half)

	This Walk	Cumulative	This Walk	Cumulative	Grading	Timing
Ascent	2,995ft	16,866ft	913m	5,141m	Strenuous	6 hours
Distance	11.2mi	98.7mi	18.0km	158.8km		

For detailed directions see our Westward Ho! to Clovelly Path Description booklet.

This Section is one of cliffs and woods. The eastern half is an area of undulating cliffs, cut in places by substantial valleys, though in the length closest to Westward Ho!, where the line of an old railway is used, the path is generally level. The western half passes through lengthy wooded stretches, much of it along the old carriage road known as the Hobby Drive. At the western end, Clovelly is probably one of the most picturesque villages in England.

Directions

There is no direct bus route between Westward Ho! and Clovelly. However, there is one between Bideford and Clovelly, as well as a frequent link to Bideford from Westward Ho! Buck's Mills, about two thirds of the way along this length towards Clovelly, is on the Bideford-Clovelly bus route, giving a possible bus-walk at this end.

At Westward Ho! walk along the path above the beach. After passing the last of the holiday chalets, the path follows the track of the long-disused Bideford to Westward Ho! railway. This makes a fine easy scenic walk. Where the railway turns inland, the path continues along the cliffs, rising and falling to cross a short pebble beach before climbing again. At Peppercombe turn inland to cross the stream and then continue through woodland. Note that some old maps may not show the correct route at Worthygate Wood. The path drops to Buck's Mills, a picturesque little spot, then climbs again into more woods. On leaving Barton Wood, keep to the bottom edge of the field until crossing a bridge to the Hobby Drive at the end of a second field. The Hobby Drive section is nearly 3 miles/5km long, and although very pleasant offers sea glimpses rather than sea views. The path arrives at Clovelly at the top of the steep village street. Clovelly is very picturesque and has most facilities, though perhaps limited in range.

Clovelly

Week 2 - Day 2

OS Maps: Landranger 190; Explorer 126

	This Walk	Cumulative	This Walk	Cumulative	Grading	Timing
Ascent	2,382ft	19,248ft	726m	5,867m	Moderate to strenuous	5 hours
Distance	10.3mi	109.0mi	16.6km	175.4km		

For detailed directions see our Clovelly to Hartland Quay Path Description booklet.

There is a great contrast in this Section between east and west. In the east the landscape is one of parkland, the domesticated and partly ornamental landscape of the grounds of Clovelly Court. After leaving the parkland a run of high cliffs culminates at Hartland Point, one of the great defining headlands of the Coast Path. Here the coast turns from east-west to north-south and its character changes into one of the Coast Path's most breathtaking stretches, with dark brooding cliffs behind jagged fingers of rock stretching into the Atlantic Ocean. Experiencing its magnificent scenery is well worth the effort of crossing the spectacular deep valleys which cut the coast. The Section ends at the pub and hotel at Hartland Quay, which has a wonderful remote atmosphere.

Viewpoint near Clovelly Court

Directions

Hartland Quay has no public transport. However, there are numerous walking links from the Coast Path to Hartland village, 2.5 miles/4km inland, which is on the bus route to Clovelly.

If using Clovelly as a base, it is requested that walkers use the main car park. If you are only walking the Path and not visiting the village, car parking is £7.50. If you are on your own however, it is cheaper to pay for the village visit which is £6.75. Enquire at the Visitor Centre.

From the main car park walk out of the entrance and turn right down the road for some 220 yards/200m to a black gate on the left. Go through and follow the track first right and through a gap in the wall, then leave the track and follow the marked path down to the right. After a while go through a kissing-gate then follow the fence on the right to another gate into shrubbery. Continue through the shrubbery through more gates. Turn right at a T-junction and right again at the next fork. Soon the path arrives at an unusual seat known as the "Angel's Wings". At the track, turn hard right - not along the track. After passing a superb viewpoint the path descends steeply into a valley to another track. Go right here. The signed detour to the viewpoint is well worth the effort.

The Coast Path goes down the valley to the shore at Mouth Mill. Cross the stream then follow the grass track inland past the lime kiln. At times of storm, high water or heavy rain the stepping stones across the stream do get washed away, making it difficult to cross. A bridge is planned to help with this problem.

Shortly, turn right and climb the valley side. Half-way up, follow the steps to the right. On reaching the top pass through fields to a stile on the right leading to some descending zigzags. Cross the bridge at the bottom, turn left then take the first right.

After the prehistoric earthwork of Windbury Castle the path continues on the cliff-top to Shipload Bay and then on to Hartland Point, where there are seasonal refreshments. The Coast Path turns sharp left off the lighthouse track towards the coastguard lookout before the lighthouse gate. A short diversion gives a good view of a wreck on the rocks below.

From Hartland Point the path descends into an unusual valley, almost parallel to the coast, at Smoothlands, before climbing again. Descending then to the valley at the Abbey River the path goes inland to cross at a stone bridge. At the next cliff top, past an old folly tower, the path arrives at a road by the old Rocket House. Bear right to follow the path downhill to Hartland Quay, a lonely outpost with car park, toilets and refreshments, as well as an hotel.

Week 2 - Day 3

OS Maps: **Landranger 190; Explorer 126 (most of length); Explorer 111 (Bude)**

	This Walk	Cumulative	This Walk	Cumulative	Grading	Timing
Ascent	4,170ft	23,418ft	1,271m	7,138m	Severe	8.5 hours
Distance	15.4mi	124.4mi	24.8km	200.2km		

For detailed directions see our Hartland Quay to Bude Path Description booklet.

This is an awe-inspiring and dramatic coastline. Great jagged ridges of rock stretch out into the Atlantic Ocean, backed by high, surf-fringed cliffs. The coast is punctuated by jutting headlands and tiny, often inaccessible beaches. In the south, towards Bude, the coast softens a little and, at low tide, long sandy beaches appear. This is a spectacular Section.

Directions

Hartland Quay has no public transport connections. There is, however, an infrequent bus service between Bude and Morwenstow, half-way along, which could be used for a bus-walk on the southern half of this Section.

Note that this is probably the most arduous of all the days in the suggested itinerary. It is necessary to cross ten river valleys to complete the length, all of them steep and deep. Because of this, many may prefer to split the length at Morwenstow.

From Hartland Quay a track then a grassy path passes behind St Catherine's Tor. There is a climb then the cliff path reaches the dramatic waterfall at Speke's Mill Mouth. Keep to the eastern side of the stream here for some 150 yards/135m then cross by the wooden footbridge. Follow the signs up the valley inland of Swansford Hill. Take care at Sandhole Cliff, after joining the metalled road, to look out for the signpost after about 0.3 mile/0.5km indicating the turn right back to the coast. (It is hoped this length of road may be eliminated in the near future.) After Welcombe Mouth, Marsland Mouth marks the Cornish border, indicated by a wooden sign. The ascents and descents continue, and a diversion to Morwenstow might be worth considering. The church is picturesque and interesting and there are seasonal refreshments nearby. At the radio dishes do not miss the sign directing right towards the cliff edge. Descending to Duckpool, cross the stream by a footbridge. There are toilets here. Continue on to Sandy Mouth where there are more toilets and seasonal refreshments. The going now eases at last and after passing over the open cliffs at Maer Down the path arrives at Crooklets Beach at Bude. Follow the path along the low cliffs behind the beaches into the town, which has all facilities.

Stanbury Mouth

Week 2 - Day 4

OS Maps: **Landranger 190; Explorer 111**

	This Walk	Cumulative	This Walk	Cumulative	Grading	Timing
Ascent	2,494ft	25,912ft	760m	7,898m	Easy then strenuous	4.75 hours
Distance	10.2mi	134.6mi	16.4km	216.6km		

For detailed directions see our Bude to Crackington Haven Path Description booklet.

Low grassy cliffs and surfing beaches south of Bude give way to an ever higher and more rugged coastline fronted by rough rock ledges and cut by deep and steep valleys. There are some superb viewpoints along this later quiet and remote-feeling length which reward the effort. Crackington Haven is a pleasant spot and on the cliffs above, St Gennys Church is a superb spot for contemplation.

Directions

A regular bus service links Bude with Crackington Haven, and also serves Widemouth Bay, about 3 miles/7km from Bude, thus offering a number of bus-walk options.

The path south from Bude starts at the sea lock on the historic Bude Canal, then climbs to the cliff top at Compass Point and on to Efford Beacon. There are excellent views from here. The path over Efford Down to Upton and on to Widemouth Bay is easy to follow. Widemouth has toilets and refreshments, the last before Crackington Haven. (There are further refreshment facilities a little inland at Whalesborough, reached by a scenic footpath from Widemouth.)

South of Widemouth the path follows the low cliff for a short distance then diverts inland slightly at Wanson Mouth to join the coast road in the stream valley. Turn right and follow the road as it climbs steeply to Penhalt Cliff. There are more magnificent views from the cliff-top car park.

From the southern end of the car park the Coast Path crosses a field and descends steeply to Millook Haven. Now follow the steep road uphill for a short distance then turn right onto the cliff top at Raven's Beak. From here the path climbs steadily past the stunted oak woodland at Dizzard Point and on to Chipman Point. Two further deep and steep valleys are crossed, then a ridge walk leads to Castle Point, which gives tremendous views. Another steep valley crossing leads on to Pencannow Point and views over Crackington Haven. The path descends easily into the cove, where there are toilets, refreshments, buses and accommodation.

Bude Canal

Week 2 - Day 5 (half day)

OS Maps: **Landranger 190; Explorer 111**

	This Walk	Cumulative	This Walk	Cumulative	Grading	Timing
Ascent	2,264ft	28,176ft	690m	8,588m	Strenuous	3.75 hours
Distance	6.8mi	141.4mi	10.9km	227.5km		

For detailed directions see our Crackington Haven to Tintagel Path Description booklet.

This is a Section of high cliffs, the highest, indeed in Cornwall. Not only are they high, but they also present an appearance of bulk, of being literally massive, and the walker will often feel dwarfed by them, especially on a climb or descent or perhaps on a headland. Much of this Section is also quite lonely, and this combination makes this a coast with an imposing character.

Directions

Crackington Haven and Boscastle are linked by a regular bus service, making this an option for a bus-walk.

There are toilets and seasonal shops, cafes and a pub at Crackington Haven. Leave behind the beach near the toilets and head out for the headland of Cambeak. Rounding the headland, keep away from its high and sheer cliff edges. Beyond Cambeak the path is relatively level, passing above the landslip zone at Strangles Beach. Ahead looms High Cliff, the appropriately-named highest cliff in Cornwall. There is a steady ascent but the descent on the south side is very steep. The path then climbs through a landfall at Rusey Cliff, twisting and turning to the top. A cliff top section through fields follows to the sheer black cliff at Buckator. The path then dips slightly before continuing at high level to Fire Beacon Point. Here the descent is steep, but helped by attractive slate steps. The path then follows the cliff face into the inlet of Pentargon, with its impressive waterfall. This is best seen from the southern side - do not be tempted to leave the path for a better view.

Shortly afterwards the path passes refreshment facilities at Boscastle Farm Shop (call 01840 250827 for details).

The now easy path continues on to Boscastle. Aim for the white mast on Penally Hill, then follow the path alongside the beautiful harbour inlet into Boscastle, now happily restored after its 2004 experiences.

Boscastle

Week 2 - Day 5 (half day)

OS Maps: Landranger 190 (eastern half); Landranger 200 (western half); Explorer 111

	This Walk	Cumulative	This Walk	Cumulative	Grading	Timing
Ascent	1,230ft	29,406ft	375m	8,963m	Moderate	2.25 hours
Distance	4.6mi	146.0mi	7.4km	234.9km		

For detailed directions see our Crackington Haven to Tintagel Path Description booklet.

This fairly short Section is a great local favourite, as it combines all the best of the Coast Path - headlands, sandy bays, historic features and, yes, steep valleys, all in a manageable but picturesque length which is not too taxing. In addition, although popular, it never seems crowded and is, indeed, a "real" walk. With all this and its convenient bus links it is a perfect Coast Path taster.

Directions

Boscastle and Tintagel are linked by a regular bus service. It also serves Rocky Valley, half-way between the two, enabling a variety of bus-walks to be undertaken.

Boscastle has been attractively rebuilt after the floods of 2004, and has all facilities.

The Coast Path leaves the south side of the harbour over the new stone bridge and climbs towards the headland of Willapark, with its prominent white watch tower. The path cuts across the neck of the headland, but a diversion to the end is worthwhile.

After a steep descent and climb at Grower Gut the path continues easily, turning seaward of the Manor House at Trevalga. The headland beyond gives views over the rocky offshore islands important for breeding seabirds. The path continues past Firebeacon Hill - look out for the Ladies Window rock arch in the gully to the right - then passes seaward of a cliff-top caravan and camping site. There is then a des cent into the exquisite Rocky Valley. There is a path up the valley to a bus stop on the coast road, passing prehistoric carvings in the cliff wall.

From the footbridge in the valley the path climbs again, round the edge of the grassy Bossiney Common and above the sandy bay at Bossiney Haven. Another climb then leads to another headland also, confusingly, called Willapark. Again the Coast Path cuts across the neck of the headland and, again, a diversion to the end is worthwhile.

The path now continues to Barras Nose headland, from where it descends to Tintagel Haven below the castle ruins. Here are toilets, cafe and English Heritage gift shop. A good but steep path leads inland to the village.

Barras Nose

17 · Tintagel to Port Isaac

Week 2 - Day 6

OS Maps: Landranger 200; Explorer 111 (eastern half); Explorer 106 (western half)

	This Walk	Cumulative	This Walk	Cumulative	Grading	Timing
Ascent	2,589ft	31,995ft	789m	9,752m	Severe	4.75 hours
Distance	9.1mi	155.1mi	14.7km	249.6km		

For detailed directions see our Tintagel to Port Isaac Path Description booklet.

Both ends of this Section are relatively popular and accessible. At Tintagel the Coast Path passes the remains of the medieval castle perched on its isolated headland then the atmospherically located cliff-top church and the now picturesque evidence of coastal slate quarrying. At the other end is the beautifully quaint village of Port Isaac in its scenic bay. The long central length, though, comprises high cliffs cut by sometimes precipitously steep valleys. It is remote, lonely and often tough, and will be especially appreciated by those who relish an empty, arduous and dramatic coastline.

Trebarwith Strand

Directions

There is a regular bus service between Tintagel and Port Isaac; occasionally a change at Camelford is needed. A bus-walk is therefore possible on this Section.

Tintagel has all necessary facilities. Surprisingly, however, little in the village is very old other than the Old Post Office, once a local manor house.

From the village walk down the path to Tintagel Haven. From here the Coast Path climbs past the entrance to the Castle and gives excellent views over the headland which forms the castle site. A good path continues seaward of the church and on beyond past the Youth Hostel in its former quarry building and round Penhallic Point with its superb views.

The path drops steeply to Trebarwith Strand, where there are toilets, refreshments and pub, the last facilities before Port Isaac. The next part is particularly tough as it climbs steeply out of the Trebarwith valley then almost immediately drops down to sea level and up again at Backways Cove. There follows a level stretch of about a mile/1.5km to the stream valley behind Tregardock Beach. Descend on the inland side of the detached piece of cliff known as The Mountain, then climb again to Tregardock Cliff. Another level length follows, before the deepest and steepest valley yet at Jacket's Point. At the top yet another deep valley almost immediately follows. Then comes a further valley, at Barrett's Zawn. This is an area of massive rock falls. The next valley follows, this one with exceptionally steep and stony sides.

At last the path levels out again through cliff-top meadows, with just a small valley to cross at St Illickswell Gug. Eventually, the path reaches the road at Cartway Cove. Take the path on the right and round the headland to Port Gaverne, a charming spot. Follow the road uphill to the car park at the edge of Port Isaac. Go through this and follow the well-signed path above the attractive harbour inlet into the village.

Port Isaac is a very picturesque village clustered round the little harbour at the head of a sheltered bay. It has all facilities.

Port Isaac

Week 2 - Day 7

OS Maps: **Landranger 200; Explorer 106**

	This Walk	Cumulative	This Walk	Cumulative	Grading	Timing
Ascent	2,923ft	34,918ft	891m	10,643m	Strenuous then easy	5.5 hours
Distance	11.7mi	166.8mi	18.9km	268.5km		

For detailed directions see our Port Isaac to Padstow Path Description booklet.

This Section can be divided into three distinct characters. From Port Isaac to Port Quin is a rollercoaster of a path, closely following the ups and downs and ins and outs of the quiet, scenic but energy-sapping coast. From Port Quin to Polzeath the character becomes rather more open, if still very scenic, including the broad headland of The Rumps and Pentire Point, a wonderful airy lookout. From Polzeath to the Padstow ferry the landscape is tamer, more domesticated, often with housing or tourist development and more estuarine than maritime as it reaches the mouth of the River Camel.

Directions

There is a regular bus service between Port Isaac and Rock, the ferry point for Padstow. This service also passes through Polzeath at the mouth of the Camel estuary, giving several scenic bus-walk options, including an almost level estuary-side one. There is a popular circuit using the Coast Path between Port Isaac and Port Quin and others from Polzeath around Pentire Point.

Port Isaac has all necessary facilities, and is a scenic gem. To leave the village, take the road to the right behind the fish market. Climbing, it bears right and becomes a cliff path, soon dropping into Pine Haven. From here to Port Quin the path is magnificent and clear, but tough as it follows the cliff edge next to a prominent fence line. There is an optional diversion to the end of Varley Head.

The path enters the beautiful Port Quin inlet, descending to what was once a busy pilchard port, though there are no facilities here now. Follow the road westbound up the steep hill and a little way up the Coast Path leaves to the right, towards Doyden Point. The path follows above the cove, keeping seaward of and below the large house. Head to a prominent stone cairn, then continue ahead on a grassy path and past some old mineshafts. From the cairn a diversion to the right goes to

St Enodoc Church

Padstow Ferry at Rock

the folly of Doyden Castle and to Doyden Point, where there is a superb view back to Port Quin.

There is a sharp descent to Epphaven Cove then the path passes through a delightful little wooded valley before climbing past the impressive Lundy Hole. The clear cliff path now heads for the Iron Age fortress on The Rumps headland. A detour to the end is well worthwhile.

From The Rumps the path climbs through a little former quarry area then continues at high level round Pentire Point, giving spectacular views. An easy descent follows to Polzeath, all well marked. Polzeath has all necessary facilities, including now an all-year café, "Tubestation", open Wednesday-Saturday during the winter. The path follows the road past the beach car park then goes right by the cottages, where the road bends sharp left on the steep hill. It now follows a low cliff to Daymer Bay, where there are toilets and a seasonal cafe, then down steps to the beach. At the far end of the beach it leaves through dunes and over a footbridge below Brea Hill. It is possible to detour to visit the little St Enodoc Church from here.

To continue on the Coast Path follow the path clinging to the side of Brea Hill, though it is possible to go over the top or, at low tide, along the beach. On the far, south, side of Brea Hill the well-signed path continues through dunes to arrive at Rock car park. The ferry to Padstow is in the estuary just below. However, be warned that at exceptionally low tides the ferry may sail from some way downstream, in front of the dunes.

For ferry details see page 18.

A water taxi service operates between Rock and Padstow between 19:00 and midnight from Easter to 31st October, weather and tides permitting. For further details see page 18.

Note that it is possible to walk Coast to Coast across Cornwall between Padstow and Fowey on the south coast, using the Saints' Way. A guidebook is available from Padstow TIC.

Week 3 - Day 1 (half day)

OS Maps: **Landranger 200: Explorer 106**

	This Walk	Cumulative	This Walk	Cumulative	Grading	Timing
Ascent	744ft	35,662ft	227m	10,870m	Easy	2.5 hours
Distance	5.7mi	172.5mi	9.1km	277.6km		

For detailed directions see our Padstow to Porthcothan Path Description booklet.

The length from Padstow to Stepper Point, at the mouth of the Camel, is a scenic length of ever-changing estuarine views with sandy stretches, especially at low tide. Beyond, the coast is an easy but picturesque length of cliffs, which include occasional views right across the headland at the mouth of the estuary and up the Camel as well as west to Trevose Head. The two elements of this Section combine to form a popular local walk.

Directions

A regular bus service links Padstow with the inland end of Trevone, about one mile/1.5 km from the Coast Path. This allows for a possible bus-walk. There are also a number of possible circular walks from Padstow using the Coast Path which take in the Stepper Point headland.

Padstow is a charming and bustling little harbour town a short way up the Camel Estuary. If arriving from Rock, notice that normally this arrives in Padstow at the harbour, but at low tide it lands a short distance downstream at St Saviour's Point. In either event, it is well worthwhile taking time to explore the town.

The Coast Path leaves the north end of the harbour past the TIC and proceeds on low cliffs alongside the estuary. After passing a wooded little stream valley at St George's Cove the path heads inland of a marshy area before going back to the cliffs and on to Hawker's Cove. Refreshments are available at Hawker's Cove at the "Rest a While" tea garden. The cafe is normally open 10.30am to 4.30pm, mid March until late October, weather permitting. It may be best to telephone 01841 532919 to check opening times. Pass behind the old pilots' houses here then fork right to climb to Stepper Point, with its Daymark tower. From here there are remarkable views, inland to Bodmin Moor as well as along the coast.

The path is now on the exposed Atlantic coast. Go round the precipitous inlet of Butter Hole Cove, looking out for the small Pepper Hole to the right of the path just before. An easy length to Gunver Head follows, with excellent sea views. Approaching Trevone the path skirts the impressive Round Hole collapsed cave - approach this with caution as the sides are sheer. Follow the cliffs round into the bay at Trevone, which has toilets, cafe and pub, as well as a car park.

Stile at Padstow

Week 3 - Day 1 (half day)

OS Maps: **Landranger 200; Explorer 106**

	This Walk	Cumulative	This Walk	Cumulative	Grading	Timing
Ascent	817ft	36,479ft	249m	11,119m	Easy	3.5 hours
Distance	7.9mi	180.4mi	12.7km	290.3km		

For detailed directions see our Padstow to Porthcothan Path description booklet.

This is a popular Section, never far from a variety of holiday accommodation. It is perhaps most associated with a range of scenic sandy surfing beaches, some of them quite extensive. As a contrast, around the middle of the length is the great landmark of Trevose Head and its lighthouse, visible from great swathes of the North Cornwall coast and an atmospheric location.

Directions

A regular bus service passes the inland end of Trevone, about one mile/1.6km from the Coast Path, and links to Porthcothan. The same route serves Constantine Bay, about two-thirds of the way along the coast from Trevone, giving a potential for a variety of bus-walks.

Trevone has all necessary facilities. The path crosses the rear of the beach and leaves behind the little headland on the south-west side of the bay, following the cliff edge round rocky Newtrain Bay. Reaching Harlyn there are refreshments and toilets. Cross the stream on the road bridge then follow the beach below the low cliff for some 330 yards/300m before climbing left onto the cliff and then continuing to the headland at Cataclews Point.

The path passes inland of Padstow's lifeboat station, accessible by a cul-de-sac path, and then goes on to Trevose Head, passing the lighthouse. On a clear day the coastal views are incredibly extensive, ranging from the satellite dishes north of Bude to the granite hills of West Penwith behind St Ives. This is an atmospheric headland.

After an old quarry the path passes a Round Hole collapsed cave and descends to the partly rocky Booby's Bay. Continue on to the rear of Constantine Bay, a very attractive and extensive beach at low tide. Walk the length of the beach. There are toilets and seasonal refreshments at the far end and a bus stop a little way inland. Beyond the dunes the path rounds Treyarnon Head to cross another attractive beach at Treyarnon Bay, with seasonal toilets and refreshments.

An unusually indented coastline follows, with sheer-sided headlands and impressive coves. Near Pepper Cove the ramparts of an Iron Age cliff fort may be seen, and the whole coastline is quite spectacular. The path then turns into another sandy cove, at Porthcothan Bay, which has toilets and refreshments and also has a pub, the Tredrea Inn, about 500 yards/458m inland up the road.

Porthcothan Bay

Week 3 - Day 2

OS Maps: Landranger 200; Explorer 106

	This Walk	Cumulative	This Walk	Cumulative	Grading	Timing
Ascent	1,447ft	37,926ft	441m	11,560m	Moderate	5 hours
Distance	11.1mi	191.5mi	17.9km	308.2km		

For detailed directions see our Porthcothan to Newquay Path Description booklet.

This is a relatively well-walked Section, particularly around Newquay. It shows the interplay of high cliffs and sandy beaches particularly well. Almost the whole length is characterised by high, flat-topped cliffs, sometimes with prominent headlands, which for long stretches form the back of extensive attractive sandy beaches, many of them popular with surfers. While never a lonely Section, its cliffs and bays make it one well worth exploring, helped by the relatively easy terrain.

Directions

Porthcothan and Newquay are linked by a regular bus service. This route follows a road parallel and close to the coast, meaning that there are a number of possible links to the Coast Path from this bus, allowing for quite a range of possible bus-walks.

Porthcothan has all facilities that may be needed. The Coast Path leaves past the shop and keeps in front of the houses and on around the headland. After a short steep descent and climb, an easy level walk leads to Park Head, an excellent viewpoint. There have been numerous landslips here so keep to the path inland of the white posts. The whole headland is worth wandering over and exploring. Ahead now is the National Trust's Carnewas property, with its spectacular beach. The Trust's cafe and Information Centre are open through the summer. On the beach below are the massive stacks forming Bedruthan Steps.

The Bedruthan Steps area can be busy, but the steps to the beach are closed in the winter months. A quieter length follows to Trenance Point and into the sandy bay of Mawgan Porth, where there are toilets, refreshments and a pub as well as a bus stop. Surprisingly, this was once the site of an unfinished canal project.

Cross the stream using the road then leave it to the right on the sharp bend on the hill out of Mawgan Porth. There then follows a long high level length to Watergate Bay on airy flat-topped cliffs, cut by a couple of minor descents. The path passes Iron Age remains here while inland is the contrast of Newquay Airport. The path continues on the cliff top behind the magnificent Watergate Beach, much used for surfing and other activities. The path then descends to the road by the Watergate Bay Hotel, and here there are toilets, refreshments and another bus stop.

Cross the stream at the road then turn right by the car park and climb back to the cliffs, which are now followed to the outskirts of Newquay. The coastal view ahead to the town and its headlands is excellent. The Coast Path leaves the road to pass round the headland of Trevelgue Head, an important prehistoric location. Although

Bethruthan Steps

the path bypasses the island at the very end, this can be visited via the footbridge, and is worth the diversion for the views. The path returns to the road by Porth Beach before leaving it at steps down on the left, to pass underneath the main road and cross the next little headland to emerge above Lusty Glaze beach - look for the information board here relating to the canal previously encountered at Mawgan Porth.

The path continues into the park at Barrowfields, skirting its seaward side, to reach the main road into Newquay town centre. Follow this just past the railway station then take the old tramway road on the right. At the overbridge climb the steps on the right and go down to Trebarwith Crescent. Go left here then right into Island Crescent. Follow this then turn right along the footpath above Towan Beach.

At the corner go down the steps on the right then from the car park cross Beach Road and follow the tarmac path ahead. At the end follow the steps on the left to pass a bowling green and public toilets to Fore Street. Turn right here as far as the Red Lion and here turn right again to the harbour down North Quay Hill.

As well as all facilities, Newquay has a branch line railway station linking to the main line to Penzance and is the centre of a network of local bus routes.

The aptly named Seaside Tea Garden on Newquay Harbour is open from Easter to October, selling light lunches, cream teas & all the usual extras.

Week 3 - Day 3 (half day)

OS Maps: Landranger 200; Explorer 104

	This Walk	Cumulative	This Walk	Cumulative	Grading	Timing
Ascent	1,145ft	39,071ft	349m	11,909m	Moderate	3.5 hours
Distance	6.3mi	197.8mi	10.2km	318.4km		

For detailed directions see our Newquay to Perranporth Path Description booklet.

This Section includes some superb viewpoints from headlands in and around Newquay, the panoramas quite unspoiled by the proximity of the large town. Beyond Newquay a range of landscapes is experienced, from wide sandy beaches to exposed cliff tops to small sandy bays to dune systems. In addition, unexpectedly, the wooded estuary valley of the river known as The Gannel is crossed at the edge of Newquay. This variety, and the proximity to a range of facilities and accommodation, make this a popular, well-used length.

Directions

A regular bus service links Newquay with Holywell Bay, and also serves Crantock, between the two. This gives a number of bus-walk possibilities.

Newquay is the biggest town on Cornwall's north coast. Although usually busy, being especially popular with surfers and also with groups of young holidaymakers, it is in a very attractive setting of beaches and headlands. All the facilities are here, and there is a branch railway linking to the main line to Penzance.

From Newquay Harbour the Coast Path climbs past the old Huer's Hut to Towan Head. This is a good lookout spot, and is excellent for seabird watching. From Towan Head the path then follows the back of Fistral Beach. This is probably the country's most popular surfing beach and international competitions are held here. The path climbs to the cliffs at the southern end and then crosses the road to go along Pentire Crescent which leads into Penmere Drive. The path then arrives above the Gannel Estuary. However, this misses the major headland of Pentire Point East, which is well worth the diversion to the end. (If following the diversion round the headland, on returning from the end aim for the far bottom of the car park at the neck of the headland. From here head along the suburban road parallel to the Gannel. Follow this to the Fern Pit Cafe.)

There are four options from here for crossing the Gannel, depending on the tide and time of year.

OPTION 1: FERN PIT FERRY (deduct 2 miles/3km from total mileage)
The first option is to use the Fern Pit Ferry from behind the cafe. The cafe is approximately 0.7 mile/1.1km west of Penmere Drive. The ferry operates continuously, 7 days a week, 10.00-18.00 mid May until mid September weather dependent - telephone 01637 873181. For further details see page 18.

OPTION 2: PENPOL CROSSING (official route)

Go along Penmere Drive then turn right into Trevean Way. Follow the waymarks right and go downhill across a grassy area. At the foot of the grass bank turn right along the footpath then take the steps on the left down to the tidal Penpol Footbridge across the Gannel Estuary.This can be used 3-4 hours either side of low water. Cross the Gannel here. (If coming from the headland circuit, continue past the Fern Pit Cafe and on along Riverside Avenue, then ahead and right. At a junction where there is a footpath to the right keep ahead, ignoring the footpath. Bear right into Penmere Drive and re-join the main route following the directions above.

OPTION 3: TRENANCE FOOTBRIDGE (add 3 miles/4.8km to total mileage)

This route is usable at most states of the tide. From the Newquay side of the Penpol crossing continue upstream on the path parallel to the river until it arrives at the A392 Gannel Road. There is a footbridge on the right just before the junction with the A3058 Trevemper Road. Cross the bridge and continue ahead, following the bridleway to Trevemper. Turn right just before reaching the tarmac and follow the footpath through Treringey to arrive at the south side of the Penpol tidal footbridge.

OPTION 4: MAIN ROAD ROUTE (add 4.5 miles/7.2km to total mileage)

Continue past the Trenance footbridge and along the A392 Trevemper Road from the roundabout. At the next roundabout turn right and after about 100 yards/90m take the little unsigned lane on the right. This leads to Trevemper, going forward and right as the lane goes left. After the gate turn left on the route described under Option 3 through Treringey.

Options 2, 3 and 4 come together at Penpol. Follow the lane then take the signed path on the right above the estuary. After passing the ferry landing for Option 1 this path leads to Crantock Beach car park. Crantock village with its facilities and bus stop is a little way inland. Cross the car park to the dunes; bear left at the junction of grassy paths on entering the dune area and follow this inland of the main dune area to re-emerge at a coastal path which leads to the cliffs of Pentire Point West where the Bowgie Inn provides meals and refreshments. The path goes round Porth Joke (known locally as Polly Joke), then on around Kelsey Head to Holywell Bay, descending across more dunes either into the village or to cross the river on a seaward footbridge. There are facilities, some seasonal, here.

River Gannel from Fern Pit Cafe Gardens

Week 3 - Day 3 (half day)

OS Maps: **Landranger 200; Explorer 104**

	This Walk	Cumulative	This Walk	Cumulative	Grading	Timing
Ascent	755ft	39,826ft	230m	12,139m	Moderate	2 hours
Distance	4.5mi	202.3mi	7.3km	325.7km		

For detailed directions see our Newquay to Perranporth Path Description booklet.

Perranporth sundial

The theme of this Section is sand, in the form of both dunes and beaches, although it begins by rounding headlands at Penhale and Ligger Points. However, even at Penhale the inland vista is dominated by dunes, although the adjacent Army camp is also prominent. For the bulk of this Section sand is everywhere around, on the seemingly endless length of Perran Beach and the dunes which back it. Both ends, Holywell and Perranporth, are busy holiday settlements but the more remote areas of Perran Beach can be surprisingly quiet.

Directions

Holywell Bay and Perranporth are linked by a regular bus service, making a bus-walk a feasible option here.

Holywell Bay has all facilities, some seasonal.

From Holywell Bay the path rounds Penhale Point, skirting the seaward edge of the somewhat unattractive Penhale army camp. It then goes on out to Ligger Point, where there is a panoramic view of the length of Perran Beach. The path heads towards the dunes then descends behind the cliff quarry to the beach. It now follows the back of the beach for some 1.5 miles/2.5km. This is possible even at high tide, and usually on firm sand. At Cotty's Point the tide often makes it necessary to climb the steps leading to Perran Sands holiday park. At the top of the steps turn right following the slate Coast Path waymarks. The path descends back to the beach on the south side and then crosses the stream by the footbridge when nearly at Perranporth, where there are again all needed facilities.

Week 3 - Day 4

OS Maps: Landranger 200 (Perranporth); Landranger 203 (remainder); Explorer 104

	This Walk	Cumulative	This Walk	Cumulative	Grading	Timing
Ascent	2,250ft	42,076ft	686m	12,825m	Moderate then strenuous	5.75 hours
Distance	12.2mi	214.5mi	19.7km	345.4km		

For detailed directions see our Perranporth to Portreath Path Description booklet.

This Section is one in which Cornwall's coastal mining heritage is paramount. There is much evidence of former mining activity, this including somewhat stark areas of spoil and sometimes slightly sad building relics, but also some grand and imposing engine houses and chimneys. In some locations, the large-scale level of the activity is difficult to imagine now. Nevertheless, the scale and grandeur of the cliffs, the beaches and the surf mean that nature always re-asserts itself.

Directions

A summer bus service links Perranporth to Portreath, also passing St Agnes and Porthtowan along the way, giving numerous bus-walk options.

Perranporth is a busy holiday centre with all facilities. The Coast Path goes west from the main car park and follows the hill up Cliff Road. Keep left of the castellated building then along Tregundy Lane. Go half left at the entrance to the Youth Hostel and on to the cliffs, the path clinging to the cliff face out to Cligga Head. Here the path enters quarry and mine workings, but is well signposted. There is then a level stretch alongside Perranporth Aerodrome before the steep descent to Trevellas Porth, a valley marked by many relics of the mining industry. Go upstream to cross at the road bridge, then back to the cliffs and back down again into Trevaunance Cove, where there are toilets and refreshments. The bus stop at St Agnes is a little way inland.

On reaching the road at Trevaunance Cove go straight across passing the Driftwood Spars car park and a large tall house on the right. Follow the waymarked footpath immediately right along a metalled lane then fork right along a footpath. Soon the path climbs steeply to the cliff top. A long and scenic high-level path now goes around St Agnes Head, giving superb views ahead, then past the iconic engine house at Towanroath before descending to Chapel Porth, a small and attractive cove with toilets and seasonal refreshments. Refreshments are available at the Chapel Porth Beach Cafe daily in the holiday season and weather permitting at weekends during the winter. Phone 01872 552487 to check opening times. The toilets here are only unlocked when the cafe is open. Follow the stream inland for 200 yards/185m then turn right and up to the cliffs, before it is back down again into Porthtowan. Again there are toilets and refreshments and a magnificent beach. There is a bus stop a little inland.

Follow the road inland then turn right up West Beach Road, then left up the narrow road to the cliff top. More mine workings are passed, then the path runs alongside a prominent fence next to MOD land before reaching a road which descends into Portreath. This former industrial harbour town has all facilities.

Wheal Coates Mine

Week 3 - Day 5

OS Maps: **Landranger 203; Explorer 104 (eastern half); Explorer 102 (western half)**

	This Walk	Cumulative	This Walk	Cumulative	Grading	Timing
Ascent	1,362ft	43,438ft	415m	13,240m	Moderate/ easy	5.5 hours
Distance	12.4mi	226.9mi	19.9km	365.3km		

For detailed directions see our Portreath to Hayle Path Description booklet.

There are two distinct characters to the coast of this Section. Between Portreath and Godrevy it is one of high, level cliffs, the sea far below. In contrast, between Godrevy and Hayle the walk focuses on sand, either dunes or beach, on the focal view of Godrevy lighthouse and on the great colourful sweep of St Ives Bay. This is never a lonely or remote length, but it is a scenic, fascinating and rewarding one.

Directions

A summer bus service links Portreath and Hayle, and also passes Godrevy, half-way between the two. This allows for bus-walk options over the whole Section or over either of the two distinct character lengths.

Portreath has all facilities and a nice beach. Leave the town crossing the bridge next to the car park then right, up Battery Hill. Continue ahead, meandering between properties at the end, turning right just beyond them up steps to the top of Western Hill, with its excellent views. After a couple of noticeable valleys the path then embarks on a long easy cliff-top walk along Reskajeague Downs, eventually arriving at Hell's Mouth, where there is a seasonal cafe. The path then narrows and turns right at an obvious T-junction. Cross a stile next to a gate and cross the seaward side of a field before continuing easily round Navax and Godrevy Points, the lighthouse becoming a focal point offshore. Keep seaward of the car park and access road and follow the signs along the low cliffs and over the dunes to another car park, at the Godrevy Cafe. Follow the boardwalk from the car park to cross the Red River. Turn left for 30 yards/29m then go right, following the large slate waymarks through the former quarry, now a nature reserve.

Keep ahead through the dunes, following the signposts. Note it is often possible to walk along the beach here but beware the incoming tide which can mean being cut off below the cliffs. If the tide is right, leave the beach at the lifeguard hut near the foot of Black Cliff. If coming through the dunes, keep ahead above the hut. Then, with either option, turn left up some steps just before two chalets. Turn right towards a house, leaving it on the right, and walk along a line of chalets on the left. The path is slightly overgrown but then opens out at a car park. Follow the access track ahead then bear right onto the raised walkway parallel to the harbour and continue ahead on this level. Descend the steps at the far end and follow the pavement ahead then cross the old swing bridge to the road. Turn right to reach the railway viaduct in the centre of Hayle.

Hayle

Week 3 - Day 6

OS Maps: **Landranger 203; Explorer 102**

	This Walk	Cumulative	This Walk	Cumulative	Grading	Timing
Ascent	617ft	44,055ft	188m	13,428m	Easy	2.5 hours
Distance	5.6mi	232.5mi	9.0km	374.3km		

For detailed directions see our Hayle to Pendeen Watch Path Description booklet.

This Section is never far from roads and houses, so often has a suburban air. However, this is outweighed by the views over the River Hayle estuary and, particularly, by the vistas over the great sweep of St Ives Bay with its vast sandy beaches and dunes, the iconic offshore Godrevy Lighthouse as a focal point and the fabulous sea colours, turquoises, greens and blues, whenever the sun shines on this length.

Directions

Towards St Ives

A regular bus service links Hayle and St Ives, giving a bus-walk option. In addition, a branch-line railway plies between Lelant and St Ives, and this gives marvellous sea views. This makes for an unusual and especially scenic train-walk option.

Hayle has all facilities, including a railway station on the main line to Penzance. Walk to the viaduct and turn right on the path immediately before it. Go ahead to Carnsew Road and continue on the pavement, turning right on a narrow path at the end of a stone building, by the pedestrian traffic lights. A short way down this path turn left next to a fence to arrive alongside a large lagoon. Keep on to the end then bear left to the road. Continue as the road passes alongside the River Hayle estuary on The Causeway, a birdwatchers' delight. Cross to the far side of the road then back to the riverside again before forking right at the Old Quay House - take care on the road here. Under the bridge turn right, signed to St Ives Park and Ride. At the car park attendant's kiosk turn left to a lane, then turn right here. Follow the lane next to the railway and estuary all the way to Lelant Church. Go along the path next to the church to pass under the railway. Just before the beach turn left along the seaward side of the railway through dunes. (NB this is also the route of the St Michael's Way, a cross-peninsula path from Lelant to Marazion - a guide leaflet is available at St Ives TIC.)

Follow the clear path parallel to the magnificent Porthkidney Beach. Approaching the headland of Carrack Gladden the path forks - keep right then continue ahead. Descend the road to Carbis Bay, where there are toilets and seasonal refreshments, walking inland of the cafe but seaward of the hotel. Climb over a railway bridge then continue as the path becomes a minor road. Pass the path taking St Michael's Way inland then at a little cross-roads go straight ahead, steeply downhill. (Turning right shortly after the St Michael's Way turning down a private, pedestrians only path gives a more scenic alternative to the official route, re-joining at the little cross-roads.) Cross the railway bridge and double back right then left to arrive at Porthminster Beach, just below St Ives railway station.

Week 4 - Day 1

OS Maps: **Landranger 203; Explorer 102**

	This Walk	Cumulative	This Walk	Cumulative	Grading	Timing
Ascent	3,428ft	47,483ft	1,045m	14,473m	Severe	7 hours
Distance	13.9mi	246.4mi	22.3km	396.6km		

For detailed directions see our Hayle to Pendeen Watch Path Description booklet.

There are no settlements on this Section and the character is lonely and remote. It is also tough going, with rocky scrambles and boggy lengths. But it can only be described as a magnificent length. Stark cliffs, rock pinnacles, tiny scenic coves with translucent water, rugged exposed headlands - all are here. Inland the view is often of empty moorland. This is the Coast Path at its most awe-inspiring. Prepare for its rigours, then enjoy the wonderful experience.

Directions

A regular summer bus service links St Ives and Pendeen village, a little inland of the Coast Path. It also passes through other inland settlements linked by footpath to the Coast Path, principally Zennor, Treen (Gurnard's Head) and Morvah, allowing for various bus-walks options.

A warning:- this is a tough and deserted length of the Coast Path. There are no settlements or refreshment facilities, though there are some path links inland to small settlements. The terrain is often rough and rocky and in places can be boggy. But a compensation:- this is a length of wonderfully dramatic coastal scenery.

From the path below St Ives railway station keep along as close as possible to the sea and harbour. The official route goes round the green St Ives Head, usually known as The Island. This is reached by following signs to the museum from the far end of the harbour and on through a small car park. From The Island go through the old "Downlong" quarter to Porthmeor Beach and the Tate. There are also short cuts direct to here - follow signs to the Tate.

Go along the rear of Porthmeor Beach then bear off right along the path next to the putting green. The Coast Path now leads out to the rugged Clodgy Point and then on round Hor Point to Pen Enys Point, where it cuts across the neck of the headland. Pass the trig point on Carn Naun, where there are extensive views forward and back, then descend to cross the stream at River Cove. Just beyond the path passes the offshore Carracks, where seals are regularly seen. Approaching Zennor Head the path forks - keep right to follow the seaward path round the headland. From Zennor Head the path heads inland - look out for the signed Coast Path descending steeply to the right. If in need of refreshments, or for the bus, continue along the path inland to Zennor, where there is a pub and seasonal cafe.

Standing Stone at Trevalgan Cliff

On the Coast Path, more ups and downs lead to the distinctive headland of Gurnard's Head. The path cuts across its neck, but a diversion onto the headland, an Iron Age fortified site, is worth the effort. There are also diversions inland here to Treen, where refreshments are available at the Gurnard's Head Inn and there is a bus stop.

The Coast Path continues, generally easy to follow if not always an easy walk. Approaching Bosigran, another Iron Age fortification, can be confusing. Aim for the high point of the rocky ridge ahead and follow the most obvious path towards it. It is likely to lead just inland of the summit - turn right to reach it then follow the clear path down the other side. Cross the stream on a small bridge near a ruined building then follow the path uphill, just seaward of an obvious stone wall. There is a diversion path inland here to a bus stop at Rosemergy.

Further on the Coast Path, look out for a path inland to Morvah for another bus stop if needed. Otherwise keep on the obvious Coast Path round the back of Portheras Cove and on to the lighthouse at Pendeen Watch. Pendeen village, with its pubs, cafe, shop, toilets and bus stop, is about 1 mile/1.5km inland.

28 · Pendeen Watch to Sennen Cove

Week 4 - Day 2

OS Maps: Landranger 203; Explorer 102

	This Walk	Cumulative	This Walk	Cumulative	Grading	Timing
Ascent	1,683ft	49,166ft	513m	14,986m	Moderate	4.25 hours
Distance	9.0mi	255.4mi	14.6km	411.2km		

For detailed directions see our Pendeen Watch to Porthcurno Path Description booklet.

This Section offers a wide range of walking experiences. Between Pendeen Watch and Botallack the overriding experience is of Cornwall's coastal mining heritage. This ranges from unattractive early 20th century industrial relics to romantic stone-built cliff-face engine houses, all this next to sheer cliffs and often wild seas. Beyond Botallack is a superb length of scenic exposed cliffs, highlighted by the magnificent headland of Cape Cornwall. This Section has all that is best on the Cornish coast - rugged cliffs, mining relics, translucent water, turquoise coves, purple heather, rocky scrambles, the view of a lighthouse. Then, approaching Sennen Cove, there is a sweep of broad sandy beaches backed by dunes, and the length ends with a scenic harbour and a lifeboat station. A wonderful length.

Crowns engine houses, Botallack

Directions

A regular summer bus service links Pendeen village, a little inland of the Coast Path, with Sennen Cove. It also serves St Just, inland of Cape Cornwall, which is used as the centre of various Coast Path-based circular walks. Bus-walks are also possible from Geevor and Botallack, reached by footpath from the coast.

Priest's Cove at Cape Cornwall

From Pendeen Watch the path goes along the road to the end of the row of cottages, then turns right at a granite marker. (The road continues into Pendeen village, with its range of facilities.) The Coast Path is clear and leads to the old mining area at Geevor. A diversion inland leads to refreshments and toilets at the mining museum, which is itself well worth a visit if possible. Follow the signed track beyond Geevor to the National Trust's Levant Beam Engine House, open for steaming at certain times. From here the official path follows the clear track parallel to the coast, but a narrower path to seaward with better views leads from the far end of the car park. The two options come together as more mines are passed at Botallack. Look to seaward to see the famous Crowns Mine engine houses perched improbably on the cliff.

Beyond Botallack, as the mines give way, look for the signed path to the right which leads to the headland at Kenidjack Castle. A lot of the waymarking in this area uses granite stones, perfect for the landscape setting. From the old building on the headland descend left to a track, go left then quickly right to another track. Go left here then turn right to cross the floor of the Kenidjack Valley. Climb to the top and turn right. Ahead now is the distinctive shape of Cape Cornwall, surmounted by its chimney. Turn right immediately before the road and then bear right across a field past the ruins of a chapel to a stone stile. Cross this, turn left and then climb right to reach the top of the headland. Savour the views, then join the path which descends over the seaward side of the Cape by zigzags and steps to reach the National Coastwatch Institution watchhouse. This recent addition to the Coast Path provides a superb experience. Go to the left of the watchhouse then down the steps and along a path past some stone buildings and through a gate to reach another set of granite steps descending to the right. In the nearby car park are seasonal refreshments and toilets. St Just is about 1 mile/1.5km up the road.

At the bottom of the steps go left then climb right to a road at the top. Bear off right at the sign and follow the clear path into the Cot Valley. Turn right at the road to the cove at Porth Nanven, and here cross the stream and climb onto the cliffs. There is a good clear cliff-face path to the beach at Gwynver, although with one awkward scramble. From Gwynver the path continues through the dunes behind the sandy beaches, which can be walked at low tide, to the car park at Sennen Cove. This is a popular family and surfing spot with all facilities.

Week 4 - Day 3 (half day)

OS Maps: Landranger 203; Explorer 102

	This Walk	Cumulative	This Walk	Cumulative	Grading	Timing
Ascent	1,542ft	50,708ft	470m	15,456m	Moderate	3.25 hours
Distance	6.6mi	262.0mi	10.6km	421.8km		

For detailed directions see our Pendeen Watch to Porthcurno Path description booklet.

This is the most westerly length of coast in England. Much of it has the character of moorland meeting the sea, with great granite headlands and massive rock outcrops interspersed with isolated coves with exquisite sea colours. Towards Porthcurno the moorland is replaced by a more pastoral landscape, but the cliffs and coves continue. Much of this Section has a quiet character, interrupted only by the visitor mecca of Land's End.

Porthcurno Cliffs

Directions

Sennen Cove and Porthcurno are linked by a regular bus service, which also goes to Land's End. This allows for a choice of bus-walks and there are also numerous circuits possible based on the Land's End area.

Sennen Cove has all facilities. Leave the village passing the Round House gallery into the car park. Turn left up steps then right, towards the lookout. From here a range of parallel paths all lead to Land's End. Bear right to the First and Last House, at England's most westerly point, then keep seaward of the main complex to the outpost at Greeb Cottage. The complex has toilets and refreshments if needed. The path goes behind Greeb Cottage; then again a choice of paths all lead towards the beautiful bay of Nanjizal. At the far end of the bay head inland up the track then turn right steeply uphill on a stepped path. After passing through a gate look out for the official, unsigned, path leaving the main track to go seaward over a little rocky scramble. The path descends then climbs to the Coastwatch station on Gwennap Head. The main track also leads here, but less scenically.

The official path is clear from Gwennap Head down into Porthgwarra. An alternative, in good conditions only and for the sure-footed only, is to leave the main path to the right some 150 yards/140m after the Coastwatch station, then pass the hole of Tol-Pedn-Penwith ("the holed headland of Penwith") before bearing left to re-join the main path.

Porthgwarra is a charming little hamlet with toilets and seasonal refreshments and unusual passages through the cliffs. Leave along a track next to some cottages, climbing again to the cliffs. The clear path descends to Porth Chapel, passing St Levan's Holy Well. Bear left above the beach, climbing again to arrive at the car park of the unique cliff-face Minack Theatre. Leave by the path next to the theatre entrance. The path drops very steeply, with deep steps, to Porthcurno Beach. If in doubt, because of the conditions or possible vertigo, follow the road. At the bottom of the steps keep left above the beach to Porthcurno's facilities.

Week 4 - Day 3 (half day)

OS Maps: Landranger 203; Explorer 102

	This Walk	Cumulative	This Walk	Cumulative	Grading	Timing
Ascent	1,381ft	52,089ft	421m	15,877m	Strenuous	3.25 hours
Distance	5.5mi	267.5mi	8.8km	430.6km		

For detailed directions see our Porthcurno to Penzance Path Description booklet.

This is a quiet, remote and very scenic Section of cliffs and headlands, punctuated by some picturesque coves and a lighthouse. The larger coves, at each end, Porthcurno and Lamorna, are particularly attractive and are the only access points for cars, so are more popular, Otherwise, the sound of the sea and seabirds are likely to be the only disturbances in this beautiful length.

Directions

A regular bus service goes to Porthcurno and passes about 1 mile/1.5km inland of Lamorna Cove, making a bus-walk feasible. Many undertake one of a variety of circular walks between Porthcurno and Treen using the Coast Path.

Porthcurno has all facilities in summer. The Coast Path leaves at the back of the beach, climbing a steep track to Percella Point before turning to run parallel to the sea. A seaward loop gives a good view of the beautiful Pednvounder Beach, but requires a little scramble to return to the official route. The path then reaches the neck of Treen Head, or Treryn Dinas, the site of an Iron Age fortification. A cul-de-sac diversion heads for the end and the Logan Rock.

Continue on the clear path over the cliff to descend into Penberth Cove, a superb little fishing hamlet with an old capstan. There are toilets but no refreshments. There is a necessary inland diversion loop for dog walkers here.

After climbing away from Penberth the path continues along the cliff top, with one steep descent and climb at Porthguarnon, then starts to head inland. After passing a seaward house look out for the signed path to the right which descends into the wooded valley of St Loy and on to the boulder beach. Keep along the top of the beach for 55 yards/50m before leaving up the path. This climbs to pass above the lighthouse of Tater-du. Approaching Lamorna Point the path crosses a length of tumbled rocks, making for slow going, until it suddenly descends to the car park at Lamorna Cove. Here are toilets and seasonal refreshments.

Penberth Cove

Week 4 - Day 4

OS Maps: Landranger 203; Explorer 102

	This Walk	Cumulative	This Walk	Cumulative	Grading	Timing
Ascent	725ft	52,814ft	221m	16,098m	Strenuous then easy	3.5 hours
Distance	9.4mi	276.9mi	15.1km	445.7km		

For detailed directions see our Porthcurno to Penzance and Penzance to Porthleven Path Description booklets.

West of Mousehole this Section is one of lushly vegetated cliffs, but most of it is urban or semi-urban in character as it passes through Newlyn and Penzance. However, it is really defined by its views over the magnificent Mount's Bay, dominated by the iconic sight of St Michael's Mount and its castle, which give this coast a magical character.

Directions

A regular bus service passes about 1 mile/1.5km inland of Lamorna Cove and also serves Newlyn, Penzance and Marazion, giving a variety of possible bus-walk options.

Lamorna Cove has a seasonal cafe, toilets and, a little way inland, a pub. The Coast Path leaves the cove behind the harbour, bearing right to the cliffs. The well-marked path eventually leads to a road which descends into Mousehole. The road leads to the harbour; however, the official route turns right opposite "Lowena" then continues towards the sea, turning left along a terrace to a car park. It briefly passes along the harbour before turning left then right to reach the main harbour-side road. Mousehole has all facilities and is very picturesque.

At the far end of the harbour go through the car park, on along a concrete walkway then up some steps. Turn right along the road, then along a seaward track to arrive at Newlyn. Follow the road round the harbour and past the fish market, turning right just after the Seamen's Mission to cross a bridge. Bear right past the Tolcarne Inn then follow the promenade to Penzance. Pass the harbour then go right through the large car park to where a walkway leaves from its far right-hand end. Penzance has all facilities, is the end stop of the main-line railway and is the hub of local bus services. The train and bus stations are next to the car park.

The walkway follows the sea wall to the edge of Marazion. At the end of the walkway and cycle route either cross over and follow the road or cross the dunes to a large car park, cross this and continue behind the sea wall into Marazion.

Marazion is the centre for access to St Michael's Mount and is the southern end of the cross-peninsula St Michael's Way from Lelant. The little town of Marazion has all facilities.

Lamorna Valley

Week 4 - Day 5

OS Maps: Landranger 203; Explorer 103 (Porthleven); Explorer 102 (remainder)

	This Walk	Cumulative	This Walk	Cumulative	Grading	Timing
Ascent	1,916ft	54,730ft	584m	16,682m	Moderate then strenuous	4.75 hours
Distance	10.6mi	287.5mi	17.1km	462.8km		

For detailed directions see our Penzance to Porthleven Path Description booklet.

Between Marazion and Cudden Point this Section is dominated by the sweep of Mount's Bay and its iconic focal point of St Michael's Mount. It is a charming length of low cliffs and small fields. East of Cudden Point the Mount is lost but the local landscape is bolder, with craggy headlands, long sandy beaches, inaccessible coves and picturesque cliff-top engine houses.

Directions

There are regular bus services which link Marazion and Porthleven and also serve Perranuthnoe and Praa Sands between the two, making a variety of bus-walks possible, Marazion is a pleasant little town with all facilities and the causeway to St Michael's Mount.

St Michael's Mount

The Coast Path leaves along the main road, following it for some way to the speed restriction sign. Turn right before the cemetery, then bear left on a concrete path down steps and follow the path to the beach. Cross the top of the beach to some metal steps, climb them and continue ahead. Just after Trenow Cove the path turns inland. Look out for the signed right turn after 275 yards/250m, which goes back to the low cliffs and on to Perranuthnoe. There are toilets and seasonal refreshments here.

Take the lane on the seaward side of the car park, bearing right and then left into a field. The well-marked path leads to Cudden Point, with magnificent views over Mount's Bay. It descends past Little Cudden to Bessy's Cove, where it joins a track. Go ahead, bearing right at some granite gate posts, then through Prussia Cove on a lane between large stone buildings. Keep ahead on the path which passes above Kenneggy Sand and then descends to Praa Sands, where there are toilets and seasonal refreshments. Go down the slipway to the beach then along in front of the shop, taking the steps up beside the cafe. Keep along the top of the grassy dunes, turning left when signed at the end then right into a housing estate. At the end bear right and climb to the cliffs. The path skirts behind Rinsey Head then through a car park and down to a restored engine house. It continues to Trewavas Head, inland of more restored engine houses. Beyond there have been numerous cliff falls - be sure to follow the signed path. This then enters Porthleven on a lane - fork right entering the town to pass alongside the harbour to its head. Porthleven has all facilities.

33 • Porthleven to Mullion Cove

Week 4 - Day 6 (half day)

OS Maps: **Landranger 203; Explorer 103**

	This Walk	Cumulative	This Walk	Cumulative	Grading	Timing
Ascent	1,109ft	55,839ft	338m	17,020m	Moderate	3.25 hours
Distance	7.1mi	294.6mi	11.4km	474.2km		

For detailed directions see our Porthleven to The Lizard Path Description booklet.

This is a Section mostly of low cliffs with cliff-face paths, long stretches being above extensive beaches. It harbours a couple of unexpected features, firstly in the shape of Loe Bar, a large strip of shingle barring the freshwater Loe Pool from the sea, and secondly in the unusual position of Gunwalloe Church, hidden away in the corner of a sandy cove. Add a cliff-top monument to Marconi, a couple of picturesque coves and the rocky and atmospheric harbour at Mullion Cove and it makes for a fascinating length.

Directions

Porthleven and Mullion village, which is some 0.5 mile/1km from the Coast Path, are both served by regular but separate bus routes, which meet at Helston. The Mullion bus also serves Poldhu Cove, 1.5 miles/2.5km along the coast from Mullion Cove, allowing various bus-walks.

Porthleven has all facilities. The Coast Path goes alongside the harbour towards the clock-tower at the end near the pier. Follow the road past this building, going right at the fork and keep on out of the town to a car park. Climb the steps and continue ahead on the track to Loe Bar. Cross the bar to the far side, forking right, downhill, shortly after the memorial. After passing a renovated fishery building the path arrives at Gunwalloe Fishing Cove. Go ahead onto the National Trust's Baulk Head, then above Halzephron Cove to a road. Bear right to a small car park then go right again, away from the road, on the cliffs down to Gunwalloe Church Cove. There are toilets and seasonal refreshments here. The picturesque church is tucked away at the right-hand end of the cove.

Skirt the beach to a road, then take the signed path over a footbridge and over the rear of the beach to the path rising away. Immediately after the car park at the top turn right along the cliff top before returning to the road and dropping into Poldhu Cove, where there is a bus stop, toilets and refreshments. Cross the stream on the road and turn right up the driveway signed to the Marconi Centre, leaving this after 110 yards/100m for a path to the right. This passes the Marconi monument on the cliffs then drops into Polurrian Cove. Climb away past the Polurrian Hotel and along the slightly suburban path to the Mullion Cove Hotel.

Keep to seaward and drop down to the harbour, where there are seasonal refreshments. There are toilets 110 yards/100m up the road.

Towards Loe Bar

Week 4 - Day 6 (half day)

OS Maps: **Landranger 203; Explorer 103**

	This Walk	Cumulative	This Walk	Cumulative	Grading	Timing
Ascent	1,303ft	57,142ft	397m	17,417m	Moderate	3.25 hours
Distance	6.8mi	301.4mi	10.9km	485.1km		

For detailed directions see our Porthleven to The Lizard Path Description booklet.

This is an exposed Section of high, flat-topped cliffs and spectacular coves and bays. The coastal landscape is superb throughout, but punctuated by some real scenic gems, of which Kynance Cove is probably the pick. The combination of steep cliffs, unusual geology and flora, beautiful sea colours and long stretches of easy walking make this a rewarding length. And watch out for choughs, Cornwall's iconic bird now returned to re-colonise this coast.

Directions

A regular bus service links Mullion village with Lizard Town, each settlement about 0.5 mile/1km inland from its respective end, thus giving a possible bus-walk. In addition, there are many easy local circuits based on the Coast Path in the Lizard-Kynance area.

Mullion Cove has seasonal refreshments and there are toilets a little way inland. The Coast Path leaves the quay slightly inland to the right, up the hill just after the cafe. Climb to the cliffs, keeping to the right to hug the coastline. There is an information board on the unique flora and fauna of the area here.

The easy and clear path rounds Parc Bean Cove and Lower Predannack Cliff. Approaching Vellan Head, be sure to keep close to the coast for the official route - the more obvious track misses the views. After the deep valley at Gew Graze the path rounds Rill Point and descends to Kynance Cove. The steep descent leads to a footbridge by the seasonal cafe. There are also toilets here. If the sun is shining the sea is brilliant turquoise.

From the cafe either follow the main track up towards the car park or cross the little beach (at low tide) and climb a partly stepped path to the cliffs, leaving this at a sign pointing right. This passes adjacent to the car park, where the main track arrives, and the Coast Path then continues clearly and easily above Pentreath Beach at Caerthillian and round Old Lizard Head, and on to Lizard Point, England's most southerly point, where there are cafes, gift shops and toilets. The nearby lighthouse is open to visitors at certain times. A path leads inland to Lizard Town, which has all facilities including regular bus services.

Mullion Cove

35 • The Lizard to Coverack

Week 5 - Day 1

OS Maps: Landranger 203 (Lizard); Landranger 204 (remainder); Explorer 103

	This Walk	Cumulative	This Walk	Cumulative	Grading	Timing
Ascent	2,293ft	59,435ft	699m	18,116m	Moderate, strenuous in places	5.75 hours
Distance	10.6mi	312.0mi	17.1km	502.2km		

For detailed directions see our The Lizard to Coverack Path Description booklet.

This is a Section of cliffs and coves, punctuated by headlands giving excellent views along the coastline. Here and there are areas of sandy beach at the foot of the cliffs, but only at Kennack are they very extensive. This coast is largely sheltered from the worst of the prevailing south-westerly winds, and consequently has a lush, well-vegetated character. This being a relatively unfrequented stretch, substantial lengths are quiet and remote.

Downas Cove GSWW Project

Directions

Lizard Town, about 0.5 mile/1km inland of the Coast Path, has a bus service which also passes a little inland of Cadgwith, about half-way along this length, which presents a bus-walk possibility. In addition, there are numerous easy circuits based on The Lizard using the Coast Path which are popular and attractive.

Lizard Point has cafes and toilets, while Lizard Town, inland, has all necessary facilities. Lizard Point has the distinction of being England's most southerly point and is a fine location. The Coast Path leaves the Point alongside the car parking area and on in front of the lighthouse. There is a Heritage Centre at the lighthouse and both lighthouse and Heritage Centre are open to the public at certain times (www.lizardlighthouse.co.uk). After passing the lighthouse descend to cross a footbridge then climb, passing in front of the Housel Bay Hotel and on past the Lloyds Signal Station, bearing right here. The route passes Bass Point National Coastwatch Institution lookout, the first in the country to be established. At Kilcobben Cove the path goes behind The Lizard lifeboat station with its new boathouse which was completed in 2011. It then arrives at Church Cove. Go left for a short distance then take the path through the gate on the right. There are some ups and downs to a path junction just after a stone stile at Polgwidden Cove; keep right here. A little further on the path skirts the dramatic collapsed cave of the Devil's Frying Pan. Follow the signed path past the cottages and down into the picturesque little fishing hamlet of Cadgwith.

Cadgwith has a pub, shop, refreshments and toilets. There is a superb little beach here where the fishing boats are hauled up. This is overlooked by a convenient grassy knoll with seats known as The Todn (Cornish for lawn). Walk through Cadgwith and up the hill, turning right on the signed path a little way up. The Path then descends to Poltesco, crossing a footbridge. There is a diversion to the right leading to the attractive and interesting cove, complete with old serpentine works, where the local colourful rock was made into useful items. Climbing out of Poltesco, the path then joins a road which leads to the beach at Kennack Sands. There are toilets here and seasonal refreshments.

Follow the path behind the beaches and on to the cliffs to reach the neck of the long promontory of Carrick Luz, the site of an Iron Age cliff fort. The path cuts across the neck and then negotiates the steep valley at Downas Cove. Another, shallower valley crossing leads to the end of Black Head and its lookout hut. The path now descends over the cliffs towards Chynhalls Point going amongst the natural rock outcrops which can be slippery in wet weather. Beyond the Point the path soon reaches Coverack.

An alternative inland path avoids the slippery Chynhalls Cliff. At the top of the Coast Path descent, the wide alternative path goes through gorse and passes a Sculpture Park, then the edge of a caravan park before arriving at a bungalow on a tarmac road. Turn right towards the hotel and then almost immediately bear left down a narrower path to rejoin the Coast Path at Chynhalls Point.

Reaching the road at Coverack, the path soon veers off right down some steps to arrive at a car park at the end of the village. Follow the road past the harbour. Coverack, a pretty place, has all facilities, including a regular bus service into Helston.

Week 5 - Day 2

OS Maps: **Landranger 204; Explorer 103**

	This Walk	Cumulative	This Walk	Cumulative	Grading	Timing
Ascent	2,192ft	61,627ft	668m	18,784m	Moderate	5.75 hours
Distance	13.1mi	325.1mi	21.1km	523.3km		

For detailed directions, see our Coverack to Helford Path Description booklet.

This is a sheltered Section of the Coast Path. It includes low cliffs facing away from the prevailing winds, but also lengths of pleasant rural field paths, a little inland, necessary to avoid inaccessible coastal working and former quarries. In addition this Section has substantial lengths which fringe a tidal creek and on wooded estuary-side paths passing pretty beaches where the Coast Path reaches the Helford River. While not as dramatic as some Sections, it is an attractive stretch with a quiet charm of its own.

Directions

Separate bus routes from Helston serve Coverack and Helford Passage, across the river via ferry (Good Friday or 1st April to October) from Helford, allowing a bus-walk based on Helston. There is an attractive local circuit using the Coast Path between Helford and Gillan Creek.

There are all necessary facilities at Coverack. The Coast Path follows the road away from the pub and past the harbour, continuing straight ahead on a narrow lane when the road goes left. Look out for the sign pointing right, just before the end of the lane. The path goes over sometimes boggy ground next to the coast to arrive at Lowland Point. Next, the old workings at Dean Quarry are passed on their seaward side. The well-signed path then arrives at the open area at Godrevy Cove. The next length of coast is inaccessible due to operating quarries, so the Coast Path heads across the open area inland to pick up a signed path going uphill between fields. This leads to the little hamlet of Rosenithon. At the T-junction, turn right on the lane, uphill, turning left into a field just after the right-hand bend. Cross three fields in the same direction, stone stiles between them, to emerge on a lane. Go left then, at a junction, right, which leads to Porthoustock, a coastal hamlet with public toilets.

The route of the next stretch, to another coastal hamlet, Porthallow, is also a rural inland walk. It leaves Porthoustock past the telephone box and up the hill. Where the road bears right go straight ahead on a narrower lane. Go past a row of thatched cottages and over a little grassy bank at the end next to a greenhouse to a kissing-gate. Just past the gate there is a fork in the path. Bear right and follow the path climbing to the far top corner of the field to cross a lifting-bar stile and a Cornish stile (a sort of stone cattle grid) into another field. Turn right in this field alongside the hedge, then bear away left at the top to cross another Cornish stile to a road. At the road go left, passing through the tiny hamlet of Trenance. Here the route follows the road round to the right to a T-junction. At the junction go slightly right and immediately left onto an enclosed path which leads to a track between buildings. Here is the charming Fat Apples Cafe, open all year though winter hours are limited.

Porthoustock

At the road turn right to arrive at Porthallow.

Porthallow has a pub, toilets and seasonal refreshments. Fat Apples Cafe is open all year with winter opening hours between October and March. Look out for the marker indicating the half-way point of the Coast Path, equidistant (at 315 miles) from Minehead and Poole. Leave Porthallow along the back of the beach and up the steps. The path now follows the coastline, keeping close to the edge round Nare Point and then past a couple of pretty beaches. Moving into the mouth of the Helford River the path continues alongside its tidal tributary, Gillan Creek.

From Easter/1st April to 31st October use the signal board to request the ferry. Telephone 01326 231357 or see page 19 for ferry details.

Otherwise, the route goes left from the creekside up the hill to a sharp left-hand bend. Here go straight ahead along the field edge, then bear right over two further fields to a road. Turn right to Carne, at the head of the creek, then right again along the north side of the creek to St Anthony Church. Past the church turn left uphill then shortly right on a farm track which leads into a field. Cross diagonally left to the top of the field to a kissing-gate.

For a short, direct route from here go through the gate and turn left. However, the Coast Path includes an optional extra of a circuit of Dennis Head. For this circuit do not pass through the gate but turn right then almost immediately left over a stile. At the next junction continue straight ahead to reach the end of the headland. The path circles around the headland, re-joining the outward route to the stile and then the kissing-gate.

Go through the gate and continue along the top of the field. The route now heads up the estuary side of the Helford River through woods and past coves. Towards the end the path reaches a track - follow to the road and go right here then quickly left. The path then emerges next to the main car park at Helford. Go down the hill into the village. Helford has a pub and shop and there are toilets and a seasonal cafe at the car park. The cafe will take telephone orders to be ready on arrival, so it is possible to phone from St Anthony and have your order ready when you reach Helford - call 01326 231893.

Week 5 - Day 3

OS Maps: **Landranger 204; Explorer 103**

	This Walk	Cumulative	This Walk	Cumulative	Grading	Timing
Ascent	1,397ft	63,024ft	426m	19,210m	Moderate	4.5 hours
Distance	10.0mi	335.1mi	16.1km	539.4km		

For detailed directions see our Helford to Falmouth Path Description booklet.

There are two contrasting parts to this Section. Between Helford and Rosemullion Head it is a sheltered walk alongside the mouth of the beautiful Helford River, with undulating, relatively low cliffs alternating with charming little beaches. Between Rosemullion Head and Falmouth the walk flanks the sweep of Falmouth Bay, with rather larger coves overlooked by the great headland of Pendennis Point at the Falmouth end, crowned by its castle. Over the bay is St Anthony Head lighthouse. None of this is a lonely or remote walk, and the Falmouth end is decidedly urban, but it is never uninteresting and always very scenic.

Directions

Helford Passage and Falmouth are linked by a regular bus service, which also serves two of the beach coves along the route, at Maenporth and Swanpool, giving numerous bus-walk options. The short circular walk round Pendennis Head in Falmouth is a great local favourite.

Helford has pub, shop and toilets; Helford Passage, over the river, has a pub and seasonal refreshments. There is a seasonal ferry link.

For ferry details see page 19.

It is possible to use local taxi services if the ferry is not operating - Autocabs, tel: 01326 573773 or Cove Cars tel. 07980 814058. Alternatively Sailaway St Anthony Ltd, tel: 01326 231357 may be able to help.

Walk around Helford River

If the ferry is not operating, a 13 mile/21km walk around the Helford River is possible. This will add another day to the itinerary. For this route, from Helford take the path up the hill in front of the Shipwright Arms to arrive at Penarvon Cove. Go round the back of the cove and turn inland up a track to a road. Turn right then left on a track to the permissive path along the atmospheric Frenchman's Creek.
At the end take the path on the right signed to Withan past Frenchman's Pill Cottage, crossing a footbridge. Follow the path through the woods and aim for the far left corner of the field, taking the stile on the left. Follow the boundary on the left past Withan Farm, then head west over the fields to a lane. Here turn left to a crossroads, turning right here towards Mawgan. The lane joins a larger road; turn right past Gear then down and up into Mawgan-in-Meneage village. Turn right just after the church on the path towards Gwarth-an-drea then left behind a bungalow to a road.
Turn right and at the junction bear right and continue downhill to the bridge at

Gweek. There is a shop and pub here. Take the road opposite the Gweek Inn and at Tolvan Cross turn right along a bridleway to a road junction. Go straight ahead, towards Porth Navas. After crossing the stream take the footpath on the left along the field edge to the road. Follow the road ahead to Nancenoy and Polwheveral. At the crossroads after Polwheveral turn right then after 140 yards/128m take the path on the left along the field edge then across the field corner to a road junction. Take the Porth Navas road opposite through the village to Trenarth Bridge, then turn right towards Falmouth. At the junction at Trebah turn right, then right again into Bar Road. At the end turn left on a footpath which leads to the Helford River, turning left to the Ferryboat Inn at Helford Passage, the landing place for the ferry from Helford.

Blockhouse at Pendennis Point

Ferry users start from here

Coast Path, Helford Passage - Falmouth

From the Ferryboat Inn, facing the pub, turn right along the river and up to a grassy hill. Keep on to a concrete track and follow this, passing behind Trebah Beach at Polgwidden Cove. Continue on the riverside to Durgan, turning sharp right to enter the little village. Go up the road, ignoring one path to the right, until the road turns left and the path continues straight ahead. Follow this path, arriving at Porth Saxon Beach behind a building and then through a field to Porthallack Beach. The path then climbs round Toll Point to arrive at a wooded area. At the fork keep right and follow the path onward to Rosemullion Head, leaving the Helford River behind.

Keep seaward round the headland then descend to go through a small wood and then on, the path becoming suburban now, to reach Maenporth where there are toilets and refreshments and a bus stop. Turn right behind the cafe and continue to Swanpool, with more toilets and refreshments and another bus stop. Take the path from the far end of the beach to arrive at Gyllyngvase, then keep along Falmouth's promenade to the far end. The official path goes around the magnificent Pendennis Point - keep to the seaward road all the way to the end then at the car park descend on the signed path up the river, parallel to the road above. The path emerges from woods and passes the Leisure Centre, descending above the docks to a T-junction. Turn right then go ahead under the railway bridge, passing the Maritime Museum and along Falmouth's main shopping street to arrive at the Prince of Wales Pier at the far end. Falmouth, of course, has all facilities, including a rail link to the main line at Truro.

Week 5 - Day 4 (half day)

OS Maps: **Landranger 204; Explorer 105**

	This Walk	Cumulative	This Walk	Cumulative	Grading	Timing
Ascent	974ft	63,998ft	297m	19,507m	Easy	2.75 hours
Distance	6.2mi	341.3mi	10.0km	549.4km		

For detailed directions see our Falmouth to Portloe Path Description booklet.

This Section includes a trip on the ferry across the mouth of the River Fal, a treat of scenery and interest in its own right. Beyond, the walk round St Anthony Head is one of superb estuarine and coastal views, followed by an easy but charming path on low cliffs, sheltered from the westerlies, while passing some fine sandy beaches and giving excellent views up the South Cornwall coast.

Directions

A regular bus route serves Portscatho and St Mawes from Truro, which is also linked to Falmouth by bus and train. There is also a very popular circular walk using the Coast Path in the St Anthony Head area and another from Portscatho.

Two ferries are required to cross between Falmouth and the Coast Path at Place, east of the large estuary. The first goes between Falmouth and St Mawes, across the mouth of the main Fal Estuary, sometimes referred to as Carrick Roads.

The ferry operates all year except winter Sundays, June-October inclusive. Telephone 01326 313201. The ferries operate from Prince of Wales Pier year round and Custom House Quay summer only.

For ferry details see page 19.

The second leg of the crossing is the ferry between St Mawes and Place, crossing the mouth of the Fal's tributary, the Percuil River. This ferry operates Easter to 31st October, 10:00 to 16:45, every half hour; telephone 07791 283884. In winter an alternative may be offered by a water taxi service, telephone 07971 846786. For details visit www.stmaweskayaks.co.uk .

For ferry details see page 19.

There is also Falmouth Water Taxi service which operates between Falmouth and St Mawes or Place, weather permitting between March and October 0900 to 1800 (2230 May to September). If needed, it is best to telephone a day in advance. Tel: 07970 242258, www.falmouthwatertaxi.co.uk.

Information is also available from the Fal River Visitor Information Centre at Prince of Wales Pier, or visit www.falriver.co.uk.

If arriving at St Mawes and wishing to proceed to Place when the Place ferry is not operating it is possible to take the regular bus service from St Mawes to Gerrans, walking from here to Place (2.5 miles/4km). For this option, go to Gerrans Church and pick up the walking

St Mawes Ferry

route described below. In addition, a local taxi company, Roseland Taxis, will carry walkers around here and throughout the Roseland Peninsula - tel: 01872 501001, M: 07817 447667, website www.roselandtaxis.co.uk

New steps at St Anthony Head

Walk between St Mawes and Place

A walking route also exists between St Mawes and Place, via Gerrans. This adds 9 miles/14km to the overall route, effectively an extra day to the itinerary. Leaving the ferry point in St Mawes, turn left along the road. Approaching the castle, take the minor lane left, which leads to a footpath at the end. This becomes a scenic path alongside the Carrick Roads - the Fal Estuary. At a minor road go right then bear left in front of the boatyard and then on a bank above the shore. This leads to the churchyard of St Just in Roseland, a beautiful spot. Pass the church and keep to the path next to the shore. Follow the path as it bears right up the hill, signed St Just Lane, to emerge on a road. Turn left, ignoring the first footpath on the right, but take the second a little afterwards. Follow the path alongside field boundaries, first to the right, then to the left, then to the right again. Go down to the road at the end of the fourth field and turn right to the A3078 at Trethem Mill. Turn left and immediately right after the bridge up some steps and through a small wood. Out of the wood, cross the field diagonally right (bearing 110) then in the next field bear diagonally right again (bearing 140), leaving it by a wooded track. Cross the stile at the top and bear diagonally right again (bearing 137) to meet a hedge, which is followed to a road. Turn right on the road. At the next junction follow the road curving to the right past Polhendra Cottage then turn left through the second gate. Descend towards the bottom of the hedge visible on the opposite side of the valley (bearing 123). Cross the bridge and climb as close as possible with the hedge to the left. Cross the stone steps behind the gorse at the top and bear slightly left across the next two fields (bearing 125) to emerge on a road. Turn right to arrive at Gerrans Church. (Those who have taken the bus from St Mawes will join here - see above.)

At the church fork left into Treloan Lane, keeping ahead past the buildings. Go through the gate at the end of the lane, crossing an open field ahead into another enclosed track, which leads to Porth Farm. At the road turn right then go left at the sign indicating "Footpath to Place by Percuil River". Follow this very scenic path which leads to the ferry landing point then on to Place itself.

Coast Path, Place - Portscatho

At Place, walk up the lane past the gates to the grand house. Turn right into the churchyard of St Anthony Church, passing behind the church and up into a wooded area. Turn right at the track then at the creek look for the sign on the left taking the path alongside the plantation. The path now gives superb views over Carrick Roads to Falmouth. Approaching St Anthony Head keep to the coastal path to the right until passing through the gate towards the lighthouse. Just after the gate climb the steps to the left to the car parking area. There are also toilets here. Leave the car park next to the coast and the superb and easy path then leads to Portscatho, which has a shop, toilets and pubs, as well as a bus service to St Mawes and Truro.

39 • Portscatho to Portloe

Week 5 - Day 4 (half day)

OS Maps: Landranger 204: Explorer 105

	This Walk	Cumulative	This Walk	Cumulative	Grading	Timing
Ascent	1,674ft	65,672ft	510m	20,017m	Strenuous	3.75 hours
Distance	7.5mi	348.8mi	12.0km	561.4km		

For detailed directions see our Falmouth to Portloe Path Description booklet.

This is a very quiet Section for the most part. Cliffs are relatively low at first, but increase in height as the great promontory of Nare Head, with its superb views, is approached. The long sandy beaches below the cliffs passed west of Nare Head are replaced by tiny isolated and inaccessible coves east of the headland. This length has a wonderfully remote atmosphere.

Directions

Portscatho and Portloe are both served by regular, but different, bus services, both linking with Truro. There are some local circular walks using the Coast Path around Nare Head, based on the inland village of Veryan.

Portscatho has a shop, pubs, toilets and bus service. The Coast Path leaves past the Harbour Club; keep right just after leaving the village at the footpath junction. The path goes round the back of Porthcurnick Beach, then up the road on the far side, turning right along the coastal edge. The path continues to undulate along the coast until it turns inland to reach a road. Turn right, past Pendower Court and down the road to its end at Pendower Beach. Cross the rear of the beach and head for the public toilets, going up the hill and turning right. The path soon diverts around the rear of the Nare Hotel to a road, descending to Carne Beach. Follow the road round the bend and up the hill for a short way, turning right to return to the cliffs. The path now heads for Nare Head, via a steep descent and ascent at Tregagle's Hole and past an old fisherman's cottage. A short diversion at the top of Nare Head reveals some stunning coastal views.

The path now goes round the seaward edge of Rosen Cliff and over the valley behind Kiberick Cove to Blouth Point. At the point enter a field and keep left for a short way before bearing right, downhill, towards some trees. The path zigzags upward to pass Broom Parc and then goes through a field to round Manare Point. After this it is downhill going over a short uneven section before joining a tarmac path which descends into Portloe. The village is very picturesque and has pubs and toilets as well as a bus service.

Portloe

Week 5 - Day 5

OS Maps: **Landranger 204; Explorer 105**

	This Walk	Cumulative	This Walk	Cumulative	Grading	Timing
Ascent	2,841ft	68,513ft	866m	20,883m	Strenuous then easy	5.75 hours
Distance	12.3mi	361.1mi	19.8km	581.2km		

For detailed directions see our Portloe to Mevagissey Path Description booklet.

This is a quiet Section of mostly high cliffs, often covered in lush vegetation. Towards Gorran Haven these cliffs reduce in height. The Section includes the great headland of Dodman Point, from where there are views to the Lizard in one direction and Devon in the other on a clear day. Below the cliffs are some sandy beaches, often all but inaccessible. This is a coastline for those preferring remoteness.

Back towards Chapel Point

Directions

There are some excellent circular walks using the Coast Path at Dodman Point and linking to Gorran Haven, giving a variety of options here.

The scenic little harbour village of Portloe has toilets, pubs and a bus service.

The Coast Path leaves behind the Lugger Hotel, leaving the road to reach a prominent converted chapel. Pass this then climb steeply to the cliffs. After a quite strenuous length the path arrives at West Portholland. Follow the road above the shore to a junction, then turn right to East Portholland. There are toilets here and a seasonal cafe and shop. Pass the cottages at the far end and climb behind them on a clear path to a field, turning right down the field edge. The path leads to a road which descends to Porthluney Cove. Here are toilets and seasonal refreshments and the picturesque setting is enhanced by the presence of Caerhayes Castle just inland. Walk behind the beach and turn right into parkland. Climb behind the field-edge trees then go to the right and follow the field edge to the woods. After crossing the rocky ridge at Greeb Point the path descends to a road behind Hemmick Beach. Cross the bridge and go right, climbing to the headland of Dodman Point ("The Dodman"), with its memorial cross and superb views. The path stays clear above the lovely sands of Bow or Vault Beach, then rounds the headland of Pen-a-maen to enter Gorran Haven. This little harbour village has a shop, pub and toilets.

Leave Gorran Haven up Church Street, turning right into Cliff Road. Turn right near the top of the hill and a stile on the left leads to the cliffs. The clear path leads to Chapel Point, where it crosses the tarmac access road to follow the path along the coast into Portmellon. Follow the road uphill and go down through the park on the right on entering Mevagissey. Steps descend to the harbour. Mevagissey is the archetypal Cornish fishing village and has all facilities.

Week 5 - Day 6

OS Maps: **Landranger 204; Explorer 105 (western half); Explorer 107 (eastern half)**

	This Walk	Cumulative	This Walk	Cumulative	Grading	Timing
Ascent	2,434ft	70,947ft	742m	21,625m	Strenuous then easy	5 hours
Distance	10.5mi	371.6mi	17.1km	598.3km		

For detailed directions see our Mevagissey to Charlestown and Charlestown to Fowey Path Description booklets.

The western half of this Section has a relatively remote feel, enhanced by some quite strenuous climbs and some attractive cliffs and headlands. To the east the coastline is more urbanised but with beaches and the lovely Georgian docks of Charlestown found among the houses, golf courses and clay industry. The cliff-top path between Porthpean and Charlestown was reinstated in late 2011, avoiding two miles of road diversion.

Directions

There are bus routes from St Austell to Mevagissey, Charlestown and Par, one of these routes serving both the latter two locations, so that a range of bus-walks is possible.

The attractive fishing village of Mevagissey has all facilities. The Coast Path goes along the back of the harbour and then turns right along its eastern side before forking left steeply uphill. After crossing some playing fields, pass seaward of the houses then continue along the undulating cliffs to descend behind the ruined fish cellars at Portgiskey Cove. Continue uphill along the seaward and far field boundaries to a fenced path at the top. Turn right here, parallel to the road. At the entrance to Pentewan Sands Holiday Park follow the B3273 road pavement and turn first right before the petrol station, signposted to Pentewan. There are a few shops, toilets and a pub in the village. The official route then follows the road through Pentewan and up the hill for about 100 yards/90m, taking the first turn sharp right along The Terrace and along a narrow path at the end to arrive at the cliffs. A more interesting alternative turns right, away from the road into the harbour area just after the public toilets then, immediately after the last cottage, goes left steeply uphill, through gardens, to arrive at the official route on the cliffs.

After some 1.25 miles/2km the path descends through a wood and reaches a track. Turn right here to arrive at another track just behind the remote Hallane Mill Beach. Turn left here then quickly right, climbing back up the cliffs to arrive at Black Head. A diversion from the memorial stone goes to the tip of this atmospheric location. Continuing from Black Head the path enters Ropehaven Woods with some confusing paths - it is important to follow the waymarking. Entering the wood turn right down a rocky and sometimes slippery path, then left. Go left again onto a walled path, ignoring descending paths on the right, to arrive beside a cottage and emerge onto a track. Go right here then leave the road to the right just after a parking area and follow the cliff-top path down, up and down again to Porthpean. Walk along the promenade to the far end and climb the steps to rejoin the newly reinstated cliff-top path all the way to Charlestown.

Charlestown has a fascinating Georgian harbour, the home of a group of tall ships, and has refreshments, toilets, pubs and buses. Note that the official Coast Path does not cross the dock gate at the mouth of the harbour, though many people use that route. On the east side climb past the public toilets and on to reach a suburban road for a short way, soon forking off right over a long grassy area. Arriving at a large car park above Carlyon Bay Beach keep to seaward then cross the beach access road where a new resort is being developed and continue ahead on the low cliffs. Keep seaward of the golf course to approach the old china clay works at Par Docks. At the little beach at Spit Point turn inland and follow the narrow path past the works and then alongside a railway line to emerge on a road. Turn right along the pavement past the docks entrance and under a railway bridge. Turn right at the junction, signposted to Fowey, over a level crossing and then under another railway bridge before forking right on the road, Par Green.

Mevagissey Harbour

To continue beyond Par on the Coast Path, walk along Par Green, looking for house no.52 and follow the path signed on the right.

Par has all facilities, including a mainline railway station; for the station turn left at the far end of Par Green along Eastcliffe Road.

Pentewan Beach from Black Head

Week 6 - Day 1 (half day)

OS Maps: **Landranger 200 or 204; Explorer 107**

	This Walk	Cumulative	This Walk	Cumulative	Grading	Timing
Ascent	1,132ft	72,079ft	345m	21,970m	Moderate	3 hours
Distance	7.0mi	378.6mi	11.1km	609.4km		

For detailed directions see our Charlestown to Fowey Path Description booklet.

This Section goes out to the prominent Gribbin Head. The west side of the headland is relatively exposed, mostly on high cliffs, with views west over St Austell Bay. The east side is more indented and sheltered, the cliffs lower, and the path passes numerous scenic little sandy coves. At its eastern end the path enters the lovely part-wooded estuary of the River Fowey, culminating in the atmospheric little town of Fowey.

Directions

Par and Fowey are linked by a bus service, making this a bus-walk option. In addition, a popular local circular walk from Fowey takes in most of Gribbin Head, using the waymarked Saints' Way path with the Coast Path.

Par has all facilities, including a mainline railway station. For the Coast Path walk along the road called Par Green and follow the path which leaves the road next to no.52. After crossing the private clay haul road, fork right along a grassy path immediately before the chalet park. Follow this path before turning left then quickly right along the road to a small car park at the western end of the sands of Par Beach. Walk along the back of the beach to another car park at the far, eastern end. This is Polmear; a pub and buses are to be found on the road outside the car park.

The Coast Path crosses the car park to a footbridge and then up the cliffs and continues on to the little harbour village of Polkerris. Here are a pub, toilets and restaurant. The path continues from the back of the beach, up a ramp to join a zigzag path through woods to the top. The path now continues to the Daymark on Gribbin Head (or "The Gribbin"). The tower is open to visitors on some summer Sundays. From the Daymark follow the path downhill to the scenic cove at Polridmouth ("Pridmouth"), said to have inspired the setting for Daphne du Maurier's "Rebecca". Cross behind the beach and go up into the woods, then on over cliff-top fields and past a couple of small coves to arrive at another woodland. Look out for the path on the right, which goes past St Catherine's Castle and gives superb views upriver to Fowey. Now follow the path down a rocky track and behind Readymoney Cove before following the lane into Fowey.

Note that it is possible to walk Coast to Coast across Cornwall between Fowey and Padstow on the north coast using the Saints' Way. A guidebook is available from Fowey TIC.

Fowey, Readymoney Cove

Week 6 - Day 1 (half day)

OS Maps: Landranger 200 or 204 (Fowey); Landranger 201 (remainder); Explorer 107

	This Walk	Cumulative	This Walk	Cumulative	Grading	Timing
Ascent	1,939ft	74,018ft	591m	22,561m	Strenuous	3.5 hours
Distance	7.1mi	385.7mi	11.5km	620.9km		

For detailed directions see our Fowey to Polperro Path Description booklet.

This is a connoisseur's Section - it is quiet and remote; it is scenic, with beautiful large sandy bays and smaller coves plus impressive headlands; it is started and finished at superbly picturesque locations, the Fowey estuary at one end and Polperro at the other; and it is quite hard work, emphasising that nothing this good should come too easily.

Polruan looking up River Fowey

Directions

Polruan and Polperro are linked by a bus service, giving a bus-walk option, though unfortunately it does not operate at weekends. There is a popular scenic circular walk taking in Fowey and Polruan and using two ferries, an estuary tributary valley and the Coast Path.

Fowey is a charming little town, well worth exploring, with all facilities.

The crossing of the river to Polruan on the opposite bank is by foot ferry. In summer it usually operates from Whitehouse Quay, along the Esplanade, and in winter from the Town Quay.

The ferry operates all year except Christmas Day at 5-10 minute intervals, telephone 01726 870232.

For ferry details see page 19.

At Polruan, a picturesque little place, go up the steps next to The Lugger. Turn right at the top in West Street then turn left up Battery Lane. At the grassy area keep left by the wall then through the car park parallel to the coast to a signed path on the right. After around 2 miles/3km the path passes above and behind the impressive Lantic Bay, climbing steeply at the far end. There is a higher path here, going to the top of the hill and turning right, or a lower one, turning off right 30 yards/28m before the top, dropping then climbing again to meet the higher path (ignore beach turnings to the right). The path goes out around Pencarrow Head then behind an old watch house to descend and pass behind two charming and remote coves at Lansallos West and East Coombes. After climbing past a marker warning shipping of an offshore rock more ups and downs follow until the path approaches the almost hidden inlet of Polperro. Follow the waymarked path to arrive at a rocky outlook point - go left here then fork right to descend to the harbour. Polperro, an impossibly picturesque harbour village, figures justifiably in most picture books and calendars of Cornwall. It has all facilities.

Week 6 - Day 2 (half day)

OS Maps: **Landranger 201; Explorer 107**

	This Walk	Cumulative	This Walk	Cumulative	Grading	Timing
Ascent	774ft	74,792ft	236m	22,797m	Moderate	2.25 hours
Distance	5.0mi	390.7mi	8.0km	628.9km		

For detailed directions see our Polperro to Looe Path Description booklet.

The cliffs on this Section, never really lofty, tend to decrease in height towards the east. This is a relatively sheltered length passing around lush bays, while offshore, Looe Island is a seaward focal point from the eastern end. Here, also, extensive rocky platforms are exposed at low tide. These factors, and the popularity of Polperro and Looe, have made this a justifiably popular length of coast.

Directions

There is a bus route between Polperro and Looe, making a bus-walk a popular option here.

Looe Island from Hore Point

Polperro is a popular visitors' destination with all facilities. The Coast Path crosses the stone bridge behind the harbour then turns right along The Warren. Climb out of the village, keeping left at the first fork and right at the second, which leads to the War Memorial on its headland. The path turns left here to descend towards Talland Bay, turning right near the bottom down a steep track towards the beach. There are toilets and seasonal refreshments here. Pass behind the beach, going left then right by the public toilets and behind a second beach to a small car parking area. The path climbs back to the cliffs from here - keep well back from the crumbling edge. It then continues very clearly (ignore all turnings towards the beach) eventually arriving at the end of a suburban road at Hannafore, the western end of Looe. Continue along the road, or the lower promenade; there are toilets and seasonal refreshments along here. At the end a short stretch of road with no pavement turns alongside the mouth of the Looe River. Take steps down on the right to the riverside of West Looe. There is a seasonal and tidal ferry from here to East Looe, the main part of the town, as an option. Otherwise continue along the West Looe riverside and over the bridge, turning right into East Looe's main street. Looe has buses to Plymouth and a branch to the mainline railway at Liskeard - for the station turn left after the bridge. Between them, East and West Looe have all necessary facilities.

Week 6 - Day 2 (half day)

OS Maps: Landranger 201; Explorer 107 (western half); Explorer 108 (eastern half)

	This Walk	Cumulative	This Walk	Cumulative	Grading	Timing
Ascent	1,965ft	76,757ft	599m	23,396m	Strenuous, moderate in places	4.5 hours
Distance	7.6mi	398.3mi	12.2km	641.1km		

For detailed directions see our Looe to Portwrinkle Path Description booklet.

Quiet and relatively remote cliff lengths in the western and eastern parts of this Section are separated by a low-level, suburban length, or by an optional route via sea wall and beach between Seaton and Downderry. The western cliffs are covered in lush vegetation, scrub and woodland, and there are stretches where the sea is only glimpsed through the trees. The eastern cliffs are more open and give some superb views along the coast in both directions, with the distinctive Rame Head a focal point.

Directions

A bus service connects Seaton, Downderry and Portwrinkle, making a bus-walk option possible over the eastern end of this section. Further bus-walk options may be possible with a change of bus from Looe at Hessenford (inland from Looe).

From East Looe's town centre, turn up Castle Street and keep climbing until it becomes a footpath above the sea. Continue, then at a road turn right, passing Plaidy Beach, and continue until just after the road veers left inland. Here go right, up a steep tarmac path then ahead at the top until the road turns left. The Coast Path descends steps between houses to Millendreath Beach. There are refreshment facilities here - for details call 01503 263651. On the far side go up the cul-de-sac road and climb the sunken lane to reach another road. Large-scale cliff falls occurred here in early 2013 resulting in loss of the Coast Path. Follow the current signing until the route descends the road to Seaton Beach. Turn right and along the road behind the beach, where there are toilets and seasonal refreshments.

Although the official path follows the narrow and busy road up the hill to Downderry, if the tide is not high it is preferable to walk along the top of the sea wall from Seaton and then the beach, taking one of the choice of footpath links into Downderry, where there are pubs, shops, toilets and seasonal refreshments. Note that the most easterly link path shown on the OS map is currently closed. Follow the road to the eastern end of Downderry, where it turns inland, and take the signed path right, which zigzags steeply upward. A superbly scenic cliff- top path, with several ups and downs, continues until it arrives at a road just above Portwrinkle. Turn right to descend to the village and the quiet sea-front road. The Gook Cafe is open all year in Portwrinkle or other facilities are at Crafthole, a 10 minute walk uphill inland.

Looe River

Week 6 - Day 3

OS Maps: **Landranger 201; Explorer 108**

	This Walk	Cumulative	This Walk	Cumulative	Grading	Timing
Ascent	2,169ft	78,926ft	661m	24,057m	Moderate	5.75 hours
Distance	13.3mi	411.6mi	21.4km	662.5km		

For detailed directions see our Portwrinkle to Plymouth Path Description booklet.

This is a Section of great interest rather than spectacular drama. There is a golf course, a gunnery range, a cliff face of wooden chalets and an historic Country Park. It also includes the magnificent and atmospheric Rame Head, which is a significant landmark for many miles along the coast in both directions, the charming twin villages of Cawsand and Kingsand and some superb views, including Plymouth Sound and, indeed, the city itself.

Directions

A bus route links Cremyll to Cawsand, part-way along the section, and also runs along the coast road adjacent to the Coast Path between Rame Head and Tregantle, giving various bus-walk options. There are a number of popular circular walks using the Coast Path based on Mount Edgcumbe Country Park, next to Cremyll, and also around Rame Head.

From Portwrinkle walk up the road, past the first footpath, which is a cul-de-sac, then turn right on the signed path opposite the golf club. After climbing, the path goes along the seaward side of the golf course. After leaving the golf course the path begins to rise towards the Tregantle Firing Ranges. When firing is not taking place it is possible to walk an excellent, well-signed permissive path through the ranges. At the time of going to print non-firing weekends (Friday to Sunday inclusive)for 2014 had not been confirmed, but will normally alternate throughout the year starting with 3rd, 4th and 5th January. But please note that live firing may still take place on these weekends if operational requirements demand. In addition there is no live firing on Bank Holiday weekends nor on any day in August. Other non-firing days are known up to two weeks in advance - telephone Andy Westcott on 01637 857157 during office hours to check. If live firing is in progress red flags will be raised and the access gates locked - do not proceed into the range. If open, keep closely to the marked path and, at the far end of the range path, emerge through another security gate onto the National Trust's cliff-top path.

If the range path is closed, continue on the official Coast Path through a field to a road, where the path initially continues inside the hedge before joining the road further along. The road is usually quite busy so take care. There is the compensation of a magnificent view up the Tamar to Plymouth from the car parking area here, where there is often a refreshment van. Follow the road then turn right at the first road junction and continue along the road (past Tregantle Fort entrance) to the cliffs, near where the range path emerges.

Cawsand

The Coast Path is then off-road, along National Trust land, before it rejoins the road for about 1.25 miles/2km. The signed path then leaves the road again to descend onto the sloping cliff face, although this cliff length had to be closed in 2013 because of subsidence, the Coast Path continuing on the road. There is a cafe just off the path down the cliff at this point. If open, the path undulates quite steeply and meanders unexpectedly among chalets and gardens - keep alert for the waymarking - climbing back to the road. The route then descends gently across the cliff slope to Polhawn Cove at the base of Rame Head. After crossing a private access road for Polhawn Fort the path climbs to reach the headland. The official Coast Path route omits the very end, with its medieval chapel, but the easy climb is worthwhile for the views and the atmosphere.

A good cliff path then goes to Penlee Point, where there are the first views of Plymouth Sound. Bear left to reach a road then fork off to the right on the signed path through woods to descend to the charming little village of Cawsand, with pubs, toilets, shops and refreshments. Go through the village square to Garrett Street and continue, turning right in front of the Post Office having, imperceptibly, crossed into Kingsand. At The Cleave turn left then first right up Heavitree Road, which leads to a gate on the right into Mount Edgcumbe Country Park. Continue through the park to a road, turning right then almost immediately left, forking uphill through woods. After a woodland drive there is a waymarked diversion to avoid a cliff fall, the route climbing left to a higher level path before continuing parallel to the coast. Once around the fallen cliff the path descends to the foreshore of Plymouth Sound. Keep on the signed path up and through a deer gate then back down towards the shore to follow into an Italianate garden, past the Orangery of Mount Edgcumbe House (refreshments), and out through the park gates to the ferry point. Cremyll has a pub and toilets, but most will use it as the staging point for the ferry across the Tamar to Plymouth, an interesting excursion in its own right.

Week 6 - Day 4 (half day)

OS Maps: **Landranger 201; Explorer 108**

	This Walk	Cumulative	This Walk	Cumulative	Grading	Timing
Ascent	463ft	79,389ft	141m	24,198m	Easy	3.5 hours
Distance	7.5mi	419.1mi	12.0km	674.5km		

For detailed directions see our Plymouth to Wembury Path Description booklet.

This is an urban walk along the waterfront of one of the country's prime historical maritime cities. It is therefore quite different to the vast majority of the Coast Path, but is nevertheless well worth doing. The view over the Sound, flanked on both sides by cliffs, is inspiring, and often referred to as the finest urban vista in the country. Elsewhere are lengths of waterside industry, historic quays and modern marinas, making this a fascinating excursion.

Directions

A range of urban bus services runs throughout Plymouth, including to and from Admiral's Hard, the ferry point for Cremyll, and Mount Batten. Though not on the same route, they link in the city centre. There is also a ferry link across the mouth of the River Plym between the historic Sutton Harbour and Mount Batten. These links make a range of public transport-walks possible.

The Coast Path from Cremyll uses the ferry across the Tamar.

The ferry operates all year, weather, tide and other circumstances permitting, generally at 30 minute intervals. Telephone 01752 822105.

For ferry details see page 19.

Plymouth's Waterfront Walk is enhanced by a variety of information plaques and pieces of artwork relating to the city's history. A companion guidebook "Plymouth's Waterfront Walkway" is available free of charge from us, you will just pay postage.

Most of the route is waymarked by white bands on lamp-posts, red metal marker signs and pavement signs.

From the ferry walk up the road and turn right, going round the car park into Cremyll Street and on to the gates of the Royal William Yard. Enter the Yard via the walkway to the right of the main entrance and go through the Yard following the sea wall. (There is a ferry from the Royal William Yard to the Barbican that will also stop at Mount Batten on request for those who want a short cut.) At the far corner of the Yard's sea wall climb the Eric Wallis Memorial Steps to Devil's Point Park. Follow the path around the Park, overlooking Drake's Island and Plymouth Sound to reach the Artillery Tower, now a restaurant. At this point bear inland into Durnford Street and continue past the Royal Marines Barracks, turning right immediately after them. Continue along Millbay Road then, after the entrance to Millbay Docks, turn right into West Hoe Road. Fork right off here into Great Western Road, then bear off right down a narrow path along the shoreline. The path returns to the road; here turn right to walk along the Hoe promenade all the way to The Barbican and Sutton Harbour,

Plymouth's original harbour. Above on the left, away from the Coast Path but worth a visit, are the lighthouse of Smeaton's Tower, Drake's statue and other points of interest.

At The Barbican on the right are the Mayflower Steps, the site of the Pilgrim Fathers' embarkation. Adjacent is the ferry point for Mount Batten, an unofficial short cut direct to the end of the Section.

The ferry operates all year, telephone 07930 838614.

For ferry details see page 19.

Continuing on the Coast Path Waterfront Walk, walk across the lock gates at the entrance to Sutton Harbour, past the Marine Aquarium and then along Teat's Hill Road past the entrance to Queen Anne's Battery. At Breakwater Road, just after the entrance to Victoria Wharves, turn right up a narrow hill and footpath and down to the industrial Cattedown Wharf area. Continue past warehouses, then left along Shapters Way, right into Maxwell Road and along Finnigan Road to Laira Bridge. Turn right to cross the River Plym then, at the first roundabout, turn right (at the rhinoceros!) Go right, into Breakwater Road, and continue for about 500 yards/450m then turn left, still in Breakwater Road, to the entrance to Yacht Haven Quay Boatyard. To the left of a mesh fence is a path, signed as the Coast Path, which is followed to Oreston Quay. At the quay walk past the grassy area into Marine Road then left into Park Road. Turn left at the top of the hill, and this path descends to

Radford Lake. From here a Coast-to-Coast walk goes to Lynmouth on the north coast, following the Erme-Plym Trail and the Two Moors Way. Guidebooks are available at Ivybridge TIC.

Go across the causeway with its old mini castle folly and turn right. Follow the path along then left and at a junction turn right down Hexton Hill Road to Hooe Lake. Skirt the lake, going along Barton Road and then turn left on a path to Turnchapel. Go through the village, bearing left at the Clovelly Bay Inn, up the hill then turn right down steps to the marina and over the slipway and along the shoreline to Mount Batten and the Sutton Harbour ferry. There are toilets, refreshments and a pub here. The short walk along the breakwater is very popular, although not part of the Coast Path.

Eric Wallis Memorial steps at Royal William Yard

Week 6 - Day 4 (half day)

OS Maps: Landranger 201; Explorer OL20

	This Walk	Cumulative	This Walk	Cumulative	Grading	Timing
Ascent	1,260ft	80,649ft	384m	24,582m	Easy	3 hours
Distance	7.3mi	426.4mi	11.8km	686.3km		

For detailed directions see our Plymouth to Wembury Path Description booklet.

This is a Section of low cliffs, much of it overlooking Plymouth Sound. Below the cliffs are extensive areas of rock platform and offshore the Great Mew Stone becomes a focal point. Caravan and chalet sites and suburban villages are never far away and this is never a lonely Section. Towards its eastern end, as the cliffs rise somewhat, is the picturesque mouth of the River Yealm, forming a dramatic wooded gap in the cliffs.

Directions

Separate bus routes serve Mount Batten and Wembury village, and also Heybrook Bay, midway along this section, all from Plymouth city centre, allowing bus-walk options. There is a popular circular walk using the Coast Path between Wembury and Warren Point and a longer, full-day circular using the waymarked Erme-Plym Trail between Wembury and Mount Batten plus the Coast Path.

Mount Batten has toilets and refreshments, as well as a direct ferry link to and from Plymouth's Sutton Harbour. From Mount Batten the Coast Path heads over the little hill and past the old fort tower to the grassy area at Jennycliff, where there are more toilets and refreshments. Keep close above the shore and at the end of the grass enter woodland. There has been a landslip here, so there may be diversion signs up to the road, turning right for a short way along the road then back into the woods. The path then undulates and emerges above Fort Bovisand. Descend steeply to a road and turn left; there are seasonal refreshments here. Follow round to the right and up to pass seaward of the chalets, past a cafe and toilets and on round the point and so to Heybrook Bay. There is a pub a little way up the road here, as well as a bus stop. Keep right and follow the path above the shore around Wembury Point and on to Wembury Beach. Yet more toilets and refreshments await here and the bus stop, together with pub and shop, are in the village a little way inland.

From Wembury Beach a Coast-to-Coast walk goes to Lynmouth on the north coast, following the Erme-Plym Trail and the Two Moors Way. Guidebooks are available from Ivybridge TIC.

Continuing on the Coast Path, climb seaward of the church and along the now higher cliffs to a junction of paths at the Rocket House. The path going inland from here leads to Wembury village and its facilities. For the Coast Path, bear right, downhill, to reach the ferry point. Note that operating times on this ferry can be limited - see page 19 and Walk 49.

Wembury Beach towards Great Mew Stone

Week 6 - Day 5

OS Maps: **Landranger 201 (western end); Landranger 202 (remainder); Explorer OL20**

	This Walk	Cumulative	This Walk	Cumulative	Grading	Timing
Ascent	2,450ft	83,099ft	747m	25,329m	Easy then strenuous	5.75 hours
Distance	13.5mi	439.9mi	21.8km	708.1km		

For detailed directions see our Wembury (Warren Point) to Bigbury-on-Sea Path Description booklet.

This is a fine Section of high-level coastal cliffs, cut mid-way by the substantial and extremely picturesque estuary of the River Erme. The western end is a particularly good length, since the superb cliff coastline is easily accessed by a scenic former carriage route. Beyond that a series of descents and ascents, some quite steep, accentuate the dramatic landscape of the coastline. At the eastern extremity is the tidally insular Burgh Island, a focal point on this part of the coast. Because of its remoteness and strenuous nature, much of this section has a quiet character which will specially appeal to those in search of a lonely coastline.

Directions

This remote length of coast only has public transport at its western end, so no bus-walks are feasible. There is a very popular local walk using the Coast Path on the carriage drive from Noss Mayo.

The ferry at Wembury's Warren Point operates three ways over the River Yealm and its tributary Newton Creek. Warren Point is thus linked with both Newton Ferrers and Noss Mayo, and these two points with each other. For the Coast Path the link between Warren Point and Noss Mayo is needed.

The ferry operates seasonally and at limited times - telephone 01752 880079.

For ferry details see page 19.

There is a signal board to summon the ferryman by the steps at Warren Point or the slipway at Noss Mayo. Alternatively, telephone beforehand.

Because of the somewhat limited nature of the ferry it may be necessary to make alternative arrangements to reach Noss Mayo. Both Wembury and Noss Mayo have a regular bus service to and from Plymouth, so it is possible to use these services as a link, perhaps combining with an overnight stop in Plymouth. Alternatively, local taxi companies are available:-

Eco-Taxi, based in Kingsbridge, will carry walkers between Plymouth and Dartmouth and from all estuaries in South Devon; telephone 01548 856347 or 07811 385275. Ivy Cabs, telephone 01752 895555, will also carry walkers round the South Devon estuaries as will John Pitcher at Wembury Cabs, details page 103.

Week 6 - Day 5

Crossing the Erme during the Great South West Walk

It is also possible to walk round the Yealm Estuary from ferry point to ferry point. This is a distance of some 9 miles/14.5km, effectively adding an extra day or half day to the itinerary.

Walk around the Yealm Estuary

Walk uphill inland from the ferry steps to the house at the top, the Rocket House. Continue inland along the track, which in turn becomes a road. Where the road bears sharp right go ahead along a public footpath into a field, then keep ahead alongside a high wall. At the end of the wall, after two gates, bear left (bearing 330) across fields, then go down a few steps. The now enclosed path goes left then right to arrive at a road. This is Knighton, on the outskirts of Wembury. The bus stop for Plymouth is a little way to the left, just before the pub.

To continue the walking route around the estuary cross the road at Knighton to a minor lane, following it left to another junction. Turn right here and continue until the road meets another, more major, road. Cross this road, going ahead and left for a short way then turn right on a signed footpath. This is part of a waymarked route, the Erme-Plym Trail, and is shown on the OS Explorer OL20 map. Follow the waymarked route across fields, over Cofflete Creek, next to a lane and on to the village of Brixton. Turn right and follow the road through the village to Brixton Church then back on the Erme-Plym Trail up Old Road, along a suburban road, over fields, along a minor lane then over more fields to arrive at another village, Yealmpton. On reaching the A379 road at Yealmpton the Erme-Plym Trail is now abandoned. Here, turn right along the A379 then quickly left, into Stray Park. At the bottom bear right along a tarmac path then, when it arrives at a road, turn left along a stony track. At the footpath sign continue ahead, eventually emerging at a road by a car park. Turn left along the road to cross Puslinch Bridge then follow the road up the hill. Take the footpath on the right near the top of the hill, crossing a couple of fields to a road. Turn right and continue to meet a more major road, which is followed ahead to Newton Ferrers. At the edge of the village turn left down the road signed to Bridgend and Noss Mayo, and at the junction at the head of the creek keep to the right. Follow the riverside road, forking right into Noss Mayo. Keep on the road round Noss Creek and continue on the creekside road out of the village until this becomes a track. A signed path on the right leaves the track for the ferry point.

Coast Path, Noss Mayo-River Erme

From the ferry point, follow the path westward through the woods as it climbs to meet a track, an old carriage drive. The drive continues through woods, past a row of former coastguard cottages, into more woods, then on a superb cliff-face shelf round Mouthstone Point. Further on keep right where the more obvious path bears left inland to a car park, the drive continuing round Stoke Point and on to Beacon Hill. A series of ups and downs now ensues as the path approaches the estuary of the River Erme, which has been fairly described as England's most unspoiled river estuary, and is possibly the most attractive. The path crosses the top of a small beach then passes through a short woodland stretch to arrive at Mothecombe slipway on the Erme. There are seasonal refreshments a little way inland.

There is no ferry at the River Erme. It is usually possible to wade the river 1 hour either side of low water along the old ford and, under normal conditions, at low tide the water is about knee deep and the river bed is of sand with pebbles. The crossing is between grid references 614 476 and 620 478, ie the road by the row of coastguard cottages at Mothecombe and the end of the inland road to Wonwell Beach. However, great care should be taken as heavy rains or high seas can make conditions dangerous. Low water is approximately at the same time as at Devonport; see tide tables on pages 21-23.

If timing makes wading impossible there are local taxi companies Eco-Taxi telephone 01548 856347 or 07811 385275, or Ivy Cabs, telephone 01752 895555.

Alternatively, it is possible to walk round the estuary. There are no riverside rights of way and for the most part minor roads must be used. The distance is approximately 8 miles/13km, adding an extra half day to the itinerary.

Walk round the Erme Estuary

From the slipway follow the road inland, following signs to Holbeton. Go through the village and leave on the minor lane to Ford and then Hole Farm. At the sharp bend after this farm follow the waymarked Erme-Plym Trail to the A379 and across the River Erme at Sequer's Bridge. Then leave the waymarked trail, continuing very carefully along the A379 for a couple of hundred yards/metres, before turning right on the lane signed to Orcheton. Follow this for about 2 miles/3km then turn right, following signs for Wonwell Beach. Follow the lane downhill to arrive at the estuary.

Coast Path, River Erme-Bigbury-on-Sea

Just inland of the Wonwell slipway a path leaves the lane into the woods then continues above the shore, emerging on cliffs which rollercoaster up and down to the holiday park at Challaborough. Here are toilets and seasonal refreshments, and the path then soon reaches Bigbury-on-Sea. Here also are toilets and seasonal refreshments; the Bay View Cafe and Bistro will also supply packed lunches. On Burgh Island offshore, reached by walking across the sands or by unusual sea tractor, is a pub.

Week 6 - Day 6 (half day)

OS Maps: **Landranger 202; Explorer OL20**

	This Walk	Cumulative	This Walk	Cumulative	Grading	Timing
Ascent	876ft	83,975ft	267m	25,596m	Moderate	2.75 hours
Distance	5.7mi	445.6mi	9.2km	717.3km		

For detailed directions see our Bigbury-on-Sea to Salcombe Path Description booklet.

This is a well-used and popular Section, never far from residential and holiday accommodation. It is a length of low cliffs and sandy beaches, the coastline providing some interesting seascapes. These include views of the tidal Burgh Island, the estuary of the River Avon, the distinctive holed Thurlestone Rock and the headland of Bolt Tail. At the end of the Section, Hope Cove is a charming little settlement with a picturesque harbour and an old centre of historic cottages.

Directions

A regular, if infrequent, bus service links Thurlestone and Hope Cove, making a bus-walk option possible. There is a popular short circular walk using the Coast Path between Bantham and Thurlestone.

From the main facilities at Bigbury-on-Sea the Coast Path goes along the road, turning right immediately after the car park entrance to follow a short cliff-top length which re-joins the road further up. Cross the road and follow the path along the field edge next to the road. Leave the field where signed and cross the road, passing through Folly Farm and down the cliffs to the flat open area of Cockleridge Ham. At the edge is the ferry point for the crossing of the mouth of the River Avon.

The ferry is seasonal and operates at limited times - telephone 01548 561196. For ferry details see page 20.

The ferryman is alerted by waving. It must be noted that if the ferry is not operating on arrival the river should NOT be forded, despite its sometimes benign appearance. There are local taxi services, ie: Eco-Taxi, telephone 01548 856347 or 07811 385275; or Ivy Cabs, telephone 01752 895555.

Alternatively, there is a waymarked walk round the estuary between Bigbury-on-Sea and Bantham on the opposite bank. This route, the Avon Estuary Walk, is signed with blue waymarks and adds about 8 miles/13km to the route, or another half day to the itinerary. The route is shown on OS Explorer map OL20.

Avon Estuary Walk

The route is accessed by continuing up the road, without turning into Folly Farm, for a further 60 yards/55m and then turning right. The path reaches the golf course, turning left on a track then off this to the right, down another track past Hexdown Farm. Follow this track to the bottom then go left along a drive which eventually arrives at a road. There is a permissive path alongside the road and at the end of this a path goes right over a field, through the top of a wood then downhill over another field to a road alongside the estuary. This tidal road is then followed to Aveton Gifford on the A379. At high tide there is a waymarked diversion which crosses the tidal road on arriving at it and re-joins it next to the village. From Aveton Gifford cross the Avon on the A379 then take the first lane on the right, which becomes a track and continues to Stadbury Farm. Bear left approaching the farm onto a footpath, following field edges towards the valley bottom to cross Stiddicombe Creek. Enter the wood on the right and climb to leave at the far top corner. Follow the top edge of fields then cross a farm track and a stream to a junction of paths. Turn right and continue to Bantham village, where there is a pub, shop, toilets and seasonal refreshments as well as the ferry point.

Coast Path, Bantham-Hope Cove

From the ferry point go through the car park and round the edge of the dunes of Bantham Ham. Follow the shore, leaving the dunes and climbing past the edge of Thurlestone Golf Club to descend to Thurlestone Sands. Cross a long footbridge at an inland lagoon (South Milton Ley), pass public toilets and seasonal refreshments then join a road for a short stretch before turning back to the shoreline and over low cliffs to Outer Hope, where there are all facilities in season. Follow the path behind the little harbour and down to the old lifeboat station at Inner Hope, where the bus stop is situated. Buses to Kingsbridge leave from here. A little inland is the old village centre of Inner Hope, at The Square, a picture-postcard location worth seeing before leaving.

Bantham Boathouse

Week 6 - Day 6 (half day)

OS Maps: **Landranger 202; Explorer OL20**

	This Walk	Cumulative	This Walk	Cumulative	Grading	Timing
Ascent	1,506ft	85,481ft	459m	26,055m	Strenuous	4 hours
Distance	8.0mi	453.6mi	12.9km	730.2km		

For detailed directions see our Bigbury-on-Sea to Salcombe Path Description booklet.

This is a very scenic Section of the coast, largely comprising quite spectacular high cliffs soaring above tiny, mostly inaccessible coves. Near both ends are dramatic headlands, Bolt Tail in the west and Bolt Head in the east, offering superb coastal views in their respective directions. At the eastern end this Section turns into the mouth of the estuary of Salcombe Harbour, and there is the contrast of softer, sandy bays. This is a length which is never really remote, but never really busy.

Directions

Separate bus routes serve Hope Cove and Salcombe from Kingsbridge, a few miles inland, making a bus-walk feasible from there. However, there are numerous popular local circuits using the Coast Path which are based on Hope Cove and Salcombe.

Leave Hope Cove from the old lifeboat station at Inner Hope up the signed Coast Path and out to the magnificent viewpoint of Bolt Tail, where the ramparts of an Iron Age cliff fort are crossed to reach the end. The path doubles back along the cliff top over Bolberry Down and then down to the splendid little Soar Mill Cove. Climbing from the cove a long level stretch of easy walking follows. Keep along the cliff top and as the path approaches Bolt Head pass through a couple of gates, staying on the closest path to the cliff top as possible. A steep descent will then lead to the headland, where a sharp turn leads to the cliff-face path round Starehole Bay and then on to the Courtenay Walk below rocky pinnacles. Passing into woodland at the National Trust's Overbecks property the path joins a road which is followed past South Sands and North Sands - toilets and seasonal refreshments at both - and then on into Salcombe town centre. For a variation, there is a summer ferry service between South Sands and Salcombe. The town is a renowned yachting centre and has all facilities.

Looking back to Soar Mill Cove

Week 6 - Day 7

OS Maps: **Landranger 202; Explorer OL20**

	This Walk	Cumulative	This Walk	Cumulative	Grading	Timing
Ascent	2,251ft	87,732ft	686m	26,741m	Strenuous	6.75 hours
Distance	12.9mi	466.5mi	20.8km	751.0km		

For detailed directions see our Salcombe to Torcross Path Description booklet.

This is a superb Section of walking. Part of it is on exposed cliff faces, the sometimes stark cliffs contrasting with numerous tiny sandy coves below. A significant length in the middle is on an old "raised beach", a low shelf a little above the sea giving an easy passage here. In the east the path crosses the rocky spine of Start Point, behind its lighthouse, a dramatic stretch, before following a lush, sheltered length into Torcross.

Directions

Salcombe and Torcross are both on regular bus routes to and from Kingsbridge, a little inland, making a bus-walk possible from that town. There is also a popular local circuit using the Coast Path from the Salcombe Ferry.

Salcombe has all necessary facilities. The ferry across the estuary leaves from steps next to the Ferry Hotel, a little way downstream from the town centre.

The ferry operates all year; telephone 01548 842061 or 01548 560558.

For ferry details see page 20.

From the ferry point on the eastern side, where there are toilets and refreshments, the Coast Path follows the road down the estuary side then, after crossing the rear of the beach at Mill Bay (toilets), passes the refreshment facilities at Gara Rock (call 01548 844810 for details), then follows a clear cliff path to Prawle Point. The path goes to the Coastwatch lookout at the very end, then descends to follow the "raised beach" shelf just above the waves before a short inland length to avoid a cliff fall leads to Lannacombe Beach. Beyond here a dramatic length goes along and up to the rocky ridge leading to Start Point, the path dropping to the lighthouse access road. From the car park at the top the path bears off right down the cliff face to Hallsands, passing above the old ruined village. A short diversion to the viewpoint is both instructive and interesting.

The path continues over low cliffs to Beesands, where there is a pub, toilets and seasonal refreshments. Continue along the shingle ridge then behind an old quarry to descend into Torcross, with a panoramic view of Slapton Ley ahead on the descent. Torcross has all facilities, and buses to Plymouth, Kingsbridge and Dartmouth.

Gara Rock Lookout

Week 7 - Day 1

OS Maps: **Landranger 202; Explorer OL20**

	This Walk	Cumulative	This Walk	Cumulative	Grading	Timing
Ascent	1,493ft	89,225ft	455m	27,196m	Easy then strenuous	4.75 hours
Distance	10.2mi	476.7mi	16.4km	767.4km		

For detailed directions see our Torcross to Dartmouth Path Description booklet.

Something like a quarter of this Section consists of the low shingle ridge known locally as the Slapton Line, cutting off the freshwater lake of Slapton Ley from the sea. Most of the remainder of the Section is cliffs and coves, partly looking to the sea and partly to the outer reaches of the picturesque wooded Dart Estuary. This Section has some lengths a little more inland than is usual and some road lengths, one of which is frankly unpleasant, but in compensation there are also some splendid stretches.

Directions

A regular bus service runs along the coast road which is, for much of the Section, adjacent to the Coast Path. With stops at most obvious locations this gives numerous bus-walk options. There is also a very popular and scenic circular walk using the Coast Path between Dartmouth and the mouth of the Dart Estuary.

Torcross & Slapton Sands

From Torcross, with all facilities, the Coast Path runs along the shingle ridge. The official route is on the landward side but it is possible, if more tiring, to walk along the seaward side. At the end, Strete Gate, follow the narrow lane uphill to reach the A379 road. It is now necessary to walk along this and for the next 400 yards/365m **THE NEED FOR CAUTION ON THIS BUSY, NARROW AND DANGEROUS ROAD CANNOT BE OVERESTIMATED.**

Follow the main road through Strete village (pub and shop) then, just after the village end, take the path to the right which passes over fields and a footbridge to reach a high point above the sea. Continuing parallel to the coast for a while it then heads inland over a deep valley, crossing the main road and over more fields to a lane. Descend the lane then leave it across more fields until, after crossing the main road again, the picturesque cove of Blackpool Sands is reached. There are toilets and seasonal refreshments. Follow the path uphill through the woods then the route enters and meanders along various paths in the village of Stoke Fleming (pub, shop and toilets), arriving at the village hall. Cross the main road again and follow a lane to a National Trust car park. From here a scenic cliff path proceeds, latterly through woods, to reach the Dart Estuary and arrive at Dartmouth Castle. An estuary-side path passes the adjacent church and joins the road which is followed into the town. Look out for some steps on the right just after the public toilets before reaching the centre; the steps lead down to Bayards Cove through its little castle and on to the Embankment at the town centre. Dartmouth, of course, has all facilities.

Week 7 - Day 2

OS Maps: Landranger 202; Explorer OL20

	This Walk	Cumulative	This Walk	Cumulative	Grading	Timing
Ascent	2,992ft	92,217ft	912m	28,108m	Strenuous	5.75 hours
Distance	10.8mi	487.5mi	17.3km	784.7km		

For detailed directions see our Dartmouth to Brixham Path Description booklet.

This is a Section of superb cliff scenery, tough going in places and often quite lonely. In the west, near the mouth of the Dart, are substantial wooded areas but further along the cliffs become higher and more open. This makes for a dramatic, steeply undulating landscape ending at the sea in steep cliff faces.

Directions

A regular bus service links Brixham and Kingswear, on the east side of the Dartmouth Ferry, making a bus-walk possible. There is also a popular circuit using the Coast Path based on Kingswear.

Walkers have two ferry options from Dartmouth town centre to cross the river, the Lower Car Ferry, which also carries foot passengers, and the Dartmouth Passenger Ferry.

The Lower Car Ferry operates all year on a continuous service telephone 01803 752342.

The Dartmouth Passenger Ferry also operates all year on a continuous service telephone 01803 555872.

For ferry details see page 20.

From either ferry landing point in Kingswear cross the road and pass through an arch to ascend Alma Steps. Turn right along Beacon Road and continue out of the village. After some 1.25 miles/2km turn right down steps and undulate sometimes steeply into and through woodland to the old Battery buildings at Froward Point. Here the path descends steeply to the right from the corner of an old lookout building, passing World War II searchlight and gun positions before continuing along the cliffs. Pass Pudcombe Cove, by the National Trust Coleton Fishacre Gardens, and then on over Scabbacombe Head and past Scabbacombe Sands and Man Sands and over Southdown Cliff to Sharkham Point - this is a particularly strenuous length. Passing holiday accommodation the path arrives at Berry Head, a Napoleonic fortified area. Divert to the end of the headland to see the unusually squat lighthouse. Berry Head has toilets and seasonal refreshments. From here descend past an old quarry to a road, where there are further refreshment facilities at the Guard House Cafe (01803 855778). Turn right then go right again through the Shoalstone Car Park and along above the shoreline, returning to the road before descending steps to Brixham Breakwater. Follow the promenade to the harbour. Brixham has all facilities.

55 • Brixham to Torquay to Babbacombe

Week 7 - Day 3

OS Maps: Landranger 202: Explorer OL20 (western half); Explorer 110 (eastern half)

	This Walk	Cumulative	This Walk	Cumulative	Grading	Timing
Ascent	1,972ft	94,189ft	601m	28,709m	Moderate	6 hours
Distance	12.8mi	500.3mi	20.5km	805.2km		

For detailed directions see our Brixham to Torquay and Torquay to Shaldon Path Description booklets.

This is mostly an urban Section, passing along the shoreline of the "English Riviera", or Tor Bay. There is a mixture of grand terraces, open green parkland, amusement parks and the elegant white buildings overlooking the sea at Torquay. At the western end there is also the old fishing town of Brixham and at the other end the almost rural wooded cliffs around Babbacombe. All in all, this is a surprisingly diverse Section.

Directions

A range of bus routes runs throughout the Torbay area, including one which follows the coast road between Brixham and Torquay, and another linking Torquay to Babbacombe. As a result, a wide variety of bus-walks is possible.

Leaving Brixham by the fish market, the Coast Path initially passes a car park and gardens before passing two small coves and climbing into woodland which takes the path to Elberry Cove. From here it passes behind the sweep of Broadsands, climbing by the railway viaduct at the far end to proceed alongside the steam railway line to the promenade at Goodrington. At the far end climb through ornamental gardens and go down a road to Paignton Harbour and so along the promenade. Paignton's railway station is inland of the pier. Turn inland at Hollicombe, at the far end of Preston Sands, going through a park to the main sea-front road which is followed to Torquay Harbour. Torquay Station is inland a little before the harbour.

Cross the pedestrian bridge across the harbour and climb the hill, turning right at the Imperial Hotel on the signed path which leads to the open area at Daddyhole Plain. Descend to the sea-front road at Meadfoot Beach, climbing again at Ilsham Marine Drive. Take the cliff path round Thatcher Point to Hope's Nose. A cul-de-sac path goes to the end of this low headland.

From Hope's Nose follow the path inland of the road, crossing the road to the Bishop's Walk, which in turn arrives at a car park above Anstey's Cove. The path now goes round the edge of the grassy downs on Walls Hill, bearing off right to descend to Babbacombe Beach. Cross a wooden footbridge to Oddicombe Beach then climb by the cliff railway to reach Babbacombe's facilities at the top.

The Old Bathing House at Elberry Cove

Week 7 - Day 4 (half day)

OS Maps: Landranger 202; Explorer 110

	This Walk	Cumulative	This Walk	Cumulative	Grading	Timing
Ascent	2,090ft	96,279ft	637m	29,346m	Strenuous	3.75 hours
Distance	6.4mi	506.7mi	10.3km	815.5km		

For detailed directions see our Torquay to Shaldon Path Description booklet.

This is a tough Section of almost constant ups and downs. The characteristic red cliffs of this part of Devon are often quite high and quite sheer, though unfortunately the terrain is such that sea and cliff views are perhaps less frequent than would be wished. Its strenuous nature makes it a relatively quiet Section, except for the two ends, although it is never far from roads or housing.

Directions

A regular bus service links Babbacombe and Teignmouth, making a bus-walk an option.

From Babbacombe, a pleasant suburb of Torquay with all facilities, the Coast Path descends next to the cliff railway and then soon climbs again to avoid a cliff fall. This diversion takes the path up a grassy area to a main road where it turns right, then right again into Petitor Road.

Shaldon Ferry

At the bottom turn left on the Coast Path again, which soon descends onto a cliff face before reaching the wooded valley at Watcombe. Cross the track running down the valley and on through a wooded length to a short rocky stretch, turning right at a junction before reaching the car park at Maidencombe. There is a pub and toilets here. Turn right after the car park and keep on the rollercoaster path which eventually climbs to go alongside the coast road, then quickly leaves it to pass alongside fields to a track. Turn right and go round the wooded Ness headland, with super views ahead, descending to the promenade at Shaldon, on the estuary of the River Teign.

The ferry service across the River Teign operates throughout the year, weather permitting - telephone 01626 215617; ferry mobile 07896 711822.

For ferry details see page 20.

Walk, Shaldon-Teignmouth

If the ferry is not operating, continue inland along the riverside roads to Shaldon Bridge and cross the Teign. On the Teignmouth side turn right into Milford Park, through Bitton Sports Ground into Park Hill, cross into Bitton Avenue then into Clay Lane and right into Willow Street. At the end bear left then right into Quay Road, then right to go along the Strand and right to the Harbour Beach and the ferry point. Teignmouth has all facilities, including a mainline rail station and buses to Exeter.

Week 7 - Day 4 (half day)

OS Maps: **Landranger 192; Explorer 110**

	This Walk	Cumulative	This Walk	Cumulative	Grading	Timing
Ascent	488ft	96,767ft	149m	29,495m	Easy	3 hours
Distance	7.9mi	514.6mi	12.7km	828.2km		

For detailed directions see our Shaldon to Exmouth Path Description booklet.

This Section primarily comprises two fairly large seaside towns, flanked by a coastline of high red cliffs at one end and marshes and a sand bar at the other. Running through it, often next to the Coast Path, is possibly the most scenic part of Brunel's GWR railway line, the embankment of which forms the sea wall for much of this length. This is a busy, largely urban and much used Section with an historic importance to the tourist trade.

Directions

A regular bus service links Teignmouth and Starcross, the ferry point for Exmouth, and also passes through Dawlish and Dawlish Warren. As there are also stations on the railway line at these places, bus or train-walks are options here.

From the ferry point at Teignmouth, or from the town centre, go to the car park at The Point, jutting out into the Teign Estuary, and begin by walking along the promenade. Leaving the town the Coast Path continues between railway and sea below the red cliffs to the end, where it descends steps to pass under the railway and then up Smugglers Lane to the A379 road at the top.

High water route, Teignmouth-Smugglers Lane

With a high sea and an onshore wind the far end of the promenade can become very wet, and for about an hour either side of high tide the steps at Smugglers Lane become impassable. In these cases, immediately after leaving the town fork left and cross the railway on a footbridge on Eastcliff Walk, and this path eventually reaches the A379 which is then followed ahead to meet the official path at the top of Smugglers Lane.

Coast Path, Smugglers Lane-Dawlish Warren

Use the footway on the inland side of the A379 and walk for about 150 yards/135m before turning right into Windward Lane, going immediately left on a path which skirts fields before returning to the A379. Bear right into Old Teignmouth Road, which in turn returns to the A379 then, very soon, turn right by some railings on a path which zigzags down to the shoreline. Follow the sea wall through Dawlish, past the station - all facilities are found beyond the railway here. The best route is then to continue on the sea wall between railway and sea, again below the red cliffs, to Dawlish Warren. Just before the amusement area cross the obvious railway footbridge to a car park, turn right and follow to the main road.

High water route, Dawlish-Dawlish Warren

At high tides the sea wall becomes impassable between Dawlish and Dawlish Warren. In this case, go under the railway at Dawlish station to the station forecourt, turning left here up a narrow path then through an arch and up some steps. Continue past a housing area then through more arches to arrive at the A379. Continue ahead then right on the road signed to Dawlish Warren then immediately right again along a signed footpath which leads to Dawlish Warren and to join the more coastal path here.

Coast Path, Dawlish Warren-Starcross

The Coast Path does not go around the large sand spit at Dawlish Warren itself, jutting out into the mouth of the River Exe, or the marshes behind it, but if there is time this can be an exhilarating experience. Otherwise continue along Warren Road on the pavement, then opposite the entrance to Dawlish Warren Sandy Park join the cycleway and footpath to Cockwood Harbour. After following the road around the harbour join the A379. Cross the road and follow the footpath and cycleway to Starcross, and the ferry point to Exmouth. Starcross has all facilities.

The ferry operates mid-April - end October, telephone 01626 862452 or 07974 022536.

For ferry details see page 20.

If there is no ferry operating on arrival at Starcross, there are several options to reach Exmouth.

Option 1: Explorer Water Taxi - this runs daily 1st April until 31st October. Check their web site before travelling as times vary: www.exeplorerwatertaxis.co.uk

Option 2: Bus or train from Starcross to Exeter, bus or train from Exeter to Exmouth.

Option 3: Walk from Starcross to Turf Lock following the waymarked Exe Valley Way on the riverside road and footpath (3 miles/5km), then ferry Turf Lock-Topsham and bus or train from Topsham to Exmouth.

Ferry operates seasonally - telephone 07778 370582.

For ferry details see page 20.

Option 4: Walk from Starcross to Topsham Lock following the waymarked Exe Valley Way on the riverside road and footpath and Exeter Canal towpath (4.5 miles/7km), then ferry Topsham Lock-Topsham and bus or train from Topsham to Exmouth.

Ferry operates seasonally - telephone 01392 274306 (office) or 07801 203338 (ferryman).

For ferry details see page 20.

Dawlish from above

Week 7 - Day 5 (half day)

OS Maps: **Landranger 192; Explorer 115**

	This Walk	Cumulative	This Walk	Cumulative	Grading	Timing
Ascent	722ft	97,489ft	220m	29,715m	Moderate	3 hours
Distance	6.2mi	520.8mi	9.9km	838.1km		

For detailed directions see our Exmouth to Sidmouth Path Description booklet.

This is a well-used and popular Section, never far from houses and passing a large caravan site and a golf course on the way. Most of this length is on relatively low cliffs, and in the west these give excellent views over the mouth of the Exe and the great sandy bar of Dawlish Warren. Further east, the high point of West Down Beacon gives exceptionally fine panoramic views, while beyond the Beacon the path becomes more enclosed. It is an easy-going Section of some variety, ideal for those not wishing to explore remote or strenuous lengths.

Directions

A regular bus service links Exmouth and Budleigh Salterton, making this a good bus-walk option. In addition, a summer service links Exmouth with Sandy Bay, approximately mid-way along the section, giving another, shorter bus-walk.

Exmouth has all facilities, including a railway station on a branch line from Exeter. The obvious route for the Coast Path is to walk along the promenade from the former, now redeveloped, docks area at the mouth of the Exe, which is also the ferry landing point. Continue to the cliffs at Orcombe Point then climb the steps and continue on the cliff top, passing the Jurassic Coast marker and on to the Devon Cliffs Caravan Site at Sandy Bay. Follow the fence line inland of the Straight Point rifle range then climb to the high point at West Down Beacon. The path then descends steadily, seaward of the golf course though offering relatively few sea views on this stretch. Approaching Budleigh Salterton, a charming and traditional small town, the path turns inland then almost immediately, at a junction, goes right to descend to the end of the promenade. The shops, pubs and other facilities are immediately inland of the path, which continues towards the distinctive line of pine trees to the east of the town.

Exmouth, Sea front in winter

Week 7 - Day 5 (half day)

OS Maps: **Landranger 192; Explorer 115**

	This Walk	Cumulative	This Walk	Cumulative	Grading	Timing
Ascent	1,037ft	98,526ft	316m	30,031m	Moderate then strenuous	3.5 hours
Distance	6.9mi	527.7mi	11.1km	849.2km		

For detailed directions see our Exmouth to Sidmouth Path Description booklet.

This pleasant Section is mostly on relatively low red cliffs with attractive views inland over an undulating pastoral countryside as well as to seaward. However, there are contrasts at both ends. The western end skirts the narrow, marsh-fringed estuary of the River Otter while the eastern end includes a wooded cliff top and high cliffs on the appropriately named High Peak and Peak Hill. This is a pleasant and quietly popular Section.

Directions

A regular bus service links Budleigh Salterton and Sidmouth, making a bus-walk a possibility.

Budleigh Salterton, a town with something of an olde-world air, has all facilities. The Coast Path goes along the promenade to the car park at the eastern end. Progress east seems tantalisingly close, but the River Otter, with no bridge at its mouth, bars the way. The path therefore passes through a gate at the rear riverside corner of the car park and follows the riverside path until it meets a road. Turn right and cross the River Otter on the road bridge, then bear right to follow the path back downriver to the sea, bearing round to the left on reaching the cliffs.

The path is clear to the caravan site at Ladram Bay, where there are toilets and seasonal refreshments. Here, descend across a field to the beach access track, going left then immediately right, past a pub and on to climb into woodland at High Peak. Here, the path goes behind the very top, emerging on a track. Turn right and climb again to the open land at Peak Hill. Follow the path down the cliff through woodland to a road, turn right then keep right along an old road length then onto a large grassy area down to a zigzag path next to the white Jacob's Ladder. At the bottom follow the seafront path to reach the main esplanade. Sidmouth is an elegant Regency town and has all facilities.

Ladram Stacks

Week 7 - Day 6

OS Maps: Landranger 192; Explorer 115 (most); Explorer 116 (eastern end)

	This Walk	Cumulative	This Walk	Cumulative	Grading	Timing
Ascent	2,408ft	100,934ft	734m	30,765m	Severe then strenuous	5.5 hours
Distance	10.4mi	538.1mi	16.7km	865.9km		

For detailed directions see our Sidmouth to Lyme Regis Path Description booklet.

This is a Section of lofty cliffs cut by deep and narrow valleys, making for a magnificent coastal landscape but a testing one to walk. In the west the cliffs are characteristically red, but this changes quite abruptly along the length as the Section reaches the most westerly chalk cliffs in England, appropriately bright white. Add an elegant Regency town, a charming picture-postcard village and a picturesque fishing town and the result is a length of great attraction.

Directions

A regular bus service links Sidmouth with Seaton, making a bus-walk an option. There are also regular, if less frequent, bus links to Branscombe and Beer, along the length, giving further options.

The Coast Path passes along the elegant esplanade at Sidmouth to the footbridge over the mouth of the River Sid at the eastern end. Some dramatic cliff falls have occurred just east of Sidmouth and a well-signed diversion is necessary past housing until, at the top of Laskeys Lane, it turns back to the cliff top. A steep climb up Salcombe Hill is soon followed by an equally steep descent and climb through the Salcombe Regis valley. The path skirts behind the hollow of Lincombe then descends to the beach at Weston Mouth. A short way along the beach the path leaves to climb steeply back to the cliffs and a good level stretch which eventually turns inland to meet a track. This descends to Branscombe Mouth, where there are refreshments and toilets. Beyond Branscombe the official path passes among some holiday chalets then along an undercliff path, with the cliffs rearing massively above, before climbing to the cliff top at Beer Head. These are the most westerly chalk cliffs in England. An alternative route from Branscombe Mouth climbs up the valley side and proceeds directly along the cliff top to Beer Head.

Follow the signed path from Beer Head, past a caravan site and into the village behind the beach. Beer, an attractive fishing village, has all facilities. Climb the path on the east side of the beach to the cliff top, descending to a road and down to Seaton Hole. If the tide is low, walk along the beach to the end of the promenade at Seaton. If not, an inland diversion must now be taken. A cliff fall caused by the extreme wet weather in 2012 has created a very large hole in Old Beer Road, necessitating permanent closure of the previous Coast Path route. At Seaton Hole one must now turn left on to Old Beer Road and walk approximately 330 yards/300m inland towards Beer. At the junction with the B3172 Beer Road, turn right towards Seaton. After approximately 1,100yards/1km, leave the Beer Road and take the path on the right through the chine and on to the promenade and so into Seaton, which has all facilities, including bus services to Exeter, Weymouth and Poole.

Week 8 - Day 1 (half day)

OS Maps: **Landranger 193; Explorer 116**

	This Walk	Cumulative	This Walk	Cumulative	Grading	Timing
Ascent	1,401ft	102,335ft	427m	31,192m	Moderate	3.5 hours
Distance	6.8mi	544.9mi	11.0km	876.9km		

For detailed directions see our Sidmouth to Lyme Regis Path Description booklet.

Most of this Section is unlike any other on the Coast Path. The western end crosses a golf course and there is a short length of cliff, but the majority of the Section passes through the National Nature Reserve of the Axmouth-Lyme Regis Undercliffs. Except for the path, this area has been undisturbed since the massive cliff fall which formed it in 1839. It is effectively a wilderness area of virtually virgin woodland and dense scrub, with an almost eerie character. For most of this length the sea will not be visible. It is an odd and impressive experience, delighting some but frustrating others.

Directions

A regular bus service links Seaton and Lyme Regis, making a bus-walk possible.

Seaton has all facilities, and has links to the railway network at Exeter and Weymouth. Leave Seaton at the east end, using the old concrete bridge to cross the River Axe. Turn inland along the road then turn right up the golf course access road, past the club house then due east over the fairway to the end of a lane. Turn right off the lane to reach the cliffs, and the path then enters the strange world of the Undercliffs.

This old landslip is a National Nature Reserve, being an area of virtual wildlife wilderness. The path through the Undercliff rarely offers sea views and can feel claustrophobic in places. There are no escape routes to the coast road inland nor safe paths to the sea shore. However, the route is well waymarked and the maps on the Natural England display boards show walkers their exact location: no one should ever feel lost. Eventually the path emerges on cliffs and is then waymarked down through woods to arrive adjacent to Lyme Regis's scenic harbour, The Cobb. Lyme Regis is a charming and attractive town and has all facilities.

Beer Head, section 60

Week 8 - Day 1 (half day)

OS Maps: **Landranger 193; Explorer 116**

	This Walk	Cumulative	This Walk	Cumulative	Grading	Timing
Ascent	1,883ft	104,218ft	574m	31,766m	Moderate then strenuous	3 hours
Distance	6.7mi	551.6mi	10.9km	887.8km		

For detailed directions see our Lyme Regis to West Bay Path Description booklet.

A major feature of this Section is the large number of cliff slippages caused by a combination of wet weather and geology. This means that as things currently stand there is effectively no proper coastal path between Lyme Regis and Charmouth (approximately 3 miles/4.5km), nor, indeed, immediately east of Charmouth. However, the remainder of this Section is a superb coastal experience, climbing as it does over the top of Golden Cap, the highest point on the entire south coast of England, with views to match as well as an energy requirement of a high level!

Directions

A regular bus service which could be used as a basis for a bus-walk links Lyme Regis, Charmouth and Chideock, which is about 0.75 mile/1.25km inland of Seatown.

Major diversions have had to be put in place in this Section, especially between Lyme Regis and Charmouth, to avoid the considerable cliff falls that have occurred. It looks likely that these diversions will remain in place for 2014. However, for up-to-date details check the Association's website (www.swcp.org.uk).

Lyme Regis is a charming and attractive town with all facilities. From the town centre the Coast Path follows Church Street and Charmouth Road (A3052) as far as Lyme Regis Football Club on the right, beyond which there is a gate at the corner of a lane to a footpath across fields to a lane where the route turns left for 100 yards/90m. Turn right at a sign up through woods and near the top is a path junction.

Official Coastal Route, Lyme Regis-Charmouth

If an official route is in place, and this is highly unlikely for 2014, turn right onto a path that runs between the cliff edge and the golf course. Take the track downhill to Charmouth and at the first junction (with Old Lyme Hill) turn sharp right to follow the signposted route back to the cliff edge. The old alternative route along the beach is also closed following a landslide.

Official Diversion, Lyme Regis-Charmouth

Dorset County Council have installed and waymarked their official diversion. At the path junction in the wood (at GR 3456 9330) turn left for 130 yards/120m to meet Timber Hill. Turn right here to join in some 440 yards/400m the A3052 road and continue on this for 110 yards/100m. Turn eastwards on a public footpath signposted to Fern Hill, crossing the golf course then north-east through woods to re-join the A3052. Turn right to the roundabout with the A35 and fork right, signposted to Charmouth, following the road into the village for 760 yards/700m. At the second road junction turn right into Higher Sea Lane. When the road bends right take a footpath south-east and continue for about 650 yards/600m to re-join the official Coast Path at GR3640 9305.

Official Diversion, Charmouth West

If the official route from Lyme Regis to the edge of Charmouth is in place, there may still be the necessity for a diversion at the western end of Charmouth. This will take the route from the west end of Old Lyme Hill north-eastwards to the main road through the village. It then turns right and, after 110 yards/100m right again into Higher Sea Lane as above.

Preferred Diversion, Lyme Regis-Charmouth

The Association recommends a preferable alternative to the official diversion above, which deviates from it at the A3052/A35 roundabout. Take the road signposted to Charmouth and shortly after the junction take steps on the right to a stile and public footpath. Follow the waymarked direction up the field to the former Lily Farm, now holiday accommodation. Cross a stile and pass between the buildings and the Dutch barn on the left and after the buildings cross a field to arrive at a tarmac lane (Old Lyme Hill). Turn right and after 90 yards/80m turn left to arrive at Old Lyme Road.

Preferred Diversion, Charmouth West

Go left along Old Lyme Road and after 80 yards/70m turn right into a private road, Westcliffe Road. Descend steeply for 330 yards/300m to a junction with Five Acres. Bear right here and at the end of the cul-de-sac take a footpath going forward into a narrow lane. Shortly it reaches a wider road (Higher Sea Lane). Turn right and continue ahead, ignoring various signs pointing off the lane, continuing round the bend to the west in the lane that rises for some 130 yards/120m to an oak signpost on the left. Here leave the lane through a metal gate to re-join the Coast Path, descending over grassy slopes to Charmouth Beach, with its toilets and refreshments.

Official Route, Charmouth East

The official route crosses a footbridge and climbs the obvious green path ahead. This is unlikely to be available for 2014.

Diversion, Charmouth East

From the approach to the footbridge go north-east along a tarmac lane (River Way) and at the end continue along a gravel path to Bridge Road. Continue to the main village road (The Street) then turn right, cross the bridge and fork right into Stonebarrow Lane. Continue up this narrow lane for nearly 0.75 mile/1.25km. At the car park at the top turn sharp right to a signpost then take a grassy track as signed south-westward to re-join the Coast Path.

Coast Path, Charmouth East-Seatown (Chideock)

There is a hefty climb to Golden Cap, the highest point on England's south coast, but the views from the top are spectacular. At the top go slightly left to the trig point which then leads to the long and steep descent. There is a minor diversion on the approach to Seatown, taking the Coast Path slightly inland then back to the coast along the access road. Seatown has toilets and refreshments. Other facilities are at Chideock, 0.75 mile/1.25km inland.

Lyme Regis Harbour

Week 8 - Day 2

OS Maps: Landranger 193 (western half); Explorer 116 (western half)
Landranger 194 (eastern half); Explorer OL15 (eastern half)

	This Walk	Cumulative	This Walk	Cumulative	Grading	Timing
Ascent	1,489ft	105,707ft	454m	32,220m	Strenuous then moderate	6.25 hours
Distance	12.4mi	564.0mi	19.9km	907.7km		

For detailed directions see our Lyme Regis to West Bay and West Bay to Abbotsbury Path Description booklets.

This is a Section of two contrasting halves. West of West Bay is a rollercoaster of steep and high cliffs, giving far-reaching views along the coast and also inland, over the deeply dissected pastoral countryside. East of West Bay a sheer red sandstone cliff rises from the sea, looking almost artificial in its straight lines, and then the coastline subsides to a low level and the Coast Path loses its ups and downs, though not its hard work, as the shingle of what is the far western end of Chesil Beach tests the legs.

Directions

A regular bus service links Chideock, which is 0.75 mile/1.25km inland of Seatown, with Abbotsbury, and also calls at West Bay and Burton Bradstock which are along the length of this Section, giving various bus-walk options. A popular circular walk based on Abbotsbury uses the Coast Path as well as the South Dorset Ridgeway.

From the pub and toilets at Seatown the Coast Path climbs the cliff slope on its way to the high point of Thorncombe Beacon. There is a descent to the little beach at Eype then a further climb and descent to the harbour at West Bay, which has most facilities. Go round the back of the harbour, pass to the right of the church and ahead to the West Bay public house, opposite which is the Coast Path sign pointing to the surprisingly steep cliff. Arriving at Burton Freshwater the path runs between the caravan park and the beach and is well signed. Following major cliff falls in the summer of 2012 the Coast Path has been reopened along Burton Cliff, although a short inland diversion is necessary around the hotel leading to Burton Beach, where there are refreshments and toilets. Further on, the path passes inland of Burton Mere before coming to West Bexington, where there are toilets and seasonal refreshments.

See Section 71 for details of the alternative Inland Coast Path (South Dorset Ridgeway) between West Bexington and Osmington Mills.

The Coast Path continues along the back of the beach, later passing another car park with toilets and seasonal refreshments and some 200 yards/185m beyond this it turns inland to Abbotsbury. There are alternative routes either going into the village or going south and east of Chapel Hill and missing the village. A permissive path alternative leaves the Coast Path and leads direct to the famous Swannery. Abbotsbury is a beautiful stone-built village with much of historic interest and most facilities.

Back towards Seatown

Week 8 - Day 3

OS Maps: Landranger 194; Explorer OL15

	This Walk	Cumulative	This Walk	Cumulative	Grading	Timing
Ascent	955ft	106,662ft	291m	32,511m	Easy. Chesil Beach route strenuous	4 hours official route
Distance	10.9mi	574.9mi	17.5km	925.2km		

For detailed directions see our Abbotsbury to Ferry Bridge Path Description booklet.

This is an untypical Section of the Coast Path. In the west, there is an inland rural high-level field route, giving views over the unusual feature of Chesil Beach and the landlocked Fleet behind. To the east, the path runs along the banks of the Fleet, with pleasant views over this attractive feature, but with views of the sea largely cut off by the shingle bank of Chesil Beach. Although never far from houses or roads, this is often a very quiet Section.

Abbotsbury, Abbey Barn

Directions

Buses to and from Abbotsbury and Ferry Bridge link at Weymouth for a potential bus-walk.

It is possible to walk direct from the beach near Abbotsbury to Ferry Bridge at Wyke Regis along the length of Chesil Beach. If this is intended, start at the beach at the inland turn (Day 2) to Abbotsbury, continuing along the beach. However, note that:

1. It is not possible to get off the beach before Ferry Bridge.
2. It is extremely hard and slow walking.
3. It is necessary to check that firing is not scheduled at the nearby Chickerell Rifle Range; telephone Major Hazard on 01305 783456, ext.8132.
4. The beach is closed to visitors from 1st May to 31st August for the bird nesting season.

Although the Coast Path does not pass through Abbotsbury most walkers will visit the attractive village and its facilities. From the village leave West Street on the path going south adjacent to Chapel Street Stores. Continue on to Nunnery Grove to the signed Coast Path, which now goes inland but is well signed and enjoyable with some excellent views. After Horsepool Farm on the edge of Abbotsbury the path climbs onto the ridge. After about a mile/1.5km turn right off the ridge then left after Hodder's Coppice. Cross a minor road then follow the field headland east then south to the north-east corner of Wyke Wood. The path then heads for the edge of the Fleet - be aware approaching Rodden Hive that the path suddenly goes through a hedge on the left. From here the path follows the edge of the Fleet. At Tidmoor Point follow the red and white posts, unless it is necessary to divert inland because of firing. The diversion is well marked. Approaching Wyke Regis there is a minor deviation behind an MOD Bridging Hard, then the path arrives at the A354 road adjacent to Ferry Bridge, the access for the Isle of Portland, at Wyke Regis, a suburb of Weymouth.

Week 8 - Day 4

OS Maps: **Landranger 194; Explorer OL15**

	This Walk	Cumulative	This Walk	Cumulative	Grading	Timing
Ascent	1,112ft	107,774ft	339m	32,850m	Moderate	6 hours
Distance	13.2mi	588.1mi	21.3km	946.5km		

For detailed directions see our Portland Path description booklet.

Portland is different. Different from the rest of Dorset and from the rest of the Coast Path. An almost-island, jutting out into the English Channel, joined to the mainland only by the end of Chesil Beach, it has an isolated air. Formed of limestone, it has been extensively quarried and these workings, some still operational, characterise much of the landscape. Elsewhere, former military buildings and those of Verne Prison and the Young Offenders' Institution are prominent. Portland is rugged rather than pretty, but it is well worth exploring with superb views and a rich natural and historic heritage.

Directions

Bus routes run the length of Portland, making a variety of bus-walks possible. This Section is, in any event, a circular walk in its own right. However, at the time of going to print there were suggestions that the service all the way to the Bill may be discontinued. Check on local bus information.

It is possible to omit this section and continue from Wyke Regis directly into Weymouth. However, Portland is officially part of the National Trail and its interest and sense of being different make it well worth the day's walk.

From Ferry Bridge cross the causeway onto Portland; this is done by simply following the shared footway/cycleway alongside the A354 road or alternatively by crossing the bridge on the A354 to beyond the boatyard and then walking along the raised bed of the old railway on the eastern bank to near the end of the causeway at the roundabout for the access road to Osprey Quay and here returning to the footway/cycleway. At the southern of the two roundabouts at Victoria Square take the main road south and shortly turn right into Pebble Lane then left just before the public toilets. Continue to the Cove House Inn and bear right up onto the promenade. About half way along, at the floodgates, cut back sharp left then right, following Coast Path signs up a steep tarmac path, past the school and up the steep path in the grass incline to the steps to the terraced path that was once the old road. Bear off right onto the signed path running between quarry banks and the cliff face, leading to 3 miles/5km of airy cliff-top walking to Portland Bill. Two short lengths of the Coast Path above West Wears have remained closed since January 2013 following movement in the cliffs. Follow the signed diversions as you proceed along the old quarrymen's tramway. At Portland Bill, as well as the lighthouse, are refreshments, toilets and buses (but see above).

Continue around the end of the low headland then start northwards, seaward of the wooden chalets, to follow a winding path along the top of low cliffs to join a road above Freshwater Bay after about 1.5 miles/2.5km. Turn right on the road (use the footway on the west side of the road) for 600 yards/550m, past Cheyne Weares car park to a signpost on the right. Follow the zigzag path into the undercliff area and follow the waymarking through disused quarry workings to Church Ope Cove.

Looking back to Portland Lighthouse

Ascend the stepped and signed path up to Rufus Castle. Here the South West Coast Path also becomes the England Coast Path, the first section of which, from here to Lulworth Cove, was formally opened on 30th June 2012. The signposting now usually indicates simply "Coast Path". Some, but not all, of the improvements to the route that the Association sought on Portland can now be walked and the new route is described below. Unfortunately the major alignment around the north-east corner of Portland was not resolved because of legal complications with Portland Ports plc and security issues.

After Rufus Castle the Coast Path soon joins the track bed of the former Weymouth to Easton railway line. This is then followed northwards for some 1,585 yards/1,450m to a pair of signposts. Here turn left to follow a rocky path that climbs up the cliffs to what appears to be an isolated chimney seen on the skyline above. At the top turn sharp right along the prison road northwards and through a gap in a high wall. On the right is the Old Engine Shed, soon to be converted into a visitor centre. On reaching a narrow road the official route is signed across the road and takes a route across open ground passing disused quarries to reach the perimeter fence of the Verne prison. However, the Association's preferred route here, which is all on public rights of way, can be followed thus:-

At the road turn right and just over the brow of a hill turn left on an access track to compounds. Continue ahead on a grassy path towards a large pinnacle of rock (Nichodemus Knob) after which, at the "rock falls" sign, bear left steeply up onto the higher escarpment, heading for a large communications mast. At the high wire perimeter fence turn left and follow it along then round to the right, to reach the south entrance to Verne Prison. Here rejoin the route of the England Coast Path.

Take a path through a little gap to the left of the entrance, passing beside railings and down steep steps. Bear right along a path that traverses under the grassy banks.

The path drops downhill towards houses to a waymark post. Ignore the left fork and continue on the level on a grass path which then passes through an underpass below a road. Descend steeply down the Castletown Incline (a former quarry tramway), crossing two footpaths and a road. Pass under a footbridge and through another underpass to reach an access road and turn left to a roundabout.

Continue ahead for some 30 yards/27m and then cross to turn right down Liberty Road, signposted to Portland Castle. Go past the castle entrance to the car park and turn right towards the harbour, heading for five black posts. Here join the footway/cycleway to follow the harbour-side to the Sailing Academy, the venue of the sailing events at the 2012 Olympics. Continue on the footway/cycleway to reach the roundabout on the A354 road. From here follow the former railway trackbed to the boatyard before the bridge over the mouth of the Fleet and follow the footway alongside the road to Ferry Bridge.

Week 8 - Day 5

OS Maps: Landranger 194; Explorer OL15

	This Walk	Cumulative	This Walk	Cumulative	Grading	Timing
Ascent	2,385ft	110,159ft	727m	33,577m	Easy to moderate to strenuous	6.25 hours
Distance	14.1mi	602.2mi	22.7km	969.2km		

For detailed directions see our Ferry Bridge to Lulworth Cove Path Description booklet.

This section is part of the first section of the England Coast Path. The signposting generally only refers to "Coast Path".

The western part of this Section is an urban walk along the various lengths of Weymouth's sea front. East of the town is a length of relatively low cliffs but then at White Nothe, two thirds of the way along the section, the coastal geology changes. East of here is a rollercoaster of often sheer white cliffs, the length punctuated by the iconic landmarks of Durdle Door and Lulworth Cove. Both ends of this Section are busy, but in the centre is an often quiet and remote length.

Directions

A regular bus service links Weymouth with Lulworth Cove, also serving Osmington, close to the Coast Path mid-way along this Section, allowing some bus-walk options.

From Ferry Bridge the signed Coast Path follows the footway/cycleway on the old railway trackbed, passing behind the sailing centre. Shortly afterwards bear off right to continue into Old Castle Road. Ignore the footpath sign to the right, a cul-de-sac as the onward cliff path is closed due to a landslip. However, except at high tides the beach can be used to reach a flight of new timber steps that rejoin the former Coast Path beyond the landslip. Instead, continue along the road and 260 yards/240m beyond turn right into Belle Vue Road. Continue for about 600 yards/560m to a crossroads and turn right into Redcliff View. At the end of this road a path leads across a grassed area back to the coast at GR 682 781 (westbound walkers follow the path worn across the grassed area here). Continue on the path to Nothe Fort and bear sharp left then turn down steps on the right to Weymouth harbourside. This is followed to the Town Bridge, which is crossed and the opposite side of the harbour followed back to the Pavilion complex. Bear left to join the Esplanade.

In summer a little ferry may cross the harbour, slightly shortening the route.

Ferry operates (rowing boat) between Easter and June 11:00 to 15:00; during July 09:30 to 17:00; during August 09:30 to 19:00; during September-October 11:00 to 15:00; all weather permitting - telephone 01305 838423.

For ferry details see page 20.

Leave Weymouth along the promenade then, at Overcombe, go up the minor road to Bowleaze Cove. After passing the Spyglass Inn the route now bears right to cross the crest of the grass public open space to reach the Beachside Centre. With the new public access rights now provided the Coast Path follows a signed route through the Beachside Leisure Centre to take a narrow path that squeezes between the

View from Swyre Head, Durdle Door

Riviera Hotel and cliff edge and follows a new signed route to Redcliff Point. A little further on, beyond an education and adventure centre, follow the signed route on a re-established length of the Coast Path. On the downhill approach to Osmington Mills the route avoids another landslip by bearing away from the cliff edge over a stile and down the edge of a field, then crosses two further stiles to meet a narrow road down to the coast.

See Section 71 for details of the alternative Inland Coast Path (South Dorset Ridgeway) between West Bexington and Osmington Mills.

The path goes slightly inland at Ringstead. Beyond the wooden church the route of the Coast Path near Holworth House is now signed to deviate north-east and south although the original route (which is a public right of way) can still be used as a more direct route.

Further on, at the coastguard cottages at White Nothe, take the left fork of the two yellow arrows. The path now traverses some quite severe gradients on its way to Lulworth Cove, passing behind Durdle Door to Hambury Tout. Follow the waymarking here - the route sometimes shown on older maps going south here is not usable. Approaching Lulworth Cove a stone-pitched path leads down through the car park to the Heritage Centre. Turn right here along the cliff past the view into Stair Hole. Pass the Jurassic Coast commemorative stone then turn down towards the Cove in front of the boathouse. Lulworth Cove has toilets and refreshments and most facilities are found here or at West Lulworth a little way inland.

Week 8 - Day 6 (half day)

OS Maps: Landranger 194 (most); Landranger 195 (eastern end); Explorer OL15

	This Walk	Cumulative	This Walk	Cumulative	Grading	Timing
Ascent	2,002ft	112,161ft	610m	34,187m	Severe	4 hours
Distance	7.3mi	609.5mi	11.8km	981.0km		

For detailed directions see our Lulworth to Kimmeridge Path Description booklet.

The coast of this Section is of geological interest and importance, largely having been formed by lines of relatively hard limestone having been breached at intervals to form coves and bays as the sea erodes the softer rocks behind. The result is a dramatic coastline of white cliffs and darker coloured coves, some prominent headlands and a succession of extremely steep slopes. Inland, the landscape of the military ranges has been unchanged by farming for some seventy years, though it is perhaps a little too obviously military in a few places.

Directions

Lulworth Cove and Kimmeridge village, about one mile/1.5km inland from Kimmeridge Bay, both have bus links to Wareham, which could provide a bus-walk option.

IMPORTANT: Note that this Section passes through the Lulworth Army Firing Ranges. Before deciding to walk this Section, check that the Ranges are open. PLEASE BE AWARE THE OFFICIAL COAST PATH FOR THIS SECTION MAY BE CLOSED TO WALKERS DURING THE WEEK. However most weekends and during school holidays it is normally open, but please read the section below to check the dates when walkers are allowed access along the official Coast Path.

The Lulworth Range walks, including the Coast Path between Lulworth Cove and Kimmeridge Bay, plus access to Tyneham village, are open to the public every weekend.

LULWORTH RANGE WALKS AND TYNEHAM VILLAGE OPENING TIMES 2014
The Lulworth Range walks and Tyneham Villages are open to the public every weekend with the exception of the following:

1. 18th/19th January 2014
2. 8th/09th March 2014
3. 11th/13th April 2014
4. 14th/15th June 2014
5. 27th/28th September 2014
6. 15th/16th November 2014

In addition to the weekends they are open every day during the following times; all dates are inclusive:

Christmas 21st December 2013 - 05th January 2014
Easter 18th - 27th April 2014, Bank Holiday 03rd - 5th May 2014
Spring 24th May - 1st June 2014, Summer 26th July - 31st August 2014
Christmas 20th December 2014 - 4th January 2015

Please note that the exhibitions in Tyneham School and Tyneham Church are open from 10.00 until 16.00. The gates to the walks are opened as near to 0900 hours on the Saturday morning as possible and remain open until 0800 hours on the Monday morning when only open at the weekends. The gate to Tyneham is locked each night at dusk. For any further information please phone 01929 404819

The abandoned village and its historical exhibition are 0.5 mile/800m inland of the Coast Path, and worth the diversion. The gates to the walks are opened as near to 09.00 on the Saturday morning as possible and remain open until 08.00 on the Monday morning when open only at weekends. The gate to Tyneham is locked each night at dusk. For any further information telephone 01929 404819 or 01929 404712, 0800-1700, Monday to Friday

If the Ranges are closed, it is strongly recommended that schedules are re-arranged so that the Coast Path is walked when open. If, however, this is not possible, two alternative inland diversions are shown below.

Coast Path - Lulworth Cove-Kimmeridge Bay
The Coast Path from Lulworth Cove leaves from behind the cafe. Higher up, a short signed alternative path avoids an eroded area close to the cliff edge. Tide permitting, walking the beach avoids a considerable ascent and descent. At most states of the tide this is possible, going up the path which rises diagonally on the far side of the beach. At the top of the steep ascent off the beach the best route proceeds seawards, the path then turning south-eastwards along the coast to the beginning of the Army Ranges. The route onward is straightforward - just follow the yellow topped posts through the ranges to arrive at Kimmeridge Bay. Here are toilets and seasonal refreshments (or all year refreshments in the village 0.6 mile/1km to the north).

If Ranges Closed - Alternative Option 1 (13.5 miles/22.0km)
This route is safer and quieter but more strenuous than Option 2; it uses mainly Rights of Way plus some permissive paths. Leave the Cove on the road inland, forking right, and take road on the left, by a bus shelter (GR 825 807), and in 100 yards/90m turn right on a footpath that heads north for 0.75 mile/1.2 km. Turn right (east) and after 100 yards/90m turn left (north) to pass Belhuish Coppice and Belhuish Farm, then cross the B3071 road at GR 835 832. At the eastern boundary of Burngate Wood (GR 845 828) use the permissive path (blue) north-east past Park Lodge and go across the road at GR 855 832 onto a bridleway. Continue north-east along the bridleway to GR 865 839, where it veers north and later north-east through Highwood to meet the road at GR872 862. Walk east along the road and then fork right (signposted Stoborough) at GR882 855. Go over the crossroads with the B3070 at GR 886 855 and walk east for a further 1.5 miles/2.5km along Holme Lane to GR 911 854. [(*) Aternative Option 2 below continues from here].

Turn right just before the railway bridge onto Doreys Farm bridleway. After 1.25 miles/2km turn right onto Creech Road. After 1.5 miles/2.5km of this road, walk up a steep gradient to a viewpoint car park. Beyond the car park, at GR 902 815, take the left road that turns back and down over the ridge. (A short cut bridleway at GR 905 817 zigzags down to meet the same road.) As the road levels out, at a left-hand bend at GR 907 812, take the bridleway ahead that leads south through Steeple Leaze Farm. About 200 yards/185m south of the farm, a footpath heads up steeply south to a bridleway on a ridge. Turn left through a gate and look for a narrow path on the right raking steeply downhill and then across three fields towards the coast ahead and Kimmeridge Bay.

If Ranges Closed - Alternative Option 2 (12 miles/19km)
This option is mainly road walking, and care is needed on narrow bends. Leave the Cove to West Lulworth on the B3070, then turn right to East Lulworth and beyond, keeping to the B3070 for some 3 miles/5km to GR 886 855. Here turn right along Holme Lane to GR 911 854. From here, follow the route described from (*) in Option 1 above.

Taxi operators Mike Whittle, Silver Cars, tel. 01929 400409, mobile 07811 328281 Adrian, Valley Taxis, tel. 01929 480507; and K Bay Taxi, tel.01929 480669, mobile 07545 776716, all offer their services in the Lulworth/Kimmeridge area.

Week 8 - Day 6 (half day)

OS Maps: Landranger 195; Explorer OL15

	This Walk	Cumulative	This Walk	Cumulative	Grading	Timing
Ascent	1,059ft	113,220ft	323m	34,510m	Severe	3.25 hours
Distance	5.2mi	614.7mi	8.3km	989.3km		

For detailed directions see our Kimmeridge to South Haven Point Path Description booklet.

This is a Section of steeply undulating cliffs, often with quite sheer faces and frequently with rock ledges at the cliff face. Houns-tout Cliff, near the eastern end of the Section, is especially steep. There are some very attractive bays formed by these cliffs, particularly at the eastern end. The tough terrain means that this Section often has a remote character, accentuated by the lack of neighbouring houses and roads.

Directions

Bus-walks are not easily undertaken on this Section. Circular walks using the Coast Path, based on inland villages such as Kimmeridge or Kingston, are possible.

The Coast Path from Kimmeridge Bay eastwards is straightforward, although care may be needed where small lengths have slipped, cracked or may be close to the cliff top. Just beyond Kimmeridge the Clavell Tower has been relocated 27 yards/25m inland and an improved Coast Path installed. There is a very steep climb to Houns-tout and the descent beyond turns inland to avoid dangerous terrain at Chapman's Pool. (For those aiming to end at Worth Matravers, which is about 1.2 miles/2km inland, the Coast Path is left where it crosses the valley at Hill Bottom Cottages. For the village head inland then turn right up a steep track past Renscombe Farm. Worth Matravers has a pub, shop and cafe.)

The four-mile length between Kimmeridge Bay and the top of Houns-tout was closed early in 2013 due to several cliff falls. It could remain closed in 2014 so walkers should plan to use an alternative route via Swyre Head and Kingston. From the public car park in Kimmeridge Bay follow the road inland to the village of Kimmeridge, continue up the hill to the disused quarry car park and turn right onto the footpath that rises up Smedmore Hill. Pause at Heaven's Gate to savour the view. From Swyre Head the path downhill takes a north-easterly direction before joining the road into Kingston, where there are refreshments. The route back to the top of Houns-tout runs along the top of Encombe valley with more stunning views back to Portland. Then re-join the Coast Path down to Chapman's Pool.

Clavell Tower

Week 8 - Day 7 (half day)

OS Maps: **Landranger 195; Explorer OL15**

	This Walk	Cumulative	This Walk	Cumulative	Grading	Timing
Ascent	1,195ft	114,415ft	364m	34,874m	Severe then Moderate	4 hours
Distance	8.1mi	622.8mi	13.1km	1,002.4km		

For detailed directions see our Kimmeridge to South Haven Point Path Description booklet.

The western part of this Section is dominated by St Aldhelm's Head, a flat-topped headland of limestone surmounted by an old chapel. There are extensive views, especially along the coast to the west. East of the headland the cliffs become increasingly disturbed by the remains of small-scale quarrying activity until the Country Park at Durlston Head marks the approach of Swanage.

Directions

Numerous footpaths cross the cliffs to the Coast Path from the outskirts of Swanage and the inland village of Langton Matravers. This allows for bus-walks which combine these link paths with the Coast Path.

(For those starting in Worth Matravers village, walk along the lane westwards past Weston Farm and Renscombe Farm then turn into the valley and on to the Coast Path at Hill Bottom Cottages.)

From the valley at Hill Bottom the Coast Path climbs on a well-signed route steeply up West Hill and on to Emmett's Hill. The path goes out round St Aldhelm's Head, with excellent coastal views west, and on as a fine high level walk to Durlston Head. Signing in Durlston Country Park is limited; keep on the low level path all the way round Durlston Head then, coming up on the north side take the second turning right (the first is a cul-de-sac to a quarry). Durlston Castle has now been converted to a Jurassic Coast Gateway Centre and includes refreshment facilities.

After leaving Durlston Castle follow a broad stony path north through the woods for some 760 yards/700m to a barrier and sign. From here there is a permanent diversion following a cliff fall. Turn left on a good path for some 125 yards/115m to reach Durlston Road at a gate. Turn right and in 185 yards/170m turn right again into Belle Vue Road. Follow the road north-eastwards to the grassed open space leading to Peveril Point. In bad weather or at high tides use the roadway and then down to the footpath at the end of the coastal buildings, otherwise use the foreshore. Continue along Swanage's sea front promenade. Swanage has all facilities.

St Aldhelm's Head, Rock Pillar

Week 8 - Day 7 (half day)

OS Maps: **Landranger 195; Explorer OL15**

	This Walk	Cumulative	This Walk	Cumulative	Grading	Timing
Ascent	492ft	114,907ft	150m	35,024m	Moderate	3.5 hours
Distance	7.6mi	630.4mi	12.2km	1,014.6km		

For detailed directions see our Kimmeridge to South Haven Point Path Description booklet.

This is an excellent and scenic Section. The southern, Swanage end comprises increasingly high cliffs, culminating in the length between Ballard Point and Handfast Point, with its offshore stacks. This is an exhilarating length with superb views over Poole Bay to Bournemouth and across the Solent to the matching cliffs of the Needles on the Isle of Wight. The northern end passes along a long sandy beach before arriving at the mouth of Poole Harbour, an enormous enclosed water area and the second largest natural harbour in the world.

Directions

A regular bus service, half hourly in summer and hourly in winter, links Swanage with South Haven Point, making a bus-walk a good option. There are also popular local circuits using the Coast Path in the Swanage-Ballard Down-Studland area.

Swanage has all facilities. The Coast Path passes along the town's sea front, following the main road (Ulwell Road) at the north end by the telephone box where it bears left and on ahead into Redcliff Road at a one-way system. At a shop and post-box turn sharp right into Ballard Way - do not be put off by "Private Estate" signs. Continue forward into the chalet estate and follow signs for the Coast Path, to emerge on a grassed area on the cliff edge. However, from the sea front road, except at very high tides or in severe weather it is possible to keep along the narrow promenade then 200 yards/185m along the beach turn up some rough steps to re-join the official route in a little valley.

The path climbs out to Ballard Down, then the obvious high-level route continues out to Handfast Point and the much-photographed rocks of Old Harry before turning west towards Studland. Studland has toilets and refreshments. For the pub turn up the road from the toilets, otherwise turn right (east) on the outskirts of the village along the signed stony path to South Beach. On reaching the shore, turn left (north) along a terrace in front of beach huts to a seasonal cafe. The route ahead was diverted in 2013 inland up a track to join the road by the public toilets. Turn right here past the pub and right again to re-join the Coast Path above the beach huts. If this short diversion is no longer necessary then continue along the beach for another 90 yards/82m and look for a Purbeck stone waymark between beach huts numbers 59 and 60B, to find a narrow path that ascends steeply up the low cliff. At the top, at another sign, turn right and follow the cliff edge past Fort Henry to join the Middle Beach access road by a barrier. Turn sharp right down to the beach then left by another cafe.

The final 2.6 miles/4.3km are on the sandy beach. Note that further along this beach a length is used by naturists - do not be surprised if nobody else is wearing

South West Coast Path end marker

clothes! There is an alternative, the Heather Walk, through the dunes, marked by yellow-topped posts, but the soft sand is tiring walking and part of the naturist area is still visible. The beach route curves round to the point at the mouth of Poole Harbour. This is South Haven Point, the end (or beginning) of the Coast Path, with an impressive commemorative marker. A ferry links the Point with Sandbanks on the opposite shore, which is linked to Poole and Bournemouth.

The ferry operates all year daily every 20 minutes, from Shell Bay (South Haven Point) 07:10 to 23:10; from Sandbanks 07:00 to 23:00; Christmas Day every half hour - telephone 01929 450203.; website www.sandbanksferry.co.uk.

Note that the ferry is usually scheduled to undergo maintenance during late October or November and may be closed for approximately four weeks. If you intend to use the ferry at this time check the Association's website under Path News or the ferry company's website above.

For ferry details see page 21.

Postscript

For those who have been with us all the way from Minehead, be it in one go or in bits and pieces over a period, a final few words seem appropriate. Alfred Wainwright, at the end of his work on the Pennine Way, said; "You have completed a mission and satisfied an ambition. You have walked the Pennine Way, as you have dreamed of doing. This will be a very satisfying moment in your life. You will be tired and hungry and travel stained. But you will feel great, just great." Just substitute the South West Coast Path for the Pennine Way and Wainwright's words will doubtless ring true. You will be glad and proud that you have walked and finished Britain's longest and finest footpath. As Wainwright said of the Pennine Way, it's a longer step than most take in their lifetime!

Alternative Inland Coast Path

OS Maps: Landranger 194; Explorer OL15

	This Walk	This Walk	Grading	Timing
Ascent	2,290ft	698m	Moderate	8 hours
Distance	16.8mi	27.0km		

For detailed directions see our West Bexington to Osmington Mills Path Description booklet.

This is a very scenic walk, parallel to the coast and a varying distance inland. For most of its length quite extensive coastal views are obtained beyond a green and rural foreground. Substantial lengths follow chalk ridges and these give impressive views north as well. Coastal features such as Portland and Chesil Beach are clearly seen, as are the flanks of the enormous Iron Age Maiden Castle inland. This is a quiet route, often feeling quite remote, and with usually no refreshments on its length it requires preparation. It is, nevertheless, a superb experience.

Directions

A regular bus service links Swyre (for West Bexington) and Osmington Mills, making this a perfect opportunity for a bus-walk.

The Dorset element of the Coast Path is unique in having an official alternative route for part of its length. This was often referred to by the apparently contradictory name of the "Inland Coast Path". It is, however, now known as the South Dorset Ridgeway (SDR) and the signposting now uses that name almost throughout. The waymarking has also been replaced and incorporates the name of the South Dorset Ridgeway. The length of the Section, and the fact that the two ends are linked by a regular bus service, make it an ideal long day's walk. However, be aware that other than one seasonal mobile refreshment van if the timing is right, no facilities are found anywhere along the route other than at the two ends, so it is necessary to be well prepared. A detailed route description is given below.

At West Bexington car park turn inland up the road and where the road turns left continue forward up the stony track, signposted "SDR. For Hardy Monument 6 Osmington Mills 16".

Near the top of the hill take the right-hand fork to reach a lay-by on the B3157 road. Take the gate or stile to the right and follow a faint path that follows the edge of the escarpment of the hill passing three waymark posts. After passing through a wall start to bear upwards to the left towards a signpost near the road. Continue eastwards through the field to reach a gate by the corner of a wall. Continue through the gate and almost immediately emerge on the B3157 road at a signpost. Cross and leave through a gate, again signposted "Hardy Monument".

Approaching Abbotsbury Castle prehistoric hill fort, where the grass path divides, take the upper, slightly right-hand fork along the top of the southern earthwork of the fort, past the trig point, from where there are superb views in all directions. It should be possible to see the Hardy Monument clearly in the distance.

Continue eastwards along the top of the earthwork and cross a minor road, signposted "SDR Hardy Monument". Proceed in an approximately easterly direction along the ridge of Wears Hill and the crest of White Hill for about 2 miles/3.2km, following the signing. Be careful not to follow any signs indicating routes down to the village of Abbotsbury in the valley below and its adjacent hilltop chapel. At the east end of White Hill bear north-east as signed and leave the field in the north-east corner through a gate on to a minor road. Continue north-east along this road for some 50 yards/46m and then turn right as signposted.

Follow the narrow and rough bridleway along the wire fence above the scrub to a path junction; where the bridleway bears right take the yellow waymarked footpath to the left and cross a stile. At the end of this short section take a headland path north-east. At the far side of the field the track then leads approximately 50 yards/46m to a further gate with a stile and waymark. Immediately adjacent to this gate is a prehistoric stone circle, a scheduled ancient monument. Continue forward on the track, leaving a small wood to the left, to reach the road between Portesham and Winterbourne Steepleton. Turn left along the road for about 60 yards/55m and then turn right over a stile into a field, signed "Hardy Monument". Continue eastwards through four fields. At a small wooded area before Black Down Barn (ruin) turn north at a signpost to Hardy Monument. Climb through the woods to the recently renovated monument. In season it may be possible to find a mobile refreshment van here.

To continue find a roadside signpost 30yards/32m east of the car park entrance. Cross the road and descend eastward on a narrow path through the bracken. Reaching the same road again, ignore the signpost "Bridleway to Coast Path" and the track opposite and turn left along the road then in another 30 yards/32m turn right, signposted "Inland Route or SDR to Bincombe" .

Now there is a good ridgeway path for some 3 miles/4.8km, with excellent views to seaward. At a point some 550 yards/500m after passing under the second set of HV power lines take the gate north of a large tumulus to stay on the north side of the fence running along the ridge. On reaching the B3159 road, marked by the Borough of Weymouth boundary stone, continue across as signposted and towards the A354 road.

Major road construction has now been completed and a new section of the busy A354 road opened over Ridgeway Hill. The former very difficult crossing of the old road has been replaced with a fine new bridleway bridge (locally known as Green Bridge). Cross the new bridge and take a new bridleway south, that at first rises and then falls, down the perimeter fence on the east side of the new road. About halfway down the hill look out for and take the old bridleway on the left.

Continue eastwards, then before the farm, with its adjacent radio mast, take care to go through the gate on the right, marked with a blue arrow. After crossing the field, leaving two tumuli on the left, reach a metalled road and turn right. At the junction at the corner of Came Wood turn right at the signpost "Bridleway to Bincombe".
At the end of the path join a metalled lane and at the road junction turn left, signposted "South Dorset Ridgeway".

Alternative Inland Coast Path (continued)

Drop down the road into the village of Bincombe and where the road turns right take the track forward leaving the small church on the right. Where the path splits take the left-hand fork, marked with a blue arrow and acorn. After the overhead HV power lines, pass through a small signposted wooden gate and then proceed forward through one field, into the next to a footpath sign. Here turn left and there is a choice of routes for the next couple of hundred yards/m.

For the best option, at a waymark post turn sharp right down a steep grassy slope to a stile at a road ahead. Cross the road to go over another stile to follow a grassy path that contours around the south and east sides of Green Hill. On reaching a road at a gate and stile turn left and in 50 yards/46m turn right through a gate signposted "White Horse Hill - Osmington Mills". The path is now easy to follow with extensive views to seaward over Weymouth and Portland. On passing a ruined building on the left the route reaches a broad track; here turn right, signposted "Osmington" and after about 200 yards/185m go through a gate as signposted. Shortly afterwards pass a trig point on the right and at the next field gate bear left and follow the field boundary along White Horse Hill. Just beyond the next gate fork right, signposted "For Osmington".

Descend to Osmington and follow the signs through the village. On reaching the main Weymouth road near the Sun Ray Inn turn left and in about 250 yards/230m turn right at a signpost, over a stile and footbridge. Follow the field boundary on the left through two fields - at the top look back to see the Hardy Monument in the distance and the white horse on the hillside. Go over the stile to the footpath sign, then turn half right to cross the field at an angle to a further stile. Cross it and turn left along the hedge side to the bottom. At the end of the field there is a very short length of enclosed footpath to the road; turn right along it, descending to Osmington Mills.

Hardy Monument

Old Harry Rocks

Accommodation

This list of accommodation has been prepared in path order.

The majority of our B&B addresses have been recommended by Coast Path walkers. The fact that they are included in this book does not indicate a recommendation by The South West Coast Path Association and their inclusion is merely for information purposes. We cannot, for financial and practical reasons, introduce vetting, inspection or any form of `Star' rating. We do have a system whereby addresses can be removed from the list. All the contact information in the following pages has been supplied by the accommodation providers themselves.

RED DISC

Many of the accommodation addresses are highlighted with a red disc. This indicates that they have joined the Association as Business Members, with a large proportion of their membership fee going towards improvements on the Coast Path.

In return for their support for the Path, we urge you to support them and use their accommodation and facilities on your walk wherever possible. Your support for them will in turn encourage them to stay with us as Business Members, with all that means for our Path Improvement Funds.

B&B Key

Facilities:

O Open All Year
EM Evening Meal
CP Car Parking
DW Dogs Welcome
PD Pick Up/Drop Service
D Drying Facilities for wet clothes
PL Packed Lunches
LSP Long Stay Parking
KT Kit Transfer
LT Luxury Tent
SO Single Occupancy
PR Per Room
W Wifi
LF Local Food

Room Type:

D Double
ES Ensuite
S Single
SS Single Supplement

Campsite Key

Facilities:

T Toilets
G Grocery Shop
LSP Long Stay Parking
O Open All Year
KT Kit Transfer
S Showers
CP Car Parking
LY Laundry
DW Dogs Welcome
PD Pick Up/Drop Service

Colour coding by walk regions

Exmoor
North Devon
North Cornwall
West Cornwall
South Cornwall
South Devon
Dorset

Pick Up/Drop (PD)

This code appears following the distance from the path and denotes a facility whereby your host is prepared to collect and return you to the Coast Path within reasonable distance. No fee should be charged for this service. Where this facility is offered, you may consider booking for two or three nights and asking them to collect you from your finishing point and return you there for your start the next day. This way the B&B gets you for more than one night and you can get to walk for a day or more with a lighter day sack. Again no fee should be charged for this service.

Distance from Path - please remember these are only approximate and may not be accurate.

Luxury Tent (LT)

Due to the Eden Project there may be accommodation problems in the St Austell Bay area, and some providers have installed superb tents in their gardens/paddocks. You will not need sleeping bags or any camping out gear.

Listed Information

The part of the address in CAPITALS is an aid to location; it does not signify the postal town. The extreme left-hand column refers to the appropriate section in the 'Coast Path Walks'; we feel it may help you to find addresses quickly. The amount quoted gives an indication of the starting rate for bed and breakfast, and may well rise. **If working on a tight budget, it is best to ask first.**

Tourist Information Centres can be an additional source of accommodation addresses. We have provided a list of TICs along the Coast Path for your use on page 181.

Most of the B&B providers operate from their own private homes so do not expect plenty of staff as there are in hotels and large guesthouses. They work hard to make you comfortable, welcome, dry you out and make you feel like one of the family.

If your chosen address does not supply evening meals you should ask, when booking, how far it is to your evening meal - you can then decide if you want to stay there.

We wish to develop this list and suggestions for inclusion in our next guide will be welcome. Details of any new accommodation should be addressed to the Administrator. Our list is not comprehensive and walkers will find many B&Bs in towns and villages along the Coast Path that are not recorded in this book.

Although there are a lot of addresses that state they are 'open all the year', some of these close for the Christmas period. Walkers should remember that during the holiday season many of our accommodation addresses could be fully booked up in advance by holidaymakers staying for a week or two. Conversely a walker could book for one night only in good time, thus preventing a guest house proprietor from taking a week or more booking later on. Accommodation problems can be frustrating to all parties concerned so bear these facts in mind when hunting for one night only.

Campsites

Individuals - but we stress not parties - usually find no problem in obtaining leave to camp away from official camp sites if they request permission to do so. In fact, our correspondence has many examples of extra kindnesses extended by farmers and others to campers. We would, however, very much emphasise the requesting of permission first. It would be so easy for the thoughtlessness of a few to undo the good relationships of many others built up over some years.

The list of campsites is thin in many areas. Suggestions for inclusions in future lists will always be welcome. Information should be addressed to the Administrator.

Important

If having booked ahead, and for any reason you are unable to get to your accommodation address, please telephone and explain your absence to your intended host. We have known instances where the host has become so worried about the non-appearance of walkers that they have informed the emergency services. The last thing we want is the emergency services out on a wild goose chase.

Walk No.	Contact name Establishment name Address Region/Postcode	Telephone no. Mobile no. Email Website	OS Map Ref. Dist. from path	Starting price Facilities Room types Notes
1 BUSINESS MEMBER	Mr A Brunt The Yarn Market Hotel 25- 31 High Street **DUNSTER** TA24 6SF	01643 821425 www.yarnmarkethotel.co.uk hotel@yarnmarkethotel.co.uk	993 438 4 km PD	£45.00 PL EM DW KT O PD D S(4) D (12) T(6) F(5) All ES
1 BUSINESS MEMBER	Mr & Mrs S H Leaker The Parks Guest House 26 The Parks **MINEHEAD** TA24 8BT	01643 703547 www.parksguesthouse.co.uk info@parksguesthouse.co.uk	965 467 500 mts	£37.00 PL EM DW D LSP CP KT PD O W LF S(2)(2ES) D(6)(6ES) T(4)(4ES) F(2)(2ES) Special dietry needs catered for on request. Excellent Trip Advisor reviews.
1 BUSINESS MEMBER	Mrs J Bakker Beverleigh Beacon Road **MINEHEAD** TA24 5SE	01643 708450 www.beverleigh.co.uk beverleighminehead@gmail.com	968 469 200 mts	£32.50 PL D LSP CP KT PD O W D(2)(2ES) T(1)(1ES) £40 single occupancy
1	Mr E Moulder Montrose Guest House 14 Tregonwell Road **MINEHEAD** TA24 5DU	01643 706473 www.montroseminehead.co.uk montroseminehead@btinternet.com	972 460 900 mts	£40.00 D CP KT O D(4)(4ES) T(1)(1ES) Price based on 2 sharing, single supplement
1	Mr & Mrs S Poingdestre Kenella House 7 Tregonwell Road **MINEHEAD** TA24 5DT	01643 703128 www.kenellahouse.co.uk kenellahouse@fsmail.net	972 462 500 mts	£32.50 PL EM CP KT O D(4)(4ES) T(2)(2ES) Single supplement
1 BUSINESS MEMBER	Mr M Lawrence Cross Lane House **ALLERFORD** Minehead TA24 8HW	01643 863276 www.crosslanehouse.com max@crosslanehouse.com	905 469 1 km PD	£50.00 PL EM DW D LSP CP KT PD O W LF D(3)(3ES) F(1)(1ES)
1 BUSINESS MEMBER	Mr & Mrs N Southwood Myrtle Cottage High Street **PORLOCK** TA24 8PU	01643 862978 Mobile 07884 233422 www.myrtleporlock.co.uk enquiries@myrtleporlock.co.uk	885 467 1 km	£30.00 DW D CP KT PD O W LF S(1)(1ES) D(4)(4ES) T(2)(2ES) F(2)(2ES) SS £5
1 BUSINESS MEMBER	Mr & Mrs C Gladstone The Cottage High Street **PORLOCK** TA24 8PU	01643 862996 www.cottageporlock.co.uk cottageporlock@gmail.com	885 467 400 mts	£35.00 PL D LSP CP KT O W LF D(2)(2ES) T(2)(2ES) F(1)(1ES) £5 single supplement
1 BUSINESS MEMBER	Mrs G Kenyon Sea View Bed & Breakfast High Bank **PORLOCK** TA24 8NP	01643 863456 www.seaviewporlock.co.uk seaview.porlock@btconnect.com	884 467 100m	£32.00 D LSP CP O LF S(1)(1ES) D(2)(2ES) T(1)(1ES) Locally sourced award winning breakfast
1	Miss E Lewis Chapel Court High Street **PORLOCK** TA24 8PS	01643 862597 lislewis@hotmail.co.uk	 1km	£30.00 DW D CP O W D(1)(0ES) T(1)(0ES) Private bathroom
1	Mrs Jane Richards Silcombe Farm **PORLOCK WEIR** TA24 8JN	01643 862248	833 482 750 mts PD	£28.00 PL EM DW D CP KT PD O LF S(1)(0ES) D(1)(1ES) T(1)(1ES) £31 single, above Culbone Woods on old route of Coast Path
1	Mrs J E Richards Ash Farm **PORLOCK WEIR** TA24 8JN	01643 862414	842 478 750 mts PD	£25.00 PL D LSP CP KT O(April to Oct) S(1)(0ES) T(1)(0ES) F(1)(0ES) Pick up for a small charge

Walk No.	Contact name Establishment name Address Region/Postcode	Telephone no. Mobile no. Email Website	OS Map Ref. Dist. from path	Starting price Facilities Room types Notes
2 BUSINESS MEMBER	Mr & Mrs A Williams The Bath Hotel **LYNMOUTH** EX35 6EL	01598 752238 www.bathhotellynmouth.co.uk info@bathhotellynmouth.co.uk	727 495 100 mts	£35.00 PL EM DW D CP KT W O S(1)(1ES) D(10)(10ES) T(7)(7ES) F(4)(4ES) £10 SS. Shut 17/11/14 to 16/1/15
2 BUSINESS MEMBER	Mr & Mrs C Parker The Old Sea Captain's House 1 Tors Road **LYNMOUTH** EX35 6ET	01598 753369 www.thecaptainshouseinlynmouth.co.uk thecaptainshouse@btinternet.com	727 494 50 mts	£28.00 PL DW D LSP CP KT W LF O(10 Jan-18 Dec) S(1)(1ES) D(6)(6ES) T(1)(1ES) F(1)(1ES)
2 BUSINESS MEMBER	Mrs C Sheppard River Lyn View 26 Watersmeet Road **LYNMOUTH** EX35 6EP	01598 753501 www.riverlynview.com riverlynview@aol.com	725 493 150 mts	£28.00 PL D CP KT O D(3)(0ES) seasonal supplement
2 BUSINESS MEMBER	Mr & Mrs I Downing North Walk House North Walk **LYNTON** EX35 6HJ	01598 753372 www.northwalkhouse.co.uk walk@northwalkhouse.co.uk	718 497 on path	£34.00 PL EM DW D CP O W LF S(1)(1ES) D(4)(4ES) T(1)(1ES) SC(1)(1ES) Also self-catering apartment
2 BUSINESS MEMBER	Mrs A Wilford Gable Lodge 35 Lee Road **LYNTON** EX35 6BS	01598 752367 www.gablelodgelynton.co.uk gablelodge@btconnect.com	717 495 400 mts PD	£33.00 PL EM D CP KT PD O W LF D(4)(4ES) T(1)(1ES) F(1)(1ES) £10 single supplement
2 BUSINESS MEMBER	Mr & Mrs J Hodges Choughs Nest Hotel North Walk **LYNTON** EX35 6HJ	01598 753315 www.choughsnesthotel.co.uk relax@choughsnesthotel.co.uk	718 497 on path	£40.00 PL EM D LSP CP PD O W LF D(5)(5ES) T(3)(3ES) SS
2	Mr & Mrs J McGowan The Denes 15 Longmead **LYNTON** EX35 6DQ	01598 753573 www.thedenes.com j.e.mcgowan@btinternet.com	715 494 400 mts PD	£32.00 PL D LSP CP KT O D(5)(4ES) T(2)(2ES) single supplement, LSP by prior arrangement
2	Mr & Mrs N Firman Sinai House Lynway **LYNTON** EX35 6AY	01598 753227 www.sinaihouse.co.uk enquires@sinaihouse.co.uk	721 492 400 mts	£36.00 PL EM D CP KT O S(2)(0ES) D(5)(5ES) T(1)(1ES) £45 single occupancy
2	Mr & Mrs A Mundell Castle Hill Guest House Castle Hill **LYNTON** EX35 6JA	01598 752291 www.castlehill.biz castlehillbiz@gmail.com	720 493 50 mts	£32.50 PL D KT O D(5)(5ES) T(2)(2ES) F(1)(1ES)
3 BUSINESS MEMBER	Mr M Cowell Heddon's Gate Hotel Heddon Valley Martinhoe **PARRACOMBE** EX31 4PZ	01598 763481 www.heddonsgatehotel.co.uk stay@heddonsgatehotel.co.uk	 1/2 mile	£50.00 PL EM DW D LSP CP KT PD O W LF S(1)(1ES) D(10)(10ES) SS
3 BUSINESS MEMBER	Mr D Orton The Hunters Inn **HEDDON VALLEY** EX31 4PY	01598 763230 www.thehuntersinn.net info@thehuntersinn.net	654 481 1500 mts PD	£50.00 PL EM DW D LSP CP KT PD O W LF D(7)(7ES) T(1)(1ES) F(2)(2ES) SS £20.00
3	Mrs FM Dallyn Mannacott Farm Nr Hunters Inn **MARTINHOE** EX31 4QS	01598 763227 francesdallyn@gmail.com	662 481 800 mts	£28.00 D CP KT O D(1)(1ES) T(1)(1ES) £28 single occupancy

Walk No.	Contact name Establishment name Address Region/Postcode	Telephone no. Mobile no. Email Website	OS Map Ref. Dist. from path	Starting price Facilities Room types Notes
3 BUSINESS MEMBER	Mrs R Brown Blair Lodge Moory Meadow, **COMBE MARTIN** EX34 0DG	01271 882294 www.blairlodge.co.uk info@blairlodge.co.uk	579 473 on path	£30.00 PL EM D LSP CP KT PD O W LF S(2)(1ES) D(5)(5ES) T(2)(2ES) F(1)(1ES)
3 BUSINESS MEMBER	Mrs P Palmer Mellstock House Woodlands, **COMBE MARTIN** EX34 0AR	01271 882592 www.mellstockhouse.co.uk enquiries@mellstockhouse.co.uk	573 472 20 metres	£27.00 PL EM D LSP CP KT PD O W LF D(5)(5ES) T(2)(2ES) F(1)(1ES) £10 single supplement
3 BUSINESS MEMBER	Mrs L Leyland Channel Vista Woodlands, **COMBE MARTIN** EX34 0AT	01271 883514 www.channelvista.co.uk channelvista@btconnect.com	574 470 100 mts	£31.00 PL EM DW D LSP CP KT O S(2)(2ES) D(4)(4ES) T(2)(2ES) F(1)(1ES) LSP by prior arrangement
3	Mrs S Davey Fontenay Woodlands, **COMBE MARTIN** EX34 0AT	01271 889368 mobile 07814 769845. www.visitfontenay.co.uk sarah@visitfontenay.co.uk	575 470 200 mts	£25.00 PL DW LSP CP KT PD O W LF S(1)(0ES) D(1)(0ES) T(1)(0ES) PL by prior arrangement, Child friendly
3	Mrs L Heard Park View Sunnyside, **COMBE MARTIN** EX34 0JH	01271 883006 www.parkview-bandb.com luzia.heard@yahoo.co.uk	587 464 800 mts PD	PL D CP KT PD O D(1)(1ES) F(1)(1ES)

Lynmouth Cliff Railway

For Combe Martin addresses see Exmoor B&Bs.

Walk No.	Contact name Establishment name Address Region/Postcode	Telephone no. Mobile no. Email Website	OS Map Ref. Dist. from path	Starting price Facilities Room types Notes
4 BUSINESS MEMBER	Mr & Mrs Jenkins Avalon 6 Capstone Crescent **ILFRACOMBE** EX34 9BT	01271 863325 www.avalon-hotel.co.uk avalon_ilfracombe@yahoo.co.uk	522 478 on path	£28.00 O(5 Jan 14 to 19 Dec) S(1)(1ES) D(4)(4ES) T(3)(3ES) F(1)(1ES) LSP low season only, Single £33
4 BUSINESS MEMBER	Mrs A Tappenden Ocean Backpackers Hostel, 29 St James Place ILFRACOMBE EX34 9BJ	01271 867835 www.oceanbackpackers.co.uk info@oceanbackpackers.co.uk	522 478 25 mts	£14.00 DW D CP O W SC (12) (10ES) kitchen for self catering.Weekend £15. 12 dorms sleeping 56 avail.
4	Mrs C Pearson Lyncott House 56 St Brannocks Road **ILFRACOMBE** EX34 8EQ	01271 862425 www.lyncotthouse.co.uk	515 468 1 km	£35.00 PL D CP O D(4)(4ES) T(1)(1ES) £5 single supplement
4	Mrs S Furmston The Collingdale 13 Larkstone Terrace **ILFRACOMBE** EX34 9NU	01271 863770 www.thecollingdale.co.uk thecollingdale@gmail.com	526 475 30 mts	£35.00 PL D KT O D(3)(0ES) T(3)(0ES) F(3)(0ES) single supplement
5 BUSINESS MEMBER	Mrs A James Watersmeet Hotel Mortehoe **WOOLACOMBE** EX34 7EB	01271 870333 www.watersmeethotel.co.uk info@watersmeethotel.co.uk	 200mts	£90.00 PL EM D LSP CP KT W LF O S(1)(1ES) D(3)(3ES) T()(3ES) F(6)(6ES) Bistro & fine dining.
5	Mr & Mrs M & W Lambert The Rocks Hotel Beach Road **WOOLACOMBE** EX34 7BT	01271 870361 www.therockshotel.co.uk enquiries@therockshotel.co.uk	460 438 500 mts	£45.00 D PL CP KT PD 5D 3T 1S 1F ALL ES
5 BUSINESS MEMBER	Mr P Milton, Trimstone Manor Country House Hotel, **TRIMSTONE**, Nr Woolacombe Ilfracombe EX34 8NR	01271 862841 www.trimstone.co.uk info@trimstone.co.uk	499 434 2 km	£54.00 EM DW LSP CP PD O S(1)(1ES) D(10) 10ES) T(2)(2ES) F(1)1ES) Also self catering & PD from Combe Martin to Barnstaple.
6 BUSINESS MEMBER	Mrs G M Adams Combas Farm **PUTSBOROUGH** Croyde EX33 1PH	01271 890398 www.combasfarm.co.uk combasfarm@hotmail.co.uk	449 396 900 mts	£33.00 PL D LSP CP KT W LF O S(1)(0ES) D(2)(2ES) T(1)(1ES) F(1)(1ES) Single supplement high season
6	Mrs V Learmonth Chapel Farm Guest House Hobbs Hill **CROYDE** EX33 1NE	01271 890429 www.chapelfarmcroyde.co.uk vall52@yahoo.co.uk	444 390 1 km	£35.00 O D(4)(3ES) T(2)(1ES) F(1)(1ES) also self catering
6	Mr & Mrs F Cannock Sandbourne Down End **CROYDE** EX33 1QE	01271 890536 fredcannock@tiscali.co.uk	436 386 300 mts	£35.00 PL D CP KT O D(2)(1ES) T(1)(1ES)
7 BUSINESS MEMBER	Mrs A Benning The Firs Higher Park Road **BRAUNTON** EX33 2LG	01271 814358 www.bennings.co.uk alisonbenning@btinternet.com	498 364 2 km PD	£35.00 PL DW D LSP CP KT O W D(1)(1ES) T(1)(1ES) single supplement
7 BUSINESS MEMBER	Mrs S Holker Silver Cottage 14 Silver Street **BRAUNTON** EX33 2EN	01271 814165 www.bedandbreakfast-braunton.co.uk silvercottage.braunton@gmail.com	487 367 400 mts PD	£30.00 O D EM PL CP KT 2D EM by prior arrangement

Walk No.	Contact name Establishment name Address Region/Postcode	Telephone no. Mobile no. Email Website	OS Map Ref. Dist. from path	Starting price Facilities Room types Notes
7 BUSINESS MEMBER	Mr C Brookes The Brookfield South Street **BRAUNTON** EX33 2AN	01271 812382 www.thebrookfield.co.uk info@thebrookfield.co.uk	487 362 400 mts	£31.50 PL D CP KT W O(Mid March to end Dec.) S(4)(4ES) D(5)(5ES) T(5)(5ES) F(1)(1ES) single supplement
7	Mr & Mrs Mrs B Watkins North Cottage 14 North Street **BRAUNTON** EX33 1AJ	01271 812703 Mobile 07779 842367 www.northcottagebraunton.co.uk north_cottage@hotmail.com	485 367 750 mts	£28.50 PL DW D CP KT O W LF S(2)(0ES) D(2)(2ES) T(1)(1ES) SS £1.50
7	Mrs K Mitchell Folly Farm Cottage 48 Saunton Road **BRAUNTON** EX33 1HD	01271 812148 Mobile 07737 420311 www.follyfarmcottage.com info@follyfarmcottage.com	481 366 3km	£34.00 PL D CP O D(2)(2ES) T(1)(1ES) Single £48
8 BUSINESS MEMBER	Mr B Abell The Old Vicarage B&B Barbican Terrace **BARNSTAPLE** EX32 9HQ	01271 328504 www.oldvicaragebarnstaple.co.uk theoldvicaragebarnstaple@gmail.com	561 328 200 mts	£40.00 D LSP CP KT O W LF S(1)(1ES) D(1)(1ES) T(1)(1ES) F(2)(2ES)
8	Mrs J Manning Herton Guesthouse Lake Hill **BARNSTAPLE** EX31 3HS	01271 323302 www.herton-guesthouse.co.uk janice@janicemanning93.wanadoo.co.uk	554 322 500 mts	£29.00 PL D LSP CP KT O D(3)(2ES) T(1)(1ES) F(1)(1ES) SC(1)(1ES) Single supplement
8	Mrs S Svenson Yeo Dale Hotel Pilton Bridge **BARNSTAPLE** EX31 1PG	01271 342954 www.yeodalehotel.co.uk stay@yeodalehotel.co.uk	557 338 600 mts	£42.50 PL EM D LSP CP KT O S(3)(3ES) D(7)(7ES) T(2)(2ES) F(2)(2ES) EM & LSP by prior arrangement
9 BUSINESS MEMBER	Mr P Day Lower Yelland Farm **FREMINGTON** Barnstaple EX31 3EN	01271 860101 www.loweryellandfarm.co.uk peterday@loweryellandfarm.co.uk	492 322 200 mts	£35.00 DW D CP KT O W LF S(2)(2ES) D(5)(5ES) £5 SS
10 BUSINESS MEMBER	Mrs J Steele Yeoldon House Hotel Durrant Lane, Northam **BIDEFORD** EX39 2RL	01237 474400 www.yeoldonhousehotel.co.uk yeoldonhouse@aol.com	on path	£60.00 PL EM DW D LSP CP W O(3/1 to 20/12) D(10)(10ES) SS £25
10	Mrs S Chapman Orchard Cottage Old Barnstaple Road **BIDEFORD** EX39 4ND	01237 422427 www.orchardstudiobideford.co.uk sylvia@orchardstudiobideford.co.uk	463 267 200 mts	£33.00 CP O T(1)(1ES) SC also SC
10 BUSINESS MEMBER	Mr M Widnell Appledore House Meeting Street **APPLEDORE** EX39 1RJ	01237 421471 Mobile 07825 141459 www.appledore-house.co.uk info@appledore-house.co.uk	463 306 500 mts	£75.00 PL D CP O W LF D(3)(3ES) T(1)(1ES) F(1)(1ES) Bikes welcome
10 BUSINESS MEMBER	Mrs P & J Hills The Seagate The Quay **APPLEDORE** EX39 1QS	01237 472589 www.theseagate.co.uk info@theseagate.co.uk	10 yards	£45.00 PL EM DW LSP CP O W LF S(1)(1ES) D(6)(6ES) T(2)(2ES) F(1)(1ES) SS
10	Ms P Lucraft 19 Bude Street **APPLEDORE** EX39 1PS	01237 477127 www.torridgehouseappledore.com pennylucraft@gmail.com	464 304 75 mts	£35.00 PL EM DW D PD O D(2)(2ES) T(1)(1ES) Single supplement

Walk No.	Contact name Establishment name Address Region/Postcode	Telephone no. Mobile no. Email Website	OS Map Ref. Dist. from path	Starting price Facilities Room types Notes
10 BUSINESS MEMBER	Mr & Mrs M Thomson Culloden House Fosketh Hill, **WESTWARD HO!** EX39 1UL	01237 479421 www.culloden-house.co.uk cullodenhouse@gmail.com	432 289 100 mts	£70.00 CP KT O W LF D(4)(4ES) T(2)(2ES) F(2)(2ES) price per room, single £56, DW by prior arrangement
10	Mrs S Clegg Mayfield Avon Lane, **WESTWARD HO!** EX39 1LR	01237 477128 www.mayfieldbandb.co.uk mayfieldbandb@hotmail.co.uk	435 291 100 mts	£28.00 PL D LSP CP KT PD O W LF D(1)(1ES) T(1)(1ES)
11 BUSINESS MEMBER	Mr & Mrs Curtis Fuchsia Cottage Burscott Lane, **HIGHER CLOVELLY** EX39 5RR	01237 431398 www.clovelly-holidays.co.uk tom@clovelly-holidays.co.uk	313 242 1km PD	£30.00 PL D LSP CP KT PD W LF O(Closed Xmas & New Year) S(1)(0ES) D(1)(1ES) T(1)(1ES) SS
11 BUSINESS MEMBER	Mr & Mrs C West Pillowery Park Burscott, **HIGHER CLOVELLY** EX39 5RR	01237 431668 www.clovellyaccommodation.com info@clovellyaccommodation.co.uk	312 241 1.5 km	£26.00 PL D LSP CP KT PD O W LF D(1)(1ES) T(2)(0ES) £10 single supplement
11 BUSINESS MEMBER	Mrs M McColl 1 Southdown Cottage **HIGHER CLOVELLY** EX39 5SA	01237 431504 maryfmcoll@hotmail.com	297 236 300m	£31.00 PL EM DW D LSP CP KT PD O S(1)(0ES) D(1)(1ES) T(1)(1ES) £14 single supplement
11	Mr & Mrs N Sanders The Old Police House Burscott Road, **HIGHER CLOVELLY** EX39 5RR	01237 431256 www.clovellybandb.co.uk norman.sanders@btinternet.com	313 241 500 mts	£30.00 PL EM DW D LSP CP KT O W LF D(1)(0ES) T(1)(1ES) £5 single supplement
12 BUSINESS MEMBER	Mr & Mrs J W George Gawlish Farm Gawlish **HARTLAND** EX39 6AT	01237 441320 gawlish@btconnect.com	256 263 300 mts PD	£30.00 PL EM D LSP CP KT O D(2)(2ES) T(2)(2ES) £5 Single supplement
12 BUSINESS MEMBER	Ms M Chesterman 2 Harton Manor The Square **HARTLAND** EX39 6BL	01237 441670 Mobile 07771 610982 www.twohartonmanor.co.uk merlyn@twohartonmanor.co.uk	258 245 3 km PD	£30.00 PL DW D LSP CP KT PD O W LF S(1)(0ES) D(1)(1ES) T(1)(1ES) PD Hartland Quay
12 BUSINESS MEMBER	Mrs Y Heard West Titchberry Farm **WEST TITCHBERRY** Hartland Point EX39 6AU	01237 441287 westtitchberry@gmail.com	242 272 250 mts PD	£27.50 PL EM D LSP CP KT PD O W LF D(1)(0ES) T(1)(0ES) F(1)(1ES) £5 single supplement
12 BUSINESS MEMBER	Mr & Mrs G Johns Hartland Quay Hotel **HARTLAND QUAY** EX39 6DU	01237 441218 www.hartlandquayhotel.com hartlandquayhotel@supanet.com	223 248 On Path	£50.00 PL EM D CP KT O W LF S(1)(1ES) D(4)(4ES) T(2)(2ES) F(6)(6ES) SS
13	Mrs A Dart 1 Coastguard Cottages **STOKE**, Hartland EX39 6DU	01237 441011 www.coastguardcottagestoke.com annajon@btinternet.com	235 246 500 mts	£35.00 PL EM DW D LSP CP KT O W LF D(2)(2ES) £10 single supplement
13	The Yarner Trust Welcombe Barton **WELCOMBE** EX39 6HF	01288 331692 www.yarnertrust.org info@yarnertrust.org		£15 D(1) T(1) F(2) SC and camping available

For addresses between Welcombe and Bude see North Cornwall B&Bs.

DEVON

CORNWALL
KERNOW
defra
This land is managed under the
Countryside
Stewardship Scheme

Walk No.	Contact name Establishment name Address Region/Postcode	Telephone no. Mobile no. Email Website	OS Map Ref. Dist. from path	Starting price Facilities Room types Notes
13 BUSINESS MEMBER	Mr Rob Tape The Bush Inn Crosstown **MORWENSTOW** EX23 9SR	01288 331242 www.bushinn-morwenstow.co.uk rob.tape@btinternet.com	208 150 600 mts	£45.00 PL EM DW LSP CP KT O W LF D(2)(2ES) T(2)(2ES) £50 single charge. Also self catering
13	Mrs C White Trelawney Crosstown **MORWENSTOW** EX23 9SR	01288 331453	208 150 800 mts	£30.00 PL D CP KT O S(1)(0ES) D(1)(0ES) £5 single supplement
13	Mrs S Bramhill West Point **CRIMP** Morwenstow Bude EX23 9PB	01288 331594 www.budebedandbreakfast.co.uk bramhill@hotmail.co.uk	255 155 5.5 kms PD	£30.00 PL LSP CP KT PD O D(1)(1ES) T(1)(1ES) F(1)(1ES)
13 BUSINESS MEMBER	Mrs J Steadman Tee-Side Guest House 2 Burn View **BUDE** EX23 8BY	01288 352351 www.tee-side.co.uk teeside.bude@gmail.com	208 066 400 mts	£30.00 PL D KT W O S(4)(4ES) D(4)(4ES) T(4)(4ES)
13 BUSINESS MEMBER	Mr M Safdar-Wallace Sea Jade 15 Burn View **BUDE** EX23 8BZ	01288 353404 www.seajadeguesthouse.co.uk seajadeguesthouse@yahoo.co.uk	209 065 450 mts	£30.00 PL EM D KT PD O W LF D(7)(4ES) £3 single supplement, Rooms are D/T/F
13 BUSINESS MEMBER	Miss S Turner Brendon Arms Falcon Terrace **BUDE** EX23 8SD	01288 354542 www.brendonarms.co.uk enquiries@brendonarms.co.uk	214 061 20 mts	£35.00 LSP CP O W LF S(1)(1ES) D(5)(5ES) T(3)(3ES)
13	Mrs E Payne Pencarrol Guest House 21 Downs View **BUDE** EX23 8RF	01288 352478 pencarrolbude@aol.com	209 070 300 mts	£33.00 PL D KT O S(1)(0ES) D(2)(2ES) T(2)(2ES) F(1)(1ES) single supplement in D
13	Mr M Fly Fairway Guest House 8 Downs View **BUDE** EX23 8RF	01288 355059 www.fairwayguesthouse.co.uk enquiries@fairwayguesthouse.co.uk	209 070 300 mts	 PL D KT O(Feb-Nov) S(3)(1ES) D(5)(5ES) T(2)(2ES) F(1)(1ES) PL by prior arrangement
13	Mrs L Kelly Links Side 7 Burn View **BUDE** EX23 8BY	01288 352410 www.linkssidebude.co.uk linksidebude@hotmail.com	208 067 400 mts	£25.00 PL D CP KT O S(1)(1ES) D(4)(3ES) T(1)(1ES) F(1)(1ES)
13	Mrs C Simmons Palms Guesthouse 17 Burn View Road **BUDE** EX23 8BZ	01288 353962 palmsguesthouse@tiscali.co.uk	210 066 500 mts	£28.00 D PL CP LSP KT 1D 2T 1S 1F ALL ES
14	Mr & Mrs R Holmes Bears & Boxes Penrose, **DIZZARD** St Gennys EX23 0NX	01840 230318 www.bearsandboxes.com rwfrh@btinternet.com	168 990 500 mts PD	£37.00 PL EM DW D LSP CP O S(2)(2ES) D(2)(2ES)
14 BUSINESS MEMBER	Mrs EK de Haan Higher Tresmorn Farm **ST GENNYS** Bude EX23 0NU	01840 230371 www.highertresmorn.co.uk tresmorn@btinternet.com	 100	 PL EM DW D LSP CP KT PD O W LF D(1)(1ES) F(1)(1ES) SC(4)(4ES)

Walk No.	Contact name Establishment name Address Region/Postcode	Telephone no. Mobile no. Email Website	OS Map Ref. Dist. from path	Starting price Facilities Room types Notes
14	Mr R Tape The Old Wainhouse Inn Wainhouse Corner **ST GENNYS** Bude EX23 0EA	01840 230711 www.oldwainhouseinn.co.uk wainhouse10@yahoo.co.uk	220 006 2.5 km	£42.50 PL EM DW LSP CP KT O W LF D(2)(2ES) T(2)(2ES) £7.50 single supplement
14 BUSINESS MEMBER	Mr & Mrs F Mussell Trewartha St Gennys **CRACKINGTON HAVEN** EX23 0NN	01840 230420 www.bychy.co.uk francismussell@btinternet.com	150 967 750 mts	£30.00 PL EM DW D CP KT PD O WS(1)(1ES) D(3)(3ES) F(1)(1ES) SC(4)(4ES) some chalet accommodation. £5 SS
14 BUSINESS MEMBER	Mr & Mrs C Morgan Coombe Barton Inn **CRACKINGTON HAVEN** EX23 0JG	01840 230345 www.thecoombebartoninn.co.uk thecoombebartininn@btconnect.com	144 967 50m	£45.00 PL EM DW D LSP CP KT O W LF D(3)(2ES) T(2)(2ES) F(1)(1ES) Limited LSP. £10 SS
14	Mr & Mrs J May Ludon Hill CRACKINGTON HAVEN EX23 0JZ	01840 230584 johnanniemay@btinternet.com	144 966 300 mts	£30.00 D KT O D(1)(0ES) T(1)(0ES)
14	Mrs J Morris 14 Lundy Drive **CRACKINGTON HAVEN** EX23 0PA	01840 230106 www.crackingtonhavenbandb.co.uk julie@crackingtonhavenbandb.co.uk	154 959 1.5 km	£27.50 PL D LSP CP PD O D(1)(1ES) T(1)(0ES)
15 BUSINESS MEMBER	Mr J Scott The Wellington Hotel The Harbour, **BOSCASTLE** Cornwall PL35 0AQ	01840 250202 www.wellingtonhotelboscastle.com info@wellingtonhotelboscastle.com	098 913 200 mts	£40.00 PL EM DW D CP KT O W LF S(3)(3ES) D(9)(9ES) T(3)(3ES) F(1)(1ES)
15	Mr & Mrs G Barratt Orchard Lodge Gunpool Lane **BOSCASTLE** PL35 0AT	01840 250418 www.orchardlodgeboscastle.co.uk orchardlodgeboscastle@gmail.com	906 099 500 mts	£37.50 PL D CP KT O D(3)(3ES) T(2)(2ES)
15	Mrs J Horwell The Old Coach House Tintagel Road **BOSCASTLE** PL35 0AS	01840 250398 www.old-coach.co.uk stay@old-coach.co.uk	098 906 400 mts	£36.00 PL D KT O D(3)(3ES) T(3)(3ES) F(2)(2ES) Price based on 2 sharing
16	Mrs A Jones Grange Cottage **BOSSINEY** Tintagel PL34 0AX	01840 770487	066 888 200 mts	£32.00 PL D CP KT W LF O(April - Oct) S(1)(0ES) D(1)(1ES) SS £6
16	Mrs P Tinney Bossinney Cottage **BOSSINEY** Tintagel PL34 0AY	01840 770327 bossinney@tinney.org	066 888 200 mts	£30.00 PL EM D LSP CP KT O S(1)(0ES) D(1)(0ES) F(1)(0ES)
16	Mr & Mrs Chamberlain Westcote House **BOSSINEY** PL34 0AX	01840 779194 www.westcotehouse.co.uk nevchamberlain@btinternet.com	064 888 300 mts	D LSP CP KT O D(1)(1ES) T(1)(1ES)
16 BUSINESS MEMBER	Mr K Walker Bosayne Guest House Atlantic Road **TINTAGEL** PL34 0DE	01840 770514 www.bosayne.co.uk enquiries@bosayne.co.uk	056 888 300 mts	£26.00 PL D CP KT O W LF S(3)(0ES) D(3)(3ES) T(1)(1ES) F(1)(0ES) SC(1)(0ES)

Walk No.	Contact name Establishment name Address Region/Postcode	Telephone no. Mobile no. Email Website	OS Map Ref. Dist. from path	Starting price Facilities Room types Notes
17	Mrs V Mackay Trenowan B&B **TREKNOW** Tintagel PL34 0EJ	01840 770554 www.cornwall-online.co.uk/trenowanbandb trenowanbandb@btinternet.com	055 872 300 mts	£30.00 O D PL CP LSP KT 1D[1] 1D/T[1] 1S Occasional DW
17	Mr & Mrs B Nutt Hillscroft, **TREKNOW** Tintagel, Nr Trebarwith Strand PL34 0EN	01840 770551 brian.nutt@btinternet.com	056 866 800 mts PD	£30.00 PL LSP CP KT PD O D(1)(1ES) £10 single supplement
17 BUSINESS MEMBER	Mr & Mrs G Sylvester Port Gaverne Hotel PORT GAVERNE Port Isaac PL29 3SQ	01208 880244 www.port-gaverne-hotel.co.uk graham@port-governe-hotel.co.uk	003 807 30 mts	£45.00 O D EM PL CP LSP DW KT 9D 3T 3F ALL ES
17 BUSINESS MEMBER	Mr & Mrs N Monk Lane End Farm Pendoggett **PORT ISAAC** PL30 3HH	01208 880013 Mobile: 07724 133820 www.laneendcornwall.co.uk nabmonk@tiscali.co.uk	026 793 2.5 km PD	£36.00 PL D LSP CP KT PD W LF O S(1)(1ES) T(1)(1ES) also self catering
17	Mrs N March Penderris House B & B 7 Tintagel Terrace **PORT ISAAC** PL29 3SE	01208 880419 mobile: 07816 918041 nancymarch@live.com	999 808 200m	£30.00 PL DW LSP CP KT O D(1)(1ES) T(2)(0ES) £10 single supplement
18	Mr & Mrs P Cullinan 4 Riverside **PADSTOW** PL28 8BY	01841 532383 www.southquaybedandbreakfastpadstow.co.uk cullinan@madasafish.com	920 754 190 mts	£35.00 DW O D(2)(1ES) single supplement, DW in one room only
18	Mrs A Crowley Trealaw Guest House & Tea Room, 72 Duke Street, **PADSTOW** PL28 8AB	01841 533161 www.trealaw.com anthea.crowley@btinternet.com	918 754 300 mts	£80.00 PL EM O W LF D(1)(1ES) price per room, single £50
18	Mrs E Cortis 'Ere Tis 3 Egerton Road **PADSTOW** PL28 8DJ	01841 532320	920 748 100 mts	£35.00 D CP W O(Easter - End Sept) S(1)(0ES) D(1)(0ES) T(1)(1ES) SS
20	Mrs E Kennerley Penhalonga **CONSTANTINE BAY** PL28 8JG	01841 521122 mobile: 07815 833158 lizkennerley@btinternet.com	869 743	£70.00 PL LSP CP W LF O S(1)(1ES) D(1)(1ES) T(1)(1ES) Price for 2 sharing; single £40
20 BUSINESS MEMBER	Mrs M Neale Penlan **PORTHCOTHAN BAY** PL28 8LP	01841 520440 Mobile 07525 940404 www.porthcothanbay.co.uk/pcb2_bandb mary@idenna.com	859 719 200 mts	£35.00 PL EM DW D LSP CP KT O W LF D(2)(2ES) T(1)(0ES)
20 BUSINESS MEMBER	Mr & Mrs J Nederpel Old MacDonald's Farm **PORTHCOTHAN BAY** PL28 8LW	01841 540829 www.oldmacdonalds.co.uk enquiries@oldmacdonalds.co.uk	867 877 1 km	£40.00 PL EM CP KT O T(1)(1ES) F(2)(2ES)
20	Mrs P Mcowen Greylands, Treburrick **PORTHCOTHAN** WADEBRIDGE PL27 7UR	01841 540451 www.greylands.moonfruit.com greylandscottage@gmail.com	862 707 500 mts PD	£65.00 PL EM DW D LSP CP KT PD O D(2)(1ES) Price per room, £45 single occupancy.

Walk No.	Contact name Establishment name Address Region/Postcode	Telephone no. Mobile no. Email Website	OS Map Ref. Dist. from path	Starting price Facilities Room types Notes
21 BUSINESS MEMBER	Mrs R Vickers Trevarrian Lodge Trevarrian, **MAWGAN PORTH** TR8 4AQ	01637 860156 www.trevarrianlodge.com trevarrianlodge@gmail.com	850 661 400 mts	£30.00 PL DW D LSP CP KT O S(1)(1ES) D(1)(1ES) T(2)(2ES) F(2)(2ES) DW by prior arrangement only
21	Mrs B Bradley Dimora, Gwel-an-Mor **MAWGAN PORTH** TR8 4DW	01637 860511 Mobile 07712590509 www.dimorabed.breakfast.co.uk abbholist@yahoo.co.uk	853 674 500 mts	 PL DW D LSP CP O W D(1)(1ES) F(1)(1ES)
21	Miss L Balls Kenton Hotel Watergate Road **PORTH** TR7 3LX	01637 872736 www.hotelsinnewquay.co.uk info@hotelsinnewquay.co.uk	532 632 200 mts	£37.00 EM DW CP KT O S(2)(2ES) D(5)(5ES) T(5)(5ES) F(4)(4ES) Single supplement in August
21 BUSINESS MEMBER	Mr G Dolan The Three Tees Hotel 21 Carminow Way **NEWQUAY** TR7 3AY	01637 872055 www.3tees.co.uk greg@3tees.co.uk	824 621 250 mts	£34.00 PL DW D LSP CP KT O D(4)(4ES) T(2)(2ES) F(3)(3ES)
21 BUSINESS MEMBER	Mrs B Watts Tir Chonaill Lodge 106 Mount Wise **NEWQUAY** TR7 1QP	01637 876492 www.tirchonaill.co.uk tirchonailhotel@talk21.com	814 617 500m	£25.00 PL DW D LSP CP KT W LF O(March - Oct) S(2)(2ES) D(2)(2ES) T(2)(2ES) F(3)(3ES) Cornish, Irish Gaelic & French spoken
22	Mr & Mrs B Clark Carden Cottage Halwyn Hill **CRANTOCK** TR8 5RR	01637 830806 www.cardencottagecrantock.com cardencottage@btinternet.com	791 603 500 mts	£40.00 PL D LSP CP KT PD O D(2)(2ES) T(1)(1ES) £4 supplement for D ES
23 BUSINESS MEMBER	Mrs S Stirling & Mrs Sue Lawrie St Georges Country Hotel, St Georges Hill **PERRANPORTH** TR6 0ED	01872 572184 www.stgeorgescountryhouse.co.uk info@stgeorgescountryhouse.co.uk	746 533 400 mts PD	£40.00 PL EM DW D CP KT PD O W LF D(5)(5ES) F(2)(2ES) SS £20
24	Mr & Mrs N York Kimberley West Polberro **ST AGNES** TR5 0SS	01872 552044 mobile 07790 048616 www.kimberleybedandbreakfast.co.uk kimberley_sta@hotmail.com	716 515 500 mts	£65.00 D LSP CP KT O D(2)(1ES) T(1)(1ES) £45 single occupancy, 4 night discount
25 BUSINESS MEMBER	Mr & Mrs S Haywood Cliff House Cliff Terrace **PORTREATH** TR16 4LE	01209 843847 www.cliffhouseportreath.co.uk cliffhousebookinginfo@gmail.com	656 455 On path	£35.00 DW CP KT O S(2)(0ES) D(2)(2ES) T(2)(2ES) F(1)(1ES) Single supplement
25	Mr & Mrs J Urban Moor House Bridge Moor **PORTREATH** TR16 4QA	01209 843120 www.moor-house-uk.com maria.urban@earthlink.net	664 452 200 mts	£40.00 PL LSP CP KT O S(1)(1ES) D(2)(2ES) Single supplement

Trevose Head

For Portreath addresses see North Cornwall B&Bs.

Walk No.	Contact name Establishment name Address Region/Postcode	Telephone no. Mobile no. Email Website	OS Map Ref. Dist. from path	Starting price Facilities Room types Notes
25 BUSINESS MEMBER	Mrs L Davies Nanterrow Farm **GWITHIAN** TR27 5BP	01209 712282 www.nanterrowfarm.co.uk nanterrow@hotmail.com	599 412 1.5km PD	£35.00 D LSP CP PD W LF O(Feb-Nov) D(1) (0ES) single supplement
25	Mr T Greenaway Godrevy House Prosper Hill **GWITHIAN** TR27 5BW	01736 755493 www.gwithianholidays.com enquiries@gwithianholidays.com	588 409 1 km	£30.00 DW CP KT PD O D(2)(2ES) F(2)(2ES)
25	Mrs P Ellis The Mad Hatter 73 Fore Street **HAYLE** TR27 4DX	01736 754241 Mobile: 07871 165381 www.cornwall-online.co.uk/madhatter paulineellis-madhatter.org@tesco.net	566 378 1 km	£30.00 PL EM DW D LSP CP PD O S(2)(1ES) D(2)(1ES) T(2)(1ES) F(1)(0ES)
25	Mrs E Cooper 54 Penpol Terrace **HAYLE** TR27 4BQ	01736 752855 jacoop@talktalk.net	558 374 on path	£45.00 PL D LSP CP W LF O(Jan - Nov) S(1)(0ES) T(1)(0ES)
25	Mrs L Eddy Wilcuma Cottage B & B 15 Wheal Alfred Road **HAYLE** TR27 5JT	01736 757357 www.eddycottage.co.uk lyndaeddy@btinternet.com	 2 kms	£35.00 CP KT PD O W D(2)(2ES) T(1)(1ES) SS £10
26	Mrs L Bowden Carlill 9 Porthminster Terrace **ST IVES** TR26 2DQ	01736 796738 www.carlillguesthouse.co.uk carlillguesthouse@hotmail.co.uk	 300m	£40.00 PL LSP CP KT O W S(2)(1ES) D(5)(2ES) T(4)(2ES) F(2)(1ES)
26	Mrs S Martin 8 Ayr Lane **ST IVES** TR26 1JL	01736 793172	517 405 100 mts	£30.00 D O(Jul-Aug) S(1)(1ES) T(1)(1ES)
27	Mrs N Mann Trewey Farm Zennor **TREWEY** Zennor TR26 3DA	01736 796936	456 381 700 mts	£40.00 PL D CP O S(1)(0ES) D(2)(0ES) T(1)(0ES) F(2)(0ES)
27	Mrs E Thompson Boswednack Manor **BOSWEDNACK** Zennor TR26 3DD	01736 794183 www.boswednackmanor.co.uk boswednack@ravenfield.co.uk	442 378 1.5 km	£27.00 PL CP KT O S(1)(0ES) D(2)(2ES) T(1)(0ES) F(1)(0ES) also SC for 5 people
28 BUSINESS MEMBER	Ms H Hurkett, Gypsy Caravan B&B, Primrose Cottage, Levant Road **TREWELLARD**, Pendeen TR19 7SU	01736 787585 mobile 07900 631268 www.gypsycaravanbandb.co.uk holiday@gypsycaravanbandb.co.uk	373 339 300 mts	£28.00 D LSP CP KT O LF S(1)(0ES) D(1)(0ES) £5 charge for dog, cold supper provided on request
28 BUSINESS MEMBER	Mrs J Hoather The Old Chapel **BOSCASWELL DOWNS** Pendeen TR19 7DR	01736 786006 Mobile 07789 547806 www.cornwallfarwest.co.uk geoffgoatherd@aol.com	385 344 1 km	£30.00 DW D LSP CP KT O W D(2)(0ES) T(2)(0ES) SC(3)(0ES) also self catering
28 BUSINESS MEMBER	Mrs M Keogh St Johns House **PENDEEN** TR19 7DW	01736 786605 Mobile 07795 570605 www.stjohnshousebedandbreakfast.co.uk moriakeogh@btinternet.com	696 184 1km	£35.00 PL EM D CP O W LF S(1)(0ES) D(1)(1ES) T()(ES)

Walk No.	Contact name Establishment name Address Region/Postcode	Telephone no. Mobile no. Email Website	OS Map Ref. Dist. from path	Starting price Facilities Room types Notes
28	Mr E J Coak The North Inn **PENDEEN** TR19 7DN	01736 788417 www.thenorthinnpendeen.co.uk ernestjohncoak@aol.com	383 344 1 km	 PL EM DW LSP CP O D(1)(1ES) T(3)(3ES) Also camping
28	Mr & Mrs T Dymond The Old Count House **BOSCASWELL DOWNS** Pendeen TR19 7EE	01736 788058 www.cornwallonline.co.uk dymondep@aol.com	383 344 1 km	£25.00 PL D LSP CP KT O D(2)(0ES)
28	Mr & Mrs P & W Michelmore St Just B&B 2 Fore Street **St JUST** TR19 7LL	01736 787784 www.stjustbandb.com enquiries@stjustbandb.com	372 314 1.75 kms	£32.50 PL KT O D(1)(0ES) T(1)(0ES) F(1)(0ES) Single £15
28	Mrs J Eccleston Nanquidno Farm **ST JUST** TR19 7NU	01736 788463 www.nanquidnofarm.co.uk joeccleston3@hotmail.co.uk	363 292 695 mts	£27.00 SS £3 EM DW D CP KT PD W LF O (Mar to end Oct EXCL Aug) D(1)(0ES) T(1)(0ES)
28 BUSINESS MEMBER	Mrs C Collinson Bosavern House **BOSAVERN** St Just TR19 7RD	01736 788301 www.bosavern.com info@bosavern.com	370 305 1 km	£38.00 PL D CP KT O W LF S(1)(1ES) D(3)(3ES) T(2)(1ES) F(2)(2ES) PL by prior arrangement, SS
28	Mrs J Pengelly Pengelly House **SENNEN COVE** Penzance TR19 7DF	01736 871866 mobile 07810 361739 www.pengellyhouse.com stay@pengellyhouse.com	352 265 40 mts	£30.00 PL D LSP CP KT PD O W S(1)(1ES) D(1)(1ES) T(1)(1ES) Continental breakfast in room
28 BUSINESS MEMBER	Mrs J Mitchell Mayon Farmhouse **SENNEN** TR19 7AD	01736 871757 www.mayonfarmhouse.co.uk mayonfarmhouse@hotmail.co.uk	356 257 400 mts	£45.00 PL D LSP CP KT O W LF D(3)(3ES) T(1)(0ES) F(1)(1ES) single supplement
29 BUSINESS MEMBER	Miss & Mr Bance & Hicks Land's End Hostel Accomm Mill Barn, Trevescan Nr **LAND'S END** TR19 7AQ	07519 309 908 www.landsendhostelaccommodation.co.uk susie@landsendhostelaccommodation.co.uk	355 248 400 mts	£25.00 DW CP KT O S(1)(0ES) D(1)(1ES) T(1)(1ES) F(2)(1ES) Hostel Accommodation
29 BUSINESS MEMBER	Ms P Willows Sea View House The Valley **PORTHCURNO** TR19 6JX	01736 810638 www.seaviewhouseporthcurno.com svhouse@btinternet.com	383 227 400 mts PD	£38.00 PL D LSP CP KT PD O S(1)(0ES) D(5)(3ES) T(1)(1ES) F(1)(1ES) Single supplement
29	Mrs S Wear The Wearhouse The Valley **PORTHCURNO** TR19 6JX	01736 810129 susan.wear@me.com	383 226 200 mts	£35.00 D LSP CP KT O D(2)(2ES)
29	Mr & Mrs C Hatton Rose Cottage **PORTHCURNO** TR19 6JY	01736 810082 mobile 07926 084610 www.porthcurno.org.uk chris@chrisswcpa.co.uk	382 229 500 mts	£28.00 PL D CP KT PD O S(1)(0ES) D(1)(0ES) guided walks Land's End & Lizard
30 BUSINESS MEMBER	Mrs R Hood Castallack Farm **LAMORNA** Penzance TR19 6NL	01736 731969 www.castallackfarm.co.uk info@castallackfarm.co.uk	452 254 1.75 km	£37.50 PL EM DW D CP KT O W LF D(1)(1ES) T(1)(1ES) SS £17.50

For Portreath addresses see North Cornwall B&Bs.

Walk No.	Contact name Establishment name Address Region/Postcode	Telephone no. Mobile no. Email Website	OS Map Ref. Dist. from path	Starting price Facilities Room types Notes
31	Mrs E Reynolds Renovelle 6 The Parade **MOUSEHOLE**	TR19 6PN 01736 731258	469 264 on path	£27.00 PL D CP KT O(Easter-Oct) S(1)(0ES) D(2)(1ES)
31	Mrs D Waters White Gates Cliff Lane **MOUSEHOLE** TR19 6PU	01736 731691 www.chycor.co.uk	471 267 on path	£35.00 DW D CP W O(Easter-Oct) D(1)(0ES) T(1)(0ES) F(1)(1ES) single supplement
31 BUSINESS MEMBER	Ms L Brown Panorama Guest House Chywoone Hill, **NEWLYN** Penzance TR18 5AR	01736 360798 www.panorama-guesthouse.co.uk lyndabrown1806@btinternet.com	461 283 400 mts	£42.50 PL EM DW D LSP CP KT O W LF S(2)(2ES) D(2)(2ES) T(1)(1ES) F(1)(1ES) single supplement.
31 BUSINESS MEMBER	Mr & Mrs A Stott Glencree House 2 Mennaye Road **PENZANCE** TR18 4NG	01736 362026 www.glencreehouse.co.uk stay@glencreehouse.co.uk	469 297 50 mts	£33.00 PL KT PD O W LF S(2)(1ES) D(3)(3ES) T(1)(1ES) F(1)(1ES)
31 BUSINESS MEMBER	Mrs C Edwards Tremont Guest Accomm Alexandra Road **PENZANCE** TR18 4LZ	01736 362614 www.tremonthotel.co.uk info@tremonthotel.co.uk	465 300 200 mts	£34.00 PL D KT W LF O(March to Dec 20th) S(2)(2ES) D(3)(3ES) T(3)(3ES) single supplement
31 BUSINESS MEMBER	Mr S Sprague Treventon Guest House Alexandra Place **PENZANCE** TR18 4NE	01736 332730 www.penzance-bed-and-breakfast.co.uk info@penzance-bed-and-breakfast.co.uk	 100m	£37.50 PL D LSP CP KT O W LF S(2)(2ES) D(4)(4ES) T(2)(2ES) F(1)(1ES) Local butcher, dairy & preserves
31	Mr M Martens Cornerways 5 Leskinnick Street **PENZANCE** TR18 2HA	01736 364645 mobile 07582 722510 www.cornerways-penzance.co.uk enquires@cornerways-penzance.co.uk	475 308 300 mts	£35.00 PL EM D O W LF S(2)(2ES) D(1)(1ES) T(1)(1ES) single supplement
31	Mr & Mrs P Vincent Blue Horizon Fore Street **MARAZION** TR17 0AW	01736 711199 www.bluehorizon-marazion.co.uk stay@bluehorizon-marazion.co.uk	521 306 on path	 PL D CP PD W O(Easter-Oct) S(1)(0ES) D(3)(3ES) T(2)(2ES) PD & LSP low season
32	Mrs C Boston Rowena Trebarvah Perranuthnoe **PENZANCE** TR20 9NG	01736 710467 www.rowenabandb.co.uk cavcarter@btinternet.com	 250 mts	
32 BUSINESS MEMBER	Mrs M Foy Mzima, Penlee Close **PRAA SANDS** TR20 9SR	01736 763856 marianfoy@prussia-cove-holiday.com	581 287 800 mts PD	£27.00 PL D CP KT PD O T(1)(0ES) F(1)(0ES)
32 BUSINESS MEMBER	Mrs B Rogers Wellmore End Cottage Methleigh Bottoms **PORTHLEVEN** TR13 9JP	01326 569310 www.wellmoreend-bandb.co.uk wellmoreend-bandb@tiscali.co.uk	 200m	£37.50 PL D LSP CP KT PD O W LF D(1)(1ES) F(1)(1ES) SS
32 BUSINESS MEMBER	Mrs S Kelynack An Mordros Hotel Peverell Terrace **PORTHLEVEN** TR13 9DZ	01326 562236 www.anmordroshotel.com enquiries@anmordroshotel.com	630 255 100 mts	£35.50 PL D KT W LF O D(5)(5ES) T(1)(1ES)

Walk No.	Contact name Establishment name Address Region/Postcode	Telephone no. Mobile no. Email Website	OS Map Ref. Dist. from path	Starting price Facilities Room types Notes
33 BUSINESS MEMBER	Mr T Martin Nantrisack Farm **SITHNEY** **HELSTON** TR13 0AE	0774 0514188 www.cornwall-backpackers.co.uk tom@cornwall-backpackers.co.uk	638 298 3 miles	£10.00 LSP CP KT PD O W D(2)(1ES) T()(ES) SC(10)(10ES) B&B £25. Continental breakfast. Pick up £4.
33 BUSINESS MEMBER	Mr D Jeffery Strathallan Guest House 6 Monument Road **HELSTON** TR13 8HF	01326 573683 www.strathallangh.co.uk enquiries@strathangh.co.uk		£35.00 PL EM D CP O W LF D(6)(6ES) T()(1ES) 2 mins from town centre. Ideally situated to explore The Lizard. SS £10
33	Mr & Mrs I Paterson Tregathenan House B&B The Old Farmhouse Tregathenan **HELSTON** TR13 0RZ	01326 569840 Mob 07796 697865 www.tregathenan.co.uk tregathenan@hotmail.com	654 306 6 km PD	£28.50 PL D LSP CP PD O W LF D(2)(1ES) T(1)(1ES) SC(3)(3ES) SS £6.50
33	Mrs T Payne Lyndale Cottage Guest House 4 Greenbank, Meneage Road **HELSTON** TR13 8JA	01326 561082 www.lyndalecottage.co.uk enquiries@lyndalecottage.co.uk	662 269 3.5 km	£35.00 CP O S(1)(1ES) D(3)(3ES) T(2)(2ES) Single supplement
33	Mr and Mrs P W Savage The Mounts Bay Guest House & Inn, Churchtown **MULLION** TR12 7HN	01326 241761 www.mountsbayguesthouse.co.uk mountsbaybandb@btinternet.com	678 192 1 km	£35.00 EM D KT O S(1)(1ES) D(4)(4ES) T(2)(2ES) F(1)(1ES)
33 BUSINESS MEMBER	Ms S Allen Mullion Cove Hotel **MULLION COVE** **TR12 7EP**	01326 240328 www.mullion-cove.co.uk enquiries@mullion-cove.co.uk	668 181 on path £60.00	PL EM DW LSP CP KT O W LF D(17)(17ES) T(10)(10ES) F(3)(3ES) Single supplement
34 BUSINESS MEMBER	Mrs A Bunnetat Treluswell Main Road, **LIZARD** Helston TR12 7NZ	01326 290286 Mobile 07967 193976 www.treluswellb&b.co.uk anniebunnetat@yahoo.co.uk		£35.00 PL DW D CP KT O W LF S(1)(0ES) D(2)(0ES) SS £15
34 BUSINESS MEMBER	D Glosby Top House Inn **THE LIZARD** TR12 7NQ	01326 290974 www.thetophouselizard.co.uk mail@thetophouselizard.co.uk	704 125 1km	£42.50 PL EM LSP CP KT O W LF T(2)(2ES) SS £27.50
34	Mrs C Barker Stormfield **THE LIZARD** TR12 7NZ	01326 290184 carol.annetts@hotmail.com	703 126 400 mts	£35.00 D LSP CP KT O W LF D(1)(0ES) T(1)(0ES) single supplement
34	Mr & Mrs A H Pratt The Caerthillian **THE LIZARD** TR12 7NQ	01326 290019 www.thecaerthillian.co.uk caerthillian@hotmail.com	703 125 500 mts	£35.00 PL DW D LSP CP KT O W LF S(1)(0ES) D(2)(2ES) T(1)(1ES) F(1)(1ES) SS from £10
35	Mrs A Rogers Fernleigh Chymbloth Way **COVERACK** TR12 6TB	01326 280626 www.fernleighcoverack.co.uk sudan-ann03@hotmail.co.uk	781 183 50 mts	£35.00 PL EM DW D LSP CP KT O D(2)(1ES) T(1)(1ES) F(1)(1ES)
35	Mrs G Wood Arlyn, Chymbloth Way **COVERACK** TR12 6TB	01326 280926 www.coverack.org.uk/pages/Arlyn woodpgs@tesco.net	781 183 300 mts	£30.00 D LSP CP O D(2)(1ES) F(1)(0ES)

West Cornwall B&Bs

For Portreath addresses see North Cornwall B&Bs.

Walk No.	Contact name Establishment name Address Region/Postcode	Telephone no. Mobile no. Email Website	OS Map Ref. Dist. from path	Starting price Facilities Room types Notes
35	Mr & Mrs D Powell Penmarth House **COVERACK**, The Lizard Peninsula TR12 6TQ	01326 280240 www.coverack-bandb.co.uk francine@coverack-bandb.co.uk	781 185 150 mts	£25.00 PL EM D LSP CP KT O D(2)(2ES) T(2)(2ES) F(1)(1ES) single supplement
36	Mr & Mrs W Sanger Tregoning Lea Laddenvean, St Keverne **HELSTON** TR12 6QE	01326 280947 waltersanger@aol.com	788 214 1 km	£30.00 PL DW D LSP CP KT PD O W S(1)(0ES) D(1)(1ES) T(1)(0ES) SS £10
36 BUSINESS MEMBER	Mr & Mrs Jourdan, FAT APPLES CAFE, THE OLD VINEYARD, **PORTHALLOW** Nr Helston TR12 6QH	01326 281559 fatapplescafe@gmail.com	On the path	 PL D O W LF
36	Mr & Mrs D Lambrick The Five Pilchards Inn **PORTHALLOW** TR12 6PP	01326 280256 www.thefivepilchards.co.uk fivepilchards@btinternet.com	796 232 5m	£0.00 PL EM D LSP CP KT O T(4)(4ES)
36	Mrs E Whale Porthvean **GILLAN** TR12 6HL	01326 231204 ewhale@hotmail.co.uk	782 252 on path	£25.00 PL DW D LSP CP KT O T(1)(1ES) facilities to prepare own EM
36	Mr & Mrs J Moore Landre Vicarage Lane **MANACCAN** TR12 6JH	01326 231556 johnandwendymoor@gmail.com	767 251 500 mts	£35.00 D CP O D(1)(1ES) Self contained unit
36	Mrs P Royall **POINT** Helford TR12 6JY	01326 231083 pamroyall@btinternet.com	758 262 on path	£37.50 D CP O W LF T(1)(1ES) Single supplement
37	Mrs S P Annan Chynoweth Carwinion Lane **MAWNAN SMITH** TR11 5JB	01326 250534 mobile 07900 274230 www.chynoweth.helfordriver.net sallyannan2@gmail.com	781 283 800 mts PD	£35.00 D CP KT O D(1)(1ES) T(1)(1ES) £50 single
37	Mrs C Lake Gold Martin Carlidnack Road **MAWNAN SMITH** TR11 5HA	01326 250666 www.goldmartin.co.uk gold_martin@hotmail.com	779 291 1.6 km PD	£34.00 PL D CP KT PD O S(1)(1ES) D(2)(2ES) T(1)(1ES) Single only let with double room
37 BUSINESS MEMBER	Mr & Mrs M Cook The Rosemary 22 Gyllyngvase Terrace **FALMOUTH** TR11 4DL	01326 314669 www.therosemary.co.uk stay@therosemary.co.uk	810 318 100 mts	£40.00 DW W LF O(Feb to end Oct) S(1)(1ES) D(5)(5ES) T(2)(2ES) F(2)(2ES) Single supplement
37 BUSINESS MEMBER	Ms J Goodchild Falmouth Backpackers 9 Gyllyngvase Terrace **FALMOUTH** TR11 4DL	01326 319996 www.falmouthbackpackers.co.uk judi@falmouthlodge.co.uk	811 319 150 mts	£19.00 D LSP CP KT O S(1)(0ES) D(1)(1ES) T(2)(0ES) 3 DORMS, price includes simple breakfast
37 BUSINESS MEMBER	Mrs S Humphreys The Westcott Gyllyngvase Hill **FALMOUTH** TR11 4DN	01326 311309 www.westcottguesthousefalmouth.co.uk westcotthotel@btinternet.com	809 317	£35.00 PL D CP KT O W LF S(1)(1ES) D(5)(5ES) T(2)(2ES) F(1)(1ES)

Walk No.	Contact name Establishment name Address Region/Postcode	Telephone no. Mobile no. Email Website	OS Map Ref. Dist. from path	Starting price Facilities Room types Notes
37 BUSINESS MEMBER	Mr A Oliver The Seaview Inn Wodehouse Terrace **FALMOUTH** TR11 3EP	01326 311359 Mobile 07805 171018 www.seaviewinnfalmouth.co.uk seaviewinn@hotmail.co.uk	808 326	£35.00 PL EM DW D LSP CP O W LF D(2)(2ES) T(1)(1ES) SS £20
37	Mr P Lower Gyllyngvase House Hotel Gyllyngvase Road **FALMOUTH** TR11 4GH	01326 312956 www.gyllyngvase.co.uk info@gyllyngvase.co.uk	810 318 50 mts	£38.00 PL EM D LSP CP KT O S(2)(0ES) D(7)(7ES) T(2)(2ES) F(1)(1ES)
37	Mrs R Riddette-Gregory 26 Melvill Road **FALMOUTH** TR11 4AR	01326 319947 www.wellingtonhouse.co.uk info@wellingtonhousefalmouth.co.uk		 £30.00 DW D CP KT O W LF S(1)(1ES) D(3)(3ES) T()(1ES)
37	Mrs T Farthing Trelawney Guesthouse 6 Melville Road **FALMOUTH** TR11 4AS	01326 316607 mobile 07792 679553 www.trelawney-guesthouse.co.uk trelawney@hotmail.co.uk	816 321 100 mts £35.00	PL D O S(2)(1ES) D(2)(2ES) T(1)(1ES) F(1)(1ES) Single supplement, Breakfast extra charge
37	Mrs Kevern Lynford, 20 Avenue Road **FALMOUTH** TR11 4AZ	01326 314258	811 320 200 mts	£32.50 PL D CP KT O W S(1)(0ES) D(3)(2ES) T(1)(1ES)

Lands End

Walk No.	Contact name Establishment name Address Region/Postcode	Telephone no. Mobile no. Email Website	OS Map Ref. Dist. from path	Starting price Facilities Room types Notes
38	Mrs K Moseley Braganza Grove Hill **ST MAWES** TR2 5BJ	01326 270281 Mobile: 078999 67367 www.braganza-stmawes.co.uk braganzak@googlemail.com	846 331 300 mts	£55.00 PL DW LSP CP KT W O T(5) (4ES) SS. PL, LSP & DW by prior arrangement.
39	Mrs W Penhaligon Trewithian **TRURO** TR2 5EJ	01872 580293 enquiries@trewithian-farm.co.uk	1.5km	£35.00 PL D LSP CP KT O W LF T(2)(2ES) SS £15
39	Mr T Blasdale Treverbyn House Tollyfrank Hill **VERYAN** TR2 5QL	01872 501201 www.treverbyn.co.uk info@treverbyn.co.uk	914 393 2 km PD	£35.00 PL D CP KT PD O S(1)(1ES) D(1)(1ES) T(1)(1ES) single supplement
39	Mrs L Righton Broom Parc Camels Veryan **PORTLOE** TR2 5PJ	01872 501803 www.broomparc.co.uk lindsay@broomparc.co.uk	930 390 on path	£46.00 PL DW D LSP CP KT O(Feb-Nov) D(1)(0ES) T(2)(2ES)
39	Mrs D Spears Threeways Cottage Crohans, **VERYAN** Truro TR2 5PR	01872 501823 demelzaspears@gmail.com		
39 BUSINESS MEMBER	Mr & Mrs I Lydall Field Cottage Treviskey **PORTLOE** TR2 5PN	01872 501045 ianlydall@verbenacornwall.fsnet.co.uk	936 404 1000	£30.00 PL D LSP CP PD O D(1)(1ES) continental b'fast only
39	Mrs B Leach Carradale **PORTLOE** TR2 5RB	01872 501508 barbara495@btinternet.com	935 394 300 mts	£35.00 PL D LSP CP KT O D(1)(1ES) T(1)(1ES) Single Supplement
40 BUSINESS MEMBER	Mr B Bennett Lower Penvose **TREGONY** Truro TR2 5SS	01872 501789 mobile 07982 306702 www.penvose.co.uk penvose@phonecoop.coop	949 415 300 mts	£35.00 EM LSP CP O W D(1)(1ES)
40	Mr & Mrs P Calcraft Grenville B&B 1 Quilver Close **GORRAN HAVEN** PL26 6JT	01726 843243	011 414 300 mts	£32.50 PL D CP KT PD O D(1)(0ES) T(1)(0ES) SS £2.50. Private bathrooms. Badger watching.
40	Mrs W Bennett 20 Perhaver Park **GORRAN HAVEN** PL26 6NZ	01726 843777 contact@penvose.co.uk	012 417 500 mts	£30.00 PL D LSP CP KT PD O W LF D(2)(1ES) SS £5
40 BUSINESS MEMBER	Mr & Mrs I Soper Honeycombe House 61 Polkirt Hill **MEVAGISSEY** PL26 6UR	01726 843750 Mobile 07710 593913 www.honeycombehouse.co.uk enquiries@honeycombehouse.co.uk	015 446 10 mts	£35.00 D LSP CP KT W LF O(mid Jan to mid Dec) S(1)(0ES) D(3)(3ES) T(1)(1ES)
40	Mrs F Thomas 35 Cliff Street **MEVAGISSEY** PL26 6QJ	01726 844656 www.trixology.com/cornwall franormthomas@btinternet.com	015 448 50 mts	£30.00 PL D KT PD O T(2)(1ES) £5 single supplement

For Falmouth addresses see West Cornwall B&Bs.

Walk No.	Contact name Establishment name Address Region/Postcode	Telephone no. Mobile no. Email Website	OS Map Ref. Dist. from path	Starting price Facilities Room types Notes
41	Ms V Casatello Peruppa Farmhouse **PENTEWAN** St Austell PL26 6EJ	01726 844728 www.peruppa.co.uk info@peruppa.co.uk	1 Mile	
41	Mr & Mrs R Callis Ardenconnel 179 Charlestown Road **CHARLESTOWN** PL25 3NN	01726 75469 ardenconnel@tiscali.co.uk	036 520 400 mts	£27.50 O D PL CP LSP KT S(4)(3ES) D(3)(2ES) T(3)(2ES) F(3)(2ES)
41	Mr & Mrs P Dormand Emm's Cottage 19 St Austell Road **ST BLAZEY GATE** PL24 2EF	01726 817155 www.emmscottage.co.uk emmscot@aol.com	059 535	
41 BUSINESS MEMBER	Mr M Bailey The Par Inn 2 Harbour Road **PAR** PL24 2BD	01726 815695 www.parinn.co.uk mattybailey1@hotmail.co.uk	25m	£35.00 PL EM D LSP CP KT PD O W LF D(2)(0ES)
41	Mrs S Clyne Boslowen 96 Par Green **PAR** PL24 2AG	01726 813720 mobile 07980 838578 www.boslowen.co.uk boslowen@gmail.com	079 536 10 mts	£32.50 D LSP CP O D(3)(3ES) T(2 (2ES) £45 single occupancy
42	Mrs S Hoddinott Trekelyn 3 Hanson Drive **FOWEY** PL23 1ET	01726 833375	120 514 200 mts	£35.00 D CP O W LF D(1)(0ES) T(1)(0ES) SS £10
43 BUSINESS MEMBER	Mr S Shephard The House on Props Talland Street **POLPERRO** PL13 2RE	01503 272310 www.houseonprops.co.uk houseonprops@btinternet.com	208 509 on path	£40.00 PL EM DW D LSP CP W LF O(Easter-Dec) S(2)(2ES) D(2)(2ES) T(2)(2ES) Single supplement, DW by prior arrangement, discounted rates possible
43	Mrs A Pidcock Penryn House The Coombes **POLPERRO** PL13 2RQ	01503 272157 www.penrynhouse.co.uk enquiries@penrynhouse.co.uk	205 511 500 mts	£36.00 PL DW D CP O S(1)(1ES) D(7)(7ES) T(2)(2ES) F(2)(2ES)
44 BUSINESS MEMBER	Mrs C Neal Schooner Point 1 Trelawney Terrace **WEST LOOE** PL13 2AG	01503 262670 www.schoonerpoint.co.uk enquiries@schoonerpoint.co.uk	252 536 on path	£30.00 PL D LSP CP KT O W LF S(1)(0ES) D(3)(3ES) T(1)(1ES) Single supplement in D room
44 BUSINESS MEMBER	Mrs S Lever Sea Breeze Lower Chapel Street **EAST LOOE** PL13 1AT	01503 263131 www.seabreezelooe.com seabreezelooe@live.co.uk	256 531 100 mts	£50.00 LSP CP KT O W LF D(5)(5ES) T(1)(1ES) Price per room, LSP by prior arrangement
44	Mr & Mrs P & C Calvert Meneglaze Shutta **EAST LOOE** PL13 1LU	01503 269227 www.looebedandbreakfast.com stay@meneglaze.com	255 540 500 mts	£34.00 O D PL CP KT PD 4D 1T ALL ES Price based on 2 sharing
45	Mrs S Broad Treliddon Farmhouse **DOWNDERRY** PL11 3DP	01503 250288	324 551 1.4km	£30.00 DW D LSP CP O W S(1)(0ES) D(2)(2ES) F(2)(2ES) £10 Single supplement

Walk No.	Contact name Establishment name Address Region/Postcode	Telephone no. Mobile no. Email Website	OS Map Ref. Dist. from path	Starting price Facilities Room types Notes
46	Mrs F M Harvey The Bungalow Cliff Road **PORTWRINKLE** PL11 3BY	01503 230334 www.portwrinklebedandbreakfast.co.uk fiona.harvey334@btinternet.com	355 541 220 mts	£30.00 PL CP KT O D(1)(0ES) T(1)(0ES) PL by prior arrangement
46	Mrs J Pape Polhawn Cottage **POLHAWN COVE** Whitsand Bay PL10 1LL	01752 822657 www.polhawncovecottage.co.uk polhawn@btinternet.com	213 937 5 mts	£32.50 PL LSP CP PD O D(2)(2ES) T(1)(0ES) Single supplement
46 BUSINESS MEMBER	Miss J Earle Finnygook Inn **CRAFTHOLE** Torpoint PL11 3BQ	01503 230655 www.finnygook.co.uk eat@finnygook.co.uk	366 542 200 mts	£30.00 PL EM DW D LSP CP KT O W LF D(2)(2ES) T(3)(3ES) SS £10
46	Ms A Heasman Cliff House Devonport Hill **KINGSAND** PL10 1NJ	01752 823110 www.cliffhouse-kingsand.co.uk chkingsand@aol.com	434 506 20 mts	£37.50 PL EM D CP KT PD O D(2)(2ES) T(1)(1ES) SC(0)(0ES) single supplement £20
46	Mrs J King Coombe House B&B Coombe Farm, Fourlanesend **KINGSAND** PL10 1LR	01752 823925 www.coombehouse-cawsand.co.uk info@coombehouse-cawsand.co.uk	429 512 500 mts	£37.50 D LSP CP KT O W D(2)(1ES) T(1)(0ES) F(2)(1ES) SS £12.50
46 BUSINESS MEMBER	Mrs J A Southward The Edgcumbe Arms **CREMYLL** PL10 1HX	01752 822294 www.edgcumbearms.co.uk info@edgcumbearms.co.uk	453 534 on path	£80.00 EM CP O W LF D(3)(3ES) T(1)(1ES) price per room, phone for single prices, also SC

Kingsand

Walk No.	Contact name Establishment name Address Region/Postcode	Telephone no. Mobile no. Email Website	OS Map Ref. Dist. from path	Starting price Facilities Room types Notes
47 BUSINESS MEMBER	Mrs J Kirsop-Taylor Rusty Anchor, 30 Grand Parade, West Hoe **PLYMOUTH** PL1 3DJ	01752 663924 Mobile 07855 333993 www.therustyanchor-plymouth.co.uk enquiries@therustyanchor-plymouth.co.uk	473 534 on path	£35.00 PL EM DW D CP KT O LF D(2)(2ES) F(2)(2ES)
47 BUSINESS MEMBER	Ms C M Williams Edgcumbe Guest House 50 Pier Street, West Hoe **PLYMOUTH** PL1 3BT	01752 660675 Mobile: 07941 242228 www.edgcumbeguesthouse.co.uk enquiries@edgcumbeguesthouse.co.uk	473 537 15 mts	£35.00 PL DW D CP KT O S(3)(2ES) D(4)(4ES) T(2)(2ES) F(2)(2ES) single supplement, also SC
47 BUSINESS MEMBER	Mr & Mrs D Radford Rainbow Lodge 29 Athenaeum Street The Hoe **PLYMOUTH** PL1 2RQ	01752 229699 www.rainbowlodgeplymouth.co.uk info@rainbowlodgeplymouth.co.uk	474 545 100 mts	£24.50 D CP KT O W LF S(2)(0ES) D(7)(6ES) T(4)(3ES) F(2)(2ES) SS
47	Mr B Huxley No. 1 The Esplanade The Hoe **PLYMOUTH** PL1 2PJ	07775 798567 barryhuxley@hotmail.com	476 539 on path	£30.00 D O D(2)(2ES)
47	Mrs J Tooze Coombe House The Quay, **ORESTON** Plymstock PL9 7NE	01752 482660 jet-28@hotmail.co.uk	500 534 on path	£30.00 PL D CP PD O D(2)(2ES) T(2)(2ES) single supplement
48 BUSINESS MEMBER	Mrs J Lockett The Boundary Hexton Hill Road, **HOOE** Plymouth PL9 9RD	01752 491446 theboundary1@sky.com	on path	£30.00 PL D CP KT O W S(1)(0ES) D(1)(0ES) T(1)(0ES)
48	Mrs G Shelford Heybrook Bay Guest House Beach Road, **HEYBROOK BAY**, NR Wembury PL9 0BS	01752 862345 www.heybrookguesthouse.co.uk heybrookgh@btinternet.com	496 488 on path	£29.00 PL DW LSP CP KT S(1)(0ES) D(2)(0ES) T(2)(0ES) single supplement
48 BUSINESS MEMBER	Mr & Mrs J Pitcher 1 Barton Close **WEMBURY** PL9 0LF	01752 863710 lorraine.pitcher123@btinternet.com	527 494 1 km PD	£30.00 PL D LSP CP KT PD O W T(1)(1ES)
48	Mrs M R Denby 107 Southland Park Road **WEMBURY** PL9 0HH	01752 862036 Mobile: 07803 827165 davidpdenby88@btinternet.com	523 489 500 mts	£30.00 PL EM LSP CP O S(1)(0ES) D(1)(1ES) T(1)(1ES)
48	Mrs J Mills 11 Valley Drive **WEMBURY** PL9 0EZ	01752 862581	523 493 750 mts	£30.00 D CP KT O F(1)(1ES)
49 BUSINESS MEMBER	Mrs S Spooner Rogers Cellars Passage Wood Road **NOSS MAYO** PL8 1EU	01752 872771 suespoonerrogers@btinternet.com	534 475 on path	£40.00 PL DW D LSP CP KT PD O W LF S(1) D(1) T(1) F(1) All ES SS £5
49 BUSINESS MEMBER	Mrs J Rogers Worswell Barton Farmhouse Worswell Barton **NOSS MAYO** PL8 1HB	01752 872977 www.worswellbarton.co.uk info@worswellbarton.co.uk	537 470 800 mts	£35.00 PL LSP CP KT O D(3)(2ES) T(1)(0ES) SC(1)(0ES) single supplement, also SC

Walk No.	Contact name Establishment name Address Region/Postcode	Telephone no. Mobile no. Email Website	OS Map Ref. Dist. from path	Starting price Facilities Room types Notes
49	Mrs J Barnett Revelstoke Coombe Hannaford Road **NOSS MAYO** PL8 1EJ	01752 872663 www.nossmayobandb.net mrandmrsbarnett@gmail.com	546 469 850 mts	£40.00 PL DW D LSP CP KT PD W LF O D(3)(1ES) D Rooms can be Twin or Singles. SS £10
49	Mrs L Proctor The Ivy Barn Fore Street **HOLBETON** PL8 1NA	01752 830293 Mobile 07960524271 www.theivybarnbnb.com theivybarn@gmail.com	4km	£50.00 PL DW CP KT O W D(3)(3ES) T(2)(2ES) F(1)(1ES)
49 BUSINESS MEMBER	Mr R Baker Kimberley **RINGMORE** Nr Kingsbridge TQ7 4HJ	01548 811115 www.kimberley-annex.co.uk info@kimberley-annex.co.uk	652 462 1500 mts	£35.00 D LSP CP KT PD O D(1)(1ES) T(1)(0ES) Pick up Mothecombe, boat across R. Erme charged, T room let with D room as family suite
49	Mrs K Purdy Ringmore Vean **RINGMORE** TQ7 4HL	01548 810382 www.ringmorevean.co.uk enquiries@ringmorevean.co.uk	651 459 900 mts	£40.00 O
49 BUSINESS MEMBER	Mrs P Dolby 1 Coastguard Cottages **CHALLABOROUGH** Nr Kingsbridge TQ7 4HT	01548 810894 patdolby1951@hotmail.co.uk	648 451 50 mts	£20.00 PL D CP KT O D(2)(0ES)
49	Mr A J Roberts Summer Winds Marine Drive **BIGBURY-ON-SEA** TQ7 4AS	01548 810669 Mobile 07540 533854 pritchard212@btinternet.com	651 443 on path	£37.50 PL D CP O D(2)(2ES) T(1)(1ES) Single Supplement £7.50
50	Mrs C Righton Cob Cottage **THURLESTONE** TQ7 3NJ	 www.southdevontv.com/cob-cottage-thurlestone-bb caroline@carolinerighton.com	676 430 Half a mile from path	£40.00 PL EM DW D LSP CP KT O D(1)(1ES) T(1)(0ES) £10 single supplement
50 BUSINESS MEMBER	Miss S Ireland The Cottage Hotel **HOPE COVE** Kingsbridge TQ7 3HJ	01548 561555 www.hopecove.com info@hopecove.com	675 401 25 mts	£56.00 PL EM DW D LSP CP KT W LF O S(2)(2ES) D(24)(24ES) F(5)(5ES) Price includes dinner, Dbl rooms can be twin
50 BUSINESS MEMBER	Miss S Ireland Tanfield B & B **HOPE COVE** TQ7 3HJ	01548 561555 www.hopecove.com info@hopecove.com	675 401 300 mts	£27.00 PL EM D LSP CP KT O S(1) D(5) T(2) All ES Book in EM & LSP at Cottage Hotel, PL ordered at hotel
51	Miss M L Coleman Sun Bay Hotel **INNER HOPE COVE** Kingsbridge TQ7 3HH	01548 561371 www.sunbayhotel-hopecove.co.uk sunbayhotel@btconnect.com	676 399 on path	£30.00 PL EM DW CP T(12)(6ES) Phone for single prices
51	Mr & Mrs R Petty-Brown Rocarno Grenville Road **SALCOMBE** TQ8 8BJ	01548 842732 www.rocarno.co.uk rocarno@aol.com	736 389 500 mts	£34.00 PL D CP KT PD O W LF D(1)(1ES) T(1)(1ES) SS £12
51	Mrs P Snelson Waverley Devon Road **SALCOMBE** TQ8 8HL	01548 842633 mobile: 07980 012608 www.waverleybandb.co.uk pauline@waverleybandb.co.uk	738 388 500 mts	£35.00 W LF O S(1)(1ES) D(6)(5ES) T(6)(5ES) F(3)(3ES) £15-£20 single supplement, also SC

South Sands Ferry, Salcombe

Walk No.	Contact name Establishment name Address Region/Postcode	Telephone no. Mobile no. Email Website	OS Map Ref. Dist. from path	Starting price Facilities Room types Notes
51	Mrs M Weymouth Motherhill Farm Main Road **SALCOMBE** TQ8 8NB	01548 842552 djweymouth@tiscali.co.uk	730 393 1.5 km	£24.00 D LSP CP O S(1)(0ES) D(1)(0ES) T(1)(0ES)
51	Ms A Woodhatch Rainbow's End 11 Platt Close **SALCOMBE** TQ8 8NZ	01548 843654 Mobile: 07974 773451 annwoodhatch@btinternet.com	730 393 1.5 km	£32.00 PL D LSP CP KT PD O W T(1)(1ES) F(1)(1ES) Single supplement
51	Mr & Mrs R Agar Ashleigh House Ashleigh Road **KINGSBRIDGE** TQ7 1HB	01548 852893 mobile 07732 194393 www.ashleigh-house.co.uk reception@ashleigh-house.co.uk	731 439 6 km	£40.00 PL DW D LSP CP KT O W LF D(5)(5ES) T(2)(2ES) F(1)(1ES) £10 single supplement
51	Mrs P Jackson 33 Knowle House Close **KINGSBRIDGE** TQ7 1AN	01548 853820 Mobile: 07792 152750 trish.j@hotmail.co.uk	735 446 5 km	£30.00 PL D LSP KT PD O S(1)(0ES) D(1)(0ES) £5 single supplement in D room
52	Mrs J Foss Down Farm **START POINT** Kingsbridge TQ7 2NQ	01548 511234 www.downfarm.co.uk downfarm@btinternet.com	806 377 1.6 Km	£37.50 PL EM DW D LSP CP O W LF D(1)(1ES) T(1)(1ES) F(1)(1ES) £45 single
52	Mrs V Johnston Valseph The Green **BEESANDS** TQ7 2EJ	01548 580650 mobile 07890 197673 www.beesands-bedandbreakfast.co.uk valseph@btinternet.com	819 406 on path	£35.00 LSP CP KT O(Mar-Nov) D(1)(1ES)
52	Ms C Ley Linger Lodge **TORCROSS** TQ7 2TJ	01548 580599 www.lingerlodge.co.uk ley@lingerlodge.co.uk	822 421 400 mts	£45.00 D LSP CP KT O D(3)(3ES) single supplement
53	Mrs V Mercer Old Walls **SLAPTON** TQ7 2QN	01548 580516 www.slaptonbandb.co.uk val.slapton@gmail.com	823 449 500mts	£35.00 PL DW D KT PD O W LF S(1)(0ES) D(1)(0ES) T(1)(0ES) F(1)(1ES) Single supplement
53	Mrs E Sharman Ley Cottage Sands Road **SLAPTON** TQ7 2QN	01548 581376 www.leycottage.co.uk elizabethsharman@hotmail.com	822 449 400 mts	£30.00 D CP KT O T(1)(1ES)
53	Mrs I Sidell Roxburgh House Dartmouth Road **STRETE** TQ6 0RW	01803 770870 www.roxburghhouse.co.uk ingrid@roxburghhouse.co.uk	841 467 on path	£40.00 PL DW D LSP CP KT PD O W LF S(1)(0ES) D(1)(0ES) T()(1ES) SS £5
53 BUSINESS MEMBER	Mr & Mrs R Jordan Cladda B&B & Self Cat Apts, 88-90 Victoria Road and Ford Valley, **DARTMOUTH** TQ6 9EF	01803 835957 Mobile 07967 060003 www.cladda-dartmouth.co.uk bandb@cladda-dartmouth.co.uk	871 511 750 mts	£35.00 PL DW D CP O W LF D(6)(6ES) T(4)(4ES) F(4)(4ES) also self catering. SS
53 BUSINESS MEMBER	Mr & Mrs A Depledge The Crow's Nest 5A Lower Street **DARTMOUTH** TQ6 9AJ	07920 053580 www.crowsnestdartmouth.co.uk info@crowsnestdartmouth.co.uk	878 512 1 km	£30.00 D CP O W D(1)(1ES) F(1)(1ES) SS £19. No breakfast.

Walk No.	Contact name Establishment name Address Region/Postcode	Telephone no. Mobile no. Email Website	OS Map Ref. Dist. from path	Starting price Facilities Room types Notes
53 BUSINESS MEMBER	Mr & Mrs C Helyer Eight Bells South Embankment **DARTMOUTH** TQ6 9BB	01803 839506 Mobile: 07813 803472 www.dartmouthbandb.com lizhelyer20@gmail.com	878 511 200 mts	£35.00 D CP O S(2) D(2) T(1) F(1) All ES £5 single supplement
53	Mrs V Ruddle Estuary View 11 Horn Hill **DARTMOUTH** TQ6 9RA	01803 834066 Mobile: 07950 852014 vjruddle@gmail.com	876 513 200 mts	£30.00 D KT PD O W LF T(1)(1ES)
53	Miss J White Hill View House 76 Victoria Road **DARTMOUTH** TQ6 9DZ	01803 839372 www.hillviewdartmouth.co.uk enquiries@hillviewdartmouth.co.uk	872 512 1 km	£35.00 D CP O W S(1)(1ES) D(3)(3ES) T(1)(1ES) price based on 2 sharing
54 BUSINESS MEMBER	Mr & Mrs G Sowerby Raddicombe Lodge Kingswear Road, Hillhead **BRIXHAM** TQ5 0EX	01803 882125 Mobile 07971882125 www.raddicombelodge.co.uk stay@raddicombelodge.co.uk	904 538 2 kms	£24.00 PL DW D LSP CP KT PD W O(mid Mar - end Dec) S(1) D(4)(T(2) F(2) SC(1) All ES SS, also SC
54	Mrs L Goodwill Midhurst B&B 132 New Road **BRIXHAM** TQ5 8DA	01803 857331 www.midhurstbnb.co.uk	917 556 1km	£30.00 PL D CP KT O W LF S(1)(0ES) D(2)(2ES) T(1)(1ES) PL by prior arrangement
54	Mrs C Robinson Westbury Guesthouse 51 New Road **BRIXHAM** TQ5 8NL	01803 851684 www.westburyguesthouse.com westburyguesthouse@gmail.com	919 560 300 mts	£30.00 PL CP O W LF D(6)(6ES) T(4)(4ES) F(2)(2ES) £5 single supplement
55	Mr & Mrs F Bamford-Dwane The Clifton Hotel 9 & 10 Kernou Road **PAIGNTON** TQ4 6BA	01803 556545 www.cliftonhotelpaignton.co.uk stay@cliftonhotelpaignton.co.uk	891 607 100 mts	£35.00 PL EM D CP W O(April to end Sept) S(2)D(4)T(4)F(2) All ES Single supplement £7
55 BUSINESS MEMBER	Mrs J Frost Garway Lodge Guesthouse 79 Avenue Road **TORQUAY** TQ2 5LL	01803 293126 Mobile: 07790 783997 www.garwaylodge.co.uk info@garwaylodge.co.uk	905 646 850 mts	£35.00 PL D LSP CP KT O S(3)(3ES) D(3)(3ES) T(2)(2ES)
55	Mr Adamson & Miss S Coombes The Haute Epine 36 Bampfylde Road **TORQUAY** TQ2 5AR	01803 296359 www.haute-epineguesthouse.co.uk gerryhauteepine@tiscali.co.uk	907 642 1/2 mile	£23.00 PL EM D O S(2)(1ES) D(3)(3ES) T(1) (1ES) F(1)(1ES)
55	Mr N D'Allen Orestone Manor Rock House Lane **MAIDENCOMBE** TQ1 4SX	01803 328098 www.orestonemanor.com info@orestonemanor.com	923 679	£50.00 PL EM DW D LSP CP O S(2) D(11) T(3) F(2) All ES Single £30
55 BUSINESS MEMBER	Mrs D Blenkinsopp Aveland House Aveland Road **BABBACOMBE** TQ1 3PT	01803 326622 www.avelandhouse.co.uk avelandhouse@aol.com	921 652 800 mts	£38.00 O D EM PL CP LSP KT 4D 2T 2S 2F ALL ES
55 BUSINESS MEMBER	Mr C Dunn Headland View 37 Babbacombe Downs Road **BABBACOMBE** TQ1 3LN	01803 312612 www.headlandview.com reception@headlandview.com	 on path	£31.00 D CP KT W LF O(Except December) S(6)(4ES) D(6)(4ES) T(1)(1ES)

Walk No.	Contact name Establishment name Address Region/Postcode	Telephone no. Mobile no. Email Website	OS Map Ref. Dist. from path	Starting price Facilities Room types Notes
55 BUSINESS MEMBER	Mr J Hannan Babbacombe Guest House 53 Babbacombe Road **BABBACOMBE** TQ1 3SN	01803 328071 www.babbacombeguesthouse.com info@babbacombeguesthouse.com	925 654 300 mts	£31.00 PL CP KT O W LF S(1)(1ES) D(3)(3ES) T(1)(1ES) F(1)(1ES)
55 BUSINESS MEMBER	Mrs K Wood The Downs Babbacombe 41-43 Babbacombe Downs Rd **BABBACOMBE** TQ1 3LN	01803 328543 www.downshotel.co.uk enquiries@downshotel.co.uk	 20 mts	 PL EM DW D LSP CP KT W LF O D(12)(12ES)
55 BUSINESS MEMBER	Mrs S Brewer Coastguard Cottage 84 Babbacombe Downs Rd **BABBACOMBE** TQ1 3LU	01803 311634 mobile 07780 661381 sheila.besidethesea@googlemail.com	927 653 100 mts	£30.00 PL D KT O W S(1)(1ES) D(1)(1ES) F(1)(1ES)
55 BUSINESS MEMBER	Mrs T Howell The Babbacombe Palms Guesthouse, 2 York Rd **BABBACOMBE** TQ1 3SG	01803 327087 www.babbacombepalms.com reception@babbacombepalms.com	922 655 100 mts	£40.00 DW D KT PD O W LF D(5)(4ES) T(1)(1ES) F(2)(2ES)
56 BUSINESS MEMBER	Mrs P Burdett 10 The Strand **SHALDON** TQ14 0DL	01626 873315 mobile: 07976 978742 maggieburdett@yahoo.com	934 722 on path	£35.00 D KT W LF O(March - Sept) D(1)(1ES) single supplement
56	Ms J Beckett West Wing, Ringmore Lodge, Salty Lane **SHALDON** TQ14 0AP	01626 872754 Mobile 07805 993890 ringmorelodge@hotmail.co.uk	927 722 1 km	£36.00 PL D CP KT PD O W D(1)(1ES) F(1)(1ES) SS £5
56	Mrs J Benjamin Port View Riverside **SHALDON** TQ14 0DJ	01626 872277 www.shaldonholiday.com jenni.benjamin@btinternet.com	933 724 on path	£30.00 O D CP LSP DW 1T £5 single supplement
56	Mr P Hockings Brunswick House 5 Brunswick Street **TEIGNMOUTH** TQ14 8AE	01626 774102 www.brunswick-house.com info@brunswick-house.com	941 727 50 mts	£30.00 PL DW D KT OS(1)(1ES) D(4)(4ES) F(3)(3ES) DW by arrangement, SS
56	Mrs D Loach Coombe Bank Guest House Landscore Road **TEIGNMOUTH** TQ14 9JL	01626 772369 mobile: 07860 782415 www.coombebankhotel.net dianne.loach@btopenworld.com	935 7327 50 mts	£28.50 PL D LSP CP KT O S(2)(1ES) D(4)(3ES) T(2)(2ES) F(1)(1ES) single supplement
56	Mr & Mrs J Allan Thomas Luny House Teign Street **TEIGNMOUTH** TQ14 8EG	01626 772976 www.thomas-luny-house.co.uk alisonandjohn@thomas-luny-house.co.uk	939 729 500 mts	£52.50 CP O W LF D(2)(2ES) T(2)(2ES) SS £22.50
57	Mrs A Ferris The Blenheim, The Seafront, 1 Marine Parade, **DAWLISH** EX7 9DJ	01626 862372 www.theblenheim.uk.net blenheimholidays@btconnect.com	962 765 10mts	£38.00 DW LSP CP KT O W LF S(3) D(6) T(4) F(4) All ES Price for D occupancy, Variable SS
57	Mr K Chambers The Croft Guest House Cockwood Harbour **STARCROSS** EX6 8QY	01626 890282 www.thecroftcockwood.com croftcockwood@aol.com	975 808 On Path	£37.50 O D PL DW 5D 3T ALL ES £51 single, bird observatory

Walk No.	Contact name Establishment name Address Region/Postcode	Telephone no. Mobile no. Email Website	OS Map Ref. Dist. from path	Starting price Facilities Room types Notes
57 BUSINESS MEMBER	Mr & Mrs P Jessen Quentence Farm, Salterton Road, **WEST DOWN BEACON** EX8 5BW	01395 442733 www.selfcatering-devon.co.uk palleandrose@hotmail.co.uk	038 820 1 km PD	£30.00 PL DW D LSP CP KT PD O W LF S(1)(0ES) D(2)(2ES) T(1)(1ES) F(1)(1ES)
58	Mrs H Morrish Appletree Cottage 23 Victoria Place **BUDLEIGH SALTERTON** EX9 6JP	01395 445433 www.appletreecottagebudleigh.co.uk hilary@appletreecottagebudleigh.co.uk	061 818 150 mts	£26.00 PL D CP KT O T(3)(1ES) single supplement
59 BUSINESS MEMBER	Mrs E Tancock Lower Pinn Farm Peak Hill **SIDMOUTH** EX10 0NN	01395 513733 Mobile: 07774 694776 www.lowerpinnfarm.co.uk liz@lowerpinnfarm.co.uk	097 865 500 mts	£37.50 DW D LSP CP KT O W LF D(1)(1ES) T(1)(1ES) F(1)(1ES) single supplement
59	Mrs L F Lever Larkstone House 22 Connaught Road **SIDMOUTH** EX10 8TT	01395 514345 davidlever22@btinternet.com	125 878 500 mts	£26.00 DW D CP KT O S(1)(0ES) D(1)(0ES) T(1)(1ES)
59	Mr & Mrs D Haslam Bramley Lodge Guest House Vicarage Road **SIDMOUTH** EX10 8UQ	01395 515710 bramleyowner@btinternet.com	127 880 650 mts	£35.00 EM CP KT W LF O(March - mid Sept) S(2)(1ES) D(2)(2ES) T(1)(1ES) F(1)(1ES) EM must be pre-booked
60	Mrs E D Jordan Lyndhurst Manor Road **SEATON** EX12 2AQ	01297 23490 davidjordan367@btinternet.com	244 902 80 mts	£30.00 DW CP O(April - Oct) S(1)(0ES) D(1)(0ES) T(1)(0ES)
60	Mr & Mrs B Rosewarne Sea Glimpses 8. Burrow Road **SEATON** EX12 2NF	01297 22664 Mobile 07527 636687 liz@seaglimpses.fsnet.co.uk	250 899 20 mts	£30.00 CP KT O S(1)(1ES) D(1)(1ES) T(1)(1ES) Single £35
60	Mr & Mrs D & S Jamieson 11 Seafield Road **SEATON** EX12 2QS	01297 21966 www.baytreedevon.co.uk info@baytreedevon.co.uk	 250 mts	 W LF O CP D1(1ES) F2(2ES) T1(1ES) S1 Bicycle lock-up available
60	Mrs G Sedgwick Holmleigh House Sea Hill **SEATON** EX12 2QT	01297 625671 Mobile 07748498948 www.holmleighhouse.com gaynorsedgwick@hotmail.co.uk	243 900 200 mts	£35.00 PL D LSP CP KT W LF O(Closed Xmas) S(2)(2ES) D(3)(3ES) T(2)(2ES) F(1)(1ES) £55 single
60	Mrs P Chapman Devonia 21 Harepath Road **SEATON** EX12 2RP	01297 625155 Mobile 07761243876 bedandbreakfastsearcher.co.uk john.walker61@btinternet.com	 1/4 mile	£30.00 PL EM D LSP CP KT O W LF D(2)T(1)

Walk No.	Contact name Establishment name Address Region/Postcode	Telephone no. Mobile no. Email Website	OS Map Ref. Dist. from path	Starting price Facilities Room types Notes
61	Mrs J Thomson Westley B&B Lyme Road, **UPLYME** Lyme Regis DT7 3UY	01297 445104 mobile: 07982 302038 www.westleybedandbreakfast.wordpress.com westleybandb@btinternet.com	324 934 1.8 km	£32.50 D CP PD O D(2)(1ES) T(1)(1ES) £5 single supplement
61 BUSINESS MEMBER	Miss E Saunders Berrydown Highcliff Road **LYME REGIS** DT7 3EW	01297 792299 emmabsaunders1@hotmail.co.uk	333 920 500 mts PD	£45.00 O S(1)(1ES) D(1)(1ES) T(2)(0ES)
61	Mr O Lovell Lucerne View Road **LYME REGIS** DT7 3AA	01297 443752 lucernelyme.co.uk lucernelyme@btopenworld.com	338 923 500 mts	£35.00 PL D CP O S(1)(1ES) D(3)(3ES) T(1)(1ES) SC(1)(1ES) PL by prior arrangement
61	Mr L Hatfield Devonia 2 Woodmead Road **LYME REGIS** DT7 3AB	01297 442869 www.lymeregisbandb.com devonia@lymeregisbandb.com	337 925 450 mts	£42.00 D CP O S(1)(1ES) D(4)(4ES)
62 BUSINESS MEMBER	Mrs J C Elliot Warren House Main Street **CHIDEOCK** DT6 6JW	01297 489996 Mobile: 07759 274905 www.warren-house.com jane@warren-house.com	419 928 1 km	£37.50 PL D LSP CP KT O W D(2)(2ES) T(1)(1ES) F(1)(1ES) SC(1)(1ES)
62 BUSINESS MEMBER	Mr J Taylor Brook Cottage Mill Lane **CHIDEOCK** Bridport DT6 6JS	01297 489528 www.chideockandseatown.co.uk jim@chideockandseatown.co.uk	423 926 400 mts	£40.00 D CP KT O W LF S(1)(1ES) D(1)(1ES) T(1)(1ES) Continental breakfast
62	Mr & Mrs M Kelson Rose Cottage Main Street **CHIDEOCK** DT6 6JQ	01297 489994 www.rosecottage-chideock.co.uk enquire@rosecottage-chideock.co.uk	423 927 200m	D CP KT O D(1)(1ES) T(1)(1ES)
62	Mr & Mrs C Crawford Mervyn House **CHIDEOCK** Near Bridport DT6 6JN	01297 489578 www.chideockandseatown.co.uk callbrig@gmail.com	422 928 500 mts	£32.50 D CP O S(1)(0ES) T(1)(0ES)
63	Mrs PA Bale Highway Farm West Road **BRIDPORT** DT6 6AE	01308 424321 Mobile: 07791 915228 www.highwayfarm.co.uk bale@highwayfarm.co.uk	443 928 1.5 km	£40.00 PL D LSP CP KT O D(2)(2ES) T(1)(1ES) F(1)(1ES) on bus route, Self catering also available
63	Mr A Hardy Britmead House 154 West Bay Road **BRIDPORT** DT6 4EG	01308 422941 www.britmeadhouse.co.uk britmead@talk21.com	465 912 500 mts	DW CP KT O D(5)(5ES) T(2)(2ES) F(2)(2ES)
63	Mr W Vickers & Ms D Clarke Seacroft 24 West Bay, **WEST BAY** Bridport DT6 4HD	01308 423407 mobile 07855 457875 www.seacroftbandb.co.uk seacroft24@btinternet.com	461 905 50 mts	£32.50 PL D LSP CP KT O S(1)(1ES) D(2)(2ES) T(1)(1ES) F(1)(1ES)
63 BUSINESS MEMBER	Mr A Bailey Barn Cottage, Graston Farm, Annings Lane, **BURTON BRADSTOCK** DT6 4NG	07778 261796 www.grastonfarm.co.uk ababredy@fwi.co.uk	503 899 1750m	£35.00 PL EM DW D LSP CP KT PD O W LF D(2)(1ES) T(1) (1ES)

Walk No.	Contact name Establishment name Address Region/Postcode	Telephone no. Mobile no. Email Website	OS Map Ref. Dist. from path	Starting price Facilities Room types Notes
63	Mrs E M Edwards Sea Fret House Coast Road **PUNCKNOWLE** DT2 9DQ	01308 897435 www.seafret.co.uk enquiries@seafret.co.uk	537 874 800m	£35.00 PL DW D LSP CP KT PD O W LF D(1)(1ES) F(1)(1ES) 100 mts from inland alternative route Section 80
63 BUSINESS MEMBER	Mrs I Donnelly Cowards Lake Farmhouse 13 West Street **ABBOTSBURY** DT3 4JT	01305 871421 www.cowardslakebandb.com cowards-lake@btconnect.com	573 853 800 mts	£37.50 DW LSP CP KT PD O W LF D(1)(1ES) T(1)(1ES) SS £12.50.
63 BUSINESS MEMBER	Mr R Halfhead Abbotsbury Tea Rooms 26 Rodden Row **ABBOTSBURY** DT3 4JL	01305 871143 www.abbotsbury-tearooms.co.uk atr@uwclub.net	578 852 600 mts	£80.00 PL KT W LF O(end Mar - end Oct) D(3)(3ES) Price per room
63	Mrs P Crockett 21 Rodden Row **ABBOTSBURY** DT3 4JL	01305 871465 Mobile 07925 350023 pat21rr01@hotmail.co.uk	579 855 750 mts	£27.50 PL O W D(1)(0ES) T(1)(0ES) Prior booking preferred
63	C Rawlings Upalong 8 West Street **ABBOTSBURY** DT3 4JT	01305 871882 mobile 07887 981850 www.upalongwestdorset.co.uk clarerawlings@sky.com	573 853 500 mts	£30.00 CP O W LF D(1)(0ES) T(1)(0ES) EM by prior arrangement, £10 single supplement
63	Mrs M Peach 6 Market Street **ABBOTSBURY** DT3 4JR	01305 871364 www.abbotsburybandb.co.uk enquiries@abbotsburybandb.co.uk	576 853 1200 mts	£35.00 KT O W S(1)(1ES) D(1)(1ES) £10 single supplement
64 BUSINESS MEMBER	Mrs J Furlong Swallows Rest, Marleaves Farm, South Rd, **WYKE REGIS** DT4 9NR	01305 785244 www.swallowsrestselfcatering.co.uk jane.furlong@swallowsrestselfcatering.co.uk	662 770 300m	£35.00 PL DW D LSP CP KT O W LF S(1)(1ES) D(3)(2ES) T(1)(1ES) F(1)(1ES) SC(6)(6ES)
65 BUSINESS MEMBER	Mr G Bisogno Alessandria House 71 Wakeham Road **EASTON** Portland DT5 1HW	01305 822270	694 716 20 mts	£30.00 DW D LSP CP O W S(3)(2ES) D(5)(4ES) T(2)(2ES) F(4)(4ES) £5 single supplement. Please call to book.
65	Mrs K Smith Fairview Cottage 14 Old Coastguard Cottages **PORTLAND BILL** DT5 2JT	01305 820368 www.portlandbill.net grahamsmith.14@btinternet.com	678 688 on path	£40.00 D CP KT O S(1)(0ES) D(1)(0ES)
66 BUSINESS MEMBER	Mrs D Quick Harbour Lights Guest House 20 Buxton Road **WEYMOUTH** DT4 9PJ	01305 783273 www.harbourlightsguesthouse.com harbourlights@btconnect.com	673 779 200 mts	£35.00 O(March-Nov inc) S(4)(2ES) D(5)(5ES) T(2)(2ES) F(2)(2ES)
66 BUSINESS MEMBER	Mrs S Pitman Florian 59 Abbotsbury Road **WEYMOUTH** DT4 0AQ	01305 773836 www.florianguesthouse.co.uk enquiryflorian@aol.com	671 791 500 mts	£30.00 PL D CP KT O W LF D(4)(3ES) T(2)(2ES) F(1)(1ES) £10 SS. EM in winter. 1885 Building.
66 BUSINESS MEMBER	Mr & Mrs Stephenson Wadham Guesthouse 22 East Street **WEYMOUTH** DT4 8BN	01305 779640 www.wadhamhouse.co.uk stay@wadhamhouse.co.uk		O W S(6)(3ES) D(6)(3ES) T(2)(1ES) F(4)(2ES)

Walk No.	Contact name Establishment name Address Region/Postcode	Telephone no. Mobile no. Email Website	OS Map Ref. Dist. from path	Starting price Facilities Room types Notes
66 BUSINESS MEMBER	Mr Saxton Gloucester House B&B 96 The Esplanade **WEYMOUTH** DT4 7AT	01305 785191 www.gloucesterhouseweymouth.co.uk gloucesterhouse@hotmail.co.uk	3km	PL CP KT O W S(3)(3ES) D(6)(6ES) T(2)(2ES) F(4)(4ES)
66 BUSINESS MEMBER	Ms J Rolph The Beach House 2 Brunswick Terrace **WEYMOUTH** DT4 7RR	01305 789353 www.thebeachhouseweymouth.co.uk stay@thebeachhouseweymouth.co.uk	10 mtrs	PL CP W O (Dec to Oct generally) S(3)(1ES) D(4)(4ES) T(1)(1ES) F(1)(1ES)
66 BUSINESS MEMBER	Mr M Clark Oaklands Edwardian Guesthouse 1 Glendinning Avenue **WEYMOUTH** DT4 7QF	01305 767081 www.oaklands-guesthouse.co.uk stay@oaklands-guesthouse.co.uk	678 800 500 mts	£34.00 PL EM D CP O(February to November) D(6)(6ES) T(2)(2ES) F(1)(1ES) Single supplement
66	Mr Penman Horizon Guest House 16 Brunswick Terrace **WEYMOUTH** DT4 7RW	01305 784916 www.horizonguesthouse.co.uk info@horizonguesthouse.co.uk	682 799 on path	O S(1)(1ES) D(2)(2ES) T(1)(0ES) F(1)(1ES)
66	Mrs S Leach Sunnyside B&B 15 Brunswick Terrace **WEYMOUTH** DT4 7SA	01305 786358 www.sunnysideweymouth.com sunnysideweymouth@hotmail.co.uk	682 799 10 mts	£30.00 DW D KT PD O D(1)(0ES) T(1)(0ES) F(3)(3ES)
66	Mr & Mrs J Green Tara Guest House 10 Market Street **WEYMOUTH** DT4 8DD	01305 766235 www.taraweymouth.co.uk lesley_john@btinternet.com	681 787 150 mts	£32.00 O S(2)(2ES) D(3)(3ES) T(1)(1ES)
66	Mr & Mrs Horvath 1 Old Coastguard Cottages **OSMINGTON MILLS** DT3 6HQ	01305 832663 www.heritagecoastbandb.co.uk	736 817 20 mts	£38.50 PL D LSP CP KT O S(1)(1ES) D(1)(1ES) Excellent cooked breakfast
67	Mrs G Hole Bradle Farm **CHURCH KNOWLE** Kimmeridge BH20 5NU	01929 480712 mobile 07764 950920 www.bradlefarmhouse.co.uk info@bradlefarmhouse.co.uk	930 806 4 km PD	£40.00 PL D CP KT PD O W LF D(2)(2ES) T(1)(1ES) single supplement, EM at café owned by farm
68	Mr D Ensor Chiltern Lodge 8 Newfoundland Close **WORTH MATRAVERS** BH19 3LX	01929 439337 mobile 07906 508125 www.chilternlodge.co.uk densor@btopenworld.com	976 778 1 km	£30.00 PL EM D CP KT O W LF D(1)(0ES) T(1)(0ES) single supplement
69 BUSINESS MEMBER	Mr & Mrs J Aslett Jonti, Studland Road **CORFE CASTLE** BH20 5JG	01929 480975 Mobile 07775 724871 www.jontibedandbreakfast.co.uk cj.aslett@btinternet.com		£37.50 PL DW D LSP CP KT O W LF D(2)(2ES) £12.50 SS. One dog only
69 BUSINESS MEMBER	Mrs L Fegan The Limes 48 Park Road **SWANAGE** BH19 2AE	01929 422664 www.limeshotel.net info@limeshotel.net	033 783 250 mts	£44.00 PL DW D CP O S(3)(1ES) D(2)(2ES) T(4)(4ES) F(3)(3ES) LSP by prior arrangement only. Families welcome
69	Mr & Mrs A Preston Sunny Bay House 17 Cluny Crescent **SWANAGE** BH19 2BP	01929 422650 Mobile 07799298767 www.sunnybay.co.uk gillgc@aol.com	031 784 1 km	£30.00 D CP O W S(1)(0ES) D(1)(1ES) T(1)(1ES) F(1)(1ES)

Portland Bill Statue

Walk No.	Contact name Establishment name Address Region/Postcode	Telephone no. Fax / Reservation / Mobile no. Website Email	OS Map Ref. Dist. from path	Starting price Months Open Facilities Info
1	Camping Club Site North Hill **MINEHEAD** Somerset TA24 5LB	01643 704138 www.campingandcaravaningclub.co.uk minehead-site@thefriendlyclub.co.uk	958 471	£4.00 end April-Sept T S LY DW CP KT
1	Mr P R Weaver Sparkhayes Farm Camp Site Sparkhayes Lane **PORLOCK** Somerset TA24 8NE	01643 862470 www.porlock.co.uk	886 469 on path	£7.00 O T S LY G CP LSP DW KT on 300 coast bus route
2	Mr C Onley Sunny Lyn Camp & Caravan Site, **LYNBRIDGE LYNTON** North Devon EX35 6NS	01598 753384 www.caravandevon.co.uk info@caravandevon.co.uk	719 485 800 mts	£6.00 Mar-Oct T S LY G CP LSP DW

Bossington

Walk No.	Contact name Establishment name Address Region/Postcode	Telephone no. Fax / Reservation / Mobile no. Website Email	OS Map Ref. Dist. from path	Starting price Months Open Facilities Info
3	Mr & Mrs A Mortimer Lower Campscott Farm **LEE** Devon EX34 8LS	01271 863479 www.lowercampscott.co.uk holidays@lowercampscott.co.uk	495 455 2 km	£6.00 O T S LY CP LSP DW
5	Mr & Mrs B Gilbert North Morte Farm Campsite **MORTEHOE** Devon EX34 7EG	01271 870381 www.northmortefarm.co.uk info@northmortefarm.co.uk	459 455 500 mts	£6.00 Apr-end Oct T S LY G CP LSP DW
5	Mrs H Lethbridge Damage Barton **MORTEHOE** Woolacombe, Devon EX34 7EJ	01271 870502 www.damagebarton.co.uk enquiries@damagebarton.co.uk	476 457 2 km	£11.00 Mar-Nov T S LY G DW
11	Mr & Mrs R Croslegh Steart Farm Touring Park **HORNS CROSS** Devon EX39 5DW	01237 431836 www.steartfarmtouringpark.co.uk steartenquiries@btconnect.com	356 229 1 km	£6.00 Easter - 30 Sept T S LY CP LSP DW Campers MUST check dates with site before arrival.

Castle Rock from Valley of Rocks

North Cornwall Campsites

Walk No.	Contact name Establishment name Address Region/Postcode	Telephone no. Fax / Reservation / Mobile no. Website Email	OS Map Ref. Dist. from path	Starting price Months Open Facilities Info
15	Mr C Heard Lower Pennycrocker Farm **BOSCASTLE** Cornwall PL35 0BY	07967 605392 www.pennycrocker.com karyn.heard@yahoo.com	124 925 500mts	£6.00 Easter - end Oct T S CP DW G LSP
20	Mrs C Pawley Carnevas Farm Holiday Park PORTHCOTHAN BAY Cornwall PL28 8PN	01841 520230 www.carnevasholidaypark.co.uk carnevascampsite@aol.com	862 728 800 mts	£10.50 Apr-Oct T S LY G DW
21	Mrs L Lightfoot Magic Cove Touring Park **MAWGAN PORTH** Newquay, Cornwall TR8 4BZ	01637 860263 www.magiccove.co.uk magic@magiccove.co.uk	850 679 300 mts	£6.00 Easter-end Sept T S LY DW G 250 mts from site
21	Mrs S Eastlake Treago Farm Caravan & Camping Site, **CRANTOCK** Newquay, Cornwall TR8 5QS	01637 830277 www.treagofarm.co.uk info@treagofarm.co.uk	781 600 400 mts	£5.00 Easter-early Oct T S LY G CP DW
24	Ms J. Sawle Beacon Cottage Farm Touring Park, Beacon Drive, **ST AGNES** Cornwall TR5 0NU	01872 552347 Mobile 07879 413862 www.beaconcottagefarmholidays.co.uk beaconcottagefarm@lineone.net	705 505 400 mts	£8.00 Apr-Sept T S LY CP LSP DW
24	Mrs P Williams Presingoll Farm Caravan & Camping Park, **ST AGNES** Cornwall TR5 0PB	01872 552333 www.presingollfarm.co.uk pam@presingollfarm.co.uk	720 495 1.6 km	£7.00 Easter-Oct T S LY G CP LSP DW

Tintagel Castle

Walk No.	Contact name Establishment name Address Region/Postcode	Telephone no. Fax / Reservation / Mobile no. Website Email	OS Map Ref. Dist. from path	Starting price Months Open Facilities Info
28	Mr K Hall Treen Farm Campsite **TREEN**, Cornwall TR19 6LF	01736 810273 Mobile: 07598 469322 www.treenfarmcampsite.co.uk	392 228 200 mts	£7.00 Apr-Oct T S LY G CP DW
28	Mr E J Coak The North Inn **PENDEEN** Cornwall TR19 7DN	01736 788417 www.thenorthinnpendeen.co.uk ernestjohncoak@aol.com	383 344 1 km	£4.00 O T S CP LSP DW Also B&B
30	Miss J A Boyns Levant Campsite Trewellard House,**PENDEEN** Cornwall TR19 7SX	01736 788795	375 337 500 mts	from April 1st T S CP LSP DW LY
28	Mr & Mrs A Collinson Secret Garden Caravan & Camping Park, Bosavern House **ST JUST IN PENWITH** TR19 7RD	01736 788301 www.secretbosavern.com mail@bosavern.com	371 305 1 km	£17.00 Mar-Oct T S LY CP Also B&B
28	Mr J Stock St Just Campsite **CAPE CORNWALL** Cornwall	07533 002762		£7.00 Mid July - Mid Sept T CP DW
33	Mr & Mrs N Whittle Silver Sands Holiday Park Gwendreath, **HELSTON** Cornwall TR12 7LZ	01326 290631 www.silversandsholidaypark.co.uk info@silversandsholidaypark.co.uk'	729 169 1km	£12.50 end Mar-early Nov T S LY CP DW
33	Mr S Cook National Trust, Teneriffe Farm Campsite, Predannack **MULLION** Cornwall TR12 7EZ	01326 240293 www.nationaltrust.org.uk teneriffefarmcampsite@nationaltrust.org.uk	672 167 1km	£6.50 1 Apr. - 2 Nov T S LY CP DW
34	Mr & Mrs R H Lyne Henry's Campsite Caerthillian Farm, **THE LIZARD**, Cornwall TR12 7NX	01326 290596 www.henryscampsite.co.uk	701 125 500 mts PD	£7.00 Open all year O T S LY G CP DW Dogs off peak only

Near Zennor

Walk No.	Contact name Establishment name Address Region/Postcode	Telephone no. Fax / Reservation / Mobile no. Website Email	OS Map Ref. Dist. from path	Starting price Months Open Facilities Info
40	Seaview International Campsite **BOSWINGER**, Gorran Haven, Cornwall PL26 6LL	01726 843425 www.seaviewinternational.com holidays@seaviewinternational.com	989 412 500 mts	£7.00 Easter-Oct T S LY G DW
40	Dr J Whetter Trelispen Caravan & Camping Park, **GORRAN HAVEN**, Cornwall PL26 6NR	01726 843501 www.trelispen.co.uk trelispen@care4free.net	005 421 1 km	£10.00 Apr-Oct T S LY CP DW
43	Mr & Mrs K Cox Polruan Camping & Caravanning, **POLRUAN** Cornwall PL23 1QH	01726 870263 www.polruanholidays.co.uk polholiday@aol.com	132 5072 50 mts	£14.00 Apr-Oct T S LY G DW
43	Mrs J Williams Great Kellow Caravan & Campsite, **POLPERRO** Cornwall PL13 2QL	01503 272387 www.bestofsecornwall.co.uk kellow.farm@virgin.net	200 521 500 mts	£5.00 Mar-Jan 3rd T S CP LSP DW
44	Mr S R Cox Camping Caradon Park Trelawne, **LOOE** Cornwall PL13 2NA	01503 272388 www.campingcaradon.co.uk enquiries@campingcaradon.co.uk	542 218 2.4 km	£13.00 O T S LY G CP DW

Polperro Harbour

Walk No.	Contact name Establishment name Address Region/Postcode	Telephone no. Fax / Reservation / Mobile no. Website Email	OS Map Ref. Dist. from path	Starting price Months Open Facilities Info
52	Mrs M Tucker Higher House Farm Little Holloway, **EAST PRAWLE**, Devon TQ7 2BU	01548 511422 www.eastprawlefarmholidays.co.uk marilynjtucker@btinternet.com	781 365 250 mts	£5.00 Whitsun-Sept T CP LSP DW Dogs must be tethered.
54	Mr & Mrs W Hosking Upton Manor Farm Camping St Mary's Road, **BRIXHAM** Devon TQ5 9QH	01803 882384 www.uptonmanorfarm.co.uk uptoncamp@aol.com	549 926 650 mts	Easter - Sept T S LY CP All parking charged. Grocery nearby.
56	Mrs A Mann Long Meadow Farm Combe Road, **SHALDON** Devon TQ14 0EX	01626 872732 www.longmeadowfarm.co.uk anne@longmeadowfarm.co.uk	922 721 2 kms	£10.00 Easter-end Sept T S LY CP LSP DW Also self catering
57	Mr A Bulpin Leadstone Camping Warren Road, **DAWLISH** Devon EX7 0NG	01626 864411 www.leadstonecamping.co.uk post@leadstonecamping.co.uk	974 782 800 mts	£7.50 23/5-1/9 T S LY G CP DW
57	Mr T Murdin Cofton Country Holidays **STARCROSS** Devon EX6 8RP	01626 890111 tobias@coftonholidays.co.uk	1km	£13.50 O T S LY G CP LSP DW KT
58	Ms M Marsden Prattshayes Farmhouse **LITTLEHAM** Devon EX8 5DB	01395 276626 mary.marsden@nationaltrust.org.uk	025 807 1.5 km	£12.00 mid Mar-end Oct T S CP DW

Goodrington

Walk No.	Contact name Establishment name Address Region/Postcode	Telephone no. Fax / Reservation / Mobile no. Website Email	OS Map Ref. Dist. from path	Starting price Months Open Facilities Info
62	Mr R Loosmore Manor Farm Holiday Centre **CHARMOUTH** Dorset DT6 6QL	01297 560226 www.manorfarmholidaycentre.co.uk enquiries@manorfarmholidaycentre.co.uk	368 937 500 mts	£12.00 Open all year O T S LY G CP LSP DW
62	Mr M J Cox Golden Cap Holiday Park **SEATOWN**, Chideock Dorset DT6 6JX	01308 422139 www.wdlh.co.uk holidays@wdlh.co.uk	425 919 50 mts	£13.70 21/3-2/11 T S LY G CP DW
63	Mrs K Batten Freshwater Beach Holiday Park, **BURTON BRADSTOCK** Dorset DT6 4PT	01308 897317 www.freshwaterbeach.co.uk enquiries@freshwaterbeach.co.uk	898 479 on path	mid Mar-mid Nov T S LY G CP DW On-site restaurant
63	Mr R Cox Graston Copse Holiday Park Annings Lane Dorset DT6 4QP	01308 426947 www.wdlh.co.uk holidays@wdlh.co.uk	497 899 2 km	£12.35 25 Apr - 7 Sep T S LY CP DW
64	Mrs K Kennedy Bagwell Farm Touring Park **CHICKERELL**, Weymouth, Dorset DT3 4EA	01305 782575 www.bagwellfarm.co.uk sw@bagwellfarm.co.uk	634 812 1 km	£13.00 O T S LY G CP LSP DW
64	East Fleet Farm Touring Park **CHICKERELL**, Weymouth, Dorset DT3 4DW	01305 785768 www.eastfleet.co.uk enquiries@eastfleet.co.uk	641 795 on path	£14.50 mid Mar-end Oct T S LY G CP DW KT
66	Mrs M Green, Rosewall Camping, East Farm Dairy, **OSMINGTON MILLS** Weymouth, Dorset DT3 6HA	01305 832248 www.weymouthcamping.com holidays@weymouthcamping.com	733 824 50 mts	£10.00 Easter-Oct T S LY G CP LSP DW
69	Mr & Mrs J Wootton Toms Field Campsite & Shop, Toms Field Road SWANAGE, Dorset BH19 3HN	01929 427110 www.tomsfieldcamping.co.uk tomsfield@hotmail.com	995 785 1.5 km	£7.00 mid Mar-end Oct T S LY G CP LSP DW Walkers Barn also available, open all year

Coast Path plaque in pavement

Looking back from Tilly Whim Info Board, near Swanage

Youth Hostels

There is an amazing variety of Youth Hostels along the South West Coast Path, 19 in total and all offering comfortable, friendly accommodation.

Prices start from £9.95 (U18) £12.95 (Adult) per night, including bed linen, the use of self-catering kitchens, drying rooms and cycle sheds. The YHA is a membership organisation, however non-members are welcome to join on arrival at the hostel. Membership enables you to take advantage of more than 4000 Youth Hostels world wide, and discounts with online and high street retailers as well as local tourist attractions.

YHA annual membership costs are currently:

Under 26 - £10, Individual - £20, Household £30. Discounts for direct debit payments.

The meals are excellent value, with kids under 10 eating for free with adults buying main meals. Buffet breakfasts, lunches and evening meals all available.

Book directly with the Youth Hostel of your choice or for further assistance, please contact YHA Customer Services, Tel: 01629 592700, or why not visit their website at www.yha.org.uk

YHA (England & Wales), Trevelyan House, Dimple Road, Matlock, Derbyshire, DE4 3YH
Email: customerservices@yha.org.uk

Youth Hostels

Town	Address	Phone	OS Ref
Minehead	Alcombe Combe MINEHEAD TA24 6EW	0845 371 9033	973 442
Elmscott	Hartland, BIDEFORD EX39 6ES *Self Catering Only*	0845 371 9736	231 217
Boscastle	Palace Stables BOSCASTLE PL35 0HD	0845 371 9006	096 915
Tintagel	Dunderhole Point TINTAGEL PL34 0DW *Self Catering Only*	0845 371 9145	047 881
Treyarnon	Tregonnan Treyarnon PADSTOW PL28 8JR	0845 371 9664	859 741
Perranporth	Droskyn Point PERRANPORTH TR6 0GS *Self Catering Only*	0845 371 9755	752 544
Portreath	Nance Farm, Illogan, PORTREATH TR16 4QX	01209 842244	668 443
Land's End	Letcha Vean ST JUST TR19 7NT	0845 371 9643	364 305
Penzance	Horneck, PENZANCE TR20 8TF	0845 371 9653	457 302
Lizard	The Lizard HELSTON TR12 7NT *Self Catering Only*	0845 371 9550	704 116
Coverack	Parc Behan, School Hill HELSTON TR12 6SA	0845 371 9014	782 184
Boswinger	GORRAN PL26 6LL	0845 371 9107	991 411
Golant	Penquite House, Golant FOWEY PL23 1LA	0845 371 9019	116 556
Salcombe	Sharpitor SALCOMBE TQ8 8LW	0845 371 9341	728 374
Beer	Bovey Combe, Townsend SEATON EX12 3LL	0845 371 9502	223 896
Litton Cheney	Litton Cheney DORCHESTER DT2 9AT *Self Catering Only*	0845 371 9329	548 900
Lulworth Cove	School Lane WEST LULWORTH BH20 5SA	0845 371 9331	832 806
Portland	Castle Road, Castle Town PORTLAND DT5 1AU	0845 371 9339	685 741
Swanage	Cluny Crescent SWANAGE BH19 2BS	0845 371 9346	031 785

Tourist Information Centres

Town	Address	Phone	Website
Minehead	19 The Avenue, Minehead TA24 5AY	01643 702624	www.minehead.co.uk
Porlock	West End, Porlock TA24 8QD	01643 863150	www.porlock.co.uk
Lynton	Town Hall, Lee Road, Lynton EX35 6BT	01598 752225	www.lynton-lynmouth-tourism.co.uk
Combe Martin	Museum, Cross Street EX34 0DH	01271 889031	www.combe-martin-museum.co.uk
Ilfracombe	The Landmark, Sea Front EX34 9BX	01271 863001	www.visitilfracombe.co.uk
Woolacombe	The Esplanade, Woolacombe EX34 7DL	01271 870553	www.woolacombetourism.co.uk
Braunton	Bakehouse Centre, Caen Street EX33 1AA	01271 816400	www.brauntontic.co.uk
Barnstaple	The Square, Barnstaple EX32 8LN	01271 375000	www.staynorthdevon.co.uk
Bideford	Victoria Park, The Quay, EX39 2QQ	01237 477676	www.bidefordtic@torridge.gov.uk
Bude	The Crescent, Bude EX23 8LE	01288 354240	www.visitbude.info
Boscastle	The Harbour, Boscastle PL35 0HD	01840 280010	www.visitboscastleandtintagel.com
Padstow	North Quay, Padstow PL28 8AF	01841 533449	www.padstowlive.com
Newquay	Marcus Hill, Newquay TR7 1BD	01637 854020	www.visitnewquay.org
Perranporth	Westcott House, St Pirans Road TR6 0BH	01872 575254	www.perranporthinfo.co.uk
Hayle	Hayle Library, Commercial Road TR27 4DE	01736 754399	www.hayle.co.uk
St Ives	The Guildhall, Street An Pol TR26 2DS	09052 522250	www.stives-cornwall.co.uk
Penzance	Station Approach, Penzance TR18 2NF	01736 335530	www.westcornwall.org.uk
Falmouth	Prince Of Wales Pier, Falmouth TR11 3DF	01326 741194	www.falmouth.co.uk
Mevagissey	St George's Square, Mevagissey PL26 6UB	01726 844440	www.mevagissey-cornwall.co.uk
Fowey	5 South Street, Fowey PL23 1AR	01726 833616	www.fowey.co.uk
Looe	The Guildhall, Fore Street, Looe PL13 1AA	01503 262072	www.looeguide.co.uk
Plymouth	3-5 Plymouth Mayflower, Barbican PL1 2LR	01752 306330	www.visitplymouth.co.uk
Ivybridge	The Watermark, Ivybridge PL21 0SZ	01752 897035	www.ivybridgewatermark.co.uk
Salcombe	Market Street, Salcombe TQ8 8DE	01548 843927	www.salcombeinformation.co.uk
Kingsbridge	The Quay, Kingsbridge TQ7 1HS	01548 853195	www.welcomesouthdevon.co.uk
Dartmouth	The Engine House, Mayors Ave TQ6 9YY	01803 834224	www.englishriviera.co.uk
Brixham	Hobb Nobs Gift Shop, The Quay TQ5 8AW	08444 742233	www.englishriviera.co.uk
Torquay	5 Vaughan Parade, Torquay TQ2 5JG	01803 297428	www.englishriviera.co.uk
Shaldon	Shaldon Car Park, Ness Drive TQ14 0HP	01626 873723	www.visitsouthdevon.co.uk
Teignmouth	The Den, Sea Front, Teignmouth TQ14 8BE	01626 215666	www.visitsouthdevon.co.uk
Dawlish	The Lawn, Dawlish EX7 9PW	01626 215665	www.visitsouthdevon.co.uk
Exmouth	3 Rolle Street, Exmouth EX8 1HL	01395 222299	www.exmouth-guide.co.uk
Budleigh Salterton	Fore Street, Budleigh Salterton EX9 6NG	01395 445275	www.visitbudleigh.com
Sidmouth	Ham Lane, Sidmouth EX10 8XR	01395 516441	www.visitsidmouth.co.uk
Seaton	The Underfleet, Seaton EX12 2TB	01297 21660	www.seatontic.com
Lyme Regis	Guildhall Cottage, Church Street DT7 3BS	01297 442138	www.westdorset.com
Bridport	South Street, Bridport DT6 3LF	01308 424901	www.visit-dorset.com
Weymouth	Pavillion Theatre, The Esplanade DT2 8ED	01305 785747	www.visit-dorset.com
Swanage	The White House, Shore Road BH19 1LB	01929 422885	www.swanage.gov.uk
Wareham	Trinity Church, South Street BH20 4LU	01929 552740	www.visit-dorset.org.uk
Poole	19 The Quay, Poole BH13 1HJ	01202 253253	www.pooletourism.com

Land's End

We are sometimes asked what we have achieved and have set out below some of the things in which we have been involved in one way or another. We do as well send a steady flow of reports on path deficiencies, both as regards maintenance and the route of the path to the local authorities and the Natural England and the South West Coast Path Team.

1973 Official Formation in May. Attendance Cornish opening at Newquay. First information sheets produced.

1974 Attendance at South Devon and Dorset opening in September at Beer. Registration as a Charity.

1975 Clematon Hill, Bigbury, small new section of Coast Path agreed at SWWA's instigation.

Attendance at opening of so-called Exmoor Coast Path.

Bideford Public Enquiry - successful opposition to golf course on the Coast Path at Abbotsham.

Hartland Point success in getting path south from Hartland Point over Blagdon and Upright Cliffs.

Lulworth walk the new range Coast Path.

1976 First Footpath Guide issued. Thurlestone Diversion opposed.

North Cliffs improvements between Portreath and Hayle secured, thanks to National Trust.

Watermouth consulted by Devon County Council. Abbotsbury consulted by Dorset County Council.

1977 Evidence presented to Lord Porchester's Exmoor study.

Evidence given to Devon County Council for Taw/Torridge Estuary survey.

1978 Westward Ho! Attendance at Somerset/N. Devon opening.

Hartland new path seaward of radar station obtained, thanks to South West Way Association.

1979 Evidence given at Public Enquiries at Abbotsbury and Lulworth Cove.

First printed News Letters and Descriptions (illustrated)

1980 Dialogues with Countryside Commission about path deficiencies.

Alternative Coast Path open Glenthorne Estate, Somerset

1981 Path improvements at Watermouth; Braunton to Barnstaple; Dean Quarry; Clematon Hill; Bigbury; Mothecombe and Maidencombe.

1982 Further openings at: Cleave Farm (N Cornwall) Pentewan and Mount Edgcumbe, (S Cornwall) Higher Brownstone Farm, Kingswear and a short section west of Berry Head in South Devon.

Also agreement for a high tide route at Mothecombe (S Devon).

1983 Opening of the Widmouth Head section (N Devon), Kingswear and Mansands

(S Devon) Crackington Haven (N Cornwall) with major improvements to path on the western side.

1984 New Sections of path opened on the east bank of the mouth of the River Dart near Kingswear giving access to Mill Bay Cove. And Trebarwith Strand to Backways Cove (N Cornwall).

1985 Culbone - Foreland Point - path at the Glenthorne Estate waymarked as official route.

Pinehaven - Port Quin (N Cornwall) new path opened.

1986 Minehead - Porlock Weir New path between North Hill and Hurlstone Point waymarked.

Black Head (Cornwall) purchased by the National Trust so allowing a coastal route.

1987 Barnstaple/Bideford/Northam new route completed along old railway track.

Bude - attendance at Public Enquiry to prevent development adjacent to footpath.

Chynhalls Point path moved to seaward of hotel.

Branscombe - Attendance at Public Enquiry for true coast path - route adopted.

Bidna/Northam - sea wall breached, acceptable diversion negotiated.

1988 Woody Bay- Trentishoe - Devon County Council adopts our recommended, nearer the coast route.

1989 Fire Beacon Point/Pentargon Cornwall County Council installs new path.

Wembury - attend public meeting to successfully oppose erection of locked gates across Coast Path by Royal Navy.

1991 Buckator - at our request Cornwall County Council re-route official path around the headland.

1992 Watcombe and Maidencombe Our recommended route installed by Devon County Council.

Worthygate Wood - our suggested path installed by National Trust.

1993 Foreland Point - successful opposition to stop closure of path on west side.

Buck's Mills - success with our request for a Path to avoid the holiday complex.

Port Quin - our suggested path installed by National Trust.

Reverse Guide from Poole to Minehead introduced.

1994 Invited by Countryside Commission to become a member of the South West Coast Path Steering Group to review the management of the South West Coast Path.

1995 Culbone - section re-opened by Exmoor National Park.

Association details on the Internet. See details on page 2.

1996 Path Descriptions for the whole Coast Path published.

Lyme Regis - golf course route reinstated by Dorset County Council.

1997 The SWCP Project published its strategy for the future management of the Coast Path.

The Association becomes a member of the SWCP Management Group.

1998 Our Silver Jubilee Year (25 years old).

The Association launches its Silver Jubilee Appeal to raise funds towards markers at each end of the Coast Path.

Mount Batten, Plymouth - Coast Path opened

1999 Name changed to South West Coast Path Association.

2000 Crock Pits - Exmoor National Park installs a coastal route recommended by Association.

Chapel, St Aldelm's Head, Dorset

2001 Eight Winter Cliff Falls Disrupt Dorset Coast Path.

Celebratory marker installed at Minehead.

Foot & Mouth Crisis - whole Coast Path closed for 3 months.

11 August - Whole Coast Path walked on one day by Association members to celebrate the re-opening of the Coast Path.

2002 Celebratory marker installed at South Haven Point, Poole Harbour.

St German's Beacon - True coastal route installed between Downderry & Portwrinkle

2003 South West Coast Path Association is 30 years old

Easter Saturday - Association arranges 'Walk the whole path in one day' to celebrate the 25th anniversary of the official inclusion of the Somerset and North Devon sections

Chynhalls Cliff -desired realignment is installed by Cornwall County Council.

Isle of Portland - Countryside Agency accepts the route around the Island.

Tregantle Cliff - desired realignment throughout the rifle ranges is installed by the MoD as permissive path. For this we award the MoD our Annual Award.

2004 Annual award presented to Brian Muelaner and National Trust Team for their work at Lansallos.

2005 Strete to Stoke Fleming - realigned Coast Path opened.

Wembury Point -Association donates £1000 to National Trust fundraising to buy this land.

2006 After 33 years in members' homes, our Administration department moves to new office at Lee Mill.

Cain's Folly -Path reinstated after 6 years of an unsatisfactory diversion.

2007 Minehead - Porlock Marsh - Thatcher Point -our requested realignments installed.

Watermouth - Major funding pledged by Association for off road Path realignment.

Porthallow - Design and artists chosen for the halfway marker.

2008 Association On-Line Shop opened.

5000th Member - Jill Fletcher, of Portishead given a presentation at Minehead.

2009 Honorary Secretary, Eric Wallis, listed in New Year's Honours, to receive MBE for his voluntary service to this registered charity.

Porthallow Halfway marker unveiled in May.

2010 Death of Eric Wallis MBE Hon Secretary since 1986 after short illness.

Coast Path re-routed around Cape Cornwall

Planning for new style Annual Guide.

Planning and surveying the first stretch of the new English Coast Path from Portland to Lulworth commenced by Natural England.

2011 Association moves to larger office at Lee Mill.

2012 Association funding is used to help progress no fewer than twelve improvement projects around the Coast Path, at Baggy Point, near Northam, between Westward Ho! and Bucks Mills, at Hartland, at Trevaunance Cove (St Agnes), in West Cornwall at Trevega, Tregerthen and Trevean Cliffs, near Millendreath (Looe), at Challaborough (South Devon), at St Mary's Bay (Torbay) and at Durlston near Swanage.

2013 Association celebrates its 40th anniversary with the Great South West Walk. Sponsorship of this walk along the whole length of the Coast Path by local holiday companies, providers of accommodation and other facilities, as well as the walkers themselves, raises over half a million pounds for Coast Path improvements when match funding is added in, enabling over 100 improvements. A fitting birthday present!

Eric Wallis Memorial Steps opened at Royal William Yard, Plymouth

Watermouth improvements opened. Path moved off busy A399 to give walkers a safe walk regardless of the state of the tide.

FUNDING IMPROVEMENTS TO THE SOUTH WEST COAST PATH

As well as the improvements funded by the Great South West Walk, a further range of improvements has had contributions from the Association over the last two years from funds from members' subscriptions. These improvements have been at:-

Durlston, Dorset; stone walling and waymarking
St Mary's Bay, Torbay; drainage
Challabrough and Ayrmer Cove, South Devon; fencing
Reskajeague and North Cliffs, North Cornwall; easy access for wheelchairs
Hartland, North Devon; replacing stiles with gates
Baggy Point, North Devon; replacing stiles with gates
Trevaunance Cove, St Agnes, North Cornwall; news steps and surface improvements
Gwennap Head, West Cornwall; new steps and surface improvements
Nanjizal, West Cornwall; surface improvements
Burrough Farm, North Devon; fencing and surface improvements
Babbacombe, North Devon; new boardwalk, steps and short re-routing
Tregerthen Cliff, West Cornwall; erosion control, new steps and drainage
Trevean Cliff, West Cornwall; drainage
Trevega Cliff, West Cornwall; erosion control and new steps
Readymoney Cove to Looe, South Cornwall; new steps, drainage and surfacing
Kemyel Crease, Lamorna, West Cornwall; drainage
Perranporth, North Cornwall; granite waymarks through dunes
Hayle, West Cornwall; granite waymarks through dunes
Tye Rock, Porthleven, West Cornwall; easy access route
Struddicks, Millendreath, South Cornwall; improved surface
Durgan, Helford, West Cornwall; replacing stiles with gates
Croyde, North Devon; drainage
Upton Towans, Hayle, West Cornwall; granite waymarks through dunes
Porthmeor, Zennor, West Cornwall; replacement of clapper bridge
Bosigran, Morvah, West Cornwall; surface improvements
Bideford, North Devon; waymark footsteps through town
Westward Ho! North Devon; waymark footsteps through town
Portheras Cove, Pendeen, West Cornwall; new footbridge.

- This is just a small selection of products available. Please refer to our website for full shop listings and colour availability. Alternatively, we would be happy to take your order over the phone, or answer any query you may have regarding any of our products.
- Order at **www.swcp.org.uk** or by telephone **01752 896237**.

Bobble Hat

Complete with two-tone pom pom in 8 fun colours (embroidered with the new SWCPA logo). The perfect accessory to keep the head warm. 100% soft touch acrylic, heavy gauge knit with ribbed cuff. Also available in children's sizing.

£10.00 (Adult) plus postage
£8.00 (Children) plus postage

Front Row Top

Half Zip neck sweatshirt, 100% cotton. Contrast tape to neck and left hem. Panel detail to body sides. Available in navy/white or red/navy both with embroidered logo. Sizes: XS, S, M, L, XL, XXL

£35.00 plus postage

Sweat Shirt

In a range of colours embroidered with the embroidered logo. (70% polyester/30% cotton). Sizes: S, M, Large, XL, XXL.

£25.00 plus postage

Baseball Cap

Available in Dark Green or Stone. 100% cotton with embroidered logo. One size adjustable to fit.

£9.95 plus postage

Sleeveless Fleece

Available in a variety of colours, with embroidered with embroidered logo and two zip pockets. 100% pill resistant polyester and unlined. Sizes: S, M, L, XL, XXL.

£25.00 plus postage

Hoodie

Available as one block colour or two-colour with contrasting hood, embroidered SWCPA logo in over 50 assorted colours - be as colourful as you dare! 80% cotton, 20% polyester. Also available in children's sizing.

£25.00/£27.50 (Adult) plus postage
£18/£20 (Children) plus postage

As from 2014, the Peninsula map logo will be replaced with the SWCPA heart logo.

Metal Badge

30mm quality enamel badge suitable for clothing, rucksacks etc. Secure with 'butterfly' pin.

£3.50 plus postage

Polo Shirt

Polo Shirt available in various colours with embroidered logo. A good quality garment, easy to wash (65% polyester/35% cotton). Sizes: S, M, L, XL and XXL.

£19.25 plus postage

Morf Snoods

Morf Suprafleece multi-function snood/hat/neckwarmer/headband. 100% polyester microfibre, anti-microbial. Available in Black, Royal, Red or Grey. Embroidered with the Coast Path logo.

£9.00 plus postage

Light waterproof and windproof Jacket

With SWCPA logo available in 6 enticing colours. 100% polyester, microfleece body and sleeve lining, concealed waterproof hood, 2 side pockets and safety tape across lower back panel.

£30.00 plus postage

Cloth Badge

Good quality cloth badge, showing the Peninsula map, with 'South West Coast Path' embroidered below, approximate size 4" x 3" (10cm x 8cm). Suitable for sewing onto shirt or rucksack.

£3.00 plus postage

Polar Fleece Jacket

Available in various colours with embroidered logo and two zip pockets. 100% pill resistant, unlined, elasticated hem and cuffs. Sizes: S, M, L, XL and XXL.

£29.00 plus postage

Tea Towel

Full cotton tea towel 48cm x 78cm, depicting the end markers and scenes and flowers from locations on the trail. In the centre is a clear map of the whole South West Coast Path.

£3.85 plus postage

To order:

- Order at **www.swcp.org.uk** or by telephone **01752 896237**.

Backpack

With SWCPA logo available in 11 colours, the perfect accompaniment for any activity. Dimensions 40x28x14cm. Zip front pocket, adjustable padded and reinforced straps, padded back.

£15.00 plus postage

Boot Bag

With handle for easy transportation with 4 plastic stud feet, made from polyester easy to spongeclean. Sizing 33x26x18.5cm

£15.00 plus postage

Membership Gift

Complete with covering letter which can be sent out to the recipient on your behalf.

£14.50 Single / £16.00 Joint Membership includes postage

£22.00 Overseas Membership includes postage

Glassware

Cut glass Tumblers or Tankards with the Peninsula map sand-blasted on the glass. Suitably packaged.

£16.00 Tumbler plus postage

£15.00 Tankard plus postage

Certificate

These lovely colour certificates are available to people who have walked the whole path. Contact the Administrator. Members can have them presented by the Chairman at our next AGM.

FREE (members)

£3.50 (non-members plus postage)

Map Poster

A large sized map poster showing the South West Coast Path with the path printed in white enabling walkers to mark off sections walked. Size 64cm x 45cm (251/4" x 173/4").

£5.75 plus postage

We accept the followingcredit/debit cards:

To order:

- Order at **www.swcp.org.uk** or by telephone **01752 896237**.

Log Book

Keep a day by day record of your walk in an easy to carry, pocket size booklet, with a page per section in which to record your journey around some of the most beautiful countryside in the British Isles. Supplied with Waterproof Cover.

£3.50 plus postage

Coast Path Notelets

Pack of 8 Notelets in 4 designs with white envelopes, all depicting Coast Path images. Approximate size 15cm x 10.5cm.

£3.75 plus postage

Reverse Guide

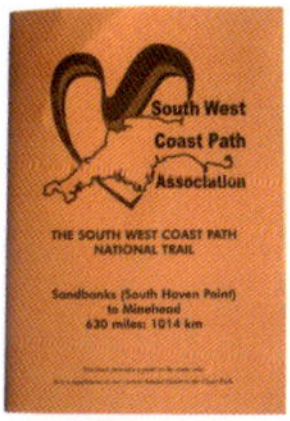

REVISED 2011 A trail description of the whole 630 miles in the direction Poole to Minehead.

£4.00 plus postage

A-Z Maps

A collection of 5 Maps in the South West Coast Path series - simply turn the pages!

£7.95 each plus postage

Also available direct from the artist...

A Calligraphic Map of the South West Coast Path

This quality calligraphic map of the South West Coast Path has been designed, illustrated and written by James Skinner of Gloucester.

The printed calligraphic map has been written entirely by hand, complemented by fine pen and ink drawings illustrating many of the sights to be found whilst walking the path.

The calligraphic map would make a superb gift, or an ideal memento for anyone having walked part or all of the path.

Overall size: approx 560 mm deep x 760 mm wide

£10.99 including free postage and packing

A £5 donation is made to the SWCPA for each map sold

View the map at www.jamesskinnercalligrapher.co.uk
or telephone 01452 611614 for further details

You may be one of those who have either bought this guide from us or a book shop. You can guarantee receipt of next year's updated, revised edition by joining the Association.

The South West Coast Path Association is a charity which represents all users of the Coast Path, be they serious hikers or afternoon strollers.

As well as producing information guides about the Coast Path, the Association raises money to help the authorities provide the best possible standard for Coast Path walkers.

If you would like to join the Association, and see your subscription go towards improving the path and its publications, you would be very welcome. Membership includes a free copy of the updated annual guide each year.

This annual guide is updated every year and published at the end of February.

Annual Subscriptions:

Single	**£14.50**
Joint	**£16.00**
Life Membership	**£220.00**
Joint Life Membership	**£250.00**
Non-UK Membership	**£22.00**

To join online visit www.swcp.org.uk or telephone 01752 896237

Looking towards Barras Nose, Boscastle

I wish to join the South West Coast Path Association.

Name ______________________________

Address ______________________________

____

____

Postcode ______________________________

Telephone ______________________________

Email ______________________________

Payment Details:

Payment made by:

☐ Cheque ☐ Visa/Mastercard

Expiry ________/________ Security Number ____________

Card Number ______________________________

Gift Aid

Under the Gift Aid Scheme the Association can reclaim the income tax paid on any donation or membership subscription received, provided you are a UK tax payer. If you would like to help us in this way then please indicate below and sign. All that we ask is if you cease to pay income tax in the future, please let us know.

I am a UK tax payer and would like South West Coast Path Association to reclaim the tax paid on any subscriptions or donations that I make to them.

Signature(s) Date

Please send completed form to:
The Administrator, South West Coast Path Association, Bowker House, Lee Mill Bridge, Ivybridge PL21 9EF • Tel: 01752 896237

BLANK FOR YOUR NOTES

Whilst walking on the path, or on any other occasion, should you meet someone interested in this book, the Association, or the Coast Path, do not worry if no one has a pencil and paper, just tear off one of these:

The South West Coast Path Association was formed 41 years ago to promote the interest of users of our Coast Path. We continue to press the authorities to maintain it properly and to complete the path. An annually updated guide to the whole 630 miles (1014km) of the South West Coast Path is issued to members every Spring. They also receive newsletters that provide the latest news about the state of the path.

For information about membership and how to obtain this annual guide contact:
South West Coast Path Association, Bowker House, Lee Mill Bridge, Ivybridge PL21 9EF
T: 01752 896237 **E:** info@swcp.org.uk **W:** www.swcp.org.uk

The South West Coast Path Association was formed 41 years ago to promote the interest of users of our Coast Path. We continue to press the authorities to maintain it properly and to complete the path. An annually updated guide to the whole 630 miles (1014km) of the South West Coast Path is issued to members every Spring. They also receive newsletters that provide the latest news about the state of the path.

For information about membership and how to obtain this annual guide contact:
South West Coast Path Association, Bowker House, Lee Mill Bridge, Ivybridge PL21 9EF
T: 01752 896237 **E:** info@swcp.org.uk **W:** www.swcp.org.uk

The South West Coast Path Association was formed 41 years ago to promote the interest of users of our Coast Path. We continue to press the authorities to maintain it properly and to complete the path. An annually updated guide to the whole 630 miles (1014km) of the South West Coast Path is issued to members every Spring. They also receive newsletters that provide the latest news about the state of the path.

For information about membership and how to obtain this annual guide contact:
South West Coast Path Association, Bowker House, Lee Mill Bridge, Ivybridge PL21 9EF
T: 01752 896237 **E:** info@swcp.org.uk **W:** www.swcp.org.uk

The South West Coast Path Association was formed 41 years ago to promote the interest of users of our Coast Path. We continue to press the authorities to maintain it properly and to complete the path. An annually updated guide to the whole 630 miles (1014km) of the South West Coast Path is issued to members every Spring. They also receive newsletters that provide the latest news about the state of the path.

For information about membership and how to obtain this annual guide contact:
South West Coast Path Association, Bowker House, Lee Mill Bridge, Ivybridge PL21 9EF
T: 01752 896237 **E:** info@swcp.org.uk **W:** www.swcp.org.uk

The South West Coast Path Association was formed 41 years ago to promote the interest of users of our Coast Path. We continue to press the authorities to maintain it properly and to complete the path. An annually updated guide to the whole 630 miles (1014km) of the South West Coast Path is issued to members every Spring. They also receive newsletters that provide the latest news about the state of the path.

For information about membership and how to obtain this annual guide contact:
South West Coast Path Association, Bowker House, Lee Mill Bridge, Ivybridge PL21 9EF
T: 01752 896237 **E:** info@swcp.org.uk **W:** www.swcp.org.uk

PLEASE CUT ALONG DOTTED LINES